Praise for *Where Ivy Dares to Grow*

"In *Where Ivy Dares to Grow*, Marielle Thompson weaves a story that is at once a haunting Gothic novel, a swoon-worthy romantic tale, and an unflinching look at what it can be to live with mental illness. This story of a woman discovering—and coming to accept—all facets of herself is rendered in beautiful, lyrical prose that will have you rereading sentences multiple times, the better to savor them. A captivating debut!" —**Alyssa Palombo, author of *The Spellbook of Katrina Van Tassel***

"Langdon Hall is imposing, numbingly cold, and isolating. But places, like people, contain multitudes, and this old house still has a heart. In *Where Ivy Dares to Grow*, Marielle Thompson tells a story about love in its many forms—and the aches it sometimes brings. A Gothic daydream of a read!" —**Briana Una McGuckin, author of *On Good Authority***

"Richly drawn and evocative, *Where Ivy Dares to Grow* is a sophisticated and masterful tale with the perfect Gothic elements: an eerie manor house that lives and breathes with atmosphere, a heroine with a core of quiet, inner strength, and inventive and surprising twists. I couldn't put this one down. Marielle Thompson is a writer to watch!" —**Paulette Kennedy, author of *Parting the Veil***

"Rich, immersive, and heartachingly romantic. A supernatural, lush tale that is equal parts Gothic mystery and forbidden love. *Where Ivy Dares to Grow* is a hauntingly addictive story of one woman's struggle to find the strength to choose her true destiny—even up to the last page, I was holding my breath."—**B. R. Myers, bestselling author of *A Dreadful Sp***

T0204958

"With a house full of secrets, a compelling love story, and atmosphere aplenty, *Where Ivy Dares to Grow* delivers all the hallmarks of a classic Gothic novel told in a lyrical and hauntingly beautiful new voice." —**Hester Fox, author of** *A Lullaby for Witches*

"The novel tugs at the heart, filled with yearning for a real love who sees you as you really are and the journey to step from the shadows to the sun." —**Kim Taylor Blakemore, author of** *The Deception*

"Thompson combines a Gothic novel, a time-travel romance, and a frank depiction of living with mental illness. Most compellingly, the protagonist's mental state is central to the narrative without driving the plot." —*Library Journal*

"*Where Ivy Dares to Grow*, an immersive debut, does a great deal to counter the stigma of mental illness." —*Shelf Awareness*

"Marielle Thompson excels at crafting an atmospheric novel populated by villainous characters and creepy houses. The descriptions practically ooze with Gothic flavor. . . . Readers who enjoy moody, Gothic-style novels or time-slip plot lines will find much to enjoy in *Where Ivy Dares to Grow*." —**Historical Novel Society**

THE

LAST WITCH

IN

EDINBURGH

Also by Marielle Thompson

Where Ivy Dares to Grow

THE

LAST WITCH

IN

EDINBURGH

MARIELLE THOMPSON

KENSINGTON
PUBLISHING CORP.

www.kensingtonbooks.com

Content warning: emotional abuse, verbal abuse, alcoholism, parental death, death or dying, murder, abortion, infertility, miscarriage, sexism/misogyny, sexual assault, swearing or cursing, violence.

For Juniper, who makes the world more magical

And for my sister, who taught me it's okay to be ambitious, to be independent, to be angry

And yet the place establishes an interest in people's hearts; go where they will, they find no city of the same distinction . . .
—Robert Louis Stevenson, *Edinburgh*

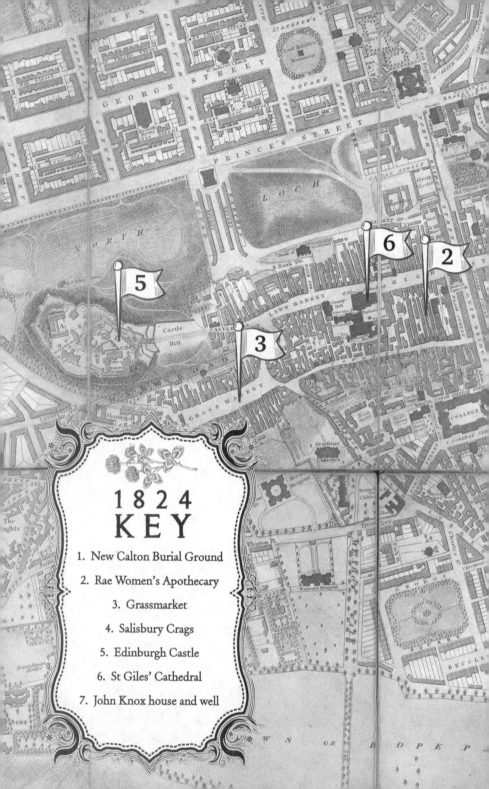

1824
KEY

1. New Calton Burial Ground

2. Rae Women's Apothecary

3. Grassmarket

4. Salisbury Crags

5. Edinburgh Castle

6. St Giles' Cathedral

7. John Knox house and well

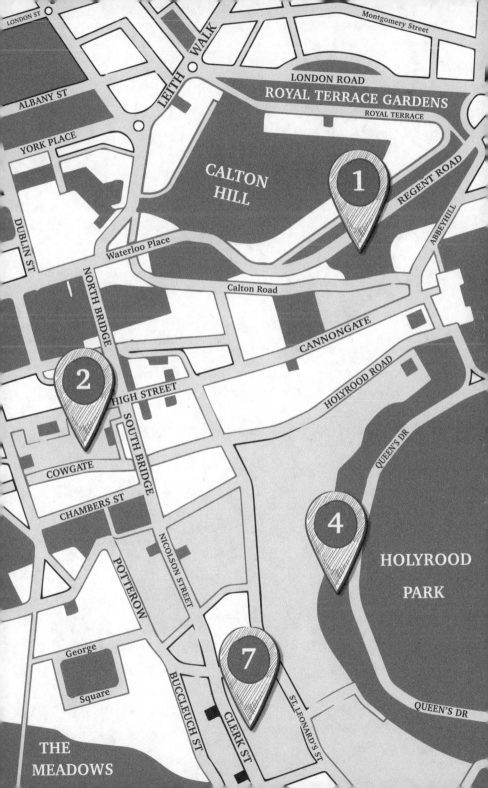

CHAPTER 1

Edinburgh, Scotland
18 September, *1824*

The day was gray and faded—as so many of them were—but any sun there was spotlighted the length of rope as it was thrown over the gallows in the center of Grassmarket. Black-gloved hands pulled it taut, weaving and knotting with a stomach-twisting familiarity. The very air of the square felt thick, not with fear—not anymore—but with anticipation.

If there was one thing Edinburgh had learned about itself in the past three months, it was that its people loved to see a witch swing. Time is perhaps an illusion, but cruelty, it seems, is just as enduring.

Nellie Duncan felt a solid lump wedge itself in the middle of her throat, as if it were her neck the hangman was preparing to weave the noose around. Thankfully, it was not, though Nellie knew full well it could be. Lady MacDonald's threats were still echoing in her ear over the din of the crowd. She dropped her gaze to her feet, which were nearly invisible due to the many shoes and their occupants that crowded Grass-market, eagerly waiting to bear witness to the hangman's jig.

I should've known better than to follow the swarm of red-faced people down here from the market, Nellie scolded herself. *I should have known what I would find.* Some people whispered that the abnormally warm summer had driven the city mad, lit a fire in people's minds, turning them against their neighbors. Nellie thought that stringing up women by their throats far surpassed madness, but she said naught.

Edinburgh seemed to have morphed over the summer. A man no one knew had been brought in from Glasgow to form a committee resolved on stamping out the city's crime once and for all. Who knew there was so many criminals in their midst, all in skirts? The new head of the Commission of Inquiry seemed to have rooted out endless witches who dwelled in the city, undiscovered, since the last wave of witch killings. The hangings had been happening all summer long. Women—witches—swinging from the gallows so often that they seemed to be as common to the Edinburgh summer as a sun sprinkle. Though one certainly fell from the air heavier than the other.

It had been nearly a century since Scotland had last been gripped by a witch trial. Many, Nellie included, had thought they were a thing of the past, an archaic fixture of cruelty that Edinburgh had outgrown. The fervor and fury the new commissioner had stirred seemed to prove that Edinburgh was not so modern a city as it claimed, that progress could be shifted backward on its axis. Its people still loved any excuse to come for a woman's blood.

It had started with the young girl—hardly anyone remembered her name anymore—James Grant's maid, the one he had gotten with child. Of course James couldn't have a lowborn bastard running about. So he'd rid himself of the girl, accused her of siring the devil's child, right under James's own roof.

James's words had given voice to all the men. Suddenly everyone knew a witch. As months passed and the summer hot spell didn't break, as crops withered and men lost coin and needed a place to take out their sweating anger . . . the hangman had found himself well employed.

Nellie wasn't sure she believed in witches, but she did believe in the power of a man's anger. And was that not the same thing?

Every few days the gallows would rise with the sun, just as inevitable. Grassmarket sat empty, normal, for days. Then one morning the people would blearily emerge from their tilted houses to find the gallows looming large in the street's center, the scaffolding around it like some wicked protector. The double ladder leaned against it, waiting for executioner and woman alike to climb up, and for only one to come down its rungs.

Gone one day and there the next, as though the hangings were so a part of the city that the beastly contraption grew straight out of the Scottish soil. No announcement was required, no declarations of criminals that shall come to their end. The appearance of the gallows was all that was needed, and its insidious whispers rippled through the city like a raging fire. The common criminals were still hung in the normal spot off Lawnmarket, but the witch hangings had moved down the way to Grassmarket. It was needed, to accommodate the great crowds it drew.

"Seems an awful waste, doesn't it?" the woman beside Nellie whispered, her voice meant to reach no one in particular and everyone all at once.

"Aye," responded a man, glancing over his shoulder quickly, afraid to miss a moment of the action before them.

His eyes caught on Nellie for a moment as he turned, pupils darkening. She looked to her shoes, an instinctive response to the gazes of men that came about too soon in her girlhood. She tucked her hands away within the folds of her cloak, holding still as could be.

"Why bother putting 'em in the ground when those bloody resurrection men will just be digging 'em back up by nightfall?" A spray of spittle flew from the man's mouth with the fervor of his words, but Nellie was busy being grateful that the gallows had grabbed his attention once more.

There were two plagues that haunted Edinburgh—witches and grave robbers. Before the soil could even settle over their graves, the hung witches were dug up, ending up a slab on a table in the medical school, ten shillings jingling in the robbers' pockets. No one minded *that* much that the resurrection men disturbed the slumber of the witches, but it wasn't just the wicked women they came for. Most criminals' corpses were offered readily by the government to the medical school, all legal. But the commissioner had put a ban on the surgeons studying witches, insisting that they were to be in the ground untouched. Of course that didn't stop the resurrection men; witch or not, a body was a body. For now, what with all the hangings, the witches seemed to always be the freshest. The medical students needed something to study after all, legal or not—and who wouldn't want to slice open a witch?

A few people chuckled in response to the man, but many more nodded, somber, gazes already locked once more on the gallows, eager to get the fill of death for which they sniffed their way to Grassmarket. Nellie swallowed heavy, but the lump in her throat persisted.

"Who's to say it's the resurrection men?" another man jibed. "Maybe the witches are digging up bodies for their nasty little spells. Or coming back to life or the like."

Nellie didn't know if the others around her believed that, but no one laughed this time.

None of the women hung were formally charged as witches— such a thing wasn't allowed anymore. But no matter what the formal charges were, it was clear to everyone that witchcraft was their crime. The fact that they were treated and hung separately from other criminals only confirmed as much; they were a different kind of threat.

The air was split as the wooden ladder creaked, two bodies making their climb—the black-gloved executioner, his hat sitting askew as he made his ashen-faced ascent, and ahead of him—the witch. She placidly faced the crowd as the noose was swung over her neck, her eyes the same gray as the sky, looking out into the crowd not with a challenge but with resignation.

She looked about the age Nellie's mother would be, silver sprouting out at the roots of her hair before fading into a light, frosty brown. *She must have been locked up only a few weeks, but it surely robbed years from her face.* Nellie felt sweat blossom along her spine, her skin growing both flushed and cool all at once.

For just a moment, as the witch's gaze swept across the crowd that had gathered to watch her take her final breath, her face met Nellie's directly. Or at least that was how it felt, though Nellie knew she was nestled well among the congregation. Nevertheless, it seemed like the witch had sought out her eyes.

Nellie's dress began to cling to her as the sweat fell in rivulets. What could the wicked woman spot in her eyes, what could she see and curse and steal? Nellie whispered a silent prayer, feeling a fool all the while for calling upon a God that she had forgotten and that had long since turned his back on her. On them all.

A witch even catching her eye could be enough to set Nellie on the gallows next. But then the executioner was nudging the witch up the last rung with an ungentle hand, and the connection between the women broke. The stone houses loomed behind the gallows like another executioner, flanking it on both sides. No escape. The castle stood just beyond, looking down with a gaze as blank and eager as the people. Even the city it-self had turned against witches it seemed.

Nellie looked away, because she must, her eyes finding a darkly outfitted man standing just beneath the gallows. The commissioner, she'd venture. He was about Da's age perhaps, but slight, hair the ashy shade of blond meeting silver. His hair was as carefully curated as his clothes, a certain levelness to his appearance that matched a man of his occupation. Con-trolled. Calculated. His white skin was flushed pink, and his hands were clasped behind him. He looked up at the woman coming to meet her end with a small sort of smile on his face, below blue eyes so singularly focused that the lump in Nellie's throat swelled.

This is mad, Nellie though suddenly. *Archaic.* But she did nothing, for what could she do? She was merely a woman, just like the one who was about to hang.

Raucous cheers swept through the crowd as the hangman tightened the rope around the witch's neck. The people of Ed-inburgh had become a beast, and they were out for blood. Be-fore the past few months, Nellie never had to consider if she had the stomach to watch a person die. Now she knew that she did not.

I never should have come.

As the witch's left foot stepped from the rung of the ladder, already prepared to walk on air and dance for the crowd, Nel-lie turned away. She pushed and shoved through the people, head down, as she scurried from the gallows. She broke through the thickest part of the crowd at last, the bucket she clutched bumping against her leg angrily as she made the climb up toward Lawnmarket. There the awaiting crowd had thinned but still lingered.

There was a moment where the city fell silent, where the only sound seemed to be Nellie's quick steps, the people hold-ing their collective breath. Then a booming cheer shook the city, and Nellie could practically hear the creak of the swing-ing rope far, far behind her.

Another morning in Edinburgh, another witch dancing on air.

Nellie's skirts collected the wetness on the ground as she raced, but she did not bother to lift the fabric. She had never quite managed to mend her hems enough for the threads to hold them at just the right height between propriety and prac-ticality. Nellie had no other dress to wear, but it was no matter if this one was dirty—she was no longer the servant of a house, no longer needed to place being presentable over being practical. Besides, she would not dare allow too much of her skin to be seen, not even an ankle. Her family's funds had grown fewer by the minute it seemed, but not so much that she had become a woman of the night. Not yet.

Nellie passed beneath the shadow of the looming kirk, its courtyard clear of a parish, as it so often was now. It seemed the people of Edinburgh had no need for a God when they could worship the divine apparition of the gallows.

Despite the crowds down on Grassmarket, a small queue snaked out before the stone well just outside the old John Knox house. It was populated by those who had to place duty above entertainment, or perhaps others who couldn't stomach the horrors. Women, like Nellie, mostly house servants as she had been, waiting to collect water in their buckets. The queue used to be abustle with chatter, whispered gossip, and raised brows, a place for the women of that lower class to convene, to trade their own kind of currency. Now, it was silent.

The women could barely meet one another's eyes. Too many women in one place was dangerous enough, but to speak to one another brought about unwanted attention that none of them could bear the burden of. They all knew that there was just too much risk in it now, the men passing by on the street like a flame hovering over skin, always applying heat, pressure, waiting to burn at the slightest provocation.

A young girl stepped up to the well, clunking her bucket beneath the spew of water. She placed her left hand on the stone step to balance and leverage herself as the water pounded into the wooden contraption. Nellie's chest tightened in panic at the sight. The girl could not have more than fourteen years, the look in her eyes still bright, surely new to her role, fresh from the safety of her mother's kitchen. It was why she was such a fool.

Nellie could feel the tension in the air, the way the rest of the women froze but no one stepped forth to stop the girl from her folly, no one spoke a word to save her. Nellie knew she should tell her. But then she imagined Thomas and her father without her. She could not be seen talking to the girl should trouble now befall her, did not want to get involved at all. Minding one's business was the only way to stay safe. Her breath coming in quick, shallow spurts, Nellie did not even let her eyes rest upon the girl, but that left hand pressed to stone burned through the edge of her vision.

Be quick about it, you foolish girl, before a man walks by and sees you. We cannot trust any of them anymore. We never could.

A ripple of surprise and fear made its way down the queue as an older woman, skin darkened by an ever-present layer of the city's grime, stepped up beside the girl. The woman turned, angling the width of her body to block the younger girl from the eyes of passing men. She leaned forth slightly, her whispered words coming out in gravelly grunts.

"Put your left foot on the stone instead, lass. No good can come from using yer hand, understand?"

Instantly the young girl's pale skin flushed scarlet, eyes growing in fear. She stepped away with her bucket only half filled, water sloshing across her worn skirts. The words had not been spoken, but it seemed the girl realized them anyway:

only witches used their left hands. One grab of the fingers, one bit of weight upon the palm, could buy a woman her ticket to swing.

Nellie stepped up to the well quickly, anxious to take her water and be on her way; the well suddenly seemed tainted and dangerous by the girl's error. They could all be punished for such stupidity. She let her bucket fill, propping it along the bone of her right shin, a permanent bruise where the bucket had rested there every day for as many years as Nellie could remember. She ignored the tremble in her fingers, a quiver caused not by winter in the air but by the fear that lurked there as well. The decorative stone face on the well that spit the water forth was so worn that the sight sent an uncomfortable tingle up Nellie's spine. The iron expressions had grown grotesque in their weathering, teetering between horror and amusement. Nellie was all too happy to step away when the water sloshed up over the rim, carrying on down the street without so much as a glance over her shoulder at the other women.

CHAPTER 2

Edinburgh, Scotland
18 September, 1824

Thomas was sitting on the crumbling steps of their tilted building when Nellie arrived home, right arm burning from the strain of carrying the water bucket one-handed.

Things used to be so much easier.

"Hiya, Nel." The young boy burst forth at the sight of her, reaching his hands out for the bucket.

With a shake of her head, Nellie carried on past him, water swaying precariously.

Nellie's stomach knotted as she looked at her young brother, so much slighter than he should be for a boy of ten years. His arms were narrow, the visible bones of his elbows and shoulders creating mountains in the worn wool coat draped across him.

"How was school, then?" she asked.

Tommy's face withered, as it often did when the matter of his schooling came up. The boy didn't understand just how lucky he was. Sending him on to school instead of a workhouse cost more coin than they had to spare, but it was an expense Nellie would always front.

"Same as." Tommy shrugged, the little bones in his shoulders poking up with the movement.

"Come on inside, laddie." Nellie hooked an arm over Thomas's shoulder as she passed, guiding him into the building alongside her.

As it so often seemed to do, rain began to beat down, the gray clouds knitting themselves together, preparing for afternoon to slide into evening.

"Let's get yer supper."

They made their way up to the higher floors, knowing which steps to skip as they climbed. The building was closer to tumbling ruins than a homestead. The door to their little flat creaked open as Nellie pressed her shoulder into it, the one-room space awash in gloom from what little light trickled in through the far window. Nellie made quick work of a fire in the grate, dumping the last of the roots and potatoes into the roiling water.

We'll need more. Perhaps if Da gets some coin tonight we can buy a bit, but we owe for last week's tater, so maybe I could—

"Was there any meat at the market?" Thomas asked, peering into the pot around his sister's waist.

None that we could afford.

Nellie's stomach tightened with worry as she ran a soft hand over her brother's head, his hair the fiery hues that he and Nellie both had gotten from their mother.

"Not tonight." Nellie knew then that her stomach would remain empty this supper so that maybe Thomas's could be filled, just a bit.

The boy heaved a sigh, stepping away.

"The stew hardly fills me up without it."

Nellie thought she may be sick, that the worry and guilt might build up so much in her belly that it came tumbling out her mouth. She knew it was her fault that Thomas must go hungry because there was no coin for food. Nearly a decade of service in the MacDonald house, nearly a decade of being able to feed Thomas and Da, gone.

Nellie had been lucky to get that post, she had known that even though she knew so little of the world then. Lady Mac-Donald had been kind when Nellie had first begun there, just a girl, newly motherless and scared beyond her wit. But the lady had treated Nellie like more than a servant, had picked up the girl's education where her mother had left off. Nellie had come to think of the lady as something like a mother. Which was why it had hurt so much to lose her.

Around the age Nellie took up her post in the MacDonald household she started to feel the flutter of desires in the pit of her belly. To experience those childlike crushes that were little more than lingering gazes and pink cheeks, at both the boys and, quietly, so quietly, the girls who also worked about the house. Romance and want in Nellie's young life was innocent, the pinnacle being a chaste kiss with the boy from her street that made her blood sing. Nellie was so busy feeling want for the first time, feeling the confidence of coin in her pocket, the warmth of a mother figure once more, that she did not notice that, while her own eyes roamed, a gaze had fallen, heavy, upon her.

Lord MacDonald's eyes had started wandering to Nellie, lingering on the young girl not too long after she'd taken the post. It took years for Nellie to notice, to even identify that the itching burn on her body as she moved about the house was his leering. It took even longer for Nellie to realize that the lady saw the looks too, that the hard pinch that formed around her eyes was not compassion. It was as though the lady believed that with each year as the two women aged in tandem, Nellie was stealing from her all the beauty that the mistress lost. It did not take long for Nellie to realize that being especially beautiful was a curse.

It had been only in the past year, just shy of Nellie's twenty-second birthday that Lord MacDonald's hands had started following the trail of his eyes. *At least he waited until I was no longer a girl,* Nellie had thought to herself the first time she had stood there, frozen with fear, as his fingers grazed down her spine and then lower as she passed by him.

Nellie knew from the steeliness in Lady MacDonald's gaze that she no longer had a protector in the lady. So she stayed silent as she knew she must. But it did not matter. For last month the lady had screamed at Nellie, though Nellie cried and swore that she had never laid with the lord, that she did not know what to do to make his touches stop, that she was sorry, so sorry. Nellie would have loved and served Lady Mac-Donald until the end of her days if the woman had let her. But she would not, it seemed.

"You leave this house and you are not to return," Lady MacDonald had said, voice as flat as her eyes.

In that moment, Nellie was more afraid of the woman she had once loved like a mother than she ever was of the lord.

"If I ever see your face again, I will go to the new commissioner myself. A lowborn woman who can read and write and is without a husband at your age? You leave at once or I will make sure the gallows appear for you, Eleanor Duncan."

Nellie did not know that she was far from being the first servant girl the lord had set his sights and hands upon. Did not know that she was the first Lady MacDonald had loved like a daughter, that the lady had shut herself in her room and wept as soon as she had finished admonishing the girl, now a woman. Nellie did not know that she was not the only one who had been robbed of something by Lord MacDonald. The two women's tears hit the soil in tandem, but nothing beautiful grew, for this was no climate made for women.

So Nellie had left. And her family had been penniless and pocketless since. For Lady MacDonald may not have gone to the commissioner, but it seems she had gone to every other lady in Edinburgh. None would even allow Nellie to pass through their door. She'd even tried for a position at one of the girls' schools, hoping her education would prove useful rather than dangerous. But either Lady MacDonald had gotten to them or they'd simply smelled the poor on her. Nothing had come of it. And now Thomas, the boy her mother had died to bring into the world, would die of hunger and it would be Nellie's fault.

Nellie told herself she did not miss the peacefulness she had only ever known from being in the company of women alone. She told herself that she did not miss Lady MacDonald. It was time for her to be an adult, a woman, to care for her family as a mother would, though she bore no such title—girls rarely got a childhood as it was. Now hers was gone.

"You eat up, then." Nellie spooned the stew in a bowl for her brother, the darkening evening light dimming his pale face.

"Will Da not be home for supper?" her brother asked, already eagerly attacking the meager meal.

It was only then that Nellie took note of her father's absence. It should have been obvious from the way the two siblings were able to be in peace for a moment, from the silence of the little room they all shared.

"Has he not been at home today?" Nellie asked.

Thomas shook his head, his red curls jostling across his forehead.

Nellie sighed heavily, doing her best to ignore the quaking of her stomach as she inhaled the wafting scent of cooked veg. Da's absence was not usually a cause for concern. In fact, it was usually the reason for a bit of joy. But Nellie knew, come nightfall, he was meant to take up his post standing guard at the new kirkyard down the way. On his last shift Da had fallen into a drunken slumber in the guard's tower, only to awake to the morning sun glinting off freshly overturned death soil and resurrection men somewhere in the city richer for it. If he missed another shift, Nellie knew there would no longer be a position for him at all. The three of them could not survive the loss of the only income they had left.

"You stay here, Tommy." Nellie draped her heaviest cloak over her shoulders. The wool was damp from the last rainfall, but there was little else that could keep the autumn chill from frosting her down to the bone, as surely the season's cold would soon arrive. It was a wonder it had not already.

"Where ye going?" he mumbled.

"I'm going to get Da." *There's only one place he could be.* "I'll be back. Be good."

Pulling her coat tight around her shoulders and tipping up the hood so she had a chance of blending into the gloom of Edinburgh, Nellie stepped out into the darkening gray of evening.

☾

The door of old Mr. Beaton's tavern opened with an echoing creak as Nellie ducked in, but thankfully there was enough raucous chatter to keep the sound from drawing eyes. The same could not be said for Nellie herself—she knew by now that it did not matter how silent she was, her presence could nevertheless incite the gazes of a roomful of men without trying.

Nellie pulled her cloak tighter around herself, despite knowing it wasn't enough to hide her figure. As dozens of eyes, glazed dark by the haze of too much whiskey, stared out at her over leering smiles, Nellie wished she could simply slip out of her skin and walk about without it. But no such luck.

Nellie gazed about the pub, too many men too deep in their pints all around her, but none of them her da. The black wood bar glistened with spilled beer and liquor, the wavering of the candles in their sconces catching the gleam. Many of the men turned away, lulled once more into their boisterous conversations. But a few eyes continued to press into her skin with the same shivering, leering presence as Lord MacDonald's hands.

To be a woman was to have a body that belonged to everyone but yourself.

Nellie ran a hand down the front of her dress, ignoring her trembling as much as she tried to ignore the looks. But some men simply would not let things rest. Or perhaps some men just liked to watch a woman squirm.

"How much for ya, then?" a man called from the far end of the room. Despite the distance, Nellie could see the spittle that arched from his mouth as a sloppy smile split his face.

"Ye'll have to get in line, Hamish, I'll give the ginger a ride first!" another man, who had many more years even than Nellie's father, bellowed.

The exchange drew back any eyes that had drifted, gazes and smiles that seemed to hold something darker than jokes all pointed at Nellie.

Though she wanted to flee, Nellie forced herself to step farther into the pub. Her eyes roved across the small room, desperate for her father, hoping against hope that he would be there, on his first pint, eyes bright and ready for his work. She knew that was the best she could hope for.

Nellie could feel her face flushing as red as her hair and pushed her hands into the folds of her coat. She tried to shallow the quick heave of her chest, fear gripping her too tight for air to make its way through. She desperately wished the men would look away from her. Wished no man would ever look at her again.

There were many dark-haired men perched before her, but none had her da's crooked twice-broken nose, none had the gentle smile he'd wear when he was sober or the dead-eyed hang to his face when he was too far gone on the drink.

"Are you fresh out of the Magdalene, dear?" The man nearest Nellie's right chuckled, eliciting a wave of chortles in response.

A man strummed in the corner, the taunts thrown Nellie's way nearly in tune with the melody, a chorus that made her want to shrink in her skin.

"What's all this?"

Nellie had never been so happy to see a man before as she was when Mr. Beaton stepped out from behind the bar. The familiar tavern keeper spotted Nellie easily.

"Come, Nellie." His voice and grip were brusque as he reached out to pull Nellie behind the bar. He led her down into the bowels of the old pub, where the barrels were stored. Nellie's stomach flipped. If Mr. Beaton was bringing her down with the wares, she knew all hope was lost that her da would be in any condition to make it to the graveyard. Hope was water through her fingers, fleeting and leaving a numbness in its wake.

"You shouldn't come round here, Nellie. You're too grown now, you know how the men will react."

The same as they acted when I was not yet grown.

Nellie nodded into the darkness of the rickety steps as they descended, though she knew Mr. Beaton could not see the gesture from where he led her.

"Your da shouldn't come round anymore either. He owes me too much; I can't keep letting him get pissed and running up a debt."

"I know. I am sorry." Nellie knew it was not her fault, but she also knew that it fell to her to apologize.

The room was dim, but she spotted her father's crumpled form easily as Mr. Beaton pointed to him with a mocking flourish. Da was propped against one of the barrels, shoulders slumped in on himself, dark-haired head lolled over to rest on his left shoulder, his limbs sprawled out like a forgotten doll. If it wasn't for the slow rise and fall of his chest—and the familiarity of this sight—one might think he was dead.

"Ta, Mr. Beaton. I'm sorry," Nellie said again, stooping to drape her father's arm over her shoulder and hoist him to his feet. His lids fluttered open just the slightest bit, mouth slurring "Oi, geheroff" before he stumbled and leaned his full weight on her once more.

"Out through the cellar door with ye. I won't have him disturbing my other customers no more." Mr. Beaton's face was a stone mask.

Nellie guided her father toward the door that let out into the alley opposite the tavern's entrance in fumbling steps, the deep ache in her right shoulder flaring up once more.

"You and Tommy take care of yourselves, Nell." Mr. Beaton said, his voice a bit softer, as Nellie and her half-conscious father stepped out into the navy darkness of night.

"Da," Nellie whispered, rising her shoulder as much as she was able, hoping to jostle her father into some state of consciousness. "Da, please, you've got to work tonight. Ye should already be headed round the burial ground."

Her da gave little more than a rumbling, shut-eyed, incoherent reply to show that he had heard her at all. Nellie knew it was hopeless. Even if she could drag her father to the cemetery, even if she could hoist him up the many steps to the top of the guard tower, it would just be another place he'd be slumbering in a corner. It was no use. He would not make it. He would miss his shift, lose his job, and her family would remain with empty bellies until they withered away into nothing. And Tommy would suffer the consequences.

Nellie began to drag her father across the streets, toward

home, their journey interrupted every few steps by the toe of his boots catching on a wobbly stone or his sudden, angry awakenings before slipping once more into his hazy half-world. They headed west up Canongate, but Nellie knew her night was far from over.

CHAPTER 3

Edinburgh, Scotland
19 September, 1824

This is an awful idea, Nellie chided herself.

Although Nellie did not have those often, she knew enough to recognize a terrible plan when she brewed one up, especially when she was daft enough to act on it. Like this, as she wove her way down Canongate, toward the city's new cemetery. Her path hugged the edges so that, between the shadows of the towering stone buildings and the vast black wool of her father's coat upon her, maybe she could blend into the night. Or, at the very least, not be recognized for a woman. Nellie pressed on, hoping that the violence the night's dark obscured would not allow her body to be taken from her, to be shared and split. Being a woman in daylight was more dangerous than ever before, but being a woman out on the streets at night was simply cursing oneself.

Thomas likely would have been better off going in their father's stead. But Nellie couldn't bear the thought of him out there alone all night, facing ruffians and God knows what else.

The city's many steeples hulked against the dark sky loom-ing down at Nellie. Had the city always been so terrifying, the very stones of the place like centuries-old predators? As she ducked in and out of darkness, avoiding the howling calls of men off their arses, Nellie felt more like a criminal herself rather than the person who was supposed to be stopping them. For if her da could not take his post in the cemetery watchtower, then she would have to do it herself.

Please, please, not tonight, resurrection men. Just let me be in peace.

Her head swiveled, perpetually checking over her shoulder. A tremble shivered down her body with each step, though the night was warm.

With a deep, unsteady sigh, Nellie passed beneath the stone arch that marked the entry into New Calton Burial Ground. The hill of the cemetery rose before Nellie, freshly laid head-stones dotting the green like hunched beasts crouched in wait-ing. She knew there were even more bodies beneath her feet, ones that were not worthy enough to be marked with in-scribed stone.

She did her best not to look at any of them as she walked up the hill in pursuit of the highest corner, where the stone watch-tower waited for her, looking like a castle turret removed and dropped among the headstones. The squelch of Nellie's shoes in the perpetually damp grass and her little ragged breaths from fear and exertion were the only sound that could be heard. The stone walls surrounding the cemetery made it a whole other world from the rest of Edinburgh city.

The scent of wet grass and freshly overturned earth hit Nel-lie's nose, and she clutched her da's coat as close to herself as she was able. She passed by a grave dug so recently, Nellie swore she could see the soil falling and rising as if its occupant breathed just beneath the surface.

Nellie broke into a little jog, the flame of her lantern wob-bling, until she reached the tower. She ducked in and climbed the spiraling stone steps up to its flat roof. Arthur's Seat lurked, a sleeping giant behind the cemetery, the mountain made of nothing but hulking darkness, blacker than the sky.

Standing there she could see every nook and valley of the cemetery, like she was the queen of all this stillness, presiding over her kingdom of death. Nellie had never been as alone as she was in that moment, a thought that came with a giddy little sense of freedom coursing through her.

Though between the dead beneath the ground and the resurrection men who skulked the city come nightfall, alone was really more of a hope than a guarantee.

For the first few hours, Nellie stood alert and prepared, perched at the edge of the tower roof. Her eyes scanned the expanse of the cemetery in an almost ritualistic, rigid pattern. Left to right, sweep across the bottom, scan to the top, right to left, left to right . . .

But by the time the moon had shifted in the sky and the stars had come out from behind roving clouds, fear and vigilance had been replaced by deep-boned exhaustion. On more than one occasion Nellie was sure her eyes were making their watchful rows only to discover they were simply dancing behind closed lids; she was lost in the land between waking and slumber, her legs sagging beneath her. Apparently, even the scariest thing one has ever done can quickly grow boring.

If the resurrection men were coming, surely they would have already, Nellie did her best to convince herself as she sunk down to sit on the stones of the roof, pulling out supplies from the deep folds of her coat. *It's not like I'll be going to sleep. In fact, I'll be doing my best to stay awake.*

She placed her lantern on the ground beside her, its flame swaying in the typical Scottish breeze but thankfully staying alert enough to swathe her in a fiery halo. Any lingering unease Nellie had disappeared as she gripped the nub of charcoal in her fingers, moving it across the little bit of parchment she was able to tuck along. There were not many times that Nellie

Duncan felt joy anymore, but with paper and charcoal she got as near to euphoria as she ever could. The sound of the nub scratching became the only sound Nellie could hear, lost in the warm comfort of another world she created.

The image slipped from her mind to her fingers to the page with an ease built from practice, so connected that it took Nellie a moment to realize what it was she was drawing. A face with small bowed lips, full cheeks, and round eyes that, Nellie knew, were gray though the charcoal made her world nothing but blackness. The woman who had swung from the gallows that very afternoon. The witch.

Nellie's fingers stalled, her mind racing from *How foolish, what if you were caught with this, you'd be next* to *Perhaps she cursed me from beyond the grave, planted her image into my mind forevermore.* Or perhaps witnessing death was not as mundane an occasion to Nellie as it quickly seemed to have become for those around her.

She was preparing to crumple the paper, to tear it in two and set it on the breeze when a sound made her hands freeze.

"I'm fit to freeze my wee breasts off out here. She wouldn't be amiss to help out a bit."

The sound was a gravelly, frustrated whisper, punctuated by the sound of a spade hitting ground, of earth being turned over. With a tremble that seemed to radiate from her bones outward, Nellie pushed herself up to peek over the ledge of the watchtower roof.

Two figures cloaked dark as nightfall were bent forth over the patch of fresh soil, bodies heaving as they dug into the ground with practiced quickness.

Resurrection men.

Fear weighed Nellie down, but the fear of these criminals, she found, was not quite as heavy as the fear of her da losing his job and the three of them being lost to the streets, exposed to the whims of the city's criminal underground nightly. She rushed down the steps of the tower, dress fluttering out behind her, the lantern in her hand trembling. She moved quickly toward the figures, unsure what she would do to confront them, let alone stop them. Adrenaline coursed through her, fading all thoughts. As Nellie got nearer, she was at least glad to see that the two men did not appear much larger than herself, tall as she was. She kept the hood of her cloak pulled down over her brow, in the hopes of obscuring the truth of her sex as long as she could manage. If they discovered that truth, she could wind up with a fate far worse than those beneath the soil.

Night pressed in all around her as Nellie slipped across the grass, rain beating softly down on the burial ground. She opened her mouth to call out, to warn them in a false deepness that they were breaking the law and she would not abide by it. But the sight before her made the words die on her tongue, robbed the air from her lungs, set her mind sputtering into silence, duty long forgotten. In her fear and shock the lantern slipped from Nellie's grasp, shattering on the ground with a calamitous splintering that broke the silence of the night. Three faces turned to look at Nellie, as shocked as she was to find that they were not alone.

Yes, three, for below the two diggers, the occupant of the unmarked grave had sat up in the coffin. The dead woman had seemingly made her way back to the land of the living.

Nellie thought perhaps she should flee, run screaming to the kirk and fall to her knees to repent for whatever it was that she was seeing. But the shock kept her frozen as she watched the woman in the poorly crafted casket stretch herself out of it and rise to her feet with a joyous little shake of her neck. Had the woman been prematurely buried, freed only now from her wrongful prison of dirt? Or, worse, had she been dead and buried yet *somehow* stood and breathed among the living once more?

Nellie had thought the resurrection men had earned their title by heinous acts of anatomy and science, not through means quite as literal as what she saw before her.

"Who are you?" the taller of the standing figures said to Nellie, when she found her feet bringing her nearer to the trio mindlessly, almost against her will. The voice was gravelly and annoyed, but now Nellie noticed it was a woman speaking, a high softness undertoning the gruffness. In fact, all three were women, the lanterns by their feet highlighting soft cheeks and hair tumbling over the shoulders of their cloaks. Even beneath the cover of her heavy cloak and nightfall, Nellie could see the defensive set to the gravel-voiced woman's shoulders. If Nellie could have managed to scream for help or bind their wrists or anything she should have been doing, the radiating energy of that woman would have been enough to silence her. Did the woman not know she was meant to shrink herself, not grow bigger than she was?

"I'm guarding against grave robbers," Nellie said in a waveringly false deepness. She had tried to say it like a warning, but even she could hear how weak her voice sounded. Her mind was screaming about the should-be dead woman who was now standing up, watching her with a placid expression.

"Well, as you can see we've not robbed a grave. We've just freed someone wrongly buried. No crime in that, is there?" The first woman's voice had hardened with defensiveness, was tinged with anger. But Nellie supposed she was right—one can't rob a grave that's not actually doing the job of a grave, right?

"You're not out here alone are you, dearie?" asked the newly resurrected woman, her gray eyes catching the orange glow of the lanterns.

As Nellie stepped forward into their circle of light, nodding, the hood slipped off from her head.

"Disgusting," the gruff-voiced woman with the sunken dark eyes huffed.

Nellie had gotten many comments on her appearance, but she had to admit that that was a new one.

"A woman, working for *them*." The woman continued in a mumble, arms coming to make a barrier across her chest.

Turning away from Nellie, the woman held out a glass bottle toward the newly living woman, popping the orb stopper off it.

"Quickly, drink. I think we ought be off now," she said, casting a pointed side glance Nellie's way.

As the glass bottle exchanged hands it caught the light of the lantern, and Nellie was able to make out the label on its side: *Rae Women's Apothecary.*

This was not how this was supposed to go, any of it. Dead or not, these women surely appeared to be criminals, for who else would lurk in a cemetery at nightfall? But that was the issue—Nellie's mind couldn't quite get past the fact that *dead or not* was, impossibly, decidedly not. For the formerly buried woman appeared fine as she drank the contents of the bottle in two grimacing gulps. *How could she—who could possibly survive being buried alive?*

It was only when the third, thus far silent, woman spoke that Nellie even noticed her.

"You wouldn't be Grace Duncan's girl, would you?" the oldest woman asked, raising her brows at Nellie.

The younger woman could not speak, the sound of her mother's name on the wind freezing whatever little control of her body she'd gained.

"I—yes. Yes, I am," Nellie whispered.

"I'd know Grace's locks anywhere. Sweet gal she is."

It had been so long since Nellie had heard a word about her mother. Her name was never even uttered in her household, unknown to Tommy and like a curse to Da. Her mother had had no friends to lend Nellie comfort, the women of the neighborhood knowing little of Grace Duncan and speaking of her less. Nellie was equally tempted to hug the woman before her and pick her brain for every last detail of the mother Nellie felt slipping from her memory daily. But her tongue and mind were not operating at their best, all of her a jumble of fear and shock from witnessing such satanic impossibilities.

"Sorry for any scare we might have caused ye, lass, but we'll be right out of your hair now," said the freshly reincarnated woman, plumper and shorter than her companions. The three of them began walking toward the cemetery's exit. Nellie stood frozen as the rain beat down on her, slowly filling the hole of the open grave. She watched them depart, feeling trapped in a dream.

For it was only once the women had passed beneath the arch and faded into the night beyond that Nellie realized where she had seen the gray-eyed woman before—swinging from the gallows that very afternoon.

CHAPTER 4

Edinburgh, Scotland
19 September, 1824

Nellie woke to the phantom of damp grave soil under her fingernails and the image of the gray-eyed witch burning through her brain, an unbelievable sight that even slumber could not shake. Her single hour of sleep had been fitful and shallow. The sun was already beginning to rise over the stones of the city when she returned home and fell into her cot, not bothering to change out of her rain-soaked clothing. It was a wonder she could sleep at all, her mind running and spinning—witches, real and rising. Witches speaking of her mother.

The sound of her father's heavy footsteps beside her shocked Nellie into consciousness. She pushed herself up on arms made weak by exhaustion.

"Well, girl, I hope yer happy," Da bellowed, eyes squinting against the tiniest sliver of sunlight peering in through the window. "Where were ye all night?"

Nellie's voice was hoarse with thirst and sleep. "At the cemetery. In the watchtower—"

"Ye were not! Or you're dumber than ye look. A body was stolen last night, right beneath yer nose, it seems. I've been sacked. Now we'll all starve to death, 'cause you cannot open yer eyes."

He stomped away, his broad back all that Nellie could see as he left her alone in the flat.

Of course. Though Nellie knew that no grave had been robbed, all the officials would see was a dug-up plot. And if Nellie were to go forth and say what she had seen, she'd be the next one swinging on Grassmarket.

Men caught witches; women merely exposed themselves as compatriots.

Her stomach twisted in on itself and knotted thrice over. She'd be forced into a brothel or worse, lest her family be pushed starving into the streets. Nellie knew she should worry about their fate, should already be up trying to remedy it. But she could think of little more than her mother's name on that woman's tongue. *A sweet gal she is*, the woman had said of Grace Duncan. *Is* not *was*, yet her mother was ten years gone. Maybe the woman did not know Grace had passed. Or maybe she knew more than Nellie did of her mother. Women seemed to be rising from the dead, after all.

That stranger had seemed familiar with her mother, or at least knew of her; meanwhile Nellie had hardly gotten to know her mother at all and was not even allowed to remember her. She could do nothing to help her family until she got answers and stopped chewing it over in her mind. That was what Nellie told herself, though whether she believed it cannot be said for certain.

Either way, she knew that she must find those women and ask—beg—for any scrap they knew of Grace Duncan.

For how can I know who I am if I do not even know the woman I came from?

Nellie would get answers about her mother and, perhaps,

figure out what exactly she had witnessed in the burial ground and if she was now witch-cursed as a spectator.

What a luxury it was to believe witches a fairy story just yesterday.

Something in Nellie's bones that she did not yet know well enough to call it by the name "intuition" told her she was meant to find these women.

But Edinburgh had become a dangerous place, and she knew she needed to be discreet. She knew no names, hardly knew the sight of the faces beyond vague features in the night. But she did know the name of the apothecary from which they got their witch's tonic. The name *Rae Women's Apothecary* grabbed on to nothing at all in Nellie's mind, but luckily nothing in Edinburgh occurred without the women of the city knowing of it.

It was uncharacteristically sunny that day, the cobblestones already drying from the previous night's shower. People walked about with not quite joy—not anymore—but perhaps a bit less fear and exhaustion than had become usual. Nellie spotted Helen Gordon just down the road, wrestling her bairn into his coat, purple half-moons under her eyes. Helen wasn't exactly the friendliest woman in the neighborhood, but she certainly was the biggest gossip. She was a midwife, and Nellie hoped that perhaps there was some sort of natural overlap between such a post and a women's apothecary.

"All right, Helen?" Nellie greeted, stepping up beside the woman, careful to keep her voice hushed.

"Aye," Helen turned dark, suspicious eyes on Nellie.

The women of her neighborhood may not know the details of why Nellie had lost her post in the MacDonald house, but the fact that she had had it at all—that she had thought herself above their station, and now had, once more, fallen down to it—was enough for them to take stock of her.

"I'm looking for the Rae Women's Apothecary. You wouldn't know of it, would ye?"

The suspicion in Helen's gaze hardened into cold contempt. Before the other woman spoke, Nellie could tell that she had lost her.

"I know of no apothecaries, women's or otherwise." Maybe Helen really didn't know or, more likely, she knew that knowing such things, let alone speaking of them, was too dangerous those days. Just as Nellie had Thomas to think of, Helen had her babe to worry for. "Now you leave me be, Nellie Duncan."

Grabbing her child's hand, Helen disappeared into the passing crowds headed westward to begin their days. Nellie considered being discouraged but only briefly. Perhaps she just needed to rethink her approach. Directness was too dangerous, but women have always had their own language of subtlety, communicating in measured glances and meaningful beats.

As if someone was looking down on her with caring eyes, another familiar young girl crossed to where Nellie stood. Eliza or Elsie, Nellie thought her name was, another servant girl at the MacDonald house. She and Nellie had rarely crossed paths, the younger girl not receiving the same privileges as the elder. She was rather plain, hair knotted at the base of her neck, her eyes cast down as she walked, hoping she'd become invisible. As the girl passed by, Nellie reached out a subtle hand to ghost across her forearm.

"Hi there," Nellie greeted quietly.

The girl looked up, eyes widening slightly when she saw who the hand belonged to.

"Hiya, Nellie."

Already a warmer start. Well done, Nell.

Nellie couldn't know what rumors had spread around the house in the wake of her leaving. But all she could hope was that the girl still had a bit of esteem for her, perhaps remembered the rigid hierarchy of the working girls, which had so long seen Nellie on top.

"I was hoping you could help me." Nellie continued searching her brain for the girl's name but came up blank.

"I don't know of any work, and Lady MacDonald curses your name about the house, so I cannot ask the other girls. I'm sorry."

Nellie didn't think the girl meant for her words to feel like a punch to the gut, but they certainly did.

"No, no, not that. I'm not feeling so well."

When the girl looked at her with a blank expression, Nellie scrambled for more. She tried to soften her vowels, take away some of the pristine edges Lady MacDonald had sanded onto her speech after so much time together. Nellie knew how unlikable a posh-sounding working girl was around these parts. The only thing worse than losing your station was forgetting it.

"It's my time, and, well, I've had much in the way of cramping. Perhaps ye know somewhere I could be treated. On the cheap. A place for women."

The girl's small dark eyes widened, but with recognition this time. She looked over both shoulders before speaking. Apothecaries weren't illegal per se—not yet at least—but they were a bit suspect. And a woman's anything was a risk.

"Aye, I may know of somewhere you could get help."

Nellie nodded eagerly, a wisp of crimson hair falling forth into her face. The girl's eyes caught the movement of the strand with something like longing. Plain girls always want for beauty because they don't know how dangerous it really is. Nellie tucked the hair behind her ear.

"Head down into Old Assembly Close. Ye may well find what you're looking for." Without another word the girl continued on, not sparing Nellie so much as a glance in the right direction.

Nellie couldn't be certain the girl had even indicated a real place, let alone the right one. But it was a start. As she began westward Nellie felt jittery at the prospect of finding the woman.

She longed to hear her mother's name spoken again, to make the hazy woman of memory and longing into a real person.

The weight and danger of what she was doing was not lost on her. But she had already decided that the risk of encountering those women again was worth the reward of her mother.

Nellie patted down the folds of her cloak, feeling for the chunk of charcoal tucked away against her chest. It would do no good in the face of witches or ungodly resurrection men or whatever it was those women in the graveyard had been. But it made Nellie feel safe, and that was worth much lately.

She tried to stop herself from peeking over her shoulder with every step. She prayed that no government men lurked, watching her. That the gallows was not already trailing in her wake, preparing for her. The quickest way to be deemed suspicious was to look the part. So Nellie kept her eyes on the ground and followed her feet up the street she knew so well.

The many closes of Edinburgh city split off from the high street like the threads of a spiderweb, weaving a scape of cobblestones and steps, narrow paths with reaching, tilting buildings pressing in on both sides. Nellie peeked up through her lashes at the one before her. An iron post stood atop the stone arch, marking it as Old Assembly Close. Despite the uncanny sunniness of the day, the stones beyond were darkened by the looming tops of their buildings, obscuring her view. Though she itched to check just once that she was not being watched, Nellie resisted the urge as she stepped beneath the stone arch and into the old alleyway.

Once upon a time the street had earned its name, being a home to the occasional cèilidh and gatherings of all sorts. But the times of joy and unity seemed to have been long forgotten in Edinburgh, beyond the pubs crowded full of men. Instead, the tight street was home to a few crumbling residential buildings, an engraving workshop, and there, nestled into the stones, a little black wood door with an iron sign above it. The sign had worn down until the metal letters were now flat and dull, hardly legible without sunlight to cut through the tall tenement buildings. But, squinting, Nellie could make out *Rae Women's Apothecary*, give or take a few letters. It looked more like a crumbling relic of a practitioner long since passed than it did a marker of an active business.

Nellie took a steadying breath and pushed the door open, the soft tinkle of a copper bell overhead announcing her entry. The room was made dim by the sparsity of windows and the dark wood rafters that crisscrossed the ceiling and walls, shelves packed to the brim with hundreds of dark glass bottles. A bushel of some dried plant Nellie couldn't identify hung from the ceiling, as did many of its partners, brushing her hair as she took a step into the space.

Women milled about the room, chatting to one another, with rags in hand and wiping down bottles and basins. They leaned over a bubbling cauldron like they had no fear of appearing as the witches of fairy tales Nellie now suspected them to be. A head of long, coarse black hair turned to greet Nellie, but the faint smile on the woman's face transformed into seething anger as she placed the new occupant.

"What are you doing here?" It was the gravelly-voiced woman, who Nellie could now see was younger than she had expected, likely not much older than Nellie herself. The woman had a simple, bland kind of face that was made almost beautiful in the expressiveness of her rage. She stepped forth, causing Nellie to retreat until the door pressed against her back and the dark-haired woman loomed before her.

"Have ye come to drag us to the gallows, then?"

The chatter within the shop had fallen away, the two of them suddenly grabbing the attention of all. Nellie's mouth went dry, images of being cursed or killed or both racing through her mind. Looking down the barrel of a witch's anger was probably even more dangerous than that of a man's.

"I do not—no, I have not—I have no authority, I swear it, I—"

"No authority? It's a rotten woman who would work for the men who want to see her kind strung up."

"I work for no man!" Nellie cried, raising her hands up before her chest as the dark-haired woman continued her predatory steps.

"*Ach!* You were in the cemetery keeping guard, were ye not? Yer telling me it's a woman paying yer wages, not the bloody Commission of Inquiry?" The woman's too-far apart eyes darkened black in her fury. Her face loomed near Nellie's, practically nose to nose, and that shameful thing in Nellie's belly swooped against her will. "How could you agree to work for the government men; they don't care about you! They'll string you up at the gallows off little more than suspicion. It's women like you who do in the rest of us and are happy to do it too!"

Nellie's mind was working slowly through the fear and the echoing thought of *Maybe I should not have come.* But she recognized the source of the woman's anger now. And, blessedly, it was just a misunderstanding.

"I don't work for the government boys." Nellie softened the heights of her speech once more. "My da does. He was drunk, so I went for him. I will not apologize for doing what must be done to keep food in my family's bellies."

Though it had been no use, had it?

A hand appeared on the dark-haired woman's arm, guiding her gently away, though Nellie could see that some of the anger on the woman's face was passing. The gray-eyed witch—the one who had been dead and born again—stepped forth. Nellie felt the hairs on her arms rise, though she appeared to be little more than a plump, matronly woman.

"All women deserve our services, Jean," she admonished the younger woman so softly Nellie could hardly hear it. "Hello again, how can we help you?" This last bit was said to Nellie with a smile.

Nellie knew how to be tactful—she'd spent most of her life

working in a lady's household, where tact was as necessary as knowing how to scrub a vase to shining. And she'd known that she would see this woman alive and seemingly normal again. She'd prepared herself for it.

Unfortunately, Nellie could not help the question that burst out of her.

"Are you a witch?" Nellie blurted, not giving a thought at all to tact.

"Oh, Christ." The angry woman—Jean—rolled her eyes to the ceiling.

"I'm a witch just as much as any woman is these days." The older woman shrugged easily.

"Sorry," Nellie said, her skirts balled in her nervous fists. "I don't—I *didn't* believe in witches. But you came back to life. I saw you . . . you were hanged, then popped out of the grave."

"Aye, well, that too every woman can do."

Jean startled. "Ma, maybe we shouldn't—"

"It's alright." Mother silenced daughter with a look.

Nellie was certain now that these women were making a joke of her. But she could not deny what she'd seen with her own eyes.

"Every woman . . . what? Cannot die?"

If every woman cannot die, and these women, or at least one of them, knew of her mother, then perhaps her mother was not gone into heaven as Nellie had believed for half her life.

Perhaps I do not have to be alone. In her very bones Nellie felt assured of her decision to come here, dangerous as it may prove to be.

"Don't be daft—we can still die. It's just that some of us return for another round. Not all, but those who honor the Cailleach, of course," Jean said, her face blooming with distrust.

"I don't understand," Nellie replied.

"Of course ye don't." Another eye roll.

"Jean, you ought to be nice to the gal. She said she doesn't work for the government men. It's right confusing to learn about it all, I imagine," the older woman admonished.

"We cannot just trust—"

"Would you like us to explain, dearie?" the witch said to Nellie, who could do little more than nod. Jean and her mother guided Nellie away from the door, where a few customers eyed them with curiosity knit into their pinched brows. The three women settled themselves behind a heavy standing divider, giving a semblance of privacy.

"What's yer name, love?" the older woman asked.

"Eleanor Duncan. Nellie."

"Lovely to meet you, Nellie. I'm Anne Rae. I do apologize for my daughter's brusqueness toward ye. Jean worries too much."

Considering Anne had been strung from the gallows just the day before, Nellie thought Jean was quite right to worry, but she said nothing. The black-haired woman stood nearby with a scowl. Nellie was beginning to suspect that perhaps that was just the way she always looked—angry and ready to fight the world.

"It's fine. You said— But I—" Nellie could not find any words to question or explain what the woman had said. Nellie knew it sounded unbelievable. She would not believe it, had she not seen it herself. But she had.

"Do you know of the Cailleach Bheur?" Anne asked.

Nellie shrugged, only dimly recognizing the title. She thought she could recall some semblance of the story; an old crone who appeared each autumn to welcome in the frigid winter months. Angry as could be, killing crops and starving folks, and ugly as sin.

Nellie said dubiously, "The Old Hag?"

Anne smiled. "Yes, that is one meaning of her title. She was the creator, the bringer of winter. But, true, often called a hag. Or a witch."

Nellie, instinctually, shook her head. "I don't understand.

How does this have a thing to do with stories of an old monster who brings about winter?"

"She's no monster. There is nothing monstrous about being a woman, and a defiant one at that," Jean said sternly, leaning forward so that her hair swept forth like a curtain of black across her chest.

"The Cailleach is not just a story. She never was," Anne continued. "She created the landscape of our country, forming mountains and valleys with her mighty hammer. She was the mother of the land, a giant. And it is true she brings about winter. In autumn, Samhuinn to be exact, her rule begins. In the winter months she uses her power to bring the wind and the frost and the cold. And throughout the season she ages a lifetime, becoming the old blue crone the stories paint her as, growing older with each passing month."

Jean scoffed. "Stories these days make her out as a wicked being to be feared because she was independent, powerful beyond the control of man. Because she was old and ugly and powerful, and did not apologize for it."

Anne nodded and went on. "When winter ends, and it is time for her to rest, the Cailleach drinks from the hidden well of youth. She returns to her youthful form for summer, beautiful as could be, beginning another cycle of life. Though some stories say that during the warmer season she simply slumbers, waking only on Samhuinn. But bringing about winter is hard business, and even the Cailleach cannot do it alone. Long ago, when Scotland was new, a group of eight women devoted themselves to aiding the Cailleach. They rode with her each winter, helped her bring about the season and the storms. These women came to be known as her 'hag servants.'"

Anne rolled her eyes, looking so like her daughter. "One such hag, Nessa, was turned into River Ness when she left the well that sourced the Cailleach's youth uncovered to overflow. The Cailleach was not passive with her daughters; she expected much, but she gave them much in return. They lived in her image, proudly claiming space and independence, not letting themselves be controlled by anyone, especially the men in power. They used the pieces of the Cailleach's creation—the plants, stones, sea—to aid each other and the Cailleach in bringing about winter. And though they helped their communities, of course, eventually, their craft was seen as a threat to be feared, like the Cailleach. These women—with all these traits of the Cailleach, and many of them old and unmarried and whatnot—had power, and that started to seem like a dangerous thing, something that needed to be controlled. They were labeled witches. A dangerous name, and unshakable too. Fear of witches has become as deep a part of Scotland as the mountains she built."

"We're not *witches*, of course; nobody is. It's just a title given to women they fear. We're aides to the Cailleach, her hags, her children. The title of *witch* is rooted in a hatred of women and a misunderstanding of the Cailleach. There are plenty of the Cailleach's daughters who refuse the term, and I understand that. But, as Mam said, it's stuck for centuries on us and on so many others. We're going to be called witches no matter what. We might as well try to take the word back a bit." Jean shrugged.

Nellie's mind spun, grasping on nothing to hold. "But how are you . . ."

"Alive?" Anne answered. "In thanks the Cailleach gave these servants a bit of her power. She gave them a second life, the ability to come back to life after death. And slower aging too, only a decade or so of age on the body for each century that passed. The winter the Cailleach brings may kill the plants and land, but it is so it can rise again—there cannot be rebirth without death. Just as the deity herself ages and returns each winter, so her helpers will, though only once. Cyclical as nature."

"Like Maggie Dickson?" She was an Edinburgh legend, a ghost story told to children or questioned in pubs. The woman hung on the gallows long ago, only to spring from the death cart within the hour, unable to be hung again as—by technicality, of course—she had already received the punishment for her crimes. Nellie had always thought the story was just that, like the Cailleach, a fable not rooted in any truth.

"Just like. A sweet lass, Maggie is," Anne said, speaking of one of Edinburgh's most famous women as if she were alive and hadn't been buried for good—or so Nellie had been told—a century ago.

"But women die all the time and never return." Nellie's voice quaked in tandem with her spinning mind.

"Aye, they do." Anne nodded. "But those are the women who do not take on the mantle of aiding the Cailleach. It's been passed from mother to daughter since those original eight. But any woman can choose to honor the Cailleach, to practice her craft. The craft is just any way folks choose to use and honor the Cailleach's earth, the means by which they connect to her. For some it's keeping oceans clean to swim, building stone monuments, growing crops, tending to animals or forests. I've heard of daughters who woodwork or metalsmith, weave clothing that always keeps the wearer cool in summer. I even met a lass once who made sculptures out of ice, beautiful things."

Nellie detected pride in the woman's voice as she spoke of the deity and the others who aided her, the many ways there apparently were to do so.

Anne continued. "Their actions and creations are more effective with the Cailleach's added aid. In doing these types of the craft and believing in her, we give her power, so she gives us a bit in return. Cyclical. My mam taught me how to use the earth to heal and help, so that is what we do here. A bit like traditional healing but with a little extra . . . *effectiveness* the

Cailleach gives her servants, which allows us to do things, to heal things, beyond the norm, fixing a broken heart or the heat of a panic someone can't shake. What we do in the shop goes beyond bellyaches and sleep tonics."

"And that's it?" Nellie asked, gesturing to the shop around them. "You do some kind of craft to connect to nature, and you're a *daughter*?"

"We also mirror the Cailleach's life and be independent of the control that is put on women. A daughter must claim her life as her own and live how she pleases, demand respect and space in the world, letting go of that which does not serve her. Allowing herself to be fierce-tempered and to do and be all the things women are told they should not be. This makes the woman a true hag, strengthening the Cailleach, allowing her to bring in winter each year. This also helps repaint her story, showing that the characteristics of the Cailleach are not fearsome but positive, in herself and in women. And in thanks the Cailleach rewards them with a second life."

Anne sighed heavily, her voice lowering as she continued. "But yer right. There are so few witches in these parts anymore. It's dangerous enough right now in Edinburgh just being a woman. And, for many, the way of the Cailleach doesn't look so appealing these days—it's too dangerous to live as her daughters must. And the more women's independence and agency is villainized, the more the Cailleach's tale makes her appear negatively. It is an endless loop."

Anne mindlessly rubbed a hand across her neck, where the phantom of the noose still wrapped.

Nellie knew she should be thinking many things, the first of which should be to call the authorities on these madwomen. But she had seen Anne hang, and she had seen her rise from the grave. If Anne was mad, then Nellie herself was too. And these thoughts barely occurred, for all she could think was this:

One of these women knew my mother. Maybe Ma is one of them, these daughters of the Cailleach. Maybe her death had not been the end. Maybe she is still alive. Alive again.

Despite the danger that lurked on every street corner and the fear that gnawed at the pit of her belly, Nellie knew she needed to be among these women. She needed answers that she suspected only they could provide, though the taller woman who had spoken her mother's name was nowhere to be seen in the room that day.

Nellie knew her life well, and it was not yet something she'd want to live again and again. But maybe that would be different with her mother by her side, some of the shame and loneliness gone.

Nellie was jostled forward a step as a young girl, dressed in cloth smeared with ever-present grime, knocked against the standing curtain. Though she had never truly lived it herself, Nellie easily recognized the perpetual exhaustion and dirty dresses of a servant girl.

"Sorry, sorry," the girl muttered, her face pulled down with worry as she looked at the two identical black glass bottles in her hands. Her fingers twisted over the little scraps of paper that hung from their stoppers by twine, a faint bit of moisture gathering in her blue eyes.

"Is everything all right, dear?" Anne asked, stepping forward to lay one of her calloused hands upon the girl's shoulder. "Could ye not pay, is that it?"

"Nah, I've paid."

Nellie's eyes dropped down to the bottles, taking in the contents scrawled on their markers, a few words on each. Nellie caught sight of the phrase on one of the bottles. Her throat tightened, her heart lurching out to the too-young girl that could not have been more than a few years older than Tommy. She was likely in a predicament that Nellie could have imagined befalling herself all too clearly had she not been let go from the MacDonald house. *To clear the womb* the label read.

"I cannot read. I don't know which is which or what to take," the gal said. "I don't know how I'll tell them apart!" She looked at the endless rows of identical bottles lining the shelves, their inconspicuous design made for discretion but providing no distinction.

Nellie's heart ached to hear the pure, devastating desperation in the girl's tone.

"A code," Nellie spoke before she could think. Her own reasons for being there were nearly forgotten. She saw too much of herself in this girl. She saw what far too many women had gone through, what they feared. And if Nellie could infer what the label indicated, others could too, putting the girl in danger. "Little illustrations. Pictures instead of words."

Nellie pulled a piece of half-scribbled-upon paper and the lump of charcoal from her pocket, laying the two on the surface of a nearby tabletop. Anne, Jean, and the young girl stepped up behind her to watch as the chunk of black moved across the page to keep rapid time with Nellie's brain. It was a quick, messy little thing, the half-moon she scribbled out.

"Each bottle will have a little symbol that aligns with what it contains. Then all ye must do is remember that code, simple as. And if your—if any man or anyone else at all should see the bottles, they won't know what they're for."

Nellie ripped the little square of darkened parchment, black dust sprinkling in its wake, and gently took the bottle from the girl's hands. She wrapped the twine about the little bit of paper until the half-moon hung down against the bottle, secured into place, replacing the earlier label.

"Here's a little marker on this one, so you can tell them apart. A moon. For the end of a cycle." Nellie gave the girl a heavy stare as she handed the bottle back to her.

The girl nodded, the worry in her face dissipating. "Thank you."

With only another word of thanks said to the woman who had brewed and bottled for her, the young girl passed out of the shop. Nellie became suddenly conscious of Jean's and Anne's gazes upon her. Nellie avoided their eyes, tucking the last of the paper and charcoal into the safety of her cloak.

"Do ye make many of those? Those illustrations?" Anne asked.

Nellie nodded.

"Clever. You can read?"

"Yes."

"How would you like a job here?"

Nellie was shocked into silence, but Jean certainly was not.

"Mum, ye cannot be serious."

Anne ignored her daughter.

"That was smart, what ye did there, safe. We need to be safer than ever now. If you'd like you can stay on, make those drawings for all the bits we sell."

Though she wasn't in the room then, the other, taller woman who had known Nellie's mother had been in these women's company once. Which meant she likely would be again. To be in the shop daily, it would be exactly the entrance Nellie would need to get close enough to ask questions about her ma. To find out if her mother was out there, somewhere. Alive.

"We can teach ye about the craft while you're in, help ye embrace and learn all you must of the Cailleach to become a daughter," Anne finished her offer.

In other words, Nellie thought, *they'll pay me in a chance to live another life. To be hidden from the dark hand of death.*

But, still, she could not ignore the danger. "Do you . . . cast spells? Curses?" Nellie wasn't sure what would be worse; getting hung as a witch or getting on Jean's bad side, ending up cursed beyond belief.

" 'Cause that's what witches do, curse people and crops and wreak havoc! That's what they'd have you think, all right," Jean scoffed, gesturing toward the city at large. "No, we do not. Forget everything you've heard of 'witches.' We don't consort with the devil, lay with him and do his bidding. We help the Cailleach and do our best to help people too because she gives us the means to."

Nellie was assured, but still she was nervous to fully align herself with these women and take a role in the shop. She remained silent.

"Death's part of the womanhood they've given us—we can always feel the shadow of the noose around our necks." Jean said gruffly, seeming to hear Nellie's thoughts. "But it chafes. Don't you want to be free of it?"

Nellie knew it was a reward anyone would take. A reward man had killed for and sought forever. And these women were offering to help Nellie find it for herself, if she were to believe them. Which she found she did, for she could not deny what she'd seen.

As much as everything in her, in the universe, in the very air, seemed to be telling Nellie to say yes she knew she could not. She had lost her job at the MacDonald house. Now her father was without pay, and she could not help but shoulder the blame for that too. There were no jobs, nothing for her family to live from. She could not spend her days dallying about in the apothecary for a payment that would benefit her alone while Tommy and Da withered away. Nellie's chest ached so hard she was sure her pain had become a real, physical thing.

"Thank ye, but I cannot. I must work proper. My family needs the money." She made to start toward the door, chiding herself for ever thinking all of this—a different future—could be hers. Nellie had paid the price for forgetting her station before. How foolish she was to do it again. She would forget she had ever heard talk of her mother or the Cailleach, tuck the pain and longing away with the hazy memories of her until they all faded away.

"I pay my girls well, don't worry about that. We take care of each other here, Nellie."

Anne, with her round gray eyes and her soft face smiled at Nellie. She felt herself become lighter, even with the dark, untrusting gaze of Jean lingering just beyond.

"Then yes, I'll take it." *Foolish as it is, how could I not?*

"Well, good, dearie, we'll be happy to have ye on. We'll see ye tomorrow, sunup."

Being in a space of so many women might spell danger, but it was danger Nellie was willing to risk if it meant answers about her mother. Besides, she would be among these women, but that did not mean she would be one of them, surely.

The thought of, somehow, unbelievably, receiving near immortal life was too much for Nellie to wrap her head around. But for the first time in a long time, Nellie Duncan looked forward to tomorrow.

CHAPTER 5

Edinburgh, Scotland
20 September, 1824

The sky was fading from ink to the soft silver of an Edinburgh morning as Nellie fidgeted with her fingers before the door of Rae Women's Apothecary. Should she knock? Try the door? Run home or, better yet, right to the kirkyard to repent?

Before Nellie could do any of the above, the large wooden door cracked open and Jean's unsmiling face filled the gap, her black hair hiding the shop's interior.

"You coming in or would ye rather just freeze out there instead? I'm happy enough either way."

"Oh. I'm coming in," Nellie answered.

"Aye, well go on, then." Jean stepped away, cracking the door open though she did not free the doorway. A challenge or simply making sure Nellie knew she wasn't entirely welcome, who could be sure?

So Nellie found her front pressed against Jean's as she squeezed her way into the shop, the other woman's dark gaze steely and assessing. Her eyes were a bit too far apart, her body was narrow and ridged, even under her dress. Nellie envied the other woman, the way she must be able to walk about the world without drawing leers and calls, her figure suggesting things she herself did not want. Jean was far from pretty in the conventional way, but she was so *alive*. She did not hide herself in shame or fear, in the way that had become so natural to Nellie that it felt like all she was. There was an undeniable allure in that. Nellie's breath jumped as she passed against her.

Nellie dropped her gaze and stepped away, thankful that the shop was dim, hiding the deep pink she knew her cheeks had become. That familiar, fearful swoop had returned deep in her stomach, a traitor, a part of herself that Nellie feared most.

Despite the morning air outside and the barren stone floor, the shop was warm, the fire in the grate heating the space and throwing waves of red and orange across the walls.

"Come on, then." Jean shooed her into the space fully.

Before Nellie even draped her cloak on a hook, the door creaked open and a woman strolled into the shop. Nellie's nerves rang out at the thought of facing her first customer. But the woman smiled widely, tossing her cloak onto a hook beside the door familiarly.

Jean greeted the newcomer warmly, continuing to prepare the shop for opening.

The woman fanned her heavy wool skirts for a moment, quipping, "Too hot for autumn out there." She paused as she turned, catching sight of Nellie. Her open expression became wary. "Hello there."

"This is Nellie Duncan. She's working about the shop now." Jean didn't sound much happier about it than she had the day before; Nellie was surprised Jean even remembered her name. "This is Ari."

"Nice to meet you, Nellie." Ari relaxed, beaming at Nellie.

"You too." Nellie smiled, relieved at the woman's warm welcome.

"Ari works at the shop often as well," Jean supplied. Ari walked to the far side of the shop, pulling down a bushel of purple herbs hung from the ceiling, a strand of fair blond hair slipping from her bun.

Jean wasted no time returning to work, snapping "Come on, then," at Nellie. She took piles of fresh plants from a basket and spread them across a tabletop in an organization system that was lost on Nellie.

Nellie stood beside the woman like her inverted shadow, waiting for some sort of instruction or inclusion that never came. Jean appeared lost in her work, pink tongue occasionally flicking out in mindless concentration, the thick curtain of her hair bleeding into the blackness of her dress. Three days now Nellie had seen Jean in black—in the cemetery it had made a grim sort of sense, of course—but Nellie wondered if perhaps the other woman was in mourning and for who.

Perhaps for all of them. All of us. The women of this city who have lost our home, who seem more common swinging from the rope in Grassmarket than walking and chattering upon the streets.

The door of the shop tentatively swung open. A woman who could not have had ten years more than Nellie's twenty-two entered, casting one last glance over her shoulder as she shut the door behind her.

"Morning, miss, what can we do for ye?" Jean asked, her tone friendly but a clear layer of hesitation atop her words. A stranger, then, one to be assessed before she could be helped.

The woman's clothes were of good, thick wool, quality for certain. But a layer of mud coated the hem of her skirts, telling Nellie that while she wouldn't be found in her own neighborhood, she was no lady either if she could not afford enough skirts to always have one clean while the rest laundered.

"I have heard you could help women with . . . well, with quite a variety of issues," the woman said. Her eyes flitted nervously to the bottles that lined the shelves.

"We can, sometimes. What is it ye need?"

"I don't know if this is something you can help with. My husband is . . . he's rather *enthusiastic*. I've tried talking to him, but he doesn't listen, says he can't help his . . . desires. He told me if I could find a way to stop his longing, he'd try it, but, well, he may have been in jest. He never used to be like that, until lately. He can be cruel about his loving now. Hurtful, you know?"

Nellie immediately understood the message between the woman's words, her stomach tightening. The thought of a man who could not keep his hands from a woman, who had the right and the desire to have her whenever he pleased, who did so with violence and anger . . . it was a nightmare to Nellie. Jean seemed to gather what the woman was saying just as quickly.

"I can make you an infusion that'll calm your husband, lessening his desires. Serve it as his evening tea," Jean said.

Nellie felt a pang of discomfort around the trickery of it, but she could see the desperation in the woman's eyes. She had no other means with which to protect herself, no rights.

"Thank you." The woman's nervousness broke. A small, relieved smile bloomed on her face.

"Give us just a moment," Jean said, turning to the table.

"Come now," she said to Nellie, the softness of her voice hardened once more.

She grabbed a handful of fresh herbs from a basket in the corner, laying them across the tabletop.

"We're to make a calming tea, not quite an anaphrodisiac, but something like," Jean said, continuing with a huff as she saw the confusion on Nellie's face. "It'll make her husband want to shag less." Jean smirked as Nellie's face grew hot.

With deft fingers the dark-haired woman plucked a bushel of pointed green leaves from their stem, chopping them finely with a knife that Nellie didn't quite feel comfortable with Jean having in her possession. Nellie noticed that, beneath her breath, Jean mumbled a thanks to the Cailleach and the plant alike as she worked.

"Mint," she supplied, casting a quick glance at Nellie to make sure she was paying attention. "It's quite calming and known to lessen desire. Works best in a tea, flavorful and effective."

Jean pulled forth another plant, fragrant on the air as she sliced. "The root of white water lily, found along the banks of many lochs."

Next Jean ran her fingers down a stalk of powerfully scented lavender, Nellie's eye catching on the quick finesse of the movement.

"One we have to grow in the garden ourselves, this is—"

"Lavender," Nellie finished. "Good for sleep."

Jean assessed her for a moment, and though she kept her face controlled and blank, Nellie could tell she had impressed the other woman. As much as Jean could ever be impressed, which Nellie suspected, where she was involved, was quite little.

"Aye. The fresh lavender will go in the tea." Jean sprinkled the little purple rounds into the bag, sealing it with a wrap of twine. She pulled forth another, darker stem from a bushel on the ceiling, the plant crumbling like dust as she ran her fingers down it. Jean swept the flakes into a minuscule black bottle, stopping it with a cork. "The dried is for his head."

"His head?" Nellie asked, reddish brows pulling together.

"Desire is powerful." Jean turned to Nellie with an expectant look that translated absolutely nothing to the other woman. "Well, aren't you here to make yer wee drawings?"

"Oh!" Nellie grabbed the narrow nub of charcoal and paper that sat on the far end of the table, the black piece coating her hands as she fingered it for a moment in thought. Then her eyes became hooded as she brought charcoal to paper, squiggling out a little illustration with ease. It was a basic, uninspired thing, and Nellie worried she'd lose her post, creating something that any of the women could. She needed to be there, she needed her answers. But she supposed simplicity was also best—the drawings were meant to be symbols the women could remember after all.

The drawing for the tea was a simple mug, a cloud floating atop it. For the bottle of dried lavender Nellie had drawn a pillow, rectangular and fluffed. As she attached them to the accompanying products, Jean nodded with almost approval, quickly turning to the waiting woman.

"Make him his evening tea of this for three nights, best at seven o'clock. Add nothing else and brew for seven minutes, stirring three times before serving to yer husband." Jean held out the bag first and then the bottle. "Sprinkle this beneath his pillow in a circle just the same. Three nights. That should sate his violence for at least a fortnight."

The woman took the bottle and bag gratefully, smiling her thanks at Jean and Nellie both. "I heard you do not always require coin. That you accept other payments as well?" The woman's voice was tentative once more, nerves and perhaps embarrassment making her eyes flit.

"We do." Jean was silent for a moment in thought. "Pay what you can manage."

The woman smiled gratefully as she withdrew, from a covered basket in her hands, a bushel of root vegetables along with some plants, partially wilted by the humidity. Jean accepted the pile.

"Thank you," the woman said one last time before she took her leave, a wash of lukewarm air entering the shop to bid her farewell.

"But you don't need for food or plant, do you?" Nellie asked, confused by the exchange.

"No," Jean answered simply, returning to work.

"Well, then, why—"

"We're here to help people. And help should not be for only those who can afford to part with money, or whose husbands even let them get their hands on it. We're here to aid women, to listen to them. Too many physicians or other apothecaries think only of men. They discredit women and their needs. We give them a place to be heard and believed and helped. And everyone deserves that."

It was a kindness that seemed so at odds with Jean as Nellie had seen her. Perhaps it was only her that Jean was not soft with. Or maybe she just didn't know the other woman well yet. Quietly, Nellie hoped she would.

"Come. Let's make a tincture before ye work yourself into a tizzy." Jean strolled to the far corner of the shop, and Nellie followed her obediently.

CHAPTER 6

Edinburgh, Scotland
20-21 September, 1824

Maybe it was the lack of sunlight or the rapidly revolving flood of patrons through the door, but Nellie's first day had passed in a quick blur of new faces. Some wore the hesitant weariness of new customers; these newcomers were met with distance by the Rae women in turn until the customers proved that they were not with the Commission of Inquiry, had merely heard of the shop through word of mouth. Others had the easy joy of those familiar with the space, those who found a comfort and safety within its walls that certainly did not exist for them in the city beyond anymore.

They were all Rae women, those limited few who worked at the shop, but Nellie had deduced that Jean—Jean *Rae*, that is—was the only true Rae in the apothecary that day. Jean's mother and the tall woman, who Nellie had silently gleaned from conversations to be Jean's aunt Mary, had made no appearance. Much to Nellie's chagrin.

There's always tomorrow, she reminded herself, a sentiment she would not have expected herself to have that very morning when she had pressed through the door with discomfort and gnawing curiosity heavy on her chest.

Her day in Rae's had been accompanied by an odd sense of pride at becoming a part of the well-oiled machine of the shop, even if an unsteady, often snappily-instructed part of the mechanics. To think that she had work made Nellie's body release some of the fear and worry that lived in her muscles, weighing her down.

As night had begun to creep in, too early with the incoming sweep of autumn, Jean had dismissed Nellie for the day. The redheaded woman left with little of the fear she had arrived with, though still with all the questions. Jean continued to sport her icy exterior, but Nellie was beginning to suspect there was a warmth defrosting beneath. A warmth that maybe—if she continued like she had that day, assisting with and creating illustrations for nearly a dozen prescriptions—she may get a glimmer of. It had not made Jean any less intimidating though.

Nellie had never spent so much time in the company of only women and did not comprehend how much lightness it had given her until she stepped out into the darkening Edinburgh evening and the weight of her city fell upon her once more. Paranoia and tension knotted themselves back into her muscles like a braid as she weaved her way home. An empty house greeted her when she arrived, ensuring her stomach would lace into knots as well. Thomas had lingered at a neighbor's house, eager and hungry for Nellie to arrive to give him supper. Da had not returned home, even as Nellie settled her brother in for the night. Though she had meant to pursue Da to whatever tavern or curb he inhabited, exhaustion had pulled her under too soon.

She had awoken to find the room shifted, his old boots beside the door even if Da was not there himself. She had little time to think upon it before she returned to Rae's, entering the shop with something akin not quite to comfort, but perhaps confidence. It was a new feeling, but Nellie liked the way it fit in her skin.

She was relieved to see Anne beside Jean as she entered the shop, the three of them spending the morning working in tandem.

"Is your aunt Mary in the shop often?" Nellie dared to ask at one point, her voice not quite catching on the casualness she reached for.

Jean narrowed her eyes briefly before continuing her work.

"She'll likely be about in the afternoon, if that's all right with you, Eleanor," Jean grumbled.

Nellie's cheeks flushed with the admonishment that she was not sure she had earned, but at least she had gotten her answer. She suspected it would be grueling to wait the day out, the hours crawling by, but the chime above the shop's door kept tinkling, and Jean was sure to keep Nellie busy.

At one point, Nellie found herself trailing Anne, the woman greeting each customer with her soft, open smile. Each time, it made Nellie's stomach tighten with nervous anticipation that the older woman did not seem to share.

"Should you not . . . stay away from the shop for a bit? Do you not worry someone will recognize you? As a hung witch, I mean?" Nellie finally asked when she could take the fear no longer.

Anne's smile was untroubled as ever.

"When it comes to the gallows, onlookers don't see a person. They just see a witch. I imagine I'm practically faceless to them all. They would not recognize a hung witch if she stood right before them."

Nellie knew well a woman's face was often of little importance unless it was young and beautiful. *But I remembered,* she thought, though she said nothing. *Your eyes haunted my mind until I put them on paper. I saw you.* But perhaps Nellie was different. Perhaps she was always meant to be at the apothecary.

Anne poured the tonic she was working on into a bottle. Many of the tonics and cures they sold were packaged in plain dark bottles, none with the inscription that had led Nellie to the apothecary in the first place. Nellie thought that was smart but, still, she worried that there might be some bottles headed out into the city that proudly sported their name, an arrow pointing the gallows to them. The apothecary's existence may not be a crime, but Nellie knew it was still deeply dangerous to draw any attention.

"The bottle you had when you were . . . raised," Nellie said to Anne, "it had the apothecary's name on it. That seems risky."

Jean, appearing from nowhere, answered in place of her mother. "Well, the bottle and its contents are about a century old and have been waiting up in our private rooms just in case one of us bites it and needs a little help when they wake. It just helps get the blood flowing again. But, aye, we've gotten much smarter. Nothing we sell bears our name anymore."

Nellie was glad to hear it. Because now the apothecary at risk also meant Nellie herself at risk.

As the sun—had it existed in Scotland at all—shifted to mid-sky, a beautiful young woman entered the shop with a cheerful greeting, her presence clearly commonplace. She appeared a few years younger than Nellie. Her deep green skirt trailed along the stone floor but was as spotless and crisp as the curl of honey-blond hair that was twisted up along her skull.

Nellie's heart picked up its pattering the way it always did when she passed by a beautiful woman, the way it had since she was a young girl and hadn't yet understood what the pattering meant.

"Hello, Louisa." Jean dropped the rag she was dusting with to promptly greet the young woman familiarly. For some reason Nellie's stomach swooped beneath her as she watched the fire cast a flattering glow across the gold of the woman's hair. Suddenly the quickness of Nellie's heart did not seem borne from excitement anymore.

"Jean." Louisa mirrored the other woman's knowing smile. Nellie, who had nearly forgotten the nub of charcoal in her fingers, was suddenly aware of how she must have been staring at the two women. She dropped the chunk and wiped the darkness off into the folds of her skirt self-consciously.

"Oh, hello, Mrs. Scott," Anne greeted the finely dressed woman as she passed by, making it clear to Nellie that, though Jean seemed a bit too familiar with the other woman, she was not the only one who knew her as a regular. That part of Nellie that she feared unclenched.

"Time for your hypnotic, is it?" Jean asked.

"Indeed. A bit of extra strength this time would work a charm," Louisa smiled easily.

Jean nodded, setting right to work. Nellie stepped up beside her like the dutiful assistant she had become.

"A hypnotic, to aid Louisa in sleep. She struggles with it often and receives the herb bath on a regular basis," Jean intoned automatically, now used to playing the role of teacher.

"Lavender, then?" Nellie asked. She swelled a bit when Jean greeted her with a smile, the expression still fierce and dangerous, like a viper forever coiled behind her teeth. Nellie's stomach swooped low.

"Aye, exactly," Jean answered, reaching for a fresh stalk of the purple plant, handing it to Nellie along with her knife.

Nellie took them both, careful not to brush Jean's fingers as she did. The other woman's hands had a slight tremble to them that shook the stalk as she held it. Nellie didn't know Jean well, but the woman certainly did not seem nervous. Nellie wondered if perhaps she was ill.

"Do I just . . . ?" Nellie looked hesitantly at the items in her hands, unsure of how to begin though she had seen Jean do it enough times in the past couple of days.

"Skin it of its flowers." Jean grabbed Nellie's hand holding the knife, not ungently. Together they guided the knife down the stalk of lavender, the purple flowers falling to the table and scattering the air with their heavy scent. Nellie took a deep breath, embarrassed by the way it shook from her lips as Jean's hand quaked softy atop her own. She told herself she did not miss the feel of it as Jean retreated a step.

She gathered the herb into a large cloth bag, pulling down a handful of white-petaled flowers with yellow hearts, gesturing for Nellie to cut them from their stems and deposit them alongside the lavender.

"Chamomile," Jean supplied, crossing her arms across her chest to observe Nellie. "This we have to travel to get, but it cannot be beat for sleep. Save the stems, they work a treat in vulnerary poultices."

"Mrs. Scott frequents the shop, no?" Nellie asked as Jean gathered more supplies. Her attempt at casualness sounded clunky to her own ears.

"Aye."

"Is she . . . a witch, then? Her and the other women who frequent the apothecary?" Nellie corrected herself when she saw Jean's raised brows at *witch*. It seemed she hadn't quite earned her familiarity with the volatile word. "Do they all honor the Cailleach, I mean? Have they all got their extra life?" Nellie felt ridiculous, even as she whispered the words, even as she saw Anne moving about the shop in the corner of her eye, no longer hung and buried.

Jean paused.

"No. There are so few in the city. There is only a handful of us, and all work in the shop." Her voice was heavy, something like regret weighing it down. "The Cailleach's daughters tend to be able to . . . sense each other, I suppose. It feels like a refreshing chill on the skin. One day, if you become a true child of the Cailleach, you'll know. But no, many of our customers want the result of the craft to better their lives but are too fearful to practice themselves. We mention the truth to very few. It would be dangerous. One cannot become a daughter of the Cailleach if she fears the deity and all she stands for, her independence and age and power. And these days, well, most women in the city seem to fear that exactly—they must to stay alive now."

Nellie thought she was likely never to be a witch, then, since there was so little that she did not fear.

Together they sliced and added a wispy pink-topped flower Jean identified as valerian. Nellie had seen the plant coloring the base of the crags at the city's edge. Jean then added a shaving of something with a strong earthy scent Nellie didn't recognize before plucking two red-orange poppy petals. Finally, Jean tied the bag with a length of twine while Nellie scribbled down a crescent moon nestled behind a cloud, a drop of water spilling from it, though it was clear Louisa knew well what the tonic was for.

"Soak the herbs in your nightly bath and use the bag to wash yerself," Jean said, and Nellie pinkened thinking of Louisa in her nightly bath, thinking of Jean thinking the same. "Once it's dry, put it under yer pillow and leave it there, for the scent."

Louisa muttered her understanding, tipping a gleaming pile of coin from her palm to Jean's. The dark-haired woman promptly tucked it away in the chest on the shelf. As Jean stretched onto her toes, the wave of her dark hair fell down her back, sliding along the curve of her elongated body. Nellie cast her eyes down to the stones beneath her feet.

A few customers more had paid with oddities: food or herbs. Some with more extravagant prescriptions had given forth family heirlooms, cameos, and minuscule gold chains. But most had handed forth coin for their payment, just as

Mrs. Scott did. As the customer slipped out the doorway, Mary ducked into the shop with a smiled greeting to all of them.

But Nellie could not return the smile, her body suddenly tight. This was it, her moment to find the truth of her mother at last. As the day wore on, she did her best to aid in the mindless tasks Jean had assigned to her, cleaning bottles, wiping tables. But she could not seem to forget the presence of Mary behind her as the woman silently went about her own tasks. Finally their paths crossed, Nellie finding herself working by Mary's side at a shared table. She took a deep breath, steadying herself to speak, but the older woman beat her to it.

"Hello. Nellie, yes?"

Nellie's tongue felt inexplicably coated in her mouth. She merely nodded.

"Welcome to the shop." Mary's words were so naturally quiet they were nearly a whisper.

Nellie swallowed heavily, finding her voice.

"Thank you."

Mary's eyes and attention returned to her task, and Nellie felt her opening fleeting.

"Was an odd way to meet, to be certain. But good to see you again." She tried to end her sentence with a chuckle, but it came out more like a choke.

"Aye." Mary smiled politely, continuing her work. But then she paused for a moment, eyes roving over Nellie's face in silent contemplation. "Ye really do look just like her. A face one cannot easily forget, though I'm sure yer told that often enough."

Nellie's stomach plummeted out through her feet. This was her moment. *Ask, Nellie. Do it, you coward.*

"My mother? Did you know her?"

It felt like a century before Mary answered. Her words were nearly lost on Nellie's ears, unable to hear anything beyond the thundering rush of her blood.

"A bit. Is she well, Grace?"

She's passed, Nellie knew she should answer. Or has she? Mary would know better than she.

Was she a witch? Does she live?

Nellie knew the questions were easy. But she couldn't push them through her teeth. For now, Nellie was able to hold the hope of her mother like a bird, its soft, delicate wings against her chest. She hadn't known hope in so long. She was afraid to ask questions, to hear the truth. The hope could bloom, could take flight, or it could crumble and perish in her hands, leaving her with nothing to hold on to. Nellie wasn't ready to risk losing it.

There was a quieter part of herself, one she ignored, that knew that if she asked, if she was told they knew nothing of her mother, that Grace Duncan had truly died on her birthing bed and stayed that way, then Nellie would have no excuse to be at the apothecary anymore. The coin in her pocket was not worth the risk of associating with, in their own words, real witches –even if it would be worth it to see the small smile on Thomas's face after a full belly. To hear a no would not only burst her hope but it also would give her no excuse to remain among the women of Rae's.

Nellie was not ready to face any of those feelings, not yet. Before she could say anything at all, Anne drifted by. She spoke a brusque word, catching her sister's attention, hauling her away from Nellie to help on some other task. Nellie felt the clench in her chest ease. She had another moment, to stretch as long as she wished. She did her best not to admonish herself for the coward she knew she was.

Much to Nellie's quiet relief, another moment did not form that day to catch Mary in a private aside. The chime above the apothecary door continued to ding, women from all corners of Edinburgh sweeping in and out. The women of Rae's filled the space with never-ending tasks and laughter, moving about each other with ease in the snatches of time in between. Nellie sliced plants, skinned and crushed herbs, swept the stone floor so the dust went "straight out the door, that's how ye banish negative energy from a space."

As the gray in the tiny window slanted and grew darker, Nellie breathed deep the smell of the remaining herbs. Jean, on a table nearby, held a rag, wiping down the surface, leaning far to reach each corner. She stopped suddenly, crying out, hand gripping her knee as her face split into a grimace.

"Are you all right?" Nellie asked, rushing to the woman's side.

Jean's hand trembled so heavily that the rag she held shook as if caught in a breeze.

"I'm fine," she barked, shoving the rag into Nellie's hand and limping her way to a stool. She perched there as she guided the new girl, in tones strained with discomfort, on how to carry out the task of cleaning the shop for the evening. Anne and Mary passed Jean with sympathetic glances, though they didn't seem surprised by the surly woman's ailment.

It must not be a new dilemma, Nellie thought, a twinge in her chest reaching out to Jean as she worked.

When the surfaces were clean and all the candles had been extinguished, Nellie passed through the door alongside the three Rae women. For once her stomach twisted at the thought of going home to Thomas, the knot quickly tightening even further with guilt. With easy, joyous goodbyes Mary and Anne set off deeper into the alley.

"I have to say, ye have been useful, Nell," Jean said.

Her eyes roved over Nellie, who did her best not to flush at the nickname, thankful for the growing gloom as evening sunk. Nellie liked Jean's smile enough that it made her too aware of her own mouth, the edges fluttering to find the right shape.

"We may make a witch of ye yet." And with that Jean set off in the wake of her mother and aunt, her steps tilting to favor her aching knee.

Nellie stood for a moment, eyes desperately searching the

street, throat closing at the thought that someone lurked, hearing Jean's word on the wind.

Witch.

Nellie wasn't sure she could be. But she also wasn't sure that the thought sat all that horrific in her mind anymore. She could not deny that she enjoyed the Cailleach's craft, that she admired the unapologetic independence of the Rae women, how they supported their community rather than turning against other women. If that was what the Cailleach represented, what she wanted of her "hags," Nellie thought she could grow to like her too.

Turning away from the apothecary, eyes cast down to the stone, Nellie passed through the darkening street and toward home.

CHAPTER 7

Edinburgh, Scotland
21 September, 1824

Nellie's neighborhood was usually silent come nightfall. Darkness muffled the sounds, the people with bellies too empty to bare the evening cold. But the silence that night was different. It was heavy and dangerous on the air. Nellie could nearly taste it on her tongue the moment she turned onto the narrow street she called home. The night did not even sport its characteristic chill, the same uncanny warmth that had fallen over the city was pressing in, making a bead of sweat form on Nellie's neck beneath the collar of her cloak.

As if she had conjured them from her fear and suspicions, a group of men emerged from one of the tilting stone buildings. Dark finery and hardened gazes marked them right away as government boys. Heart racing so fast she thought she may choke on it, Nellie tucked herself along the building's edge, opening her door with silent, shaking fingers. Hardly daring to breathe, Nellie made her way in and up the crumbling steps. Her feet slipped beneath her as she heard the heavy door open down below, the voices of the men carrying up the twisting stones. She prepared to hear her name on their lips, forever knit to the word *witch*.

But as Nellie stood, hand shaking along the wall to support herself, she heard them greet a neighbor down below in tones that did not bother to be quiet or respectful of suppertime. They were voices that wanted to be heard. To be feared. And it was not Nellie's name that they spoke.

"What do you know of the widow Helen Gordon?" one man asked, the others falling silent so his confident tone could carve a space into the night.

Nellie released a trembling breath, sliding into her flat and closing the door soundlessly behind her before she could hear any more.

Whatever they wanted to know of Helen, it could not be good if they were coming into her neighborhood, searching for word of her among her neighbors.

Nellie stared at the shut door, fluttering hand pressed to her chest.

"Nellie?" Thomas's small voice came from behind her. "What's happening?"

Nellie turned, spell broken. She swiped down the front of her skirts, her palm suddenly dampened. She swallowed heavily, stepping farther into the home, not a single wick lit to bring light to the space. She ran a gentle hand over Tommy's hair. "Nothing you need worry about."

Thomas followed her gaze to the unlit candle, to the last fleeting embers in the grate.

"I don't know how to do it without ye." He shrugged.

They would die without me, Nellie realized with a shock that dropped a stone in her already tight stomach. *Not just of empty belly or lack of money. Da and Tommy both, they are helpless without me.*

Perhaps at one time that would have made Nellie feel important, like she had a place, especially in the months since she had lost her position in the MacDonald house. Now it just made her stomach twist up so much tighter she was not sure she could have her supper even if she wished to.

Thomas droned on about some boy or other from school, but Nellie's mind was elsewhere as she moved about the home making him his sup, her ankles twinging with exhaustion from a day on her feet. Her body ached to rest, but instead it stayed wound tight, the presence of the government men like coals beneath her feet. Nellie noticed Thomas's voice only when it cut away, the boy falling to a hush at the sound of heavy-trodden footsteps making their way up the uneven steps. Nellie held her breath, waited, but still she jumped when the pounding, insistent knock came.

Thomas stepped forward, but Nellie laid a hand across his narrow chest.

"Go sit by the grate, Thomas," she snapped, too fearful to feel sorry for the way the boy's face widened as if struck. Nellie had never spoken harshly to him before, but then again, things had never been quite like this in Edinburgh before. She knew well that people like Thomas were not the ones the government was looking to root out and rot; the boy did not know to be as fearful as she was. And he had no reason to be—she was a woman; she was the one who consorted with witches, who was maybe even becoming one.

She swung the door open, greeted by the stoic faces of three men. Their eyes were all as dark as the clothes they wore, gazes vacant yet steely. Nellie tried to say hello, but the word died between her lips.

"We've come to ask questions about Helen Gordon," the man in the middle said in way of greeting.

Helen, of course. Not me, just Helen.

But Nellie quickly realized there was no *of course*. What could Helen have done that Nellie herself had not partaken in?

"I don't—" Nellie's word died on her tongue once more as a fourth man stepped forward, towering over Nellie, one step from her doorway. He lingered like some bloodsucker of lore who could not harm her without invitation in but could stand just beyond to bring about terror.

And that he did. His blue eyes were brighter up close, captivating. Nellie recognized the man immediately. He was the same one she had seen smiling serenely up beneath the gallows in Grassmarket when Anne was hanged—the new head of the Commission of Inquiry. As if reading her mind, the man identified himself as such with that same smile, so calm that it appeared threatening. Despite his fair appearance, Nellie could feel something unnerving within him, some unnatural thing radiating off him. It was every man who had ever leered at her, who treated her skin as their own, who laughed at the squirming discomfort they birthed in her—it all lived in his eyes at once.

The air suddenly seemed too hot, the heavy wool of her dress now clinging to Nellie's skin with an impossible weight. She had the urge to rip the cloth from her, to free herself from the heavy feeling of being pulled beneath water. Her lungs ached as if she were drowning. There was a hot gleam of sweat blooming along her neck, her head spinning and dizzy as the air grew too warm and thick to breathe.

"Helen Gordon, miss?" The commissioner asked. He smirked at the word on his lips and the implication *miss* held for a woman of her age, unwed. Or perhaps he was amused because Nellie had unconsciously pinched the bodice of her dress to pull it from her skin, desperate for air upon her though it was all hot, too hot, climbing up through her chest and tightening it. It was the feel of pure fear on the air.

"I know Helen Gordon. Not well, mind. But we've lived in this same building all my life," Nellie managed to answer.

"Many have attested to widow Gordon being a woman of

the devil." The commissioner did not blink, not wanting to miss a second of Nellie's squirming.

"A . . . what?"

"A witch." The word fell from his lips and landed heavily between them. They did not even bother to try to accuse women of other crimes now. The commissioner knew he was in charge; the paperwork that made its way up the ranks may accuse Helen of being a thief or a murderess or anything else that one could still legally be charged as—but he wanted the people of the city to know witchcraft was the true crime.

Nellie's head was swimming, and she was certain she would be sick, an acidic feeling blooming in her stomach.

"We have been told widow Gordon worked as a midwife. A bairn she birthed yesterday was born dead."

Nellie may not know much of birthing, but she did know such a thing wasn't uncommon.

"Many men have attested to feeling immense pain in their gut and groin as their wives birthed, aided by widow Gordon. As you must know, these are all signs of a witch."

Was that all it took to be labeled a witch?

Nellie nodded dumbly because she was certain if she opened her mouth she would be sick upon the commissioner's shoes.

"She was accused by a Mr. Smith, a neighbor, who says he's seen her up to all sorts of devilishness."

Nellie knew Mr. Smith, of course, the man who lived beside Helen. The one who had pursued her after her husband's death, the one she had rebuked. The man had then complained endlessly of Helen's babe's wailing through the wall, of the oddity of the woman living alone.

"Are you the mistress of this house?" The commissioner asked, voice dropping its flinty edge.

Nellie nodded.

"If you have a word of widow Gordon's crimes, we encourage you to attest to as much before the commission as a whole." The commissioner's eyes had fallen beyond Nellie's shoulder. She did not need to turn to feel Tommy's presence, to know that he had come into view.

Sick as she was, Nellie managed to lay a gentle hand across her doorway. It was a small gesture, hardly a movement at all, but the commissioner's eyes flashed. Nellie knew he saw it for what it was: a barring of his entry, a protection of her home and her boy.

"The other women of your neighborhood have said they've seen signs of the devil aplenty in Helen Gordon. Perhaps it would be wise you do the same. If you think of anything at all, do let me know."

Finally, with one last tilt of his head, he turned, placing the black hat upon his brow, leading his men down the stairs. Nellie stayed in the doorway, fingers trembling against the frame until she heard the door of the building slam. Then she slumped in on herself, closing the door. The sweat lining her body cooled immediately, as if the men had taken the flaming air with them.

Nellie's stomach flopped, and she barely made it to the empty bucket in the corner before she was heaving into it, acidic liquid burning through her chest and up her throat. She could not seem to stop. She fell to her knees as the heaves racked through her, as though she would not be well until she had spit up every bit of herself. Until she was empty.

As her stomach spasmed and squeezed, all Nellie could think was that she could not be parted from the Rae women. It was dangerous, she knew, to make herself the very thing the commission was painting all the city's women to be in broad strokes. She told herself it would be okay so long as she was never found out, so long as she could protect herself and Thomas and the Rae women. So long as the commissioner never turned his gaze on her again.

Nellie was certain that if Helen had been one of the Cailleach's hags, the Rae women would have known. Nellie would have seen her about the shop, even if she herself was not yet a proper witch, able to sense the Cailleach's other daughters. And if the commission accused women like Helen Gordon, who was surely innocent, then they would accuse them all— and though it made Nellie feel like she hardly knew herself, she figured if she was going to be suspected as a witch, she might as well be one.

CHAPTER 8

Edinburgh, Scotland
26 September, 1824

Nellie thought that, surely, the shop would feel different. Furtive, dangerous, doomed.

It did not.

Rae Women's Apothecary carried on like it always had, an oasis of safety for the women of Edinburgh and, somehow, a bit of the same for Nellie herself. The Rae women hadn't seemed shocked or terrified or ready to board up the shop for good when she told them of the terrifying presence of the government boys who had come around asking of Helen, pushing her neighbors to turn on her. They were not petrified for themselves as Nellie relayed how the commissioner and his men had returned the next night to drag the woman from her home and lock her up in the castle's dungeons at the top of the hill. The commissioner himself had overseen Helen's arrest, taking her bairn by his pudgy little arm and leading him along with them, a rattlesnake smile splitting the man's face as he did.

Nellie was infinitely glad that Anne's own arrest had been for something entirely separate from the shop. She trembled just to think of the commissioner's wicked attention being turned on the apothecary.

Still, Jean, Anne, and Mary had remained steady as Nellie recounted the tale in trembling breaths and whispered words. Ari had begun to quiver through her fingers, but she remained silent as Jean asked questions, her anger so palpable in the air that, had Nellie not gotten to know the other woman well enough by now, she would have shrunk in the face of it. Anne's eyebrows had tipped together in pity, whispering muttered sympathies for the widow and her babe, who had yet to return to the neighborhood. Mary had been silent as always, face giving no indication of her thoughts. But it was her word that had set the group back to work: "If the women of the city are in danger, we will do as we must. Thank you, Nellie."

The day continued, the women working in companionable silence, Nellie's brain in a constant whir. Jean, Mary, and Anne were off in the miniscule garden when the door opened, welcoming in a new, unfamiliar customer. Nellie expected Ari to take the lead, being far more experienced in the apothecary than herself, but the blond woman softly said, "You mind taking that, Nellie?"

"Oh, of course." She turned to the customer, an older woman with a loose bun of white hair. "How can I help you?"

Before the woman could respond, and likely immediately send Nellie out of her depth, Jean emerged, gently moving Nellie to the side to take over the interaction. Nellie couldn't deny her relief; she was beginning to feel comfortable in the apothecary, but she wasn't sure she was equipped to lead just yet.

She returned to the table beside Ari, the two twining fresh thistles for drying. Behind them, Jean quickly dealt with the customer, the door swinging closed as she left.

Ari turned to Nellie, "What with everything going on in the

city of late, I don't typically interact with the new customers myself anymore, you see. Until we know them better. Until we're sure it's safe."

"Oh?"

Ari took a deep breath. "I live my life as a woman because I am a woman. But I was born in a body that the world says doesn't align with that, with who I am in my very being, my soul. So, I have to be careful, now more than ever."

At first, Nellie simply blinked at Ari, the other woman's words not slotting into clarity. Slowly, as the silence between them stretched, she began to understand. With the world like this, Nellie couldn't imagine anyone choosing to be a woman— but of, course, Ari did not *choose* to be a woman. She simply was, as she said, in her soul, her being. Nellie thought she understood what the other woman was saying. Nellie had never lived through what Ari had, but she was grateful Ari felt safe enough to share with her. It may have taken Nellie a moment to understand, but once she did, she nodded encouragingly.

The other woman continued, breaking the moment of silence. "Being a woman isn't about what's in your pants or how ye look. Some women choose not to or aren't *safe* to express themselves as women are told we should, but that doesn't make them women any less. It's who you are. And I know who I am. The women of Rae's understand that and accept all without question. If you're a part of the shop, then I suppose you can be trusted to . . . respect that."

Nellie hated to think that Ari had to be nervous being herself, that the world may not always accept that. But Nellie did, without question. The way she saw it if she didn't accept and care for *all* women then she didn't care for women at all.

"Of course. Ye need not worry from me. Thank you for trusting me." Nellie smiled.

The two continued at their work, hours passing with the women moving in tandem, keeping busy. By midday the rate of customers slowed, and Nellie found her mind wandering. While she learned and sketched and crushed herbs and chatted with customers, Nellie nevertheless thrived in her cowardice. She told herself it was difficult to get Mary alone, that the older woman was an enigma, to the point of fearfulness. But she knew that wasn't it. She was just afraid to hear the truth. But it was time.

Afternoon showers were lining the shop's interior in stripes of darkness, the rain pattering against the window as they all worked in peaceful silence.

"Are ye well, Nellie?" Mary stepped up beside Nellie.

A pool of twine calloused Nellie's fingers as she wrapped it around unending bushels of dried herbs recently gathered from the crags.

Nellie paused, fingers twisted within the thread, the earthy smell on the air.

"Yer thoughts are quite loud. What can I do for ye?" Mary pressed, though her voice was as whispery as ever.

Nellie wasn't sure if Mary could actually read her mind or if the questions that lived and bloomed in Nellie's throat were making her swell. But either way, she knew this was her opportunity. She opened her mouth to speak, though she did not yet know what words would emerge. But she was silenced as Isobel, a motherly witch who worked in the shop twice a week, reached around for a bushel of bog myrtle.

"Sorry there, Nellie," she said as she did, taking her leave once more, allowing Nellie a moment to gather her mind and courage.

"You mentioned you knew my mother," Nellie ventured at last. "Grace Duncan."

"Aye, I do. Haven't seen her in a long time though." Mary's face was placid as it always was. Her eyes were on Nellie even as her hands continued to mindlessly squeeze a damp cloth that swaddled herbs, the mouth of a bottle catching the liquid that seeped through for a cold extract.

"That's because she died." *Or did she? Please, please tell me she did not.* "Many years ago. Or I believed she had. Did you—have you . . . Was my mother a witch, Mary?" Any tact that Nellie had planned was barreled out of the way by fear, by her need to finally just hear the truth.

Nellie held her breath, her chest growing tight as Mary's face finally shifted, the corners of her mouth tipping down as her brows threaded together in sympathy.

"I'm sorry, lass. Not that I knew of. She was something of a regular in the shop, but she didn't practice."

Nellie felt her eyes sting as she nodded, for she did not trust her voice not to break. She pressed the heel of her hand against her chest, like she could keep the hurt from spilling out, like she deserved the little presses of pain on her sternum, a punishment for daring to be hopeful. Mary waited patiently, averting her eyes, as Nellie let the wedge in her throat dissolve.

"What did she come round for?" she finally managed to ask.

"She used to speak of her little girl at home. I think she even brought you into the shop once, though you walked like a drunken sailor, likely too young to remember." Mary smiled, and without thinking Nellie found herself mirroring it. "She came in for aid in conceiving another babe. She came nearly every month for years."

Thomas. Thomas, well over a decade younger than Nellie herself was.

Upon hearing this, Nellie hated to admit that her first response was hurt, that she was not enough for her mother. Her second, truer response was to thank her mother, for knowing the joy Tommy would bring, for working to bring him forth into their lives.

"She didn't want you to be an only child, to have to bear the burden of the family alone one day."

Her mother didn't know, could not have known that that would be Nellie's fate, nevertheless. That Grace herself would give her life to bring into the world that child she had wanted so badly she had turned to the craft. That Nellie would need to be sister and mother all at once, that she would no longer have room for the title of *child*.

She hardly knew her mother, only as a child knows a parent, not as a woman grows to know a mentor, a guide. Any little piece of her mother she would welcome; she would knit the pieces together in her mind to create a whole, even if she could not have the woman herself. Nellie's insides shifted, and she felt, in the splitting of her new grief, that she knew her mother a bit more now.

"But she did not practice herself?"

"No." Mary shook her head, face somber. "Grace always seemed fearful as could be just visiting the shop."

Nellie swore then that she would not have that same fear—she would embrace it all to get the most out of life in the way that her mother never could. *For* her mother.

Mary, with her quick gray eyes that bore down to the bone, looked over Nellie, hearing the pained echoes of the younger woman's heart.

"I imagine everyone knew your mam for her beauty. Had the face of an angel, she did. But she was also one of the sweetest women I ever knew." Mary smiled softly, hands at work though she stepped beside Nellie. "There was once she came into the shop, all in a tizzy, a little bundle in her hands. I remember it like it was yesterday. She'd found a dying magpie on the street and had remembered hearing us chat about the luck a pair of the birds can bring. But it wasn't that—she couldn't bear to see the little creature suffer. She and I sat side by side for hours nursing the wee thing back to health. Anyone else would have thought it already dead—I know I would've. But not Grace and her big heart."

By the time Mary had finished recounting every story she knew of Grace Duncan—tales of kindness and wit, memories that were little more than sparks on the timeline—evening had settled in beyond the window. The others worked eagerly, embraced every customer, giving Mary and Nellie a wide berth. They knew that whatever it was they were discussing, it was a conversation that needed to be had. Jean even passed by, eyes falling on Nellie with something like kindness as she gathered snatches of the words that passed between the women.

Mary did not know Grace well, but she knew her as much as any woman, in her soul, knows another, and it was more words than Nellie had ever heard spoken of her mother. She took each tale hungrily for the little treats they were, and Mary, unquestioningly, gave them forth. When Nellie left the shop that night she feared the dim city streets a little less, for she almost felt her mother walking beside her.

CHAPTER 9

Edinburgh, Scotland
29 September, 1824

Nellie dodged the rickety passage of a carriage, the vendors packed all along Lawnmarket making the road perilously dense. Even if they did have room to move, Nellie thought she'd still be as singularly aware of Jean's presence by her side, dark hair swaying with each limping step she took. Jean's locks hung loose, unapologetically daring someone to reproach her for impropriety.

Likely she was the only woman on Lawnmarket that day with such daring; the air would have been thick with tension even if the hulking structure of the gallows had not appeared that morning just down the hill on Grassmarket. Its presence was like a flame on Nellie's neck, even as the leaning homes and crowded shoppers obscured it from view. The shadow of the castle hung heavy, its spires and points reflected on the cobblestones underfoot.

The other woman spoke to the vendor before them in a tone gruff enough to make Nellie want to shrink down inside her cloak, not for fear of Jean but fear *for* her. The old man already held a tight fist around the crate of dark glass jars Jean was haggling for, his knobbed knuckles grown white in frustration.

"Ye know full well, Willard, ye didn't charge that much last go," Jean huffed, reaching a hand out between them. But then, seeing the tremble of her fingers, she crossed her arms across her chest instead, self-consciousness masked by frustration pointed outward instead of inward. Nellie did her best not to let her eyes catch on the snake of dark hair that fell down the front of Jean's chest, looping and getting lost between the flat expanse of her breasts.

In the moment Nellie had let her mind wander, the vendor began to raise his voice, the old man's tone grown accusatory. His spewed words were angry enough to draw the eye of passersby, even over the steady ruckus of Lawnmarket.

"If ye cannot pay, then ye'll be gone!" Willard's voice trembled as much as Jean's hands. "A market is no place for women by the by, especially—"

"We'll pay the price for the lot." Nellie stepped forward, one kind of fear overpowering the other and making her tongue come alive in her mouth. The scaffolding of the gallows was already up and ready; she did not need Jean giving this man a reason to string them up on it along with whatever sorry soul it had risen for. The vendor's eyes fell to her, growing round for a moment as they swept over her face, her body. Nellie stood rigid as a stone as she was surveyed in the way men so often did. She could feel the ghost of his hands following the trail of his gaze.

"Well, now, that's a good girl," Willard cooed, the sweetness in his voice like poison. A ripple of disgust ran up Nellie's spine, but she swallowed down the feeling. "Ye oughta be careful what yer friend here says. A tongue like that can get a beautiful lass like yerself into trouble ye don't deserve."

Nellie resisted the urge to roll her eyes, tilting them up

through her lashes on instinct in the way she knew men liked, in the way that made them soften and expose their bellies like well-trained beasts.

"I will, sir." She couldn't quite make herself smile, couldn't swallow the gag that lived behind her tongue long enough to do so. But Willard flashed his teeth at her all the same. "How much for the crate?"

"Well . . ." He paused before giving her a price well below that he'd been willing to take Jean to the gallows for.

Nellie couldn't bring herself to look at the dark-haired woman, but she could feel Jean's glare burning the side of her face. Jean held out a small velvet bag, the coins within rattling softly in her unsteady grip, and Nellie ignored the swoop in her stomach, of guilt and shame and the other thing, as their fingers brushed. Once the coin passed into the eagerly awaiting palm of the vendor, his eyes lingered on Nellie for only a moment before moving on from them.

Her muscles ached as she scooped her arms beneath the crate and hoisted it up into her grip. Nellie and Jean stepped off into the human flow of the market, and as Nellie's arms quivered beneath the weight, she regretted all the years she'd spent sat like a girl of higher standing by Lady MacDonald's knee instead of working like the other servant girls. But as much as Nellie's arms ached, Jean's would be worse. Though the other woman would never utter a word, would never complain, Nellie could tell from the shake of her hands, from the dip of her dark brows, that Jean's ailment was worse that day than it oft was. Her steps jostled with a poorly hidden limp. Mary and Anne could not join Jean on her biweekly trip to the market; with the government boys' efforts increasing, Anne could not risk being recognized as a witch woman who had already swung, and Mary, characteristically, seemed hesitant to venture into public. But Nellie would have accompanied Jean anyway, regardless of the trip of her breath or the ache in her arms.

"I think if you'd been willing to let him bed ye the man would have handed over the keys to the whole warehouse." Jean did not look at Nellie, but the redhead felt the piercing dagger of her words all the same.

"Don't do that. It isn't fair," Nellie said softly, almost wishing she was a woman like Jean; a woman who was knit together by flame, who was unafraid to be loud, to sound angry when she was. But all Nellie knew was how to protect herself.

Jean's responding laugh was cruel and bitter on the air. She stepped near to Nellie as a girl with downcast eyes passed by them.

"What isn't fair is the way the world bends itself around you beautiful women. Men see yer face, and a path right through all the muck clears for ye."

"Well, it never seems to be the ones I want looking at me, does it? I do not want men's eyes upon me." Nellie's anger made her quiet, made her shrink, but so did the fear that the truth of her words would be understood. As did the fear that they would not be, not by Jean. But the other woman finally looked at her, eyes black as charcoal, an endless vat, and Nellie had to look away, her skin flushing. "Besides, it's not always good, being noticed by men. Being wanted. Sometimes I think it is as much a curse as a blessing. Desire makes men . . . cruel."

Nellie thought of the phantom of Lord MacDonald's hands on her body, and any lingering flush on her skin was swept away by a cold chill.

"That's because men are encouraged to be beasts." Jean boldly refused to step to the side as a man crossed in the way of their path, an unapologetic challenge in her eyes.

Nellie could practically see the fire flash in her pupils. *How could anyone ever take Jean for anything but a witch?* At the last moment, the man stepped out of her way.

"Men's desire angers them because it gives women power

over them. So they punish us. But when we aren't beautiful, when they don't desire us, that spells trouble too, for it's a woman's duty to be beautiful. So they punish us for that too. There is no winning because we're not meant to."

A woman the world saw as beautiful walking beside a woman the world saw as not, one a creature of fear and the other a creature of anger. And neither the better for it. Nellie knew that Jean was right. It was how things were, and who were they to think they could change the way of the world?

We may be witches, but we are just women still.

They walked through the market in silence, Jean's chin and eyes lifted in defiance, despite the crowd and the uneven sway of her step. Nellie kept her eyes upon the ground, the ache in her arms having grown familiar beneath the hard edges of the crate, the gentle rattle of the bottles the only sound between them. Crowds gathered around the vendors selling veg and wax, the things the people of Edinburgh could not live without even as the hysteria that sat on the city like a layer of smog made coin purses run dry.

Other spots stood empty, their wares on stark display, not a buyer in sight for such frivolities. One such abandoned post caught Nellie's eye immediately. A line of charcoal sticks were laid out across a swath of fabric, calling to her like a siren. She did not think she had let her eyes linger, but she must have, for Jean pulled her gaze from her companion and stepped up to the vendor. Nellie and the crate of jars tentatively followed behind her.

"We'll take three of the sticks of charcoal," Jean announced to the man who was nearly dozing with boredom.

He was quick to grab the pieces, swaddling them in fabric as Jean pulled out the coins.

"Jean—" Nellie tried to protest, but the other woman would hardly let her speak.

"Do you want them?"

So much Nellie could already feel the stains spreading on her fingers, could already hear the smooth slide of the tip upon paper, see the worlds she could create with the stick.

"Yes," she breathed.

Jean nodded, like Nellie's want was enough reason for coin to change hands, as if it was all that mattered.

Jean took the bundle of charcoal and stepped away from the vendor. Nellie followed without a word, drawn by the woman and what she held in equal, inexplicable measure.

"I don't want to trouble ye—" she tried again, but the dark-haired woman rolled her eyes.

Jean looked at Nellie's arms, trapped beneath the weight of the crate. So instead of merely handing the charcoal over, Jean ran the pad of her fingers across the folds of Nellie's coat where it covered her chest, searching for a pocket. Nellie did not dare breathe, fearing that Jean would feel the rapid staccato of her heart even through all the fabric. Jean's touch was ghostlike, gentle in a way that Nellie did not know the other woman was capable of. She should have thought of the crowds around them, of the foolishness of such a touch, innocent as it may look to outsiders.

Perhaps the touch was nothing to Jean, but it was everything to Nellie.

She could hear her blood hammering in her ears, a whoosh as the world narrowed down to those fingers grazing her body. Jean slipped her hand beneath Nellie's cloak, tucking the swaddled charcoal into her inner pocket, fingers trailing along the fabric too long as they took their leave. Nellie could not breathe.

Here Nellie was, so shaken by the very presence of Jean, by her slightest touch. Yet Jean did not soften for Nellie's beauty, only lit up when she saw Nellie learning, thinking, doing, within the shop. Nellie had never experienced it before; her beauty had always swayed those around her, men and women alike. It had opened doors for her that she, often, felt she did not deserve or did not want opened at all. But Jean demanded more of Nellie. It made Nellie want to be more. It was terrifying and hypnotizing.

"It's for the business. You need charcoal to do yer job at the apothecary, do ye not?" But there was a pink tint to Jean's pale face, and those daring eyes could not meet Nellie's own, so she knew it was more than that.

Jean mindlessly brushed her fingertips over her own clavicle, and Nellie was certain the air of the city had grown too hot, or perhaps it was just her skin. Jean's fingers twisted around the tiny copper deer that hung from a chain around her neck, the metal catching the gray light of the afternoon. The small creature was frozen in step, delicate and whimsical and everything that Jean was not.

"It's beautiful," Nellie breathed, hand itching to reach out, thankful that the weight on her arms meant she could not dare. Grateful for the excuse not to act.

Jean peered down at her necklace, the dark curtain of her hair swinging forth, falling along the line of her cheekbone.

"My ma forged it for me when I was a girl. Deer represent a connection to the supernatural world and the resilience of nature. Did ye know that?"

Nellie shook her head.

"And the stories say that of all the animals in Scotland that the Cailleach protected, it was deer that were always by her side. I wear it on me always. I'd have this deer on my neck even if there was a noose to join it. If you ever see it elsewhere, I must be deep in the soil for good already."

Before Nellie could respond, a wave of sound rippled down Lawnmarket. It was the steady beat of footsteps as the people began to move like one massive beast, down the slope and toward Grassmarket. Bodies pressed tightly around them, and Nellie and Jean found themselves carried along with them. Nellie's stomach swooped, her mind knowing that there was only one reason the people of Edinburgh gathered with such enthusiasm these days. One pointed glance told Nellie that Jean knew the same.

Even if they had wanted to run away and hide in the barren close of the apothecary, the crowd that gathered before the gallows was larger than Nellie had ever seen it. She could hardly move to stand beside Jean, let alone flee the scene. So she stood, locked shoulder to shoulder with her companion and the strangers foaming at the mouth at the very sight of the noose, dogs well trained to love cruelty that was not turned upon them. There was just barely enough space for Nellie to set down the crate, its sharp edges pressing into her calves with each sway of the crowd.

Panic bloomed its way up Nellie's throat, her palms going slick. Her eyes skittered among the crowd for an escape she knew would not come. The crowd of unknown faces, eyes pointed up at the noose swinging in the breeze like worshippers at the altar, were all she could see.

One set of eyes was not on the gallows but on her. Eyes of deep brown, streaked with green and gold, familiar even though Nellie had not seen them in months.

Lady MacDonald stood a little way away from the crowd of common folk, chest rising quick and shallow as she looked at Nellie. They were not mother and daughter by blood, had been something like it once by a love that had soured and turned cold, but still the women stood like mirror images of each other. Nellie had never known Lady MacDonald to venture into Old Town, amid the press of the tenement buildings and the sicknesses that spread like fire between their occupants. Yet there she was, packed into the sweating crowd and dirty cobblestones, as drawn to the horror of the gallows as everyone else.

Even as the lady's cruel words lashed through Nellie's mind she found herself longing to lay her head upon the lap of the older woman, to feel her warm palm upon her hair, to hear her soft voice reading aloud. But Lady MacDonald's eyes hardened, and a mask of hatred sunk as heavy upon her features as the stone in Nellie's belly.

The lock of their eyes was only broken by the roaring cheer of the crowd. Nellie's attention fell on the gallows, where a haggard woman was led up the steps. Her face was obscured by the knotted curtain of her dishwater hair, her bones sticking up through her torn dress. It took Nellie a moment to recognize the tear-tracked face of Helen Gordon.

Nellie had thought her belly could swoop no lower, and yet it found a way. Helen's eyes did not find hers, did not seem to find anything at all. There was only emptiness behind them, as though death had already curled itself around her neck. And then it did, the hangman looping the noose over her head. Nellie felt a sudden, oppressive heat drape itself across her, weighing on her. Her gaze followed the gallows down to the now familiar black-clad figure of the commissioner on the edge of the square, a wicked smile on his lips. His knuckles were white around the hand of a small, wailing boy. Helen's son. The boy was too small to know what was happening, but growing older each second he saw his mother prepare for death. He was met by her vacant gaze that was too tired and tortured to recognize him.

Nellie knew with a horrifying assuredness that every person in the square hated Helen. Not because she was a witch but because she was a woman.

Helen was no witch. Yet it didn't seem to matter to the commissioner, or the hangman, or the people of the only home Helen had ever known who stood with bated breath to watch her swing. Nellie could not help the tiny gasp of breath she took in, her head spinning with the need to do something, anything, and knowing she could not.

The crowd was swollen with eager chatter, but somehow Jean heard Nellie's shaking breath. The hand Jean slid into

Nellie's trembled softly, but Nellie suspected hers did much the same. So the two women clung tightly to each other, hands hidden within the folds of Nellie's skirt, as though their grip was enough to stop them from shaking, as if it was enough to stop everything that had gone wrong.

The rope creaked. The crowd cheered.

CHAPTER 10

Edinburgh, Scotland
1 October, 1824

"Just behind you, dear." Isobel slid past Nellie, her words nearly lost to the hum of the apothecary and the whirl of anxiety beating against Nellie's brain, clouding her senses.

There was no escaping. Nellie could not seem to silence the weighted creak of the rope and the sight of Helen Gordon's bare feet wiggling through the air, desperate for a hold, until they finally went eerily, hauntingly still. The swathed bushel of ferns she had been working on slipped through Nellie's fingertips, fanning out across the table before her. She heaved a sigh, gathering it together with shaking fingers. The leaves felt like the soft skin of Jean's hand as they'd watched an innocent woman swing, the breeze through the opening door lifting Nellie's fiery hair just as it had Helen's around her hung-down face.

It was Nellie's twenty-third birthday, but she didn't tell a soul; there seemed so little to celebrate. Besides, it felt wrong to celebrate her life continuing when Helen's had just been stolen.

At the very least, for once, Nellie was not alone. On this day or in her sorrow. The somberness that had seeped into the shop since Helen had been taken had grown along the rafters of the apothecary like a mold, a stench rotting them with worry that they all did their best to ignore. Mary laid a fluttering hand on Nellie's arm as she passed, a sign of solidarity that matched the birdlike woman. Ari had grown sparse in the shop for her own safety; Isobel's ever-present smile had dimmed. Even Anne questioned every woman who passed through the shop's doors before offering any services.

The door squeaked as the sole customer took her leave, leaving only the Rae women wandering about the dim room.

"The air in here feels quite thick," Mary said airily, stretching her long form up to hook a copper pot above the fire. It was hardly needed as the breeze drifting in with the customers held the same unseasonable warmth.

"How could it not?" Jean muttered. "We've got a fresh load of trouble on our hands."

"I've told ye, they don't know about us," Anne sighed, passing by her daughter. "There have been plenty of witch hunts. Mary and I have seen our fair share, have we not?"

Her sister nodded, but the two shared a silent conversation Nellie could not interpret. Nellie wondered just how old the two owners of the shop really were.

"It's a hatred of women and a love of power that makes these men string us up. Not any knowledge of the Cailleach or her aides." She shrugged, as though that was any comfort.

As if those in this room weren't all "witches" as much as women. As if woman and witch weren't one and the same nowadays. But she had been alone for a long time and did not want to be alone anymore, so Nellie said nothing.

The government boys may have hung women with a sweeping arm, painting witches over women with a looming brush, but had they not been right once? They were accusing women of being able to do supernatural things, of having great power and influence. And that, at least, was true of the women in Rae's, though they certainly did not work with the devil or curse or spite. Still, had Anne not been hung herself with that title of "witch" stamped on her, even if the commissioner and his men hadn't known that they had titled her correctly?

"Seems they're mostly going for poorer women these days, no?" Isobel looked at Nellie. "They were mostly rooting around your neighborhood?"

"Aye, exactly," Anne answered.

"That doesn't make it better," Jean huffed, setting down the knife in her hand with a thud, the table trembling beneath Nellie's hands—or perhaps that was just her hands themselves. "Are we not meant to help bring all women into their role? To teach and protect them all?"

"We cannot teach anything if we are dead," Anne answered with a sternness in her voice that Nellie had never heard before. Mother and daughter looked at each other with equally hard eyes, and for the first time Nellie could see that perhaps Jean's fire was hereditary.

"If they're treating any woman as a witch . . ." Nellie spoke softly, clearing her throat to be heard. "Perhaps they know any woman could choose to aid the Cailleach and be gifted her powers, if they . . . knew such a thing was possible."

Again, Mary and Anne cut a look to each other, a silent conversation passing with the intimacy of sisterhood.

"It is prejudice and little more. They don't know of us, I'm certain of it." And with Anne's words there was a sense that the conversation had reached a close. The older woman turned away from the others, returning to her work. Isobel stepped to Mary's side at the fire, the phantom of a smile living on her lips no more.

"I thought you—we were supposed to help all women," Nellie said so softly she wasn't sure anyone beyond Jean, who was standing near enough to flinch at the words, had heard her. *I thought you were supposed to help women like me.*

"We can give the lasses who come to the apothecary cures and means to protect themselves, but we cannot just tell them all about the Cailleach. If we do, we endanger ourselves, and if we're gone, the Cailleach will be worse off for it. And those who don't come to the shop at all . . . well . . . we can only do so much." The regret was heavy in Mary's voice but not heavy enough, Nellie thought.

It didn't feel quite right to Nellie, but then again nothing felt right anymore. She wouldn't have even known about the apothecary had fate and misfortune not thrown the Rae women in her path. Had she not found them she could have been the next poor woman to do the jig herself, sentenced for denying a man who wanted her, or for having a father who owed the wrong person money, or simply for existing. And no one would have helped her, for the Nellie of a few weeks ago could hardly help herself.

Anxiety twisted around Nellie's stomach like an insatiable snake, growing with each of her whirring thoughts. Jean, at the very least, seemed as uneasy as she. The dark-haired woman stepped up beside Nellie, her shoulder pressing against Nellie's own. She found that there was room in her stomach for it to swoop further.

"Things aren't right, I know it," Jean grumbled.

"They haven't been right for a while," Nellie returned.

Jean breathed shortly through her nose.

"Well, that's true enough." She looked at Nellie, saw the tightness around her light brows, the pinches of worry that had made a home in the corners of her eyes. "Don't worry. You're with us now. All will be well."

All will be well. Nellie did not choose to believe Jean, she simply did. The other woman spoke it like an incantation, as though her words could will it into truth, forcing the hand of the universe. If there's anyone who could, Nellie thought it would be Jean.

Nellie had spent a decade with her knees on the wood of a church pew before the symbol of a God she wasn't sure she believed in. But she would believe everything Jean said without question, with pleasure, would happily kneel at the altar of every word that came off the other woman's tongue.

"And we're daughters of the Cailleach. Hags. Witches. We're not so helpless as those men would like to believe women to be." The corners of Jean's lips lifted, a shallow, forced imitation of the expression she usually donned. Nellie recognized the attempt at normalcy, whether for Jean's sake or her own, she could not be sure. But she knew that it was nice to be looked out for, to be the one cared for, for once.

"That we are." Nellie knew her own answering smile, at least, was genuine. She could not help it, to smile before Jean, even as the world seemed to burn around them.

"Though are you truly a daughter of the Cailleach now, Nell?" Jean challenged, swinging the loose curtain of her hair behind her, awakening the long, bare stretch of her neck.

Nellie held up the fern in her hands, now dried and swaddled with an expert hand as she'd been taught. "I hope so."

"You're certainly a good worker in the apothecary, but there's more to being a true daughter of the Cailleach than that. She doesn't give her power out to everyone who can dry an herb."

"Oh?"

Jean nodded, a spark of mirth lighting her dark eyes.

"What else, then?" Nellie asked. "Teach me."

Jean's smirk was as dangerous as the power that ran through her veins. Nellie's insides thrilled. A bit of Jean's fire coursed through the length of her body in a flash that had Nellie pushing the heavy weight of her braid from her shoulder.

"Well, ye know a bit of the craft, though I suppose you

won't know the full effect until you're a proper daughter."
Jean swept a thin arm out to gesture at the shop around them.
"Something must be preventing you from getting there. Her
traits, what she stands for. Her hags must embrace and live
that too. Do you know how to truly tap into yourself and the
spirit of the Cailleach and believe you deserve to take up space
and have what you desire?"

Nellie felt her cheeks take on an embarrassing flush at the
word *desire* on Jean's lips.

"No," she breathed. Though perhaps that wasn't true, for
here Jean stood before her, everything Nellie feared, everything she wanted to be and simply *wanted*.

"People come to us not just for our knowledge or the products we can give them. Maybe some of our customers who
come in for things like a tea for joy or a salve to bring about a
child don't believe in the craft, deem our products working
just 'luck.' But, sometimes, it's enough just to have people who
will listen to them. Who hear their aches and problems and
ailments and believe them. Who believe they deserve to be
heard and, like the Cailleach inspires, to take up space and be
true to themselves." Jean spoke with a firm, flinty passion.
"But that's what separates customers from the Cailleach's children: believing and knowing, in themselves, that they deserve
to be heard and to speak, to want and to be. One can't be a
daughter of the Cailleach, with all the power she represents, if
they don't think they deserve that. You cannot apologize for
what you want, even if the world says someone like you
shouldn't have it."

"It's that simple?" Nellie didn't quite believe it.

"Aye. Certain things can help bring it forth, give ye a boost,
like hag stones. Also the weather, the time of day, the season,
of course." Jean shrugged. "Above all, ye must really believe
it. It's all about intention. The Cailleach is powerful, despite
the stories that try to rob her of that power, because she
knows she is and deserves to be, no matter what. Women are

so often made to feel powerless; the Cailleach can help them find strength in themselves and in each other."

There were so few things Nellie had ever fully believed in, things she knew without a doubt to be the truth. She'd spent years in the kirk and prayed to a God she was never sure she felt, that she was never sure she wanted to believe in, if He could make such heinous things occur. If she could lose her mother, lose their coin, feel the weight of men's hands and eyes, the noose around every woman's neck. But she wanted to believe in Jean. Nellie wanted to believe that she was not so helpless as she had been taught.

"Get to know the Cailleach—it'll help ye embrace all she is. Deep in the city sometimes the Cailleach can feel far. But the moon looks down on all the land and, well, sometimes I look up at it to speak to her. Especially the full moon, silver as the frost she creates," the other woman provided.

"I think I'd feel a bit foolish speaking to the moon." Nellie tried for lightness, but Jean's face was serious.

"If ye believe yourself to be a fool, ye will be. And you are no fool, Nell."

Her heart pattered out an uneven rhythm, and Nellie found it had taken up residence in her throat, making her unable to speak. As if she could hear the desire in Nellie's blood, Jean spoke on, her smile turned cutting and wicked.

"Embracing the traits of the Cailleach is different for each woman, you know. There's independence, and anger, and demanding respect. Unapologetically accepting yerself for who ye are. To do that, many find they must welcome the desire that blooms in them, that the world tells women they should be ashamed of." She waited for a beat, her eyes on Nellie, not even daring to blink. "Do you honor yourself as a sexual being, Nell?"

Nellie held her breath, for if she did not it would come out in unsteady rasps, would expose her for everything she was and everything she wanted.

"I—" But Nellie found all she knew of acting on desire had been men inflicting it upon her unwilling, moments that had made her tuck herself into her body. Nellie had never let her desire bloom out of her, spring her hands into action. But she wanted to. She wanted.

In that moment Nellie thought she knew desire like she never had before, more than the passing flash of skin above a dress, or forearms twisted with muscle, more than the sight of straight lines beneath trouser legs, or curves and valleys hidden beneath skirts. She knew that the truth of her desire was just another danger in her life as a woman who could one day be a witch. But nevertheless, Nellie nodded and knew if she had not honored that part of herself yet, she wanted to.

CHAPTER 11

Edinburgh, Scotland
5 October, 1824

Nellie pressed a hand flat to the front of her skirts, smothering her pocket down. She could not risk the sound of its contents catching the ear of any of her neighbors. With each step the coins she'd earned working at Rae's clinked against her legs, reminding her of what she had that those around her didn't—and maybe thought she shouldn't. Being a woman was enough, but a woman with coin painted a target on her back—Nellie had been at work enough of her life to know that. But still her coin was safer there, pressed possessively to her person. For it was not only her neighbors' greed she need fear; Nellie had so much more money than the bit she tossed her father every Friday, quickly washed away down a pint.

October had broken, but it was warm enough for Nellie to have forsaken her cloak. She had grown used to a certain, haunted sort of silence in her neighborhood, quiet enough that the people could tell themselves they were safe and hidden away. But that night, the shadows spoke. Or perhaps it was the walls themselves that whispered. Sometimes Nellie felt that people like her, the people birthed in the dirt and raised in the crumbling stones, were little more than the tilting structures they called home. In Rae's it was easy enough to set aside the terror that raced through their city. But in her neighborhood the night seemed darker and the noose felt like it was closing quick over their necks.

"Isn't that what the Duncan man does?" came a voice made of nightfall, whispered from the far end of the alleyway.

Nellie froze, the mention of Da stilling her feet. She snapped to attention, tucking herself behind the lopsided wood door of her building. She held her breath to hear the next words from her faceless companions.

"*Did*, more like, from what I've heard," answered a man's heavy chuckle. "Not up in the tower, like. The commissioner wants boys with boots in the soil, making rounds about the cemetery, among the dead."

Nellie tried to smother her quick intake of breath, to quiet the little gasps her breathing had become.

"The resurrection men getting that bad, are they?" The first voice asked, one that Nellie thought she recognized as Alan Kelly, a man about her Da's age who lived with his wife and bairns just beneath them.

It could be just that, Nellie told herself. Or it could be more. It could be worse. It could be that the commissioner and his men knew that some of the women they put in the ground would not stay there. Guilt twisted around Nellie's insides just to think it, but for a fleeting moment she was grateful it was Helen Gordon most freshly in the soil, a woman who didn't even know she could have had the ability to rise up again and therefore would not. A decent, innocent soul lost, but an inadvertent protection of her fellow women.

Things had never been great, never been easy. But how did they all become so, so wrong? How had it become that the killing of an innocent woman was a cause for relief?

"Aye, well, for a shilling you can pass my name along."

"I will that."

"I'd happily go keep Helen Gordon in the ground, the old bitch."

Nellie could hear the anger slither out of Alan's words like a snake. She could feel the vitriol on the air toward a woman Alan had only ever passed with smiles and civilities.

"Happy to help keep the witches out of town. Too headstrong these women are getting."

Women, witches, as if the two were interchangeable. As though it didn't really matter which they were. The two men spoke with such matched, sudden hatred, words pointed with almost rehearsed malice, like they were reading a script of loathing.

Nellie made her way up the steps to her home before the men could spot her and drag her to the commissioner themselves, reward and hatred on their mind. Their tiny room was dim and silent, the fire in the grate so poorly stoked that Nellie knew Da had been round the pub all day. Thomas, tucked away in the corner waiting for her, hadn't yet gotten the taste for keeping a fire.

He is still so small. So innocent, Nellie thought. *I do not ever want him to become like the men downstairs. Like the men who crawl across Edinburgh like poisonous spiders. I do not ever want him to hate me simply because I was born a different shape than he was.*

"Hello, my boy." She placed a soft hand atop the boy's head, pulling him against her skirts as he bounded over to greet her, following her to the hearth like an eager, obedient pup.

Sometimes looking at Thomas was painful because she loved him so much and she feared the world would not. She had thought it many times over the past decade of the boy's life, and Nellie thought it again then: *At least he is a boy, and thank God for it.* Even a poor boy could be greeted by the world with the open hands of opportunity. To be a woman was to be met with claws.

He smiled up at her, chattering away about some or other boy in the neighborhood, and Nellie realized Tommy hardly knew of their poorness, of the way the world pressed down on them. Because Nellie had stood above him, holding the world up on her caving spine so he could move freely and happily beneath it. She had never paused long enough to feel the strain before, but suddenly she felt her spine would break. All she wanted to do was lay down, alone, and rest.

But she could not. So she set about putting the porridge above the flames, Thomas's growling stomach not even aware of how much she had worked at the shop to be able to trade thin stew for oats. She tried not to envy him his ignorance. She knew well enough that had never been an option for her.

Hours later, the boy snoring softly on his cot, Nellie finally laid down on her own. The straw of it poked through to her aching bones, the little hag stone Mary had given her a lump beneath her pillow, held tightly in her fist just as it had been every night since. In her other hand she gripped the crisp line of charcoal, the black skating across a fresh sheet of parchment, only the dim moonlight cutting through the grime of the window to guide her.

She could not help the image her fingers conjured forth, the same one that lived in her mind—a wide, smirking mouth, eyes and hair as true black as the charcoal that depicted them. There was a shameful humming throughout Nellie's body, as she remembered the way Jean had placed the charcoal in her care, the way the woman had touched her. Thoughts she should not have, not ever, especially not when there were so many other things that should occupy her mind. But she felt the charcoal, coarse and gliding, across her fingertips, and she could not help but feel Jean too.

Thomas let out another snore. It was a small sound, but it was enough to scatter Nellie's brain, to let the shame take hold. She tucked away the charcoal and paper, hidden beneath her pillow alongside the stone; hiding items beneath her body was the only place she could have privacy. As if a woman's body is ever just hers.

She turned on her side, eyes finding the glint of the moon above her. It was not full, only half of its round body protruding from the dark blanket of nightfall. But it was there, and so was Nellie, the two women looking at each other.

Nellie took a deep breath, let her eyes drift closed, the silver light painting her inner lids in its image.

"I just . . . well, hello, Cailleach, if you're there. I, well, I am doing my best to aid you. To be one of your hags, to be in your service. To embrace your strength and independence into my own life." Even in her whispered words, with no one to see or hear her but Thomas's sleeping form, Nellie felt a fool. But she remembered what Jean had said. The work in the shop was not enough to make Nellie a witch in truth. She had to believe it. And she knew being a witch was dangerous, but just as much she knew there was power in it too. The Cailleach showed that, clearly. Power Nellie did not have now. Power she may not ever have otherwise. And she wanted it.

"I want Thomas to be safe, even if I am not around. He *will* be safe, even if I am not here to care for him. This is your land, your creation. If he is here, you can protect him when I cannot, right? *Please.*"

This wasn't a prayer, words said hoping for a blessing in return. This was a conversation. The Cailleach's hags were not her followers or devotees. They were her aides, her helpers.

The hazy halo around the moon remained steady and strong, but Nellie felt something swoop in her chest. Her nostrils filled, faintly and briefly, with the earthy, bitter scent of soil covered by fresh snowfall. It felt like a confirmation. A presence. A promise. She found that was all she needed to believe.

It is easy to believe something when you want to.

"I want to be safe, too," she added, almost as an afterthought. "I want to live too."

Weeks later Nellie would remember this; decades later she would recall the first time she spoke to the Cailleach through the moon. And she would wish she had changed her words. She would wish she had included more names, had realized how much they would be needed.

Some days, the darkest ones, she'd wished she had never said that last line at all.

CHAPTER 12

Edinburgh, Scotland
8 October, 1824

The Rae women all crowded about the customer, the soft lilt of accents layering atop one another. The woman's stomach kept them all at bay, protruding vastly and proudly out from her middle. Nellie stood alone along the wall, apart from the others. She had never been drawn to such an experience, never imagined herself as a mother because she'd never imagined herself in the position needed to get there. The thought of being a wife was almost warm, but the thought of being a man's wife . . . it sent a shock through her, the echo of inescapable panic.

She may find herself desiring men, wanting them, but she knew that, for far too many women, becoming a wife meant losing independence, being owned, being told to be meek and cooperative and happy, to have your body, legally, belong to another. Being a wife could mean being the very opposite of all that the Cailleach stood for, that a woman must do to become one of her witches and have a second life.

There were those like Isobel, married to a man she praised as kind and open and loving. She said that he encouraged her to embrace all that the Cailleach was, and even as his wife she was a witch—though, of course, her husband did not know this. Nellie feared that was the exception, not the norm. If anything, she told herself that Isobel's husband not knowing she was a witch was only proof that, no matter how loving a husband is, there may still be something to fear, for the world still gave him power over his wife.

She may have to fight for coin and food and shelter, but she could at least thank her poorness for that—even beauty like hers was not enough to make most men seek out a poor woman for a wife. They wanted to own her for a night, not a lifetime.

As Anne laid a gentle hand on the woman's stomach, the rest of the women breezed around the store like birds lost down an alley, eager to help. There'd been so few customers in the shop the past few days that the women of Rae's hardly remembered how to greet a newcomer with professional distance, how to move about one another seamlessly as they set to their tasks. Ari had taken to only coming into the shop once a week, but Nellie had been glad to see her there today along with the others. It was a rare day that all the Rae women were in the shop.

Ari's elbow bumped against Isobel's side, the two women trading a light chuckle at the collision. The heavy atmosphere of the shop was lifted by the presence of a customer, and one there for such a pleasant cause. Jean's hip grazed against Nellie's as the two moved, orbiting around each other. The look they shared was not one of smiles and lightness but something else that made Nellie's cheeks warm as she remembered the scribbled drawing of Jean tucked away beneath her skirts.

She gathered fresh raspberry, slicing three jagged-edged leaves from the plant. They were good in a tea during pregnancy, soothing any nausea and preparing the body for birthing. Nellie added them to the bag, Jean's and Ari's hands both quickly tossing in their additions, a heady and naturalistic scent overtaking the air of the shop. Nellie scrawled a rising sun on the little tassel hanging from it, the swell of the orb mirroring the woman's growing belly.

"It's a lad." Anne was nodding, her small hand held against the customer's bulging stomach, a smile on both of their faces.

That's safer. Be glad, Nellie thought.

"Yer carrying low. The lads like to settle in lower."

"Whoever they may be, I hope they come soon." The woman sighed, her hand finding the small of her back, holding herself aloft as the weight of the babe in her belly pulled her forth.

"This'll help that for certain." Isobel held out the bushel of teabags. "Every night before ye sleep for a week. I drank it when my wee lass was past due, and she came about before the fourth night."

The coin passed hands, for it was coin the shop needed most these days, customers becoming sparse as they had. Then the woman was out the door, the ding of the bell and the soft click of the wood marking the end of the lightness. Where the babe-to-be had brought the thought of a pleasant future, the present settled once more on the Rae women, a heavy weight.

"I suppose that'll be the last customer we see today." Jean sighed, turning from them.

"The women are scared to be seen about the shop, secretive as it may be. Can you blame them? I'm nervous myself." Ari shrugged.

Nellie felt words bubbling up on her tongue. She'd been swallowing them for days. She worried that in saying her fears aloud she'd make them real. Or worse, that if she continued to bring the bad news of her neighborhood, to report the sorry fate that awaited the women of Edinburgh, the Rae women would no longer want to count her among their ranks. That she would become a bad omen, a poppet of ill luck. That she would no longer be one of them and would learn that she never really had been.

But she didn't think she could swallow the words any longer, could carry the weight of the knowledge she had gathered, the things she feared, all on her own.

"I think the commissioner and his men know. About the Cailleach, and that some women are her witches, and have a second life . . ." She breathed deep, then told the women around her what she had overheard the other night. How the commission sought guards to stroll among the graves, watchful eyes upon every bit of upturned soil.

She expected to be met with silence when she finished. For the knowledge to sit as heavy and true upon the women as it had on her. But Anne was quick to speak.

"No, it's mere coincidence, I'm certain of it. It's the resurrection men they fear. They know nothing."

"Mum, ye cannot know that." Jean stepped forward, the firmness of her voice making her as much a presence as her towering height over her mother. "Nellie is right, it sounds like they may know."

"I know you girls are worried, I understand. But this is just the government boys looking to put a stop to crime, to win over the poorer folk whose women they come for by giving the men some coin in their pockets." Anne sounded like she was trying to convince herself as much as the rest of them. But she would not budge. "They don't know anything. How could they?"

How could they? Nellie didn't know, but it did little to comfort her.

"Ma, they hung *you*. And on little more than some horseshite charge. Now this? Yer telling me that's mere coincidence?"

Nellie had barely had a mother and could not imagine fighting with her. She took a step away to hide from the disorder her words had brought about.

"They're looking for women who disrupt their idea of what a lass should be. It does not mean they know about witches. They were not conspiring to get me. I was in the wrong place at the wrong time and was an old lady who dared to speak up, little else."

Nellie hadn't fully heard the story of how Anne had come to be upon the gallows. All she knew was that it had involved a young girl in the market struck by the hand of her father and Anne, seeing the abuse, had been unable to hold her tongue. It would not have even been the place of the child's mother to defy the father, let alone a woman unknown. And soon as Anne stepped in, the man got a coughing fit. Couldn't have been from all the smog on the air, no; she cursed him, he claimed.

"What would ye like us to do? Come out and tell the whole city every woman can be a witch, swing on by the shop to learn how?! All we can do is wait," Anne said.

They take to my neighborhood, to the poor, because they know we're the most vulnerable, Nellie thought. *And that no one will risk themselves for us. We have the least to lose and the most to gain.*

Mother and daughter stared at each other now, tension thick on the air between them. They had been here before, had stayed at this impasse, Jean and Nellie fearful, Mary and Anne exchanging glances they would not translate. Isobel and Ari stepped to the side, waiting for the tension to break.

"If it comes about that they know, then we'll figure it out from there. For now, we must stay below ground. Keep doing our craft, keep embracing the Cailleach—that is how she gets stronger. And it is nearly Winter—she needs us alive and well, she needs our help for the turning of the seasons. Getting ourselves killed will not help her or the women of the city," Anne conceded at last.

But it was not enough for her daughter.

"We can't do *nothing*." Jean's hands lifted and fell by her sides in frustration.

Nellie wasn't sure she agreed anymore, with reality knocking at their door. She wanted to be safe, for Jean to be safe, to protect the women there in that room. She wished she could be like Jean, a crusader to help all women, to do for others what they did for Nellie, taking her in and sharing their wisdom and saving her. But she wanted herself and her own's safety more than she wanted to save the world. She did not think that made her a bad person, or a worse witch, if she really was one. The Cailleach didn't give a second life to everyone, only to her hag servants who aided her. Was Nellie, too, not simply looking out for her own?

"We'll do what we must. For now, that is wait." Anne stepped away, placing a hand on her sister's arm. That silent correspondence passed between them before the two left through the far door, up to the stairs that led to the flat above, without a word.

Jean paced across the shop, her frustration painted plain across her face, dark hair trailing behind her like a lick of black flame.

"Well, I sure do hope the government boys are none the wiser," Ari said, the joking lilt of her voice slightly forced but present none the less. "I'm on my last life, and I'd like to hold on to it, thank you."

Nellie, desperate to feel the air around Jean settle, for them all to move past the questions left in the wake of the two older women's departures, followed Ari's lead.

"Are ye? Did you misplace the first one?"

Ari barked out a laugh, the echoing sound replacing Jean's footfalls as the other woman stilled. Even Isobel's smile returned, briefly.

"Seems I did, right under the wheel of a carriage when I was barely thirteen. Lucky enough my ma, rest her soul, knew me for myself and had already brought me to the shop with her, had already started teaching me the ways of the Cailleach. Suppose she was right though: kids shouldn't play in the street after all." The words were grim, the image they painted grue-some. Nellie's stomach tightened, suddenly realizing that while they had an advantage with a second life and slowed aging, the women she knew were not immortal. And danger was near, whether or not it knew them on sight.

"What about you, Nellie?" Isobel asked, her face once again devoid of its usual grin.

"What about me?"

"Do ye have both yer lives? Though I suppose unless you've died in the past few weeks and forgotten to mention ye must, being so new to the craft and all."

"Aye, I have them both." *Hopefully.* She could not feel the telltale chill she had heard of when she was in the shop. If she could not identify other daughters of the Cailleach, perhaps that meant she was not yet one herself. Nellie supposed she wouldn't know for certain if she was truly a witch until she was in need of that second life and it was too late to do any-thing for it. She hoped that time would not come as soon as she feared it might.

"As do I. Lucky lasses," Isobel said. The warm woman squeezed Nellie's arm.

"What about you?" Nellie turned her gaze to Jean. She im-mediately sensed her misstep by the sudden, jarring silence of Ari and Isobel behind her. She expected Jean to meet her with sharp eyes and tongue, to make a remark on whatever fault Nellie had unknowingly unearthed.

And while there was a defensive distance in her dark eyes, there was no anger.

"Just the one left. Horrible fever did it. Though could have been whatever all this is. Who knows?" Jean laid a hand on her hip, and Nellie knew she meant the ache that plagued her joints, the tremble it took through her body, the way it kept her bedridden for days at a time. "Seems possible, seeing as how the aching all started just a few years after. Mary found me unmoving and soaked in my bed one morning, not a breath to be found. I'm lucky I was born to witches, had been raised as a daughter of the Cailleach. I was back on my feet by nightfall and the fever passed soon after."

Accident and age, angry men and nooses, were what they all had to fear. But Jean had the killing thing right there in her bones, beating along with her blood. Nellie's stomach clenched.

"What is it like? To . . . come back?"

"Like waking up. I wouldn't have known I had even passed had Mum and Aunt Mary not told me." Jean looked to Ari for confirmation, and the other woman nodded, her light hair falling into her eyes.

"I suppose my mangled middle would have told me as well." Ari quipped, eliciting a surprised chuckle from Isobel.

But Nellie couldn't quite find laughter in her throat, looking at the haunted look that had fallen over Jean's eyes.

"Is it . . . are you different? After, I mean?"

"We heal from whatever it is that killed us, but there's usually some sort of ache left behind. I still have pain in my stomach, often. But it could be worse. I was young enough not to be bothered much, I suppose." Ari shrugged. "If I've learned one thing living with my brother's wee ones, it's that children always seem to bounce back quickly, don't they?"

"Just the same for me." Jean said. "But some women are. Mary . . . Mum says she was much *more* before. She does not talk about it, but Mum told me Mary was hanged as a witch a long time ago. Got in a squabble with a neighbor and got caught up in the madness. We might know her as a quiet woman, but she didn't used to be. It can change ye."

Nellie wasn't so sure if it was death that brought about the change so much as fear. Mary had seen just how evil man could be, and now she could not live in a world without that knowledge. Despite Anne's reassurances, which Nellie repeated to herself silently like a prayer—*They don't know of us, it is little more than government grappling, we have the power of the Cailleach and what we are*—Nellie suspected they would all soon come to know that kind of evil intimately.

CHAPTER 13

Edinburgh, Scotland
11 October, 1824

For once, there was silence. Or as much silence as Jean ever allowed, each breath carrying angry mutterings on the state of the city, the state of the woman, the state of the world. But Nellie didn't mind at all, especially out here, where it seemed like the two of them were the only people left in the world. The crags kissed the line of the city proper, perched at the end of the main street like protective giants. Down past New Calton, past the taverns at the outskirts, came flat fields of green and then a collection of proud hills, from which one could see the entirety of the city on one side and the open, freeing expanse of the water on the other. Where they were now, standing on one of the plateaued hills, was like being at the very end of the world.

Nellie sometimes forgot that Edinburgh was this too—not just shadows and cobblestones and the humid press of grime-soaked, scowling people. But also, these rolling green hills, their swells dotted in purple heather and pink thistle, jutting stones that stood sturdy amid the heavy wind. It bloomed in color in a way the city proper did not, as if this was a world created from richest paint, and Edinburgh city was a scape made by Nellie's grim charcoal. She felt the itch in her fingers to draw the crags, to make the land immortal on the page, untouchable by man. Nellie breathed deep, thankful for the chill on the air as it filled her lungs.

There was little civilization out on the crags, just a glimpse of nature untouched—the very reason they were there. That morning Jean had declared she was off to the crags to collect the last of the season's gorse—a prickled, brightest yellow flower. She'd said it was best to treat fever, a necessity to have in shop with the coming winter months, when the Cailleach and her power swelled. The plant should've been long dead with the arrival of autumn, but the season had carried in unnatural warmth that had allowed many of the spring and summer plants to hang on until the last. The rising temperature was also the very reason Jean wanted more gorse—just that morning a mother had come in, eyes fearful and shifting, looking for a treatment for the flaming forehead of herself and her babe. She wasn't the only such Nellie had seen in the last few weeks. It was too early for fevers, but more than a few women had entered the shop, sure that they were flaming up.

Nellie could not be certain; she was no physician herself. Nevertheless, she was thankful that the whipping wind out there was crisp and cool, slapping her skirt against her ankles. It was the first time she had been beyond the stone and smoke of the city since learning about the Cailleach. And there, standing on the rises and falls of her creation, large and untamed, Nellie felt closer to her than she ever had.

It was more than the fresh air that had drawn her out when Jean asked if she'd help, certain she'd need another set of hands to gather it all, to hold the bushels and baskets. Nellie wasn't so sure about that, but she was happy enough just to have a moment alone with Jean. Even if it meant pricking her fingers on spiked stems, watching Jean mindlessly place the little dots of red that bloomed on her own fingers into her mouth. Wishing she would do the same to Nellie's.

Jean muttered a word Nellie had never heard from a lady as another prick struck her finger, though she still dropped the gorse into their basket with a gentle hand. Nellie couldn't help, hardly even noticed, the smile that pushed its way up her own lips. But it wavered as she thought of the day before, seeing a similar smile on Jean's face when Louisa Scott had returned to the shop seeking a treatment for her sleep. The same flirtatious words had passed between her and Jean. Nellie's chest tightened to remember just as it did then. She dredged up a flower, tearing the roots from the soil with an unneeded harshness, the rocks pressing into her knees where she knelt.

The air smelled heavily sweet, like coconut and vanilla, the unique, distinguishable scent of gorse, strong on the nose of many, light for others. With a deep breath Nellie looked out at the city below and before them, so small and infinitesimal from up here on the crag. The city was nothing but dim closes and grimy stone, and it was easy to forget, out here, that all the horror that happened between those stones was real. That it was anything more than a dream. But Louisa Scott's flirting smile felt real, and though Nellie knew she had no right to ask, being out on the crags, away from her world, made her feel like someone else. Someone braver.

"Are you very familiar with Louisa Scott?"

Jean paused, and a yellow petal floated from her hand to land softly upon the grass. Her dark hair lifted up behind her like a cloak, the image of the witch the world feared, the witch she was. The whites of her eyes had grown pink with the sting of the wind and her lips, when they grew into that knowing smile, were stung red.

"Aye, you could say."

She did not return to her work, her eyes holding Nellie's,

nothing but the basket on the ground between them. Nellie wanted to ask exactly what she needed to know. She wanted answers and yet was terrified of getting them, of putting into words things she had hardly thought to herself.

"How familiar?" she whispered.

Jean didn't so much as blink.

"Familiar as you're thinking," she answered, voice unwavering.

"How?" Nellie's words were nearly lost to the wind. "Do you—? What I mean is are you—"

"I'm just the same as you. You know what I want just as much as you know what it is you're after."

There was a beat of silence where even the wind seemed to still, where all Nellie could hear was her heart thumping in her chest, bones ready to crack. But Jean was never one to shy away from a challenge.

"It's not just men for me. It's women too. Just as I know it is for you, Nell." Jean's dark eyes did not once look away from Nellie's.

Nellie's stomach flipped. Her throat was wedged so tightly that she could scarcely breathe around that thing, that want for something, so much want that you become afraid to have it, that you think you will die if you do and die if you do not. That was what Nellie felt as she looked at Jean kneeling so close, the energy of Jean's skin tingling on Nellie's own. The wind snapped Jean's dark hair against her face, pale skin flushed pink from the cold, and despite it all that too wide smile was on her face because being out there, on that land that was cold and quiet, was something like freedom. It suited Jean well.

Nellie wasn't sure she had ever seen anything so beautiful as Jean in that moment.

Don't you want to be free?

Nellie did not think as she leaned forward, as she pressed

her mouth to Jean's, hair tangling between their lips and beating against their faces. Nellie knew they were out in the open and they should not, but they did. They did.

Nellie could feel the smile on Jean's mouth as her lips moved against her own, and she did not taste of bitterness, did not feel brimming with harsh words and burning rage. She was warm and smooth, and everything Nellie had ever imagined. And as Jean's hand found its way to knot in her hair, Nellie met desire for the very first time and knew to call it by its name.

For once, Nellie acknowledged that she wanted something. For once she let herself have it.

Despite the warm flush on the air the sky was streaked with the pink brushstrokes of a winter twilight. Nellie was thankful for the hazy dimness, for she was certain that her red cheeks would have told any passersby that Jean's mouth had just been on her own, that she thrummed with its memory.

Thoughtlessly Nellie brought her fingers to gently touch her lips as they turned onto Old Assembly Close. Even as the darkness of the alley fell over them, the sky like a strip of colored ribbon between the rooftops overhead, she caught the sight of Jean's self-satisfied grin. She didn't even check that they were entirely alone before weaving her fingers into Nellie's and pulling her through the doorway of the apothecary. Nellie had hardly noticed they'd arrived, lost in her mind as she was, and the shop as hidden in plain sight as always.

The hanging herbs and cluttered shelves made monsters of the shadows. But Nellie noticed none of it, the feel of Jean's hand in hers the only sense she had left. The other woman deposited the basket of gorse on an empty table and turned to Nellie, the silence of the shop too heavy, too expecting. Nellie wanted Jean to never leave her side, to keep touching her. She wanted her to leave her be, to let her be alone so her body could feel like it was more than a pattering drum again.

"Do ye want to come up, then?" For that was who Jean was—she would push boundaries, she would not be coy, but she wouldn't give Nellie an easy escape either. She would make Nellie decide. "I'd like it if ye did."

And that little acquiescence, that little vulnerability—for that was what it was—was a steadying hand to Nellie's nerves. She nodded.

Jean led her through the heavy door on the far side of the shop, winding up a narrow stone staircase. Nellie's breath shallowed with exertion and fear and the unfamiliar strain of want. The staircase opened onto a dark hallway, doors dotting each side. Their steps were muffled to Nellie's ears, her mind whirring and her blood racing, as they made their way to the second door on the right. Jean's bedroom was narrow with little more than a slender bed, but it was more than Nellie had ever known for herself.

The single window looked out at the castle in the distance, its windows alight against the navy sky, casting a soft, glowing haze across the room. Nellie could just barely make out the furnishings, the deep intimacy of seeing Jean's crumpled blanket on the bed, the pillow whose body bore the imprint of her head. The world was out there, with all its faults and fears, but in this room it was just Nellie and all the little pieces that made up Jean Rae.

Finally, Jean stepped forth, pressing herself against Nellie's back. Her long fingers swept the loose hair from Nellie's neck, her lips following the path in a light dusting. Nellie's skin tightened and trembled beneath the touch, gentle as a breeze. Jean's hands wrapped around Nellie's middle, pressing against her stomach. Nellie worried Jean could feel her heart pounding through her, falling through her body to live, almost painfully, between her legs. She was too aware of her body, standing frozen as a statue, afraid that any move could be the wrong one. Her body felt too big, with too many limbs, too awkward, yet her skin felt too small to fit everything that grew and raced inside her. Nellie was aware of how her tiny, trembling breaths were the only sound in the room.

She wanted to move, wanted to reach out and touch Jean in the way she'd only ever imagined in those fearful, quiet, tumultuous moments. But fear and want froze her in equal measure.

But then Jean's left hand was sliding down Nellie's stomach, the fingers of her right splaying up Nellie's neck in an almost-grip, and Nellie's body seemed to come alive on its own. Her neck tilted back, falling against Jean's shoulder so the other woman's mouth could make its way to her ear, the thin skin of her neck, her tongue like a line of fire. Nellie's body could do as it must, arch herself to press wholly against where Jean lined her back and enveloped her.

Her touch was patient, not tentative but soft, as if Nellie was worth savoring. Like it was Nellie who Jean wanted, not just her body. With one last breath for confidence Nellie turned, her lips finding Jean's with a reborn fire. Jean's hands did not shift, simply pressing Nellie to her body, afraid to lose her.

The windowsill pressed into Nellie's lower back, and her body seemed to know what to do once she let it follow its want. She leaned onto the window's edge, lifting a leg to wrap about Jean's hips, thrilled as the woman's hand eagerly found the newly exposed skin of her thigh. Her clothing was quick to find its way to the floor, and she wasn't sure if the rising goose bumps across her body were from the nerves trembling through her or Jean's touches, growing firmer. The other woman's clothes fell away as Nellie's quivering fingers wove in and out of laces.

All the fire that lived inside Jean seemed to seep into Nellie's skin in the wake of the other woman's hands on her waist, over the swell of her hips, her thighs, her. Then Jean was falling to her knees before Nellie, and she was grateful for the cool flush of the window on her back as Jean's hands, her mouth, made Nellie bloom into opening. Night fell beyond as the moisture of Nellie's skin made the window slick, as Jean's fingerprints skated down it as they did Nellie's skin, the air of the room never seeming enough to fill the quick gasps and sighs of her lungs.

Time seemed to fade and ripple, and Nellie could judge how much of it had passed only from the gentle soreness in her body as she finally lay atop Jean's bed. Her head was nestled into the living dent in the pillow, the other woman's hair fanning across her sternum like an ink spill. She was glad Jean's head laid on her chest so she could not see the small smile on Nellie's lips, somehow embarrassing after all they had come to know of each other, an intimacy unlike anything Nellie had ever experienced. It was a softness she had only imagined, a heat she never thought she could have.

The world seemed quiet, not eerie, or haunting, but calm. Nellie wasn't sure she knew what peace was before that moment.

Jean trailed lazy fingers through the red of Nellie's hair, falling across her breasts. The other woman had no such qualms, no self-consciousness of worry, tipping her head up to flash Nellie her feline smile, so unabashedly pleased with herself. Her mouth found Nellie's chest in soft, fluttering kisses, a gentle finale not meant to incite, but Nellie's blood sang.

The stillness of them was interrupted by a frantic knock on the door of Jean's room. The other woman did not startle, did not frenzy, but her movements ceased, both holding their breath. It was not trouble or retribution Nellie feared, though she knew distantly that she should, shouldn't she? But there could not be anything wrong in so much rightness. The knock was the return of the world beyond, a stark, humbling reminder that it was only this room that held blooming beauty, that existed. That outside of it was fear and desolation. This was a candle in the darkness, this moment between them, but it was not the world.

"Jean, are ye in there?" It was Anne's voice, and even through the wood Nellie could hear the tightness in it, the fear. Panic seemed to seep in beneath the door, choking her. The women pushed themselves out of bed, skirts and cloaks finding their owners, fingers trembling with something so different than that which removed them.

Jean opened the door when they were both covered at last. Not a word passed between them, hardly even a gaze; they could not bear to see the loss of their peace, the fracturing of the safety of this room. Anne did not seem startled to find them both within, the pinch of her brow too consuming, the downturn of her lips holding words Nellie did not want to hear.

But time passed, as it always did, and trouble and death found Nellie in a way she thought perhaps it always would.

"Isobel's been arrested for witchcraft," Anne said.

The peace of the room left through the window as trouble entered through the door.

CHAPTER 14

Edinburgh, Scotland
16 October, 1824

They made quick work of Isobel, the commissioner and his team.

They don't know, Nellie repeated the words to herself like a prayer. Each day she believed them less. *It is a hatred of women, not a knowledge of true "witches."*

But Nellie was not so sure those two were not the same thing. It seemed less and less like it mattered if they knew the truth of witches—to hate witches was to hate women. To hang women was to hang witches. If anything, the sweeping, greedy arm of the commission, taking any woman they could to the gallows, made it seem as though they did know that any woman could choose to aid the Cailleach and become a "witch." Either way, it did not seem to matter so much anymore. They were in danger. Trouble had landed right at their feet.

Anne had been quick enough, had moved in silence to ensure that Isobel's little girl was safe with her husband, a kind man, Nellie knew, from Isobel's stories, even if he did not know his wife actually was the witch she had been accused as. The charges against her were little, hardly even known to the public; an already arrested woman had seemed to name Isobel as a conspirator, Isobel's open personality and helpfulness turned into evidence against her. It did not really matter—the crowds on Grassmarket did not need a reason for why a woman swung anymore. The frenzied rage of the city seemed to have seeped deep.

It is easy to believe something when you want to.

No open trial was held for Isobel—the opinion of the commission was enough. Each day for three days Jean and Nellie stood in a crowd before the gallows, waiting to see if it would be the woman they knew strung up. They did not even take the gallows down at nightfall anymore, for each morning saw a fresh rope, a new dead-eyed woman on its ladder.

The crowd seemed to be bigger than ever that day, with no hush of reverent silence. There was only excited chatter and crack-toothed smiles, as if the people of Edinburgh were attending the theatre. But was that not why the women hung— for entertainment?

Sweat bloomed on Nellie's neck as she stood, pressed tight in the crowd, but she dared not move her bun from her nape, dared not lift her eyes. For who knew what accusation could be found in her movements, what guilt lived in the blue of her eyes? Jean was not at her side, not anymore. But she could feel the presence of the other woman across the crowd, the strangers between them a necessity for safety. Though safety seemed like a distant wish, a hazy memory.

Nellie was not the only woman in the crowd with downturned eyes. That had become the way of the women in Edinburgh; they carried the weight of their sex around their necks, a heavy, dangerous burden.

The crowd swelled forth, the pressure forcing Nellie's feet

to carry her forward with them, and she knew that the day's entertainment had arrived. Not a week had passed, and yet she hardly recognized Isobel. The curtain of her brown hair had been roughly shorn, close to her head and brutally patched. Her dark eyes were vacant, her skin paled stark white and covered in blooming purple splotches across her neck and face that made Nellie's stomach tighten and twist in fear.

Twist in shame, for she did not want to step forth and help her friend. All she wanted was to flee, to hide, to protect herself from the same fate. *It is the only way to survive.*

But she stood frozen as the hangman roughly looped the rope around Isobel's neck, the air above the crowd hot and alive with their fervor as it was pulled tight.

She will return, Nellie told herself. *She is a daughter of the Cailleach with another life.*

It may have been the truth, but it did little to quell the horror of this moment, did not soothe the pain that was soon to follow for Isobel, even if it would not spell her end. Nellie thought of Jean by her side the past few days, eyes on the women on the gallows, unblinking, brave enough to look them in the eye until their last moment, a silent friend in the crowd even to those that were strangers.

We cannot do nothing. We cannot. Jean had spit with anger, as she tucked her head beneath Nellie's chin after their moments of peace, alone in her room each night.

Being brave enough to look upon a woman as she faced atrocious horrors was a defiance, was an honoring.

But Nellie was not Jean. She was not brave.

Nellie shut her eyes as Isobel stepped off the dais of the gallows, flashes of orange behind her lids as the crowd cheered.

The last time Nellie was in New Calton Burial Ground after nightfall, she had the deep, gnawing feeling in her gut that she was making a mistake, that trouble awaited her among the headstones. This time was no different.

But she would do it, for Isobel. Even though her hands trembled around the hilt of the shovel tucked beneath her coat, even though her feet seemed to slip across dry ground, as if the city itself was telling her to turn back.

The streets were more empty than usual, but the doors of the pubs shook with the sound of raucous male laughter within. Nellie's chest, instinctually, tightened with fear.

Go home, the warm breeze that lifted the ends of her hair seemed to whisper. But Jean pressed on through the night without question, so Nellie did too. Mary, silent, moved a few steps behind them, clinging to the sides of buildings and the darkness they provided. Jean had no such qualms, strolling down the center of the lane as if she belonged, as if the fire inside her welcomed a fight.

Nellie was almost grateful when the arch of New Calton's gate came into sight. To dig up a body was one thing, but she wasn't exactly keen in her own role in the night's activities. They knew to expect guards, likely strolling among the headstones rather than in the watchtower. It was morbid to think, Nellie knew, but she was almost grateful Isobel was not the only woman hung that week—the other three rested in differing cemeteries, and all they could hope was that there were only enough men for one to be on guard at New Calton that night. For Nellie wasn't sure she could distract more than one. And, unfortunately, such was her role.

"Yer beauty is already distracting," Jean had said at the shop earlier. "We might as well put it to good use." She had smirked, but the flirtation hadn't quite made it to her eyes. Nellie guessed her own gaze was as fearful then as it was now.

Their footfalls brought them nearer to the entrance, and Nellie was sure she would faint. The air felt too thick, too warm. She tried to take a steadying breath, to resist the urge to fling her coat from her body. She swallowed down the nausea that roiled up and made her tongue feel thick and fuzzy in her mouth. Her fingers slipped around the shovel, palms grown damp, body suddenly tired and melting.

"Something isn't right," Nellie barely managed to whisper. She felt the world tilt, too hot, pressing against her. "I don't feel well."

But Jean and Mary hardly heard her. As Nellie looked up she saw that they too seemed to be gripped by a wave of heat and hurt. Even in the darkness Mary's face had become pale as a ghost, the hood that had been pulled down to cover the gleam of her gray hair fallen, a trickle of sweat weaving its way across her hairline. Jean looked even worse, clawing at the neck of her dress, doubled over in silent, raging agony, her knuckles white around her shovel like a lifeline. Nellie laid a hand on Jean's curved spine and could feel the faint moisture of her sweat even through the layers of fabric.

Something isn't right.

In the absences of their footfalls upon stone, Nellie could suddenly hear the night around her. The night over the stone wall, within the cemetery, out of sight. But not out of hearing.

There was the faint whisper of voices, deep and masculine tones, words she could not make out, little more than decibels and vibrations. But she could hear enough to know that they were plentiful.

"It isn't just one guard," she whispered.

Jean's breath was haggard and quick, but she pulled herself upright.

"It doesn't matter. The plan is the plan." Jean stepped forward, but Nellie gripped her elbow, hard enough to even hurt her own hand. For fear had made her strong. And fear it was, for there was one voice that stood out among the rest, a voice that she did not even realize had haunted her dreams for a fortnight until she was met with it once more.

"The commissioner himself is in there."

Mary, who had stood like a statue in dripping shock, stepped closer, though she said nothing at all.

Holding her shallow breath, Nellie stepped up to the looming stone wall that wrapped around the burial ground, peering through the narrow slit of a window. The burn on the air suddenly seemed too much, like holding her face before a raging fire.

Even in the dark she could make out the commissioner, his slight, sandy-haired form, and she could see just how much trouble they had stepped into. He was not alone; that was for certain. Half a dozen men stood crowded around him, not perched in the watchtower, or strolling among the headstones. No, they stood guard around the rectangle of freshly overturned earth that Nellie knew housed Isobel, their backs to it on every side. Like watchdogs. Two stood facing the grave, daggers pointed down into the soil, as though they expected its occupant to emerge at any moment.

It was as if they knew that someone would come, not for any other newly buried body but for this one. As if they knew that a witch lay within the dirt and that more would come to dig her out, alive once more. As if they knew a dead witch did not stay that way. As if they knew, without a doubt, about the Cailleach and her gifted daughters. About *them*.

"We have to go. Now." Nellie turned, grabbing Jean's arm, her entire body trembling with a fear so potent she thought it might kill her before the noose ever could.

Jean ripped her arm away, the anger on her face blatant but not as fearful a thing as what awaited them on the other side.

"Don't be a coward, Nellie," she spat. The words were too ready on her tongue. Each landed on Nellie's chest like a blow.

"It doesn't matter, we cannot leave Isobel to die again in the dirt." Nellie understood Jean's meaning, knew the horror that would happen if they did not dig up Isobel—she would awaken, trapped in a box beneath ground, where she would slowly, torturously die again if they could not get to her in time to free her.

"I know, I know," Nellie begged, terror and uninvited tears crowding her throat. "But they know. There are half a dozen men, and they know. It's a trap. They're waiting for us, Jean, crowded about her grave. They *know*."

"It doesn't—"

But Mary cut off the furious words of her niece, releasing a long breath. She finally seemed to come to life.

"Nellie is right." Despite it all her voice was calm, distant. But there was a very real, unfamiliar terror in her eyes that made Nellie more afraid than anything else had. "They know."

That little part of Nellie that she hated most of all, the whimpering cowardice within her, sighed in relief.

"And what if they do?" Jean pressed. "If we don't step in, Isobel could die properly. She could get caught on her own. Who knows what they'll do to her. We can—"

"We cannot," Mary sighed. "We have been here before. This isn't the first time your mother and I have encountered this *man*. We had hoped it was different now. It is not."

"What are ye on about? We cannot leave Isobel." Jean's hair hung heavy and damp around her face. She was a frightful sight in her anger. "We'll face death if we must for one of our own, will we not?"

Mary laughed a dark, humorless sound. Nellie's stomach knotted. She wanted to be a little girl again, tucked against her mother's bosom, unaware or unworried about the world. She almost wanted to be the woman of a month ago, the woman who knew only to mind herself and her family, who had no grand ambitions of saving womankind, who was lonely and small, but almost safe. But it was too late for childish wishes, she knew that.

"This is something much worse than death," Mary said gravely. "Trust me, I've met both before."

CHAPTER 15

Edinburgh, Scotland
17 October, 1824

The silence in the Rae household was heavy with the guilt of abandoning Isobel to whatever fate may await her as she began her second and last life trapped beneath the soil of New Calton. But it was not quite as heavy as Nellie's relief at not having been caught in such a snare herself. Though the grim, knowing expressions on Mary's and Anne's faces told her such a relief would be short-lived, callous, or not. It usually took a few hours before a witch awoke to her second life—it was only a matter of time until Isobel was no longer with them.

They stood around the table in the little kitchen above the apothecary, the Rae women's private space. Night sat dense and foreboding beyond the window, as black as the expressions on the four women's faces. The room was dim, darkness swallowing them, the tiny flame of the sole candle flickering a wave of light across each of them in turn. There was nothing good to see, nothing but fear and regret on the faces of the two older women.

Nellie reached out for Jean's hand. As though touching the other woman would be enough to anchor her from the horror they were about to learn of, the horror they had just committed against a woman they knew. But Jean pulled away, crossing her arms. She did not even look Nellie's way, and Nellie was left unmoored. She sat heavily in a chair beside the table, uninvited.

The sisters stood across the room with nervous faces, the stern Jean leaning against the table beside Nellie, stance as hard as the wood beneath her. The air was blessedly cool up there in a room of witches, but the tension was thick enough that Nellie felt lightheaded. The memory of sweat remained on her skin. She laced her fingers in her lap, stared down at them, wished she could shrink, become small enough that none of this could find her.

"What are ye not telling us? What do ye know?" Jean asked. Demanded. Her voice took up all the space in the room. "What could those men possibly be capable of that we've abandoned Isobel?"

"They aren't just men. Let's start there." Anne's voice was steely, but there was a tremble of terror beneath the surface. "It's . . . we hoped it wasn't him. We didn't want to think he could be back."

Anne sighed, as though she wished someone else would come forth and say the words she was too afraid to. But her sister stood in unreadable silence by her side.

"Mary and I have encountered something like this before. When we lived over in North Berwick, down the coast. Must be nearly two, three hundred years gone now."

A cough of surprise echoed up Nellie's throat, drawing the stern attention of Jean.

The women before her were centuries old. Nellie had felt like she was playing a game, had been trying on being a new person. Suddenly it was all too real. It was no game at all, and it was just as grim as the life she'd left.

"The king and his new wife were meant to make port, but a storm rolled in. The king . . . he had some adviser by his side whispering all sort of madness into his ear, stirring up what already lived in him. They started blaming lasses in the village for the storm, accusing them as witches trying to keep the king from his visit. It wasn't true, of course. None of the accused were witches at all. There is no such thing as witches the way folks have long claimed, as Devil worshippers or those with evil, unnatural magic. But they hanged the lot of them anyway, for it wasn't really about the truth. It was as if once they started they couldn't stop; like a disease, those accusations that wouldn't stop spreading from person to person. And it persisted, all over the country, every few years for centuries."

Anne paused, looking down at her feet. Nellie held her breath, afraid the sound of it would disturb the delicate state of the story.

"Men forced their maids to confess, their wives, their mistresses. It was like they all wanted to see us hang. But then . . . well, they came for Mary. It was then my mam told us the story of this being . . . tales that had been passed down from her own mam and hers before. Down the line ever since the Cailleach's original eight hags."

Anne looked at her sister, whose eyes had gone hazy and distant.

She continued. "The Cailleach may have daughters, the women who aid her, that she gives another life to. But she had sons too. Not human sons, deities like her, powerful sons, giants. There was one such son, her fairest and most beloved, Angus, who was his mother's foil. The Cailleach ruled and brought about winter, but Angus was the king of the summer. That was the height of his power. But, long ago, he acted against his mother. Some say it was because he wanted to wed Bride—a beautiful woman he spotted in a dream and fell in love with—and rule summer together, and his mother stood in his way. In fact, Bride was one of the Cailleach's original helpers but, of course, stories say the Cailleach hated and abused her because she was jealous of the young woman's beauty."

Anne began to pace across the room, flickering in and out of candlelight. "But witches know that Angus simply wanted his mother's power as his own, he wanted her season, he wanted summer to last the whole year long, for his power to never wane with the turn of the season. The Cailleach had her hags, and it was then she decided to grant them another life because she *needed* their help more than ever. They battled Angus across Scotland during the time between seasons, a battle of frost and wind and might. He claims to have overpowered them, brought summer, been loved for it by humans; but, then again, it is often the men who get to tell and shape stories. It seemed this win went to his head. He wanted more. So Angus did as the Cailleach did and turned to humans. Turned them against the Cailleach so humans all would love him and resent her winter. He told humans that the harshness of winter was not simply the balance of nature, but a result of the Cailleach's cruelty, that she was nothing more than an evil old woman who wished them harm. Maybe he wanted revenge for how the stories say the Cailleach treated Bride. Or maybe it came from a place of greed, not love."

Anne stopped pacing, leaning against the counter, fingers twisted before her. "In trying to strip the Cailleach's power, Angus had to strip all women's, make it impossible for any to be independent and angry, and therefore able to join her hag servants. And it seems he did, he *does* so by whispering this hatred, this oppression into the ears of humans. Angus is the deity of youth, never aging. He moves about Scotland, stealing the face of a human man, a powerful one, different each time. I imagine it's lads who already have a spark of hatred in their heart and mind, who make themselves an easy host. He uses his power and position to make humans turn against women, to smother them into obedience. He's said to be a deity of love, but I'd guess he uses that, twists it, makes love fizzle and morph, turning husbands against wives, friends and sisters against one another."

"What of Bride?" Nellie whispered.

"Bride ruled by Angus's side, became everything the Cailleach was not, young and beautiful and warm, beloved for it," Anne answered. "But Bride, now, it seems only rules the summer from afar. Maybe Angus does not want to share his season with anyone. Who knows. But she does not take physical form anymore, just like the Cailleach. That is why she needs her witches—to be her body, her season's advocates and protectors, to give her the strength to start her season each year, to take the weather and land back from Angus come Samhuinn. And the longer and stronger Angus's summer, the weaker his mother and her witches get; perhaps that is why the Cailleach can no longer take physical form. Angus has made it so that stories nowadays say that it was the Cailleach and her hags who quested for winter all year, from that very first battle. But she represents balance. It is Angus that wants everything."

"That's . . ." Nellie could not find a single word to describe the confusion and terror gripping her. "But why . . ."

Anne shook her head and laughed humorlessly. "It is a smart tactic. People everywhere are far too keen to hate women anyway. It isn't just Scotland. But it is here that Angus dwells. It is this land he wants. And the more he can make women be stripped of power, be made controlled and helpless, be killed, the less they are able to become witches and aid the Cailleach. And the less the Cailleach is aided, the weaker she gets, unable to lead her witches in direct battle, and the more of her season and power he can slowly leech. He doesn't seem to know which women are daughters of the Cailleach, so he just sets out to kill us all. To keep us all too small to live in the Cailleach's image."

Mary finally spoke. "There are many places of the Cailleach's creation named for her, monuments honoring her still; the stones of Glen Cailliche, the Gulf of Corryvreckan, Ben Nevis. But down in Edinburgh, industry has wiped out so much of the land, has polluted and distorted it. So, most of her hags went elsewhere long ago, and now she's not as honored here as she once was or could be. And it's not just Angus. Between so many of our stories being smothered and the world hating women more and more, the Cailleach is too often painted negatively now. The churches have whittled away the old stories and women both for centuries, as has just the changing of the world. As times change the stories have been changing, and Angus has helped push that along, making sure she's too often remembered as just some wicked bringer of winter, vengeful against a woman more beautiful than she, rather than a creator and lover of the land, firm but fair. He doesn't create it, this hatred of women and these changing stories, they are already there, he just brings it to the forefront. He certainly saw how it could be used to his advantage and use it he has."

Nellie had never seen Mary speak with such passion.

The older woman continued, "The Cailleach represents unapologetic independence and agency and standards, and that is what she teaches her witches. It is what women must be to become her hags. If Angus can keep women small, keep those traits in a woman seen as a horrible, fearful, unnatural thing, the stories of the Cailleach will be interpreted to paint her poorly. And if hating women and keeping them beneath men keeps the Cailleach remembered poorly, keeps people from being able to aid and honor her—then he'll encourage them to hate women more. To keep women down is to keep the Cailleach simply a being to be feared, her power shrinking, winter shrinking, until Angus and his summer are all there is."

Mary fell into silence once more, all her energy seemingly spent.

While eternal summer might sound nice enough, Nellie had an inkling Angus's version wouldn't be so sweet for women.

Jean's jaw hung slightly slack. "And you've encountered him before?"

"Aye. Scotland's a big place, but he was bound to return to Edinburgh eventually. That's what he does—conquer one place with hatred and heat, then move on to the next, each a stepping stone until he controls all of Scotland and the Cailleach and her hags are entirely gone." Anne nodded. "Centuries ago, when Angus was the king's adviser . . . they used to burn accused witches' bodies after they hung them, destroying their second life immediately, if they had one. So when he hanged Mary, my mam and her own sister went in to save her when she reawakened, before she could be burned. But they were taken themselves. Angus realized they were his mother's aides."

Mary stood silent and unmoving at her sister's side, eyes far away.

"Jean was a seed in my belly already . . . I—" Anne swallowed down a heavy sob, and her sister laid a hand across her arm, her own eyes lost in the darkness of their past. "I ran. I had to. There are other communities of the Cailleach's helpers around the country, of course, but we all remain quiet. We must, to avoid Angus's attention and fury. And our community was all nearly killed back then. We could not save the women around us. Angus's poison had already spread too far, infected the roots of our village. We didn't go far, just over to Edinburgh proper, where we could stay hidden in the busy city. Soon it seemed Angus was pleased with what he had done. The hangings stopped but the hatred of women was in the veins of the people, and they passed it on. I suppose that wicked creature moved on elsewhere to start anew. But I think it's safe to say Angus has returned to Edinburgh and brought madness against women with him."

"He just . . ." Nellie finally managed to find words, though they were few. "This creature, this *deity*, just moves about Scotland, wearing the faces of ordinary men, whipping the people into a frenzy of hanging women?"

Mary shrugged, a helpless confirmation. "It wasn't always accusations of witchcraft and hangings. It's the smaller things too. It's *all* the little acts of violence against women that he kicks up. Every little bit helps his cause. If it isn't hangings it will be something else one day."

"You knew all this? You knew and you didn't tell the rest of us? Didn't try to stop him? It's been *months*!" Jean pushed off the table, striding toward her mother and aunt, the anger seeming to glow red around her person.

Anne did not retreat in the face of her daughter's rage, standing tall and calm.

"We didn't think Angus had returned, Jeanie. He's planted the hatred deep in the Scottish soil—sometimes it grows without him being there to water it. We figured if they suspected any of the executed now were truly the Cailleach's witches they'd burn them, like they used to. And since they didn't, well, we figured they didn't know in truth. It wasn't until I was arrested myself that we realized it's just not legal anymore, to burn someone for witchcraft or even formally charge them with it. That's why they're hanging women on all sort of criminal charges now."

"You suspected," Jean accused. "For *weeks*, you've suspected."

"Aye. But we only knew for certain tonight," Mary said, her voice hushed and steady. Lost somewhere else deep within her mind. "That hot dread, that feeling that yer body is dying, that the flames of hell themselves are swallowing you from the inside out? The unnatural warmth on the air, warmer every day? That's him, his summer getting stronger. It's worst, hottest, on the children of winter, the hags. It was like that last time. The sand on the beach could burn yer feet even in the dead of winter if he was nearby."

"It's the commissioner," Nellie whispered. "He's Angus. Or Angus is him, is posing as him. I've met him before. It's . . . it's just as ye say. The men around him have nothing behind their eyes but hatred. It's him."

Anne looked down at the ground, as though she had hoped she was wrong, and Nellie's confirmation had dashed that hope. Nellie wished she had been wrong. She knew she was not.

"Then let's go kill the man," Jean answered simply. "You know a gal up in Aberdeen, don't you, another hag? Tell her to come."

"I do," Anne sighed. "But Angus was up there, terrorizing their city too recently. They are still recovering. She and her community have gone to France for a bit, a few years, a decade or so, to lie low."

A decade must mean so little to women who could live for centuries, hardly aging at all. Silently, Nellie noted that the Cailleach's witches could remain as such off Scottish soil, it seemed. That even if they did not stand on her land, they held the nugget of her power once gifted, and as such retained their second life. Jean did not seem focused on this same fact.

"Then they're cowards too!" she roared. "Ye left women to die last time, to be ignorant of the power the Cailleach could give them, of the fact that she needs their help! Ye did just as Angus wished. He doesn't want us all to join together."

"He is a deity. He is older and smarter and far more powerful than we are, Jeanie," Anne replied. "And if what you saw tonight is truth, then he knows there are daughters of the Cailleach awoken in Edinburgh. He knows Isobel was one."

"And what of it?"

The flame of the candle flickered perilously with Jean's words, flashing her dark eyes with strains of yellow. The Rae women seemed to have forgotten Nellie was there. She could get up, leave the house, leave Jean and everything she'd been taught. She could forget it all. Be ignorant. Be safe.

For once, Nellie was glad her ma had not been a witch, extra life or no. Nellie thought that perhaps ignorance was safer. If she knew, it fell to her to act.

"It may be too late. Other places are better equipped, have more mountains and glens and lochs to connect to her through, have a bigger community around the Cailleach. It may be that all we can do is wait in silence for him to take his leave just as he did last time." Anne's voice was sad, but it was not uncertain.

"You want us to hide like cowards?" Jean raged.

"I want us to *live*. If we die, the true knowledge of the Cailleach in this city dies with us. Angus has been effective; there used to be more witches, they would pass down the knowledge of the Cailleach to their daughters. But he's made it too dangerous—just as he wants, it's dangerous enough to be a woman, let alone a witch. Too many women stopped sharing the craft of the Cailleach with others. Our numbers are dwindling. Best we know, in Edinburgh there is only those of us in the room and Ari."

Nellie questioned if she was even really a witch yet, with the Cailleach's gifted power, but she stayed silent.

"The Cailleach's hags battled against Angus once before, didn't they? Let's do it again!" Jean cried.

"The Cailleach doesn't take physical form anymore; her servants act as her body. So, we do what we can to power her with our belief, our craft, mirroring her qualities. Back during that first battle hag servants were able to cause storms, freeze the ground with our craft, but the stronger and closer Angus is, the less we can do, and each generation of hags seems to be weaker," Anne answered with passion. "Funny since that's what the hags, and accused witches, are most remembered and feared for, yet in my long lifetime we've never been capable of as much. Battling Angus now would be a *death sentence*. The best we can do is stay alive, stay honoring the Cailleach, in turn making her strong enough to bring her season here a bit *despite* Angus. That will push him back. It's all we can do."

In the beat of silence, Anne pressed on. "We can teach more women when this is all over. For now, we are safe. We'll re-build—"

"There may not be anything to rebuild! Yer just saving *yer-self* and letting everyone else be damned, especially those who don't have the benefits of yer situation." Jean gestured around at the shop, this space that these women owned and lived within and earned from. "We are in a position where we can try to *do something*. There are folks in this city who don't look like us or have our money or community. I'm not saying we're perfectly safe by any means, but we're in a bubble from the hatred and violence because of all we have. We need to change the system that Angus feeds, that gives him power in return. We cannot just sit around hiding, being glad it seems to work for us so far, that we can hide from it. We need to take him on directly. As if that wasn't enough, people will die be-cause of an age-old feud they don't know a thing about, caught in the crosshairs of a being that wants *us*. So it's our *re-sponsibility* to do something."

"I have said my piece and you have said yours," Anne's voice was as tired as her body, curling in on itself. "It's nearly morning. We'll keep the shop open and those who wish for our help will have it. But we'll be quiet."

She and Mary were already moving toward the door, refus-ing to turn an eye to the living flame that was Jean Rae.

"The shop opens in a few hours. Get some rest." And with-out another word the two older women were gone.

Immediately Jean began to pace restlessly across the kitchen, her stomping footfalls so heavy Nellie was sure they would wear right through the old wood. The flame of the candle flickered left to right with her movements. Nellie stayed silent in the chair.

"I cannot believe it," Jean grumbled to herself, hands clenched into fists. Finally, as though she had used up all the night's anger—though Nellie suspected she would always have more—Jean fell into the seat by her side. She slumped forward, her head rested heavy upon Nellie's shoulder, her dark hair falling over her face. On instinct, Nellie reached a hand to brush softly across her head, delicate as she would touch Tommy, gentle with fear and the trembling desire in her to run. She swallowed it. She did not want Jean to know she was not capable of the same indignation, that desire to fight. She wished she did not know it herself.

"It's so much worse than I ever imagined. And they never even told me, never warned me. I just . . . do nothing? Can ye believe that?" Jean's voice quaked.

Nellie *could* believe it. She may have been fearful, but she was not so foolish. For what difference could they possible make, witches or not—they were just women. And this was not a world made for them.

CHAPTER 16

Edinburgh, Scotland
24 October, 1824

They were almost lucky, Nellie supposed, that that aching pain in Jean's joints had flared up when it did. Maybe the wave of pain was brought about by the lack of sleep or the pressure of what lay before them. Perhaps even the fear of their future too—though Nellie doubted Jean feared the way she did. But it had made the other woman bedridden for several days and nights, a deep line between her brow showing her anger every time Nellie walked up from the shop to bring her food and drink. Her discontent was clear even as she slept, as Nellie traced Jean's slumber in swipes of charcoal; art and life spoke of a woman overflowing with her rage.

It was only when Nellie curled herself around Jean each night, the moon dim in the window beyond, that the indignation seemed to leave the other woman's face. That she seemed to get any peace from the aches and the anger. As though the presence of Nellie pressed along her body, providing what little comfort she could, left no room in the bed for anything but the two of them.

That first morning, after they knew the truth, after the world changed inescapably, Jean had been like a caged animal moving about the apothecary. She had insisted they needed to get in contact with Isobel's daughter, bring her to the shop, explain what had happened to her ma, raise her as a witch themselves. Nellie had sunk away a step as Jean raged at her mother and her aunt, the fire in her making the already warm shop maddeningly blistering. Rage does have such heat to it, Nellie was learning.

But Anne had remained calm as she told her daughter that Isobel's husband did not know the truth of what she did at the shop or what she was—even if they had dug her out in time, she would never have been able to see her girl again.

"The babe thinks her dead for good," Anne had sighed.

And now she really is, Nellie thought.

The tiny wrinkles at the corners of Anne's face seemed to have deepened overnight. "Let it rest."

Jean could not, she never could. But then her body had begun its aching, and she had been forced to rest herself. Nellie missed the sight of the other woman moving about the apothecary in tandem with her but was grateful it, at least, kept Jean safe.

The shop was quiet these days; not only with the lack of customers but because it was just Nellie, Mary, and Anne most days. Jean was stuck in bed, and Ari was staying away from the shop until it was safer. Whatever danger they as witches, as women, were in, the world was cruelly unfair, and Ari was in all that danger and more. Nellie missed the presence of the other woman's laughter, but she understood.

It wasn't even twilight when they closed the shop for the night. They were lucky to see three customers a day now, and after many hours of emptiness, Anne had declared Nellie free to go. Though she didn't go these days, not anymore, spending her days in the apothecary and her nights above it with Jean. Nellie hadn't been home—hadn't seen Tommy—since she returned home, so briefly, the day after Isobel died. She missed him like a limb. She had left them enough prepared food to survive, had a neighbor—who believed that Nellie had found a new post that kept her from home—checking in on them.

It was all she could do for Tommy; home was no longer a safe space for Nellie. Angus and his commission hadn't yet raided the apothecary, but they had stopped by Nellie's house before. He knew where she lived, and he seemed to be figuring out who was truly a witch, if Isobel was any indication. So going home was too risky, for herself, for Tommy, for her already vulnerable neighborhood. She would not bring that danger to her doorstep, doom herself and them.

The stairs creaked familiarly beneath her feet as she made her way up to the flat above the apothecary, preparing to see Jean lying, bored as ever, in bed. But the dark-haired woman was on her feet when Nellie entered, fully dressed.

"If I stay in here a moment longer, I'll go mad. Let's go on a walk," she declared immediately.

"Are you sure?" *Are we even safe outside the walls of Rae's? Are we even safe within them?*

"I feel fine." Even as she said it, Jean was leaning against the windowsill, her legs unable to hold all her weight, light as she was. But Nellie knew better than to fight with Jean. So she swallowed her worry and swallowed her fear of the world beyond and walked down and out with the other woman's elbow woven through hers. She knew she would be safe, so long as Jean was beside her.

The false invincibility of blooming love—what a fool Nellie would one day come to think of herself as.

They hardly gathered any looks, nothing inherently suspicious about the way they held each other, nothing beyond how two friends would take an evening stroll.

"One day it won't be like this," Jean said suddenly, voice tight.

"Like what?" Nellie asked. There was so much wrong, it was difficult to narrow down. "Unsafe for women?"

"Well, yes, that too. One day I'll own the apothecary, and I'll devote it entirely to the Cailleach and teaching others to be her witches. I'll make sure we don't have to hide."

Nellie could see it. If anyone could make such daring happen, it was Jean. She wished she could be about to see it. That she was truly a daughter and had another life, and Jean would want to spend all her lives with Nellie.

As if reading her mind, Jean continued. "But what I meant was this." She jostled their linked elbows as they continued their stroll. Her voice dropped as she continued. "I want to live in a world where I can walk down the street hand in hand with the woman I care for. That we won't have to pretend to be friends or sisters. That we can be lovers and the world can know. Where we can care for each other openly, without fear, be partners in every way a man and woman can."

For a moment the two women were silent, walking down the street without a word.

Then, "I want to do that with *you*, Nell," Jean whispered, voice soft as a breeze, a lover's touch hidden in public. Nellie felt like she knew nothing at all, never trusted her feelings. She knew that so little time had passed since they met. But the time that had was like Nellie had never known, never thought possible. And it was clear that Jean knew herself well and the assurance of her words, of their meaning, thrilled Nellie to her core. "I've had lovers before, of course, but . . . it's always been temporary. They've never known all of me, the Cailleach and all. But you do. You are not temporary. I don't think *this* is temporary. I will wait centuries if I must. But one day, with you, that is what I want."

Nellie could not imagine the world would ever be like that, no matter how many centuries they both lived. It seemed impossible. But Jean, for all her rage and brashness, was a dreamer. And, even if Nellie did not believe in them, she saw the beauty in Jean's dreams.

"I want that too. I will wait for that day. I will wait for you."

A passing group of laughing men stole their voices, both women tensing. As they passed, the city fell into silence once more. Nellie had pulled a hood down over her face, obstructing the attention-grabbing softness of it, and she hated to see that it helped. More than anything though, they drew so little attention because there were so few people present on the streets.

It was as if a plague had swept through Edinburgh, leaving the cobblestones untreaded, even as they headed toward Lawnmarket, the castle a hulking shadow against the slate sky. The silence of the street was unnerving, a complete sparseness to the city—no serving girls chittering and gathering water, no mothers on a walk with their babes. Only a few working men passed by, a singular rumbling carriage. It seemed women knew to hide.

What had the city become while they'd remained hidden away?

"Jean, I don't think this is a good idea. We should leave." But even as she said it, Nellie's feet kept carrying her onward, Jean's loop on her elbow like a vise.

"Don't be a coward."

A stinging ache joined the flipping of Nellie's stomach.

"We have as much a right to these streets as any."

Nellie knew that Jean was being headstrong and intentionally defiant. If Nellie was a coward, then Jean was reckless. Nellie said nothing, for she liked too much the feel of Jean's arm through her own.

Nellie felt him before she saw him. The sweat bloomed on her neck beneath her hood, the roiling nausea raged up in her belly, her skin suddenly felt too tight and too hot. Phantom hands seemed to run across her body like fingers made of fire, groping, and grabbing. Her breath quickened and shallowed, the air meeting her lungs suddenly damp and too thick to do her any good.

And then there he was, the commissioner. He crossed the square before St. Giles' Cathedral, a pleased smile on his face as he headed toward the dark steeples of the church.

Nellie prayed Jean would not see him. But even this close to a church, her prayers went unanswered.

Jean immediately cut across the street, not bothering to check for any oncoming carts, dragging Nellie along beside her. Without even taking note of the two witches barreling after him, the commissioner disappeared into the bowels of the cathedral.

"Jean, please!" Nellie whispered frantically, though the woman did not even seem to hear her.

The church, with all its worn stones, its countless peaks reaching up into the quickly darkening sky, looked less like palace of godly worship and more like an omen of doom. Jean's skin had grown hot to the touch as she passed through the heavy doors of St. Giles', Nellie at her side.

The high, domed ceiling of the church should have made a chill on the air, but it only grew hotter. The pews sat empty, two candles lit on the far end of the aisle, illuminating the space. There was no light left outside to brighten the colors of the intricate stained glass windows. Nellie and Jean stood alone in the hulking room, and for a moment Nellie hoped perhaps they were wrong. That it was not the commissioner they'd seen but an ordinary man, already lost deep inside the kirk.

But then the flames of the candles on the far side of the room flickered, and Nellie's knees nearly gave out from the heat scorching her skin. The commissioner stepped out of the shadows. He stood on the other side of the aisle, a grotesque imitation of worship, the dim light catching off the hard angle of his smile. It made Nellie's stomach turn, and she pulled from Jean's hold, her hand finding her stomach, trying to hold herself together.

She knew with a certainty she had never felt before in her life—not in a pub flooded with men, not alone on darkened streets, not even under the roaming palm of Lord MacDonald—that she should be scared. And she was. She felt frozen with it, like a sheep looking at a fox across the field, certain that she had just walked into the last moment of her life.

She felt a trickle of blood fall from her nose, too hot, too dry, the taste of metal as it slid across her lips.

Nellie wanted to race forward, to step fearlessly forth, knowing full well it was toward danger. But she was not Jean, a woman stitched together by rage. She was not Mary or Anne with their quiet, ageless stubbornness. Not Isobel or Ari with smiles that masked a fearless anger they could not help but act on. Nellie was indignant for the fate of her fellow woman, but she was not brave. She knew it in that moment as she stood frozen beneath the cross on the door.

Angus hummed a tune, the melody echoing and enveloping, and Nellie felt her mind softening, becoming compliant to the sounds. Only Jean by her side—though slack-jawed herself—kept Nellie steady. Still, she was filled with a deeply subconscious urge to flee, knowing that was the only way to survive. Nellie told herself she was not cowardice all the way down. Even standing there, unmoving, was a fight against her instinct and she fought it.

But Jean stepped forward, without thought. And while Nellie did not have courage to drive her, her body seemed to obey the other woman as if that was instinct too. She crawled forth in steps silenced by the velvet rolled across the stone floor, their hands linked. Perhaps Nellie could forsake herself, but she could not forsake those she loved.

Angus did not walk toward them. He let them cross half the aisle so they could see him clearly, face-to-face, no lies or innocent civilians caught between them. Nellie could see now that he was a slight man, soft of jaw and feature, but hand-some still. This being could have taken the body of any man and yet he did not choose a hulking specimen. Somehow, that only scared Nellie more. He knew he did not need physicality to have power over them.

"At last, Mother's *hag servants*, we meet in earnest!" There was a morbid glee in his voice. He enjoyed their fear. Angus held his arms out by his side like a showman, a crude mirror-ing of a figure on the cross. "The pleasure is all mine, I am cer-tain. So lovely to see you again, Eleanor. Or *Nellie*, rather, I suppose."

Jean said nothing, and Nellie's tongue was too thick with fear.

"Don't tell me ye've come to stop me when we've only just begun?" He asked, mocking them.

Nellie could feel the moment Jean's anger flared up.

"We have. We are not afraid of you." Jean's voice was hard as stone. "We know what ye are and you know of us. The Cailleach does not fear you, and neither do her hags." As if that was enough to stop him.

It hadn't been enough before. Mary and Anne had survived only because they'd ran. And they could not ride into battle against him, a trail of frost in their wake, the giant form of the Cailleach and her powerful hammer leading them. This was all they could do against Angus; empty words and small ac-tions behind closed doors, in the desperate hope that in doing so they were, slowly but steadily, empowering the Cailleach.

"Oh, I do know what you are. That's why I'm here!" He strolled forward casually, smile growing as both Jean and Nellie took an instinctual step away. He stopped, leaning ca-sually against a pew. "I'm older than you girls could even imagine—"

"I think we've got a good idea," Jean snapped.

The commissioner, Angus, raised his eyebrows, smiled, like her anger was a plaything to amuse him.

"Well, I've been at this a long time. And I'm good at it." He waved his arm, pointing at the destruction he'd caused in Edinburgh, the seeds of hate that already existed, that he'd come to sow. "It's almost too easy. To make men hate women is hardly a challenge anymore. They're only ever a breath away nowadays, constantly worried that their power is slipping from their hands. But I like this city. So *modern*. Well, not so much anymore."

He took another step forward, and Nellie felt her body cave into itself, much as she tried to stay upright, just a step behind Jean. That wicked smile grew. Even with Angus poisoning human minds and warping stories, how had the folklore ever painted him as the hero, dashing and beautiful, and his old crone of a mother the being to be feared? Beautiful or not, Nellie thought that, to his mother's aides at least, he was nothing but wicked terror given form.

"I've been . . . well, everywhere in Scotland. But Edinburgh's always been one of my favorite places to come. Between the churches and the government and oof, all those rich folks and poor folks mashed together right in the center of it all but thinking themselves so *different* from each other . . . Edinburgh's always been a guaranteed place for me. I may lose it easily, always changing and what not. But getting it back is always such a treat."

His blue eyes were sharp, not moving from the two witches. "In other parts of the country, sure, plenty of Mother's hags up there. That's its own kind of challenge. But, well, down here, despite being right in a city, you lot were doing so well. Folks really welcome your 'craft' here, don't they? Or, at least, they did. You girls should be proud of yourselves. I mean that. So I thought it'd be a challenge. I like a worthy opponent. Though, yer not so much as I thought."

There was actual regret in his voice. He was a hound, and they were little more than a bone for him to play with until he grew tired of the chase. Then he'd swallow them whole. Nellie knew it as surely as she knew her own name. This was a battle that had played out so many times it was nearly mundane to Angus. It was no longer done riding across the wild landscapes but in the deep hearts of crumbling communities.

Once upon a time, this may have been just nature, the flux and battle between seasons. Somewhere along the line, it had clearly warped; now it was a power struggle, rooted in old, old resentment.

"Still, I've decided not to kill you. Yet. I don't need to, to weaken my beloved mother's reach here."

"How kind of you." There was a trembling under Jean's bravado.

Nellie did not admire her bravery now; she thought it only foolishness. She wished Jean would be quiet, would see just how much danger they were in, how everything could be taken in a moment.

"I like you especially," Angus said.

Nellie was glad Jean did not spit at him, but the wicked curl of her lip was similar enough. Angus just laughed, a booming, unapologetic chuckle that echoed up into the rafters, somehow still a beautiful sound. Nellie's stomach twisted violently as she shrunk further into herself.

He stepped forward slowly, a predator cornering its prey.

"I could take you to the gallows now. Stop it all. But I'm having such fun. I think I'll break your spirits first. Or better yet, I'll let you women break yourselves and each other. I'll let it be your own kind that string the noose around your necks."

With one last lingering look, he headed toward the little door on the far end of the church. He was nearly gone, leaving Jean and Nellie frozen in silence, when he turned to look over his shoulder.

"I am so enjoying making a home in Edinburgh. I think I may stay around for a while."

Then he was gone, and the warmth of the air dropped away but the crippling nausea deep in the pit of Nellie did not sway.

She stood for a moment behind Jean, then the burns he'd left within her, the fear, and the worry, pulled her under. Nellie sat heavily on a pew, all energy gone from her body. Her head lolled back, the rafters of the cathedral spinning above her, before the fear pulled her down into the black.

The last thing she heard was Jean sitting heavily beside her, muttering.

"Fuck."

CHAPTER 17

Edinburgh, Scotland
31 October, 1824

It was a long time before Nellie felt comfortable stepping foot on the streets of Edinburgh again. Not that it mattered. No matter where she hid, Angus's words could reach her, echoing through her mind. The memory of his presence was enough to make a barrier between her and the Cailleach, to keep Nellie from stepping foot on her earth, the place of both of their power.

It was only the holiday—Samhuinn—that made Nellie venture outside. On any other year, it would welcome the Cailleach, young but aging into her crone form. The first day of her season, her power growing. But not in 1824 Edinburgh. Angus had made sure she could not find any power, could not deliver any cold there. The presence of her daughters in the apothecary was not enough to counteract the balmy air. The Cailleach's presence should have felt encompassing; it felt thin instead, a shrinking lifeline.

"Danger or not, we must honor the Cailleach tonight and

walk on her soil," Anne said hesitantly. "We cannot let Angus rob any more of the Cailleach's power or ours. Not today, of all days."

But he already had, hadn't he? They left the shop open, not that it mattered much. No one came by. Every day was eerily calm within the shop.

"We shouldn't all go out together. It may draw attention," Mary said softly.

Anne nodded. For once, Jean was quiet. She'd grown stoic since they had faced Angus in St. Giles'. The fire was there, Nellie could feel the anger in the other woman, but it seemed she knew not how to use it anymore.

"Jeanie, why don't you and I walk together? And Mary and Nellie."

Anne had started clinging to Jean, holding her daughter to her bosom, neither uttering words in anger toward each other. Nellie was thankful for the peace, but she dreaded all that had brought it about.

"Come, then," Mary said softly to Nellie, leading her out into the hazy twilight of Old Assembly Close. She was uncertain if a walk outdoors was worth the danger they faced. Empty or full, she knew the ancient being inside the commissioner controlled the streets of Edinburgh. Even just stepping beyond the shop gave her a knot in her stomach, the feeling of walking into a trap.

"Is there something we should be doing?" Nellie asked.

For a long while Mary didn't say anything. The two women kept walking in silent companionship, the city a bustling hum around them, until the castle grew from a distant shape to a real, looming being before them. It sat proudly on the swell of a hill, the rocks holding it up a reminder of the Cailleach's creation of the landscape across the country.

"No. There's nothing we can do," Mary said finally as they made their way up the slope to the space surrounding the castle.

That wasn't what Nellie had been asking, but she understood all the same.

"Witches!"

Nellie flinched, tucking herself further into the folds of her cloak. But it was not at her the man perched atop the upturned crate before the castle shouted, but at the city at large. Drawn in against her will by the horror of his words, she drifted forward to join the gathering crowd at his feet, Mary silent and stoic by her side.

"Witches everywhere! They may already be in yer beds, lads!"

The serious faces of the men around them grew red, soaking up the rage of the man before them. The force of the crowd seemed to tighten, to grow, too hot as the broad shoulders of strangers pressed against her own, folding her in on herself as tightly as she was able.

"Witchcraft is coming for them! Yer wives, yer daughters, keep them tight in their homes or soon ye'll have a witch on yer hands!"

It wasn't the crisp seams and coiffed hair of lords around them, of course, it was the common folk. The men who lived in Nellie's neighborhood and neighborhoods like it. Ordinary men with ordinary wives and daughters, whipped into a frenzy. The lords and the aristocrats shared this fear, this sentiment, she was certain, now that Angus was so close to stoke it. But they flamed behind their gilded doors.

Nellie could see on the faces of the men around her, red as beets and twice as sour, that they would do as the man said, and happily. These men feared a witch in their beds, but every woman already had to fear a man in hers—and now those same men may just serve as their executioners too.

"If she will not care for you and the babes as she should, she may well be swept into witchcraft," the man on the box continued. The moon was rising higher, the sky falling from the streaming colors of twilight to deep navy, and the castle at his back became a shadow, a beast waiting to do his bidding. "If she doesn't want to lay with ye, if she lays with ye and places herself atop—all signs of the witch!"

Nellie's stomach tilted and twisted, and she felt suffocated, sure that she would be sick on the shoes of the raging men around her. Or worse, seized herself, dragged to the gallows, merely for being the nearest woman to them in the sweeping fervor of their anger.

"Come." Her voice trembled as she grabbed Mary's hand, her knuckles prominent and trembling but unresisting as the two women shouldered their way out of the crowd, eyes cast down. Nellie was grateful men like her da and Lord MacDonald had given her so many years' experience shrinking herself, making herself near invisible.

Nellie wasn't sure even the Cailleach, on the first day of her season, with her shining moon, would be able to see them anymore. Though perhaps the divine being had already turned her back on the women of Edinburgh, seeing their imminent defeat at the hands of her son.

The walk back to Old Assembly was silent. But Nellie felt each footstep was too loud, each breath too damning of what they truly were. Though she was sure now, without doubt, that it didn't matter anymore if they were really witches. The commissioner's foul snakes of hatred had already slithered out across her city, woven into the ears and minds of every man. The commissioner wanted women's blood, and now the men of Edinburgh were ready to be the ones to hand it to him. Angus's foul words were settling into the root of the city and though she was too afraid to say it to the Rae women, she feared—she knew—it would not leave. Not ever.

Jean and Anne were already at the shop when they arrived, having journeyed out toward the crags themselves. Though mother and daughter did not share what they had seen, the flustered look in both their eyes, the silence even from Jean, told Nellie that it was much like her own expedition. The four retreated above the shop without a word.

Nellie sat at the table as they brought forth the near feast they'd spent the day cooking, watched as Jean's hand trembled with her sickness and her rage as she lit the candles around the table. Tatties, meat, gourds of three colors—it was more food than Nellie had ever seen on her plate before, but her stomach was too full with terror to eat. They were focused on honoring not only the Cailleach but also the dead—for the Rae women, too, needed all the help they could get.

The overflowing fifth plate sat untouched at the head of the table as the four women poked at their Samhuinn feast with unspoken words and trepidation, an offering to the Cailleach, to their ancestors, and to those that had passed. The Rae women had placed Isobel's apron from the shop beside the extra plate and a calfskin book that belonged to Anne and Mary's mother, which contained a version of Cailleach's creation tale, written in a looping Gaelic, centuries old and dangerous to have twice over—relics to remember the women they had no more. Nellie had nothing of her mother but flashes of an untrustworthy memory. She took the edge of a knife, raking it across a pinch of her hair. She laid the thin clump of auburn beside the plate, for she knew her beauty was all she had left of her mother. Sometimes it felt that beauty was all she had left of herself.

The Rae women and Nellie ate, grim-faced, doing their best to feel close to the deity who seemed as far as the moon. It was death that felt close by now.

CHAPTER 18

Edinburgh, Scotland
4 November, 1824

Jean sat by the hearth, a pot of tea coming to a rolling boil, though there was little more than embers burning in the grate. Anything more would have scorched the already warm air. Not that it made much difference, Nellie figured. They needed far more than calming tea now. But this seemed to be all they could do—nestle into the apothecary to hide like mice in the walls.

Even Jean put up little fight with Anne's suggestions of lying low. They had all seen what awaited them beyond these walls. They all knew they were locked in a battle they were not prepared to fight. Nellie was silently glad they were deciding not to fight at all, though her stomach squirmed with guilt every time rumor of the gallows appearing for another woman made its way to them. They did not mention Isobel's name, nor inquire about how Ari was doing, at her home with her da and brother, his wife, and their children. They did not say much of anything at all.

Nellie mashed chopped chamomile into beeswax, adding foxglove with its pink-purple heads, the roots of a royal fern, then a bulbous head of wild garlic. She'd heat the mix over the fire for the afternoon, the warmth making them combine. They'd make a salve that should, Nellie hoped, warm on contact with Jean's skin, soothing the balls of pain that lived where her limbs joined.

Nellie heard Jean's uneven approach before she felt slender arms wrap around her waist. Those familiar lips ghosted a greeting against her neck. Nellie's stomach swooshed.

This, she thought, *was worth having another life for.* She could fill centuries with the warmth of Jean's touch. With the memory that Jean wanted just the same, was willing to wait, by Nellie's side, for the world to welcome it.

Jean didn't seem to care much if her mother and aunt saw the two of them woven into each other, as they surely had before that afternoon. As for anyone else discovering the truth of what they were to each other—it seemed unlikely, empty as the shop had been and continued to be. Nellie's knife striking the wood table echoed against the silence of the apothecary. Even the light slanting in through the window was hazy and dull, illuminating the dust that settled across the high-shelved black bottles, the breeze too warm to welcome in the Autumn.

Nothing was right anymore. There was no balance left in Edinburgh. The scales had tipped beyond control.

The arms disappeared from Nellie's middle as the door clicked open. The four women tensed at the sound, everything once familiar now a surprise.

But at the sight of Louisa Scott filling the doorway, Nellie saw Jean perceptibly relax, and her chest flushed with the burn of jealousy.

"Oh! Hi there, Mrs. Scott. Yer hypnotic, no?"

Nellie had never seen Anne flustered, not even in the face of their more well-off clients. But she moved about the shop like a frantic bird, hands twittering on the air as she reached for the little herb-filled sac for Louisa's sleep-aiding baths.

"You've been good, I hope?"

Louisa said nothing. She stood by the door, spine straight as a pole, her little pointed chin lifted in silent defiance. A golden coil of hair slipped free of her twist, falling across her brow. She didn't reach to fix it, as though if she stood still enough, silent enough, they would not see her.

Anne faltered for a moment at the emptiness of a reply but dutifully packaged up the wares.

"All right, Louisa?" Jean asked in greeting. The other woman continued to stare at the window on the far side of the shop pretending she could not see any of them at all. Nellie tried to ignore the flash of hurt on Jean's face.

Nellie, skin crawling with the discomfort of the silence, hastily drew a moon and cloud, the charcoal smearing slightly as she passed it on to Anne to twine to the herbs. With long, pinching fingers Louisa reached out to take the bag from Anne, tucking it away into the folds of her pristine dress. She took out a handful of coin, but rather than place it into Anne's outstretched hand, Louisa tossed it on the floor at the older woman's feet. The sound of copper tumbling across stone echoed heavily as Louisa Scott turned toward the door.

Jean burst forward, the coin forgotten underfoot as she grabbed Louisa's wrist, pulling the woman around to face her.

"What is the matter with ye? You don't treat my mother like—"

"Do not touch me, witch!"

Louisa's outcry echoed across the apothecary, and the plant in Nellie's hands fell to the table, forgotten. Even Jean, angry, powerful Jean, was too stunned to speak. Her hand went slack enough that Louisa was able to rip her wrist away, holding it gingerly against her front. Her eyes hardened in a way that suddenly reminded Nellie of the women who would visit Lady

MacDonald in her home, the other wealthy women and their stony glances.

"I implore you to remember to whom you speak, witch." Louisa's voice was as haughty as her station, laced with a wicked coldness.

"As if you don't know us." Jean stepped forward, and Louisa took one unconscious retreating step before recollecting her ground. Nellie held her breath.

"I assure you, I do not know you." Her voice was tight, measured. "If you mind your own affairs, perhaps I shall remain silent about yours as well."

Louisa's eyes flicked out beyond Jean, to the three other women. There was that infuriating coldness in her expression and tone, but Nellie realized then it was just to hide her fear. And Louisa Scott was afraid twice over—to be associated with an apothecary, already considered a suspicious profession, especially for a woman. And to have been involved with Jean, however they were. The woman must be desperate for sleep, if she still dared come here for her hypnotic.

There was no regret in Jean's face, no sympathy toward the coldness of a woman she once knew well. She met Louisa's ice with fire.

Nellie saw now, a stone dropping into her stomach, that Angus was right. The seeds of his cruelty had already come to bloom in Edinburgh, in men and women alike, it seemed. For Nellie may have been naive, but she was not fool enough to think it was only Louisa Scott who would damn another woman to save herself. Just as Angus had said, the women of Edinburgh would, and had, turned on each other, a house rotting from the inside.

Before anyone could say another word, Louisa stepped out of the shop. As the door swung shut behind her, Nellie could just barely see the lady anxiously looking up and down the street before stepping invisibly out into the city, her wealth like a suit of armor around her.

C

"I don't want to talk about it," Jean huffed several times throughout the rest of the day, even as no one asked her to. They had all returned to their silence, and Nellie thought maybe she was not the only one whose tongue was weighed down by a sense of doom.

As Jean's mouth forged a path across Nellie's body in the dimness of her room that night, that vile, twisting part of Nellie whispered that it was Louisa, her betrayal, that lit a fire in her partner's belly and below, not the want of Nellie herself. But then Jean was dipping between Nellie's legs, and she forgot to be worried about anything at all.

The second pillow on Jean's bed had come to bear an indent just the shape of Nellie's skull, a sight that caused a thrill every time she saw it. But, afterward, she rested her head upon Jean's chest instead, their feverish skin slick together. That was just as much her place now as any pillow.

Nellie lifted the little copper deer hung from Jean's neck, that little piece of the woman, feeling the smooth curves of its tiny legs, the points of its ears. Lying with Jean had brought Nellie peace, but it seemed the same could not be said the other way.

She could feel the restless flutter of Jean's legs, the incessant tapping of her fingers on Nellie's shoulder.

"Everything has gone to shite," Jean said, each word heavy. "We cannot just do nothing."

Nellie's stomach knotted at the thought of Jean out there, recklessly challenging not just Angus but also the people of the city, their brains rotted by his proximity and power, by the strength of his influence. The city spent every moment searching for a witch, a woman, to hang. She did not want Jean to give them one so easily.

"Nothing's changed since . . . well, lately. Why don't we just lie low? Even this will pass. Angus will be pleased, he'll move on, maybe even leave us be, if we don't cause waves. Eventually the city will return to normal."

What was normal anymore? Nellie could hardly remember. She thought of a lifetime of being pawed at, hiding in shadows, shrinking. She did not want that either.

"I can't do that," Jean replied.

"You could though. You'd be fine." Nellie gestured at the room around them, the heavy layer of wool draped over their naked bodies.

"What do you mean by that?" Jean, always so defensive, even in the face of a compliment. In the face of someone speaking truth.

"You have more money than I do. You'll be fine, you and your ma and Mary," Nellie said, thinking it was obvious.

Jean laughed, a humorless thing that made Nellie feel like a child, too naive to understand.

"Well, you're beautiful." She did not say it like a compliment, and Nellie knew she didn't mean it as one. "If Angus keeps taking Edinburgh down the path it's on, beauty is a much richer currency for a woman than some coin."

Nellie didn't speak, but she withdrew her fingers from where they glided across the raised bumps of Jean's clavicle. She folded her hands across her stomach.

"Money can be taken, but that face of yours won't leave," Jean barreled on. "Some man with money of his own will see that face and all the rest of ye and buy you for a wife. You'll always be fine, Nell."

Nellie had desired men before. She knew that she could, maybe should, marry a man and then, to a degree, she would be safer. She suspected that this was true for many women who loved other women, or men who loved other men, or those who were like Ari—anyone whose *self* was not how the world wanted it to be. That to hide that self, tuck it away and behave as the world tells you you must, to live a lie, would be safer and easier. But it would be that—a lie, a constant denial of herself. And it would not be a life at all, to act like part of her very being did not exist. Nellie did not want it. She deserved more. She deserved the future Jean had dreamed of, two women together in every way. She wanted that with Jean, and Jean alone.

"You know I don't want that." Nellie's chest tightened just at the thought. She leaned up, looking down at Jean who didn't move, lying flat, eyes up at the ceiling. The other woman would not even look at her.

"It doesn't matter so much what a woman wants. I knew ye were a coward, but you're not daft. And don't play the victim." Jean's words were as cold as the stoic expression on her face.

"I am not making myself a victim! Just because my struggles are different from yours does not mean they don't exist. I would think you, for all your wanting to help women, especially those with less than yourself, would understand that."

Nellie did not back down, boring her eyes into Jean's even as the other woman looked through her. "You do not know what it's like in my home. I have no ma like you do. I had no one to teach me to be in the Cailleach's image, not just the craft, but to be myself and proud, to know that I deserve the space I take up—I have only my da, who does his damnedest to beat me down to even smaller. And it is not because I am a woman but because of who *he* is. Because he can have power over me because, as his daughter, he *owns* me. I do not want to marry a man and trade ownership from one pair of rough hands to another. But it is hardly even my choice. You have never known a life without the support of your ma and a community of strong women. The world looks at the Cailleach's strength as cruel and fearsome—and that is all I have ever known, all I've been taught. That I should be the very opposite, make myself small and obedient. Finding strength in independence, in myself, that is new to me. All I have known is the world that Angus feeds from—without the Cailleach I would just be another poor woman traded and dying, by the noose or starvation or a man's desire. Trying to survive, for me, looks different than it does for you. And my beauty might make some things easier, but it does not make all that just go away."

Jean looked at Nellie for a long moment, saying nothing. But then she cracked, sighed, softness washing over her features. She once more looked like the woman who told Nellie that she cared for her, that she wanted to change the world so they could be together in it.

Jean pulled Nellie down into her embrace, tilted the red-head's chin up so she could place a kiss on her mouth, full of gentleness and sweetness and all the things her words were not. She did not say sorry, and Nellie did not expect her to. She didn't need her to. She knew that Jean's fear turned to anger in a way her own did not. She knew Jean, and she could not blame the woman for her thorns when the world had given her need to defend herself.

But even as they spent the night tangled together, breathing each other's warm air, Nellie couldn't quite forget her words: *Don't play the victim.*

If the world kept going the way of that ancient being curled up inside the commissioner, Nellie was certain she *would* be a victim. They all would.

CHAPTER 19

Edinburgh, Scotland
9 November, 1824

The shop had sat empty for days, too silent. Not the silence of peace, but the silence that forewarned a storm. The cracked window of the apothecary brought a breeze in, but Nellie thought the scent of death also wafted in with it. The four women had hardly stepped foot outside in days, and not another soul had entered the shop. But as though the wind itself carried word of it, they knew what happened in Edinburgh. The scaffolding of the gallows no longer rose and fell with the sun. It lived on Grassmarket now, and every day the number of women in the city fell, lost to the hangman and hatred.

They may be hidden, but Nellie knew, in her bones, that she did not have much longer. Maybe none of them did.

She dared to step out beyond the apothecary when the afternoon sun was high in the sky. The moon may be a connection to the Cailleach, but nightfall provided no safety for a woman. So Nellie made her way across the high street by daylight, sure to keep her eyes on the quick pace of her feet.

The frayed ends of her dress snapped against her ankles. In her haste, the jagged hem of Nellie's skirt twisted about her foot, and she found herself stumbling, sprawling across the cobblestones on hands and knees. With a disgruntled, frustrated sigh Nellie pushed away the hair that had tumbled from her bun to fall across her eyes. As her vision cleared, she spotted a delicate white hand stretched out before her in aid. Nellie grabbed the mysterious woman's hand, standing slowly, a new ache budding along her bruised kneecaps.

"Thank ye for that, I—" Nellie's words died on the air as she stood, coming face-to-face with Lady MacDonald.

Despite everything Nellie's first thought was *How did I not recognize her by touch alone?*

The lady seemed just as shocked by the unveiling as Nellie. The two women stared at each other for what could have been only a moment but felt so much longer to Nellie. Brown eyes gazed into blue, and Nellie saw her childhood there, all the love she had and had lost.

She waited for Lady MacDonald's gentle grip to turn into a vise, to be dragged by her hair down to the gallows.

So she was shocked when the lady's face softened and she said, so softly it was nearly a whisper on the desolate street, "You never did seem to hem your skirts enough, Nell. Ever since you were a girl." The older woman laughed gently, the barbless admonishing of a mother's affection.

Please, let us heal this. I miss you.

To hear such tenderness in that familiar voice, to hear her nickname on the lady's tongue was almost too much. Nellie let out a little, quaking gasp. The sound seemed to shatter the thin veil of Lady MacDonald's remembered affection.

Her face fell into hardness once more, those warm brown eyes turning into the hard flint of a stranger. She snatched her hand back, holding it gently in front of her chest as though it were Nellie who had grabbed her, who had tried to bring her harm. As though Nellie had ever done anything but love her with every bit of herself.

"I—" Nellie began, but it did not matter.

Without another word Lady MacDonald continued past Nellie up the street, her chin lifted, mouth pursed, like Nellie was nothing more than grime on her shoe. Nellie stood frozen for a moment longer, mind spinning, chest aching. Then she remembered it was hardly safe to be out of doors, and this had only proved as much. Nellie continued toward home.

It had been days—weeks, maybe, she could not be sure— since she'd been in her neighborhood. What had once been a place so familiar now felt other, unsafe, full of eyes watching and waiting.

But then, there was Thomas, her boy, tucked away inside their home. She was hardly through the doorway before his arms were around her middle, his head pressing into her sternum, already higher than it was when she held him last. Nellie ached as she thought of how much she missed of Thomas's life. How much more she might.

But that was why she was there. Danger may come for her, but she would not let it touch a hair on her boy's head.

"Hi, laddie."

"Where've ye been, Nellie?" He did not say that he missed her, but the round eagerness of his eyes said enough.

"It's not safe for women anymore, ye know that, don't you?"

Tommy nodded, hair flopping across his eyes. *He needs a trim.* Da wouldn't give him one. Wouldn't even notice the boy, likely, let alone his hair.

"Aye." His voice was so small, deeper now, but tender. He was so delicate, so fragile.

"That's why I'm here—"

"Yer not in danger, are ye, Nell?"

"No, 'course not," she lied. She had looked into Angus's

eyes, that being old as this land and its fickle seasons. He was biding his time, not lending them any. "But that's why I'm here. I might . . . well, I might be away for a bit longer."

She did not say she might be gone even longer, might be strung up in Grassmarket any morning, only to be strung up again that very night, Angus knowing what she was and what she could do. Two lives meant nothing if a man wanted them both.

Nellie wasn't sure it mattered; how could she even be sure she was a witch at all? She didn't feel powerful or independent or believing. All she believed in anymore was her fear.

Nellie fumbled in her skirt for the little pouch of coin hidden away there, thankful it had not been lost in her fall. She drew out a handful, placing it into Thomas's small hand. His eyes widened even more at the sight of it. She closed his fingers over it, pressed his fist down hard enough that he flinched.

"This is for *you*, Tommy. You hide it in your pillow now and do not ever tell Da you have it. You keep it, and you use it for *yourself*. Do not let him touch a piece of it."

Nellie hated to think of Thomas left alone with her father. But the money in his hand could be enough to keep her brother from starving to death while Da drank the rest of their coin down, even if it could not stop his raging and wailing. Thomas said nothing, just stared at Nellie.

"Do ye understand, Tommy?" She pushed, too hard, she knew. But it did not feel like there was time left for gentleness.

"I do, Nell, I swear it." His face was painted in hues of startled white, but he nodded.

"Good lad," Nellie said just as the doorway rattled, the swollen wood dislodging from its frame as her father stormed and swayed into the room. By instinct Nellie fell into an obedient hush, closed her mouth, closed herself, for the room was hardly big enough to hold him, and she must concede herself to make the space.

Her da, towering over his children, seemed as surprised to see her as she was him.

"So yer back, then?" he spit.

Nellie remembered, just barely, the kindness Da showed when she was a girl. Before he lost himself to grief and then drink; now he looked at Nellie with only hatred, the daughter who wore his dead wife's face like a mockery of his loss.

Now he was always so dismissive of her, so plagued by her very presence. Though all she did, all she had ever done, was cut apart pieces of herself for him to use at his convenience. It still wasn't enough. It would not be. It was her role, she knew, but surely there was more to her da's than this.

He stumbled past them, the scent of alcohol burning Nellie's nostrils.

I will never truly be a witch, never be able to have the power to aid the Cailleach and be given a second life in return if this man is in my life. He will always keep me small and apologetic and trapped. That is not the Cailleach. That is not her witches. And no amount of crushing herbs or making tonics can counteract that. It was a sobering and terrifying realization, but such was Nellie's luck lately.

She felt red-hot fire flash through her blood, uncontrollable and flooring. Nellie had never realized she was allowed to be anything but dutiful, fearful.

She had never realized she was allowed to be angry.

"I need to get to work." Her voice was hard, surprising even her with its little defiance.

The alcohol in Da's blood usually made him sluggish, but it seemed her words had seeped the exhaustion from him. He stormed toward her, footsteps shaking their tiny home, eyes made bright with drunken anger. Nellie knew Da expected her to take a step back, to cower against the door. She expected herself to as well. So, when she did not flee, when she stood her ground, they were both shocked, though Da's showed more, his steps faltering for a moment.

She was not just Nellie Duncan, obedient, shrinking daughter. She was Nellie Duncan, hag of the Cailleach, the queen of winter, creator.

The advantage didn't last long. He leaned forward, his face looming over Nellie's, his large hand finding her arm, the touch light but still telling her to stay in place. He had never struck her before; no, he liked to intimidate instead, to remind her that he was her father, he was in charge of her. He didn't need to hit her to get the satisfaction of watching her shrink.

"You think you're better than us with yer fancy jobs?"

She hadn't been this close to her father in a long time. But as she stood there, chin tilted up to him, looking at those dark, bloodshot eyes, his sagging skin and sneering mouth, she saw none of herself.

She was more a Rae woman than a Duncan daughter.

Nellie wanted better for herself; she deserved to have a voice, to have safety, to have a say.

"Let go of me." Nellie swallowed her "please." Her voice trembled, her hands shook, but she said no more.

"Get out of my house, ye bitch." Da thrust her from him, turning his back on her. "Go sleep in the street where ye belong. I never want to see yer face again."

She did not remind him that her income was the only thing keeping the roof over their heads and the beer in his bloodstream. She did not want to fight for a place in this house that had stopped being her home. She may not live to see winter if Angus kept closing in, but she was choosing never to see her Da again.

It was not safe to take Tommy where she was, but she couldn't bear to leave him now in the room with their da in such a state. The commissioner knew what they were . . . and Nellie had to assume he knew where they were too. It seemed a matter of time before he came for them at the shop. She could not bring Tommy into that risk—he may be a boy, and avoid the gallows for it, but Nellie did not want to create any scenario at all where Tommy and the commissioner could be in the same room. Not again. No, he was safer at home. Tommy may be young, but he was smart. He knew as well as she to avoid the foulest of their father's moods, already moving toward the door.

"Come, Tommy, why don't you play outside? Get some more water from the fountain." She put a protective arm around Tommy's shoulders, pulling him against her as they made their way to the door.

Nellie didn't even know that when she walked out that door, when she pried her father's grip off her life and let him go—she became a true child of the Cailleach. He did not make decisions for her anymore; but, perhaps more, he did not control the way she saw herself anymore.

The last thing that kept her from her fate was the easiest of all. There had never been love there, only duty, and it was hers no longer. Her da did not even look at his daughter for the last time as she took her brother's hand and the two walked out the door.

CHAPTER 20

Edinburgh, Scotland
14 November, 1824

At this point Nellie thought they were doing the craft just for the craft's sake. Boiling herbs for salves, weighing out satchels of tea to soothe insomnia, swollen bowels, forbidden desires, for customers who no longer existed.

Why are we working so hard to remain witches when that's the most dangerous thing we can be?

Nellie would never dare say it out loud; she couldn't bear the way Jean would look at her. Staying shackled to the shop chafed at Jean, stomping around, dusting bottles on the high-up shelves only she could reach with such fervor Nellie was sure the glass's survival would reach as quick an end as theirs. Nellie was at least grateful that the humid air was broken up within the shop; because now she could feel the constantly present chill on her skin from being around the others. Finally, Nellie could sense it because, at last, she was a true daughter of the Cailleach, given her gifts in return.

When the shop door opened, it was a saving grace. All four

Rae women dropped what they were doing to give their full attention to the woman who entered now, a bushel of dried lavender fluttering from Nellie's hands to the floor with a sweet waft.

Nellie recognized the newcomer, though dimly, a fair enough woman with a sheepish, nervous sort of look on her face. Nellie would be worried were it not for the swaddled babe in her arms, it's little face peeking through the blankets like a mound of dough.

"Hello there, all," the woman said.

Anne was already stepping forth to coo at the infant.

"I hope it's all right my coming, what with all . . ." The woman's voice trailed off.

Anne flapped off the concern with a wave of her hand.

"You're more than welcome, lass. And I see the tea brought about the bairn after all."

Of course, Nellie realized; the heavily pregnant woman who had come to the shop, when their world was cracked but not yet crumbled, seeking out a tea to bring about birthing contractions. The absence of Isobel was suddenly heavy in the shop, but they all steadfastly remained fixed on the customer.

"Thank you. I wanted ye all to see the babe. But also, well, the little lad's got a rash, breaking out all wicked and red across his arms," the woman sighed heavily, and Nellie could see where the sacrifices of birth and motherhood had caused crinkles by her eyes, lent a heaviness to her very bones.

"I'll make him a salve," Mary said softly, fingers already reaching for the twined herbs overhead. "Birthing can be traumatic on the bairn's bodies as well. And it's good for babes to get some rowan tree sap—keep any evil at bay."

Anne led the woman to a seat in the corner by the grate, though the air outside surely did not necessitate such a means of hospitality.

"Sit there, Mum," Anne said gently, pouring the woman a mug of the chamomile tea that stewed on the pot, preparing lady's mantle to add, a helpful aid after giving birth. "Would you like to rest yer arms? We can hold the little lad for ye."

When the woman passed off her child to Anne's awaiting arms, it was clear it was a gift to them both. Anne looked down at the child nestled in her crook with a softness that made Nellie's stomach clench.

If her own mother had ever looked at her like that, she didn't remember.

Anne rocked the child softly, pacing about the shop in careful steps, a soft lullaby falling from her lips, gentle as a breeze. When she passed by Nellie, she caught the other woman's hesitant gaze on the babe and paused.

"Would you like to try holding the babe, dearie?"

"No," Nellie replied instinctually. But her arms were already raising. Though nerves and fear bloomed in her belly, some visceral urge drew her in.

The child settled on her forearms, too light to be a living being, his little head soft and delicate against the crook of her elbow. His tiny blue eyes winked in and out of slumber. Distantly Nellie heard the door open again, soft discussions, familiar tones.

"I'm looking for something to aid with gray hairs." The newcomer's voice was hazy on the other side of the room. "Not just a dye but a way to stop them, for good. I heard you are often able to handle . . . seemingly impossible requests."

Anne responded, "Well, there's nothing wrong with gray hair, now. It's a sign of survival and wisdom. And beauty—"

"Hmph. Well, my husband . . ."

Nellie hadn't even turned to welcome the customer, knowing the others could handle it, and she easily tuned out the conversation. It all seemed far away when the warmth of the baby was seeping into her arms, his little heart pattering just beside her own, thudding until it slowed with comfort. It reminded her of being a girl herself, holding Tommy's newly born form, realizing that this little sleeping being would become the most important thing in her world. Growing up in that moment because she had to.

Nellie had never imagined herself with a babe. But as the little boy slept peacefully in her arms, shading him from the horrors of the world, horrors that would have to make their way through her before they could reach him—well, she thought maybe she'd like to be that for someone someday. By choice, by love, now that she was grown enough to know what it meant and what it cost to protect and love another, fragile being.

"Nellie, can ye make up a label for—"

Spell broken, Nellie turned at the sound of her name. The rest of Anne's request fell into nothingness over the sound of her blood rushing in her ears. For there was Lady MacDonald, in her finery, coiffed and polished. Even though Nellie could still hear her hateful words and see her disdainful gaze on the street, her chest dipped with missing the woman. But it was not at Nellie that the woman looked, but at the child held in Nellie's arms.

Nellie watched the puzzle pieces click together in Lady MacDonald's mind, creating the wrong image. She knew the other woman well enough, knew her like a mother, to see every thought that passed across her face. Nellie knew what Lady MacDonald thought as she looked at Nellie, the babe held against her body, the body that a few months before Lady MacDonald's husband had greedily run his hands over. Nellie wanted to fall at the lady's feet and tell her it was not what she thought, it never was, beg to feel her hand on her head again, tell her she was scared, so scared, and she wanted to feel the safe embrace of the woman who had loved her like a daughter for most of her life.

Nellie breathed, longing falling from her mouth against logic. "I—"

But Lady MacDonald's face had fallen shut like a door, stony and heavy, and she was already turning, fleeing from the shop without a word. The echoing slam of the door and then silence marked her exit.

◖

Hours later, body still trembling, Nellie was guided to the door by Anne's gentle touch and softer words. She had explained everything to them, a story familiar to Jean by now, but her tongue twitched with more explanations. *I never wanted him to do that. I only ever wanted her to trust me. It wasn't what it looked like, not now and not then.*

With her other hand Anne pressed a dark glass bottle in Nellie's grip. "This is Ari's, for her stomach. She's had regular aches since the carriage accident. But since she hasn't been about the shop lately, we've been delivering it to her. Why don't you go and bring it to her at home, yeah? I'm sure she could use a friendly face."

Nellie knew what Anne was trying to do, to clear Nellie out of the shop. The outside world might be dangerous, but since Lady MacDonald had arrived, the apothecary had become even more so for Nellie.

As if to confirm Nellie's thoughts, Anne continued, "Then I think you ought to go home for the night, lass. That was a wealthy lady none too happy with you. If she returns tonight, it'll be with the law, and they won't be looking for explanations. Best be off with ye, until tomorrow."

But this is my home now. I have nowhere else to go.

But Nellie could not bear the shame of telling the Rae women how much her own kin despised her, how she had been banished from her home. They had already seen one loved one of Nellie's turn against her that day.

She knew it was likely Da would already be at the pub and would stay there through the night. She could probably sneak in and sleep until morning without his notice. Even if he did return home, there was a good chance he'd be too drunk to even remember their fight, his banishment.

"But I want to—" Nellie's eyes cut to Jean, the dark-haired woman striding forward to brush the hair from Nellie's face.

"Jean'll still be here in the morning," Anne said, gently urging.

Mary stood along the opposite wall, saying nothing, but she nodded with those deep, sympathetic eyes.

"It's just one night. Ma's right," Jean shrugged. "We'll see each other again soon enough." The smile in her voice was as shallow as the one on her face.

Nellie wanted to tell Jean to join her. Trouble or not at the door, she was not sure she could sleep without the touch of Jean's skin anymore. But she knew she would already have to sneak in herself, and Tommy would for certain be there, so she said naught.

Nellie just nodded.

"I'll see you all tomorrow, then. If she does come back, I'm sorry, I don't want to bring trouble on you either."

"Pfft. Don't worry, dearie." Anne shrugged as if the wrath of wealthy women was normal to them. Lately, it seemed to be. "We're a family, we look out for one another."

Nellie's tongue thickened with the weight of emotion.

And with one quick kiss on Jean's mouth, an almost mindless, temporary parting, Nellie shut the door on Rae's Women Apothecary.

CHAPTER 21

Edinburgh, Scotland
14 November, 1824

It took Nellie a long time to get to Ari's neighborhood. The other woman lived on the far side of the city, the thick smog slightly thinner out there. The sky was melting into a deep pink sunset between the roofs of the buildings, standing sturdy in a line.

Nellie was careful to not be seen as she passed through the doorway of Ari's family home. She made her way up the polished steps to the third floor, as Anne had instructed her. Before Nellie could knock, the door was pulled open. Nellie looked at her own hand, confused. Then she was pulled into a warm, enveloping hug. Light blond hair filled the edges of her vision as Nellie wrapped her arms around Ari, holding the other woman to her for a long moment. Her skin tingled with that cool breeze that marked another of the Cailleach's witches nearby.

Eventually Ari stepped away, casting a quick glance up and down the stairs to ensure they were alone. "I saw you out the window, heading up the street. I figured you might be coming to see me," Ari said, smiling. "I hoped, at least."

Nellie looked at the other woman properly now. The skin under her eyes was as dark as if they had been smudged with charcoal. The smile lines that usually lived on either side of her mouth had smoothed out with disuse.

"'Course I am," Nellie replied, squeezing Ari's arm comfortingly. Immediately she felt the tightness of guilt that she had not visited Ari before, that she had not considered that the other woman was not only fearful as they were but now lonely too.

"I've missed you," Ari said earnestly, lingering in the doorway. "All of you lot. I miss the apothecary desperately but . . ." She trailed off, but Nellie understood the rest of her words. But the apothecary was no longer safe. Nowhere was.

"We've missed you too. It's not the same without you around. The shop is too quiet without all your jokes." Nellie smiled.

Ari's face split into a grin, familiar once more.

"How have you been? Honestly?" Nellie asked. She hated to see the way Ari's smile wavered.

"I manage. I'm bored as a rock. And this place is loud enough to split my brain in two, I swear it." As if to prove her point, the joyous scream of a young child echoed out from the spacious flat through the doorway. Another child's answering cackle followed.

Ari grinned, holding her arms out as if to say *You see?* "I love them though. My brother's little ones."

"I'm glad. Must be nice to see more of them, I reckon." Nellie realized just how long Ari had been absent from the shop. So much she didn't know, hidden away here.

"It's . . . Ari, it's worse than we thought," Nellie began in a whisper. "The commissioner, he's—"

Nellie bit off her words as the sound of footsteps made their way up to them. A woman passed up the staircase, heading to the floor above. As she did her eyes snagged on Nellie with an uneasy assessment over her dirty hems, her hair frizzed from the humidity of the shop and the city. Nellie and Ari stayed silent until the sound of a closing door above them echoed down.

It was not safe to talk there. To tell Ari the truth, about Angus, about everything else he gleefully caused. And Nellie knew that Ari could not invite her into the home crowded with her family. She did not ask, and the other woman did not offer.

"I know. Well, I know a bit," Ari said. "About . . . who's really doing all of this. Anne has been by to see me once since. To bring me my tonic."

Nellie was relieved she would not have to be the one to tell Ari everything. It was awful enough to hear it from someone else's lips, let alone recount it herself.

"Ah, yes, here." Nellie extracted the bottle from her pockets, passing it over. "For you." The other woman took it gratefully.

Ari opened her mouth to speak, but before she could, a high-pitched woman's voice called out.

"Ari, dear, could you give me a hand with the packing?"

Ari shrugged.

"Well, that'll be my cue," she said.

"Packing?" Nellie asked.

Ari nodded, face downturned. "Aye. My family is headed . . . my father thinks it's best, safest, if we all head down to London to visit family for a bit. What with everything going on here. . . ."

Nellie understood. She knew Ari was at risk, and so, too, were all the other women in her family. Nellie's chest ached that her own father would never think to worry for her safety, but she was glad her friend had what she did not. A home full of love.

"That's good, Ari. You off soon?"

"Tonight. My father should be home any moment." Ari

said, waving the bottle. "It'll be nice to have this to bring along. It was good to see you, Nellie, truly. We should be back soon; don't be a stranger."

Nellie felt their conversation was too brief, too surface level, not nearly enough to remedy the time and distance the friends had to put between them. But she knew it was not wise to linger together, two witches.

With one more quick hug Ari slipped inside, closing the door, and Nellie was left alone. She headed toward the place she had once lived, the place she could no longer call her home.

CHAPTER 22

Edinburgh, Scotland
15 November, 1824

Nellie waded into waking in the way one only does when something is silently, terribly wrong. Her shift was damp with the sweat of a sleep made restless. The room was quiet, no sign of Da's grumbling drunken snore that would have had Nellie fleeing. There was just the faint, steady rhythm of Tommy's sleep. But it was easy enough for Nellie to find what roused her.

Waves of orange light danced beyond the window, flashing up from behind the distant buildings like the tongue of a dragon taking its fill. She surged up, hefting the window open. Immediately, her eyes were burned by the heavy smog on the air, painting Edinburgh grayer than usual. The moon was heavy and high in the sky, but the fire scorching across Edinburgh was enough—too much—for Nellie to see by, her sleep-addled eyes tearing even as she sprang to full wakefulness. Goose bumps raised across her body.

Nellie had lived in Edinburgh her entire life, knew it like she knew her own body. The city had so many closes along the high street, it could be emanating from any at all. But the sinking of Nellie's heart, down through her stomach, past her toes, the stones of the building, burrowing deep into the soil of the Cailleach's earth, told her she already knew which street burned that night.

She scrambled into her clothing with trembling fingers, bursting out the door and down the steps before her cloak was secure on her shoulders. It was past midnight she knew, but the city that greeted her was as bright as midday. She did not need to search for the home of the fire—if the light of the flames had not guided her there, the trembling figures lurking at the mouth of the street would have. Nellie pushed through the crowd that stood like a wall blocking Old Assembly Close, feet slipping as she raced toward Rae Women's Apothecary.

But it was not there. Not anymore.

There were only flames, so tall they reached the sky, grabbed at the other buildings of the alley, ripped through Edinburgh like it was paper. But here, the apothecary, this crumble of rubble and ash, was its blazing heart.

Nellie wasn't certain if blessed rain had fallen to foolishly war against the beast of fire, or if it was her own tears making lines of gray soot streak her face. She choked out a ragged cough as the ash made a home in her chest, but fear and panic lived there too, and that was all she felt.

Nellie grabbed the arm of a bystander, an officer standing uselessly slack-jawed, as they all did, staring up at the flame that was so much more than merely men could bring a stop to.

"The people who live here, have they got out?"

The man stared at her, the whites of his eyes burned red from the heat, a dusting of ash across his flushed skin.

"Are there survivors?" Her fingers pressed into the sleeve of his coat so tightly they ached. The man seemed to wake up.

"Nobody could survive that, miss."

He shook her off, stepped away to join the rest of the useless, helpless people who had come to watch their city burn.

Against logic, without sense, Nellie pressed forward toward the smoldering rubble. Maybe if she could just move a fallen beam, she would find Jean and Mary and Anne, *Jean*, God, her Jean, all untouched, all well. All holding that second, last life they had left. But they didn't—two witches hung; one girl dead in her sickbed. All three Rae women had escaped death once before. Witch or no, Nellie knew, though could hardly believe it, that there was nothing to save them now. The Cailleach gave only one extra life—and all three had used theirs up already.

Centuries of family—love, blood, and hope, burned down to nothing but ash. All that history endured in pursuit of a better future for womankind, reduced to little more than smoldering dirt.

Nellie's ankle rolled on something hard underfoot. The black smoke and scorching flame barricaded her from entering further. But then the fire caught on the tiny gleam of the thing beneath her foot, and Nellie's chest cleaved in two.

There, dulled by soot but unharmed and abandoned, lay Jean's little copper deer. Nellie squeezed the figure in her fist, wrapping the chain around her fingers. She did not know she was sobbing until a man pulled her away from the flame, patted out the fire that had seen a contemporary in the bright waves of her hair. The crowd swallowed her just as grief did, for Nellie knew that if that deer was there, Jean Rae was no longer.

There was no cool breeze on the air. There were no other witches here. They were gone.

Just as she was always there when Nellie was a crying girl, she looked across the crowd, through the smog and scent of burning death on the air, to see the stoic form of Lady MacDonald. For one moment the lady's eyes flickered to Nellie's, the raging fire between them painting her brown eyes with flashes of hellish red. Nellie knew what a sight she must be—scorched and sobbing and broken—but Lady MacDonald did not react. She just watched Nellie crumble, not so much as a sheen in her eyes. And then she turned and continued speaking to the man at her side, and Nellie knew for certain that this was exactly how Lady MacDonald had hoped to see her. Perhaps worse.

For by her side, speaking to each other in civil, familiar tones, was the commissioner. Angus looked up at the fire, the way hell had cracked open and swallowed Rae Women's Apothecary and the witches of Edinburgh, and he smiled.

He would let the women of Edinburgh be their own undoing, and there was Lady MacDonald, the woman Nellie had long loved most, who had brought about the end of her life. For Nellie may still breathe the smoggy air, but what good was life when death was so close at her heels, when the Rae women were no more?

It was all Nellie could think, again and again, a song she could not escape. *The Rae women are dead. They are not coming back. The Rae women are dead.*

The law did not matter; they would always find a way to burn witches.

Grace Duncan was the mother Nellie grieved, but she was not the one she lost. Lady Evelyn MacDonald was.

The commissioner had not yet seen Nellie, did not yet realize that any witches survived. But he didn't have to worry, his opposition was gone. Nellie would put up no fight.

Nellie pushed her way through the crowd, the heat of the raging flame on her neck as she bled into the Edinburgh night, feet falling through closes and streets and alleys. She gripped the sticks of charcoal in her pocket like a talisman.

The pocket of coin sewn into her skirt jingled with her frantic steps, and Nellie was glad that at least she had done this one thing. If there was anything left inside her to break, it splintered as Tommy's face flashed her mind. He had his coin, and soon he would sprout into a man and one day he would hardly remember the sister who had raised him like a mother, just as she had forgotten her own. Tommy was better left alone to the wiles of their da than by Nellie's side, fleeing like a criminal in the night.

Nellie hoped deeply that Ari was already long gone from the city after all. She cared about Ari too much to go to her home now and check, to risk bringing danger to her doorstep once Lady MacDonald told the commissioner Nellie still lived. Ari had a family to protect; Nellie was leaving only with herself, and only for herself. She knew that, no matter what else she told herself.

With the apothecary gone, the Raes were gone. They had burned because of Nellie, because she was the target of the flames, because death and destruction seemed to follow her. Everyone she cared for was safer with her gone.

Nellie told herself all these things so that she would not have to look at the truth of who she was.

She did not turn back to look at what she was leaving until the air around her was chilled and thick with the salt of the sea. When she looked then, there was nothing but night behind her.

The port was silent. The moon made the hulking, swaying forms of the anchored ships into monstrous shadows. Nellie looked up at the moon, full and bright. Nellie could not bring herself to speak to a being who could watch the slaughter of her daughters and do naught. Nellie loved the Cailleach proudly as a daughter, but she was slow to forgive.

Even by darkness a small crew of men worked loading wares onto one of the smaller fleets, their deep, masculine voices, for once, not making Nellie want to shrink inside herself. Sometimes salvation looks like the thing we fear most.

Nellie spoke to the captain in quiet tones, eased his refusals with a tip of her chin, the sliding of coin from one palm to another. Just before it was all over, on the warped entry from port to ship, Nellie turned to look over her shoulder at the only home she had ever known. Edinburgh was nothing but fire. Whipping orange flame taller than any building, summer taken its most insidious shape, hell reaching up to heaven.

The shop was gone; Isobel was gone; Ari was safe down in London. Nellie had hardly become a true witch, and, somehow, she was the last one left in the city. She could not take the mantle on. She could not bear the weight of it. She would rather let witchcraft die from Edinburgh's soil than bear it alone.

No one could survive that. But, somehow, Nellie had. *It should have been Jean. Then survival would have been worth something.*

Jean would never run from a fight, from danger and death. Jean would stand up for women even if she was the last witch in Edinburgh, even if she knew she would be hunted down.

But Nellie was not Jean. She was just Eleanor Duncan, a woman, a witch, and a coward. She stepped onto the boat.

☾

Perhaps due to the underpreparedness of the city's fire brigade, still in its infancy, the Great Fire of Edinburgh raged for five fatal days.

Much of the city's Old Town was destroyed irreparably. The fire damaged tenements along the high street, Borthwick's Close, Old Fishmarket Close, and Parliament Close.

Old Assembly Close, where the fire was believed to have started in a tiny apothecary shop from unknown causes, was destroyed.

Sixteen residents of the city perished in the flames.

One month later, as the new year of 1825 was welcomed in, the persecution of the women of Edinburgh for various, implied, counts of witchcraft finally came to an end.

28 February, 1826

If Nellie had ever imagined near-eternal life, living long enough to see the present become the past and make her space in the future—she would've thought she'd find the great artists, writers, thinkers of the time while they were earning that title. That she'd shape the future and make it in her image, that she would sniff out greatness like a hound while it was a seed in the soil of the soul.

5 August, 1894

Instead, she walked shadowed streets with her eyes cast down and her heart pattering in her chest.

24 April, 1922

Instead, she took a thousand, a million steps around the world so she would not have to take one step that mattered.

22 December, 1953

Instead, Nellie hid.

7 March, 1989

She went everywhere in the world except home, until the word lost its meaning.

CHAPTER 23

Buffalo, New York, USA
18 May, 2006

Nellie had thought of loneliness as an absence. But she knew now that it was not. Loneliness was a companion that walked beside her, that curled up in the pit of her belly each night, that draped its darkly clad arm across her shoulders and held her apart from the world. Through loneliness's gaze it looked as though all the world was happening without her.

Nellie could count on one hand the number of times, as she traveled the world twice over, that she had felt the telltale chill across her skin of another of the Cailleach's witches nearby. She knew that she could greet them, could mark herself as the same. Find a new community, build a new life. But she could never trust, even as she never stepped foot on Scottish soil again, that Angus too would not sense the gathering of witches. That he would not find her wherever she dwelled. So, she had never even turned her head to find the source of the sensation.

Nellie stayed alone. She kept running. When you've been away from home for so long, home just becomes yourself.

Or, at least, that was how Nellie felt for the first hundred and eighty years or so.

And then there was Rachel. It shouldn't have happened. Nellie was safe, she was careful. She was separate. But she and Rachel still found each other. Maybe Nellie would have been able to walk away from the other woman if the soft protectiveness that quickly formed between them hadn't reminded her so much of the sisterhood she'd found among the Rae women, unspoken but sure.

It wasn't like Jean, longing and passion and desire—it was friendship. And while Nellie had been with other women in fleeting moments in the past century, she had never felt that fire in her chest since Jean. But in Nellie's life friendship was even more rare.

She was selfish, and she held Rachel close.

Rachel and her little girl, Chani, were the only faces Nellie had allowed to become familiar in two centuries. It's not that she had been on the run, any more than Rachel was. Nellie just preferred to keep to herself. So she did not press why Rachel had taken herself and her daughter to live on the other side of the country from their home when the girl was only months old. If Chani's father was in the picture, he had not contacted them in the girl's four years. Nellie knew well the scars men could leave on a woman—she asked no questions. And in the silence and the almost secrets, Nellie, Rachel, and Chani had carved out their own little family.

The roads were slick that evening, the rain falling heavily around them as they twisted along the highway. Rachel's foot was lead on the gas pedal, as it always was, but the rain had cleared out most of the traffic.

"Ahh." Rachel smiled, twisting up the little knob of the radio, Stevie Nicks's crooning echoing around the car.

Nellie's life had become so comfortable, so joined, that she didn't even notice anymore just how happy she was in the moments like this. She sang along softly, Rachel's voice washing her out as it always did, boisterous and unapologetic. Nellie twisted in her seat to look at little Chani, her tiny hands pattering along to the beat on the plastic arms of her car seat, strapped tightly in the back. The girl never said much at the best of times, but her somber face bloomed into a smile as Nellie crooned and swayed for her.

Then things shifted, as they always do.

The first thing Nellie felt, before she saw the world spinning all the wrong ways beyond their window or heard Rachel's scream as her hands pawed desperately at the spinning wheel—was the bottom of her stomach falling out. An uncanny sort of weightlessness, less like flying and more like falling. Precisely, she would learn later as the police spoke to her in soft, well-trained tones, like wheels hitting pure water at a high speed, like hydroplaning. Like the car glinting off the metal rail that bordered the highway at an angle. Like it flipping, once, twice. Like the crunch of metal above and beneath her and then eerie, horrible silence. And then darkness.

The paramedics would tell Nellie she was lucky to have survived, being up in the front as she was, where metal crunched to half its size. But the moment Nellie opened her eyes, thick dark liquid clouding her vision, she knew she had not survived.

It wasn't luck that had brought her back. It was witchcraft. It was the Cailleach.

Her brain felt stuffed full of cotton, moving too slowly, not quite able to catch up. Later she would be grateful for it, for it kept the panic at bay as she looked to her side and saw Rachel, streaked with too much red to even see its source, eyes hauntingly open, head lolled. At least Nellie's mind was so addled that it wouldn't be until later that she felt the guilt for not taking Rachel to Scotland, for not teaching her the craft, for not putting her on the soil of the Cailleach's making and teaching her how to honor and aid the deity until Rachel too became a witch. Until she had a second life. But Nellie was too selfish. She was too afraid.

She knew Rachel would have adored the story of the Cail-leach, loved all the deity stood for. Nellie would always live with the guilt of never giving Rachel, who was already so brave, so independent, so unapologetic—already so like Cail-leach and like her hags had to be—the chance to save herself.

A high-pitched cry had pierced the terrible silence, and then there was Chani. She was strapped into her seat, the dark wave of her hair covering her face, little fingers gripping the crisscrossed straps of her seat so tight they had turned a ghostly white. She must have been sitting there, terrified, for a long time, for Nellie knew a witch's rebirth was not a quick process. There was not a scratch on her.

Reality came in flashes. There was sharp pain in Nellie's head that would have been too unbearable to fight if it was only her life on the line. But somehow, she pushed through. Then she was in the back seat, her shaking hands working on Chani's seat belt. Lifting the child with strength she didn't have, the scrape of metal on her body, then wet pavement and broken glass beneath them.

The rain fell heavy on their heads as Nellie sat beside the wrecked car, Chani gripped so tight in her arms she worried later that that would be what hurt the child. The rain just kept falling, as though it wasn't sorry for what it had done.

Other drivers stopped, their voices coming nearer to Nellie, hunched on the ground. There was the distant sound of sirens arriving. All Nellie could think was that she did not have Rachel anymore, that Chani did not have Rachel anymore. All she could do was hold the crying child in her arms and run a trembling hand across her head.

"It'll be okay, my girl. I'm here," Nellie chanted, like it was some sort of spell. Over and over. "I'm here. I'll protect you."

CHAPTER 24

Portland, Maine, USA
6 July, 2022

*M*ore states have gathered to vote upon the legality of birth control in the wake of Roe v. Wade *being overturned this spring. West Virginia has become the most recent state to discuss banning abortions entirely, with minimal exceptions. A recent statement from Governor—*

A heavy stone dropped through Nellie's stomach, acid flooding her throat. She flicked the television off, abandoning the house for the warm sun on the porch, the soft grass heating her bare feet.

We'll have to move soon. Leave the States again, head abroad. We should have left months ago; it's too dangerous here.

Even Portland was new to them. They had been in the city barely three months; Copenhagen for four months before, and Tokyo before that for six months, Rotterdam for nearly a year, Santiago, Helsinki, and Montreal for three months each. They were never still, Nellie could not be, and while they mostly tried to stay in the winter season, sometimes they needed a bit of warmth. The Cailleach was all about balance, after all.

Even with Chani in tow Nellie had bounced from place to place, in perpetual flux. They had moved so much, had so many papers and passports forged; the more Nellie's art became popular, mysterious, famous, enduring, the more money she had. She learned quickly that money could buy anything but peace, including birth certificates and passports, new identities and fresh starts, time and time again, if one knew the right people. Nellie had spent so long in the shadows of society she knew how to make those dark spots work for her.

Nellie told herself that she could not know how far the reach of Angus went; it felt like far too many places held the patriarchy as tight as Angus had. This was simply what the world was like. It was better to keep running, as if she could outrun misogyny.

But in truth, Nellie knew that she kept moving because no place had ever felt like home except the one. And she kept holding out hope that somewhere, finally, would.

Nellie and her girl had the means to keep running, to stay safe by never slowing. So many other women did not. But fear had made Nellie selfish—all she saw was evil at her back and the need to keep moving. For her, there was no one else in the world but her and Chani. If the two of them could survive, that was enough.

Nellie wiped the lingering dust of charcoal from her thigh as she stretched out on the chaise beside where Chani sat, eyes locked on the laptop propped on her knees, the sun glinting off her tan lines.

The sun beat warm and heavy across Nellie's legs as she extended them out before her. Even now, even with hundreds of years of space and weather behind her, Nellie's pulse still quickened when she felt heat on her skin, the thickness of summer on the air and in her lungs. As if to reassure herself of their safety Nellie glanced around their empty backyard and reached forward to lovingly squeeze Chani's arm. They had each other; they were safe.

"You're taking a break? What a miracle." Chani's smile was easy, as it always was. "Your wrist doing okay? You really should just let me make you a poultice to put on it while you work. We've got all this thyme in the garden anyway." She gestured toward the plants in the corner of the yard—primarily full of winter-flourishing growths, of course—thriving under Chani's care, just like all the gardens in all the countless temporary homes they'd had over the years. Every place they stayed, hopping from one to the other like stones, Chani left more beautiful than when they'd arrived.

"You don't need to care for me, love, I'm all right. And you're the kid, remember, I should be caring for you."

"Not much of a kid anymore," Chani said offhandedly, her attention already returning to her screen. She didn't even notice the way her words twisted Nellie's gut with an ache that was once novel but was now all too familiar.

Nellie knew the way age robbed a person of their childlike peace, their joy, the way the world robbed a girl of so much more than that. All she wanted was for Chani to keep all of herself for as long as she could. Nellie had kept herself hovered over Chani like a roof to keep the world from freezing those delicate parts of the girl, and it had worked. Somehow, and Nellie didn't know how she had done it, but Chani was *good*. Chani loved everything and everyone. It didn't matter if she was a woman, and the world didn't always love her back.

All she wanted was for Chani to be safe. So Nellie had opened up herself, cracked the door on her past, and taught the girl the craft she had spent a century and a half doing in whispers behind closed doors. They had never been to Scotland, so Chani was not a true daughter of the Cailleach yet, of course, but Nellie convinced herself that was okay. It did not stop Chani from knowing the story of the deity, honoring her even from afar. Chani never even contemplated shrinking herself or apologizing for her existence or letting herself believe that a man had more worth than her simply because the world had given him more power. And they practiced the Cailleach's naturalistic craft, though it ached Nellie to do so.

No matter where they lived, Nellie made sure to import and use the same herbs and plants that she was taught at Rae's, to do the craft with the tools from Scottish soil. And much as Nellie tried to forget, that same Scottish soil ran through her veins like blood, no matter where she ran. Chani may never have been on the Cailleach's land, but she loved the deity, wholly.

Nellie had taken on nearly every aspect of Chani's schooling herself, never staying in one place long enough for the girl to go to a proper school. Nellie had taught Chani math and science and languages, had outsourced lessons when she could. She did her best to raise Chani as Rachel would have done, eyes swelling with proud tears at the girl's bat mitzvah celebrated in a city they had hardly known, surrounded by strangers, nearly ten years ago now. She had supported Chani's interest in her Jewish heritage, that connection it held to the mother she had never really known. That, too, was in Chani's blood just as much as the Cailleach's craft was in her heart. Nellie had gotten to know the Cailleach over the past two centuries, though she never stepped foot on her land again—and she knew the Cailleach understood why she could not. But she spoke to the Cailleach through the moon every night, and knew it was the same one looking down upon Scotland.

She had not known she could love another so much until

she held Chani's small fingers in hers, until she held her breath as she watched the girl grow to a woman, looming over her like the shadow of a wolf over her cub. Nellie would have happily carved a hole in herself if Chani needed somewhere warm to rest.

The humid summer breeze lifted the girl's hair from her shoulders, the dark brown strands dancing behind her like the train of a gown. She stared intently, unblinking, at her computer screen.

"What are you staring at so hard, love?" Nellie asked.

It took Chani a moment to answer. First the shock on her face melted into joy and then shuttered into unease as she finally looked at Nellie.

"I . . . well . . . I wasn't trying to lie or anything, I promise. I *didn't* lie, I just didn't mention, which I know is just a loophole, that's just omission and we tell each other everything—"

"Chani."

"I applied to university. I *got into* university."

Nellie's stomach fell clean through. The warmth on the air did nothing to quell the chill that ran down her spine, the worry that flooded her like a sudden freezing rain. She wasn't sure if her expression betrayed her doom or if her girl just knew her well.

"I know, I know. You've told me all about how terrifying college can be for girls. But, I don't know, that shouldn't stop me, right?"

Nellie had, as Chani had gotten older, plied her with reminders that college was just as dangerous a place for a girl as the rest of the world was, more so even. Nellie's blue eyes locked on the news like it was a prophet, relaying to Chani tales of boys who slipped things in drinks, boys who had heard *no* so infrequently that they didn't seem to know the meaning of the word. Boys who were athletes or scholars or legacies, and so the institutions would tell them that they would never have to learn the meaning at all.

But now Nellie couldn't quite seem to find any words at all in the face of Chani's unmasked excitement. In the concern that laced her features, making her look so much younger than her twenty years.

"And I only applied to one place," Chani continued rapidly, as if Nellie's approval relied solely on hitting a word count. "I figured if I didn't get in then that's that, but I *did* and—"

"Deep breath, love." The reminder was for both of them. "What program is it, Chan?"

"Medicine. See, I know how much doctors write off women's pain, how they think we don't know our own bodies. The statistics on it are terrifying, but the anecdotes even more, especially for women of color. And trans women. And women with disabilities. It's a massive, *massive* problem. And health care systems just, like, *don't acknowledge it.* I mean, look at everything going on." Nellie had done her best to hide the news from Chani, but some horrors seep out everywhere. "But I can help change that, you know? Not only can I help women and listen to them, but I think the Cailleach's craft could really be integrated into healthcare more. I think it could make a huge difference in combination with mainstream medicine. I mean, natural healing was used for thousands of years for a reason, right? And there are so many other kinds of craft that could be so useful. And we don't know anything about how being in their second life affects a woman's health, if at all. I think I can help a lot of people."

It shouldn't surprise Nellie after all these years just how wonderful Chani was. *Rachel, I wish you could see our girl.*

So much of what Chani dreamed would be impossible, especially with witches still hiding. But Nellie could not deny the *goodness* of the girl's dreams. If anyone could find a way to make it work, it was Chani.

Nellie had that deep feeling in her gut that telling Chani no would be betraying not only the girl but also her mother. Chani had hope like no one else Nellie had ever met. The world deserved a shot at more of that.

She just wished the price for it wasn't putting her girl at risk. But maybe they could make it work. There was nothing in this world Nellie wouldn't do to see Chani smile the way she was then.

"Where's the school, love?

"In Scotland. Edinburgh."

There was nothing Nellie wouldn't do for Chani, except, perhaps, that.

"We've never lived in Scotland at all, but we should, shouldn't we? I mean you've said yourself I'm not really a witch until I've stepped foot on Scottish soil. And I want to. I want to see the land that the Cailleach created, climb her mountains and swim in her sea. I want to see one of her winters, be there to help bring it."

Nellie could hardly hear Chani through the whirring in her ears, the sound of her blood rushing, panic racing through her body like a drug. On instinct, Nellie's fingers twisted around the chain that hung from her neck, the little copper deer bouncing against her clavicle like an anxious drumbeat. Even after all these years, she still wore loss and memory around her neck.

Nellie told herself she didn't take Chani to Scotland because it would be too difficult to be a witch from so young, to grow from childhood at a slowed rate like Jean or Ari had, so their minds evolved and matured but were trapped in bodies so far behind. Nellie told herself that one day she would take Chani to Scotland and the girl would stand within the embrace of the Cailleach's earth and become her true child with a second life; Nellie had raised the girl as a witch in every way already, but without a foot on the Cailleach's soil she knew Chani was vulnerable, was living on the knife's edge of a single life. That, until then, there would always be a space between the girl and the deity. Nellie told herself that she would take her one day, that she did not value her own fear over her girl's—and the Cailleach's—thriving. Some days she even believed herself.

She had never told her girl a thing about what had happened to her in Edinburgh. Simply that she had been born and raised in Scotland. That she learned of the Cailleach and became one of her witches. As far as Chani knew, maybe Nellie had never even been to Edinburgh. As far as Chani knew, there was no enemy on that land to fear.

Nellie wanted Chani to have a home and a second life, but she also wanted her to be protected.

"Why don't you apply to some other universities?" Chani tried to interrupt, but Nellie continued. "And we'll take a trip to Scotland. One day, I promise."

"You've been saying that for years! And this uni has a great program! Plus, I'm homeschooled. I know that can make it hard to get into college, especially a medical program. But I did get in. *Here*. And I'm tired of waiting; I'll already be older than the other students."

"Oh, Chan, only by a couple of years—"

Chani's dark eyes narrowed. "Why don't you want me to go to Edinburgh?"

To answer Chani's question, to keep objecting, would mean telling her the truth. About Angus and the horrors he created, may continue to create for all Nellie knew. But Chani needed to go to Scotland. There was a small nibble in Nellie's gut too, like the intuition she hardly trusted, that told her that perhaps this was the Cailleach leading them to Edinburgh. Maybe the deity felt it was time for Nellie to face her fear.

"I'm tired of living in the middle. Of just, like, existing in a gray zone," Chani said softly. "Always running. Of not feeling Jewish enough without a community. Of not feeling like enough of a help to the Cailleach because I'm not on her land, because I only know one other of her children, when there must be so many. It's not that you're not enough, Auntie Nell. I just want . . . more too. I really want this."

They had the beauty and privilege of seeing the world but with it came the sense of being perpetually unmoored. Nellie may have gotten used to it, felt it a necessity, but her girl had not. Chani wanted a real home, a place she felt like herself, streets seen so often they became familiar enough to walk with her eyes shut. She could see it in Chani's face every time they packed up their life to begin anew, until eventually Chani stopped unpacking at each new destination at all. Nellie knew the feeling. Despite the centuries she could never get rid of that hollow ache in her chest, that homesickness, all the worse as home failed to be little more than a concept, than an ink-blotted memory, than the little girl she held in her arms.

Nellie wanted Chani to have a home, a true one, like she wanted the girl to have all things soft and warm and wonderful, things that made Nellie keep up her craft, to live for two centuries longer than she ever thought she would. Living two lives is worth nothing if surviving is all you have.

"If we go—" Nellie started.

"*We?*"

"You can't go on your own, Chani." Nellie's stomach dropped down to her toes at the very thought. Chani, alone, walking those cobblestones that had made and broken Nellie.

Nellie could not bear to tell her girl just how bad the world was. All she could do was give Chani a home and pray that Angus would not return. That Nellie would have to battle only her own memories and guilt in Edinburgh.

"Auntie Nell. I may not be centuries old, but I'm an adult, remember?" Chani tried for lightness, but her voice was unfamiliarly strained. The girl no doubt knew she was asking a lot of Nellie, even if she didn't comprehend just how much.

And yet here she was, with that unfiltered, unscarred lightness of a child. Because of having Nellie at her side, using her own body as a shield to protect Chani from the world so she could stay innocent, being privileged enough that it had worked.

"Together or not at all, Chan. And I'm not saying yes yet." But Nellie knew she nearly was.

And when Chani surged forward, wrapping her arms tightly around Nellie's neck, she knew there was no *nearly* about it.

CHAPTER 25

Edinburgh, Scotland
10 September, 2022

Nellie wasn't sure if it was the tilt of the cab around the backward roundabout or the haunting familiarity of the landscape beyond the window that made her mouth fill with spittle, the tasteless airplane breakfast sitting too high in her stomach. The rolling green all around them could have belonged to anywhere, to the unfamiliar eye. But Nellie knew that Scotland, that Edinburgh, was drawn in shades of green and brown like nowhere else in the world.

Even the air that slipped through the cracked window, though laced with pollution like in any city, was crisp and bright, and despite it all Nellie's body seemed to sigh in relief as it met home. Haunting, horrible, but home. She hated herself for it and hated the city more. But, she could not deny it felt settling. It felt like the Cailleach.

They'd had hours on the plane, a month prior to, that Nellie could have told Chani the truth of it all. But she didn't; she couldn't. She couldn't bear to tell the girl that the world was even worse than Nellie had taught her, that they were caught in the midst of an ancient, spiteful struggle for control. Nellie remained a coward, and she could not look at her own past, even for Chani's sake. She had told the girl only that she had lived in Edinburgh before, and she would answer no more on it.

Chani chattered excitedly with the cabdriver, talking of the university, of her program. Even in her endless joy Chani's answers were shallow and obscure, in just the way Nellie had taught her to speak to those she didn't know. The driver seemed unbothered, chatting about the beauty of campus, about the castle, Calton Hill, the country as a whole. The pride in his words gave him away as a local just as much as his voice, lightly burred and with a distinctly Scottish friendliness. Nellie had requested their destination in whispers, afraid that he would hear Edinburgh in her voice too. That he would try to find camaraderie with her that she was not sure she could give anymore. But he had said nothing of the sort, and only in hearing his voice did Nellie realize how much hers had changed. The burrs of Nellie's accent had smoothed out over the years, betraying her now as a local of no land.

The cab slid along, the houses becoming tighter together, greens exchanged for browns as they broke through toward the city proper. Nellie had seen enough of the world to know that everywhere changed. Modernity always seemed to stamp down on a city. And despite the taller, straighter houses, the cars and buses, the fast-food joints that slid past the window—Edinburgh didn't seem quite stamped down. It was blended, like a portrait with the deep hues of history swirled together with the neon of the modern world. Nellie's stomach plummeted as the castle came into view beyond the garden that stretched parallel to it. The castle's worn bricks were untouched from the last time she had seen it, even as the bustle of bright-signed shops was all around them as they moved along Princes Street.

She had never seen Edinburgh like this before, enclosed in the safe distance of a vehicle, like the outsider she now was. Nellie swallowed heavily and leaned into the seat, willing her eyes to stay shut even as Chani cooed and awed. Finally, the cab slid to a full stop.

"There you are." The driver helped deposit their suitcases on the curb, bid Chani farewell and good luck, and then the two women were left alone on the brightly lit streets of an afternoon in Edinburgh. Nostalgia and fear made a bitter taste on Nellie's tongue.

They hauled their things up the polished steps to the flat that Chani had only briefly argued against in favor of independence in student halls—Nellie had shut it down quickly with "It's too dangerous, love, let's just stay together for now." Nellie did her best not to notice how similar, yet how different, this home was to the one she had once known in this city. Chani had become so accustomed to the comfort Nellie could provide them with, but the older woman paused at the sprawling floors, the stretching windows, the idea that there was always this side of the city there, but never for people like her. Not then.

They muttered and unpacked, just as they always did, moving around each other with familiar ease. Chani paced like a caged animal until Nellie fearfully released her to the freedom of the city and her student orientation. Nellie did her best not to look at the looming crags beyond the window, memory taken rolling, roiling shape.

☾

Nellie was grateful for the chill on the air that whipped her coat around her knees, even if it did nothing to stop the perspiration that rose along the back of her neck. The snaking paths of the Meadows—the park standing between their flat and the city beyond it—were packed with students. So many young, carefree faces unlike those that haunted Nellie's memories of the stone and grass and smog of this place.

She passed through the city with muscles tensed, the tight-jawed face of a woman using the very last of her will. It is true, the past never really lets you go. But Nellie clung to hers with a white knuckled grip, a fist raised to the world.

It made her sick, in a way, to see how little the city had changed. To see how little she had changed too, walking across jutting cobblestones with her head bowed, as though she were still the fearful twenty-three-year-old she fled the city as. How was it that Nellie was the one who had fled, had traveled the world, yet she was the one who stayed exactly where she had been?

The Edinburgh Nellie had known was a dying thing, smothered by smog. And though so much of it looked the same, Edinburgh was a modern city now, alive. Some part of Nellie's brain knew this place was beautiful, that there had been times she was happy there, happier than she ever thought she could be. Thoughts of Jean, of Tommy, of Lady MacDonald before it all, stung her mind like sparks and she pushed them away.

Beauty—preservation of history—meant nothing when, for Nellie, every dark stone of this city was splashed with blood.

Only once in centuries had Nellie broken, allowed herself to search Thomas's name, his life, his death. He was a poor boy who became a poor man, not a king or an inventor or a scholar. The only world Tommy had changed was Nellie's. So, the world did not bother to remember him much. But after hours of digging and scouring Nellie had found the thinnest thread of Tommy's life after her. His signature working for a solicitor. A marriage certificate in 1837. A birth record in 1839, a little girl named Grace E. Duncan.

Nellie had sobbed for hours, had prayed that the *E* stood for herself, and hated herself for hoping because she did not deserve Tommy's continued love. She had never gotten the nerve or overcome the guilt to search for Tommy again.

There was no marked grave to visit.

She dodged the throng of tourists who passed through the Royal Mile like a tidal wave, unsure of whether she could be counted among their numbers. She knew the city, or she had once. But even though Edinburgh wore the same face—tall, tilting stone buildings walling the long stretch of road, closes spidering off like cracks in glass, reaching, pointed peaks and lopsided cobblestone—the makeup upon it was different. The dangerous rumble of carriages had been replaced by the wail of bagpipes for the entertainment of the tourists, the buildings that once held printing presses and pubs beneath the castle's looming presence now toted scarves and bags and tartan everywhere she looked, attention-grabbing booths hailing tours about ghosts and long-dead witches. It was as if the city's history, the history she had dragged herself from bloody and bruised, was a novel amusement.

As she climbed the gentle hill up toward the castle at the street's end, the barest flicker of Grassmarket caught her eye from the end of a staircase. The little white sign marking the street hit her like a gut punch, breathing down her neck like an old villain returned. Even among the din of cars and construction, Nellie could hear the echo of a rope creaking as it caught and swung around the neck of an innocent woman. A woman she did not save. *Could not have, she could have done nothing. What can one woman do?*

If loneliness walks beside you, nostalgia is a cat weaving through your ankles, tripping you with each reminder of its presence.

Nellie shouldered her way through the crowds headed up to the castle esplanade. She did her best to smother the growing fear in her throat at memories of crowds pushing down to the hangings, pushing up toward the screaming, hateful words of men inciting violence. The market that used to unfold in this very spot, the leering faces of men who would give her the world for the price of looking at her face, the doors it used to unlock for her. The world used to part for her beauty like a river to stone. Nowadays eyes simply passed over her, nothing in her stopping the tide. Nellie knew the story of the Cailleach, knew how older women were deemed hideous hags and a thing to be feared, that made others uncomfortable, more and more with each gray hair that sprouted from their heads. Women did not get to wear age or wisdom without paying a price.

Nellie used to know she was beautiful. The world told her every day, at every turn. Now it was as if age had bled her of grace, made her invisible. Nellie hated her beauty then, resented it. She hadn't realized then that the world considered a woman's beauty a ticking clock. God help the girls like her who took too long to realize that their strongest currency would not last forever. Sometimes Nellie wondered if she would have been better off having never been beautiful at all, so she would not know what the world considered her to have lost.

As she crested the top of the hill and the looming beast of the castle rose before her, a slender woman brushed against Nellie's shoulder, her black hair trailing behind. Nellie's chest squeezed, her throat clenched shut, blue eyes frantically following the woman's path. Then the stranger tilted her head, showed a face that was too soft, too joyous. Not Jean. Of course not Jean.

But Nellie could have sworn she'd seen her lover—long, long gone, she knew—in the face of every passing woman, peering from every window. A death by a thousand cuts, every one a scar still fresh and bleeding. Edinburgh wore its history proudly, but with it came the countless ghosts that crawled across the cobblestones.

The copper deer burned like a memory where it sat atop Nellie's heart.

Tucked along the edge of the space was a miniature fountain affixed to the side of a nearby building. Carved into stone, a snake coiled in the middle of two side profiles, one face calm and serene and youthful, the other threaded with signs of age, mouth split open in an enraged, terrifying scream. *Witches' Well* the plaque above marked it. Commissioned in 1894, a monument to those killed for witchcraft, the two faces meant to show that while some used their witchcraft for evil, *some* were simply misunderstood and wanted nothing but to spread kindness.

Nellie's eyes roved over the memorial, tucked away at the edge of the crowded square, already rusting green and barren. It was not even an apology. Not an acknowledgement of prejudice and wrongdoing. It was not enough. This city could fall to its cracking knees at Nellie's feet and beg for her forgiveness and, still, it would not be enough. She did not forgive Edinburgh.

From beyond the terrace railing the city stretched out, a monotone sea of stone buildings older than she was, the green humps of the crags at its back, the unfamiliar swirl of roads weaving between it all. Nellie didn't realize how distant the Cailleach had felt until she was once more on her soil and felt the deity in every leaf and stone and ache. Despite all the hatred and the fear and the darkness, that little restless creature that had lived in Nellie's stomach since the moment she saw the blazing city fade across the sea settled down with a sigh. For it does not matter how much horror there is, some places are like a mother; they make you and harm you like nowhere else could and are the only place that can soothe your soul.

Edinburgh was as much a part of Nellie as her bones and blood, and she hated it just as she had hated every other piece of herself.

Nellie could not bring herself to go toward the far end of the Royal Mile, to pass St. Giles' and the memory of Angus's mocking eyes. She could not bear the thought of seeing the street that had held her whole world until it burned to nothing but death and memory, seeing the cracked little street where she would never see her Tommy again, or the burial ground that had changed it all. Nellie could not even face herself, let alone her past. So she turned the way she had come and headed toward her easel and her charcoal and Chani, the closest thing she had to home.

CHAPTER 26

Edinburgh, Scotland
21 September, 2022

The charcoal was smooth beneath Nellie's fingers, the tips already stained with the dusting that coated her like a second skin. What with the acclaim, the infamy, and the fame she'd acquired—that she did her best to ignore—Nellie often felt many eyes on her back as she worked. Usually the feeling was figurative, but not today. The gazes were attentive, as silently distracting as the sun that splashed over her half-marred canvas through the windowed wall beside her.

No matter what she set out to create, ever since she'd returned to this city all that would bleed from Nellie's charcoal was twisting rope, flame and ash, the same pair of wide-set eyes that had found their way into her art again and again for two centuries, a ghost she could not escape. As those same eyes took shape beneath her fingers now, Nellie was too aware of the roomful of art students behind her, watching her every move with their own enraptured gazes. Their phones may be hidden away, but their own memories would be clear with the rare pleasure of watching allusive artist N Rae at work.

Nellie had spent years alone, in hiding, creating just for herself, to cope. But money had gotten sparse and selling three sketches on the streets of faraway cities had turned into more. It had turned into commissions and, naturally, portraits and portraits of the Cailleach. And with that had come attention and exhibits, mystery growing around her pieces as they continued to be made under the title of N Rae, long past one human's life span. When the critics and crowds theorized that N Rae was not one artist but a collective, a mantle passed down over the years, drawn in the same style, charcoal on canvases, haunting portraits—Nellie had allowed the world to think as much.

The gray had bled into the red of Nellie's hair and wrinkles had bloomed around her eyes, but still she did not look old enough to wear the name of the artist known to the public since the late 1950s. People had argued over the identity of the artist for decades, but not one conclusion seemed to be settled upon. Her face, her real name, was never known. She let the money from her art stream in while she hid behind it, as she always had. Until now.

Nellie could not bear the thought of those horrors she drew now being for the public again. Of those eyes being for anyone but her own. She set the nub of charcoal down, the piece before her drying and half-finished as she stepped away. As she did, Nellie caught the gazes snap back to their own work and breathed a tiny sigh that brought little relief.

Nellie trailed around the room, peaking behind the canvases that sat before each nervous student. The room was at least blessedly smaller than what the university had first pitched to her as this year's artist in residence. Nellie had taken on the position only due to her agent's reminder that her identity, while a mystery, was not entirely unknown to the public. They just believed Nellie to be the latest in a long line of artists creating under N Rae. Chani's encouragement had been a buoy, insisting that Nellie needed something of her own while in Edinburgh. Nellie had taken the post, but she hadn't agreed—she didn't need anything more than Chani and the private hours of just her and her work, no matter where she was.

Nellie was not ready to step out of her artistic hiding just yet, but affirmations of nondisclosure agreements and privacy promises had her peeking out, just the slightest. For Chani.

Laden with a dark simplicity, MoMA had described their latest N Rae exhibition.

Simple, yet so much more complex than the moon and clouds Nellie had once scribbled in this very city. Somehow that work had felt more fulfilling. Nellie could not shake the ringing hollowness of her work every day since she'd left Edinburgh two centuries before. She'd left so much more than memories and ash in this city.

Even though Nellie had spent two centuries never getting close enough to learn another's name, she did her best to remember those of the ten students who sat in a semicircle facing her as they took turns briefly introducing themselves. Just to her left was Gabby from São Paulo, a self-described painter looking to break into a new medium. Beside her was Tia, a young Black girl who'd just moved to the city from Providence, Rhode Island. She was in her first year of uni and living away from home for the first time. Next was Sam, a nervous-looking white girl from the American Midwest, and her outspoken seatmate, Charlotte, a dark-haired Glaswegian. Then Saba, a visual arts student from Toronto, who regularly used many mediums, including charcoal, to make art inspired by her Pakistani heritage. Two third-year flatmates: Liv, a willowy white girl from Sweden studying art history; and Mei, a stylish and outgoing art student from Singapore. Leila from Beirut, who proclaimed herself as a fan of the N Rae collective, and quiet Ella from Munich, who didn't say much of anything at all. And finally, to Nellie's right was a petite white girl named Catherine, an Edinburgh local who looked to be a few years older than most of the other girls.

Nellie had prompted the girls with the most basic of ice-breakers—to share their name, their artistic experience, where they're from, and what they study. Yet when the introductions circled to Nellie herself, she found she had no answers. Who was she—Nellie Duncan or N Rae or something between, someone she had forgotten in centuries of hiding? She did not know where she was from, no place feeling like home, and the perpetual fear, the need to hide, keeping her from identifying even one place she had ever lived, even here to these girls, for who could she trust beyond herself and Chani?

Nellie knew the girls were all students there already, that they had not come simply to take her class. But the weight of their expectant gazes on her, eager to learn and see her at work, was heavy as she held the charcoal in her hand. In the end, she had introduced herself simply as Nellie Duncan, the artist currently behind N Rae. She told them only of her life as an artist and nothing about who she was as a person.

This class was far from privacy but the steady thrum of these young women at work all in the same space, working around and with each other, was so reminiscent of the calm space of the apothecary. At the beginning at least. Jean would have called such a place fit for kindling the fire of the craft, but fire had never served Nellie well, and openness was a luxury she never found the budget for within herself. The only place she was vulnerable, shared herself, was behind the mask of her art.

"Have any of you worked with charcoal before?" Nellie asked the room at large.

Three tentative hands were raised: Saba, Mei, and Charlotte.

"It was the first kind of art I properly tried," the Scottish girl said, the eyes of the others rounding toward her, the first

one who had said much of anything at all beyond their introductions. "I've been a massive fan of your work since I was a
kid. Or, er, of N Rae's."

"Thank you," Nellie said tightly. As nervous as the girls
were, she was double. "It's a challenging medium. Without the
crutch of color and texture many artists struggle to infuse
emotion into their work. It's easy for charcoal pieces to fall . . .
silent."

If only Nellie's own creations would quiet down. Even in
smudges of black and gray they screamed as loud as her fears.

She continued her turn around the room, taking in the me-
thodical work of the students, the steady scratch of charcoal
on canvas a familiar, soothing rhythm. Most of the girls'
works were quiet indeed—landscapes leeched of color, two-
dimensional emotionless gazes, still lives without history or a
future. Art was about vulnerability and working with something like charcoal necessitated it. Nellie knew what it was like
to be a young woman, to raise a young woman—it was a fearful, fraught, frightening, beautiful experience. But there was
none of that on the canvases before her. Even in a roomful of
their peers, of people who had likely shared some of their unspoken experiences, the girls did not dare show the truth of
themselves.

Nellie could say nothing, for she knew she was no better.

☾

Nellie couldn't release the weight of tension that wrapped
around her shoulders. Chani didn't seem to notice, chattering
away as happily as the rest of the pub, cider in hand. Nellie
could feel the presence of every person in the boisterous room,
the men and boys whose gazes snagged on Chani once, twice,
before flitting away. Chani scooped the weight of her hair atop
her head and a boy to their left cut his eyes to her neck, her
shoulders, and Nellie's stomach sank.

Sometimes she wished she could hide Chani away from

everyone in the world, as though in being unseen she could be untouched by it. But she knew the only person that would hurt was her girl. The eyes of the world, of men, could be a terror anywhere, but they felt heavier in this city.

"You know, I'm really proud of you, Auntie Nell. Coming out of hiding finally." There was a laugh in Chani's voice, one that seemed to have taken up residence there since they'd taken it up in this city. But Nellie could hear the sincerity too.

Nellie's skin tightened with the chill of being near Chani, the girl already becoming a true child of the Cailleach, from nearly the moment she'd set foot on the deity's soil. Nellie had to fight down the panic that rose at the cool breeze, remind herself that it was just her girl and not a witch she did not know, a stranger to hide from, as she did from them all.

"I was never in *hiding.*"

"No, of course not." Chani had her mother's smile, open and good-natured, settling just right on her round face.

"How was your lab this morning?" Nellie asked around the sudden squeezing of her chest.

Chani's brown eyes, always so bright, lit up even further.

"Oh, it's amazing. We're actually getting to *do things.* It's not all theoretical, which, you know, is fun too, I guess, but this is better. And my lab mates are great, which helps."

Nellie opened her mouth, but before she could speak Chani predicted her questions.

"I know, it's a male professor, and there are a lot of guys in the lab, but they all seem nice, really."

They often do.

"There aren't too many women in STEM, which is a huge issue, obviously, but there's a few girls in the lab, and they're super cool. I think if we told them about the Cailleach and showed them the craft they could also—"

"No, Chani. You know that."

Nellie hated herself as she watched Chani's light dim. The world might have grown and expanded, but it did not change.

The louder they were, the more perilous their lives became. Nellie had fought hard, had given everything to give Chani safety. And Chani may now have a second life, but Nellie knew how easily both could be lost. She would not risk her girl's lives for anything, even if it meant giving another to every other woman in the world.

Before she could argue further, Chani's face opened once more as four shadows fell across their table. Even as Chani excitedly welcomed the classmates she recognized, Nellie took stock of the two boys, chatting and sipping easily from their pints of Tennent's. They were both taller and broader than Chani, with faces that seemed hard even beneath the smiles. But perhaps Nellie could just not see softness anywhere beyond her girl anymore.

"This is my auntie Nell," Chani introduced to a chorus of greetings from the foursome.

The taller white boy with a thick swoosh of blond hair smiled widest.

"Hi there, I'm Harry." The boy's accent was crisp and posh, English as could be. "It's nice to meet you."

The kids kept chattering among themselves, the spotlight of their eyes always falling to Chani, with her open smile and her easy laugh and her beauty that drew people in in a way that the girl did not yet resent. They hadn't been in the city a month, but Nellie could see that these people were the beginning of Chani's roots. These were faces she got to see often, a part of her routine, the same people and places each day. Nellie's heart pattered, and her instinct told her it was time to pack, to keep moving before the horrors found them, that to be known was to be in danger.

Her girl was thriving here, and she was cracking back open. Chani did not know how horrible a place, a people, could be. How horrible this place had been. How it might be again.

Nellie pushed herself up from the table.

"I'll leave you kids to have fun," she said, fighting the impulse that told her to tuck Chani against her chest, shelter her from the world in the circle of her arms. But Nellie was trying.

The four pulled up chairs and sipped pints as Nellie ran a hand across Chani's head, her hair as smooth and familiar a touch as Nellie's own skin. She pressed a kiss to the crown of the girl's head.

"Be sure to keep your drink covered, love. And keep me updated." Nellie tapped on Chani's phone, face down on the table.

Then she pressed out of the buzz of the pub and into the equally heady hum of the Royal Mile. She cut toward home and did not lift her head as St. Giles' Cathedral passed over her, heart hammering in her chest like a well-trained dog. Despite the horror she had encountered within that church, now steadily outlined in tourists, it was not the place in this city that Nellie feared most. Sometimes it was easier to accept the cruelty of others than it was to come to terms with our own capacity for evil.

Even as she lived her life, settled herself and her girl in as best she could, Nellie felt the presence of Old Assembly Close, no matter where in the city she was. It was the wound she was too afraid to poke. It lived in her mind like a hand held before a fire, untouched yet burning her all the same.

CHAPTER 27

Edinburgh, Scotland
30 September, 2022

Nellie wished it were colder. Even as heavy nightfall descended on the city, the air lacked its characteristic biting breeze that swept in from the sea, weaving between the crags and the pillared stone buildings that sat like walls around the city center. Even though the air was mild, it was still autumn, and daylight was more of a suggestion than a guarantee. The sun had retreated before the clocks struck five in the afternoon.

Like an exercise in exposure therapy, Nellie couldn't stop walking along the Royal Mile. She couldn't stop poking the old bruises, couldn't turn an ear from the siren's call. She wished the city had changed more, wished that she did not have to look at that same face, worn but not withered, memories staring back at her as if they were hardly memories at all.

It was a warped sort of early birthday gift to herself; daring herself to be brave, or something like it, in the last days of her two hundred and twenty years.

Tourists jostled down the street around her, students laughing as they set off on their Friday night quests. There were some cities that were meant to be explored alone, and Edinburgh was one—the city's history was everywhere, ghost and memory tucked within the cobblestones. So one could never *really* be alone. Edinburgh had once been known for digging up its corpses, after all.

Nellie's words were so quiet a passerby would mistake them for the wind. She'd had centuries experience becoming invisible, looking up at the moon and speaking to the Cailleach as if she spoke only to herself. For so long the deity had been her only companion. She tipped her head up to the sky now, the moon a hazy white-gray crescent, covered by the gauze of twilight. She looked out at the end of the Royal Mile, the looming, darkening presence of the crags, of nature so close.

She spoke the words so softly they tickled across her tongue. "Please, make me brave enough to meet whatever is meant for me. Whatever is coming."

Nellie checked her phone once more, her heartbeat easing its unsteady rhythm ever so slightly at the sight of Chani's check-in text, sent from the pub among her friends. Nellie wiped away the dark smear of charcoal she left across the screen, a reminder of why she was there.

She had been in the city nearly a month, and in that time, she had avoided walking far enough to encounter Old Assembly Close, or what had once been it. She had seen it die but she did not know if, like the rest of the city, it had been revitalized and preserved. Nellie had never looked back—she had never needed to, her memories always walked before her anyway. But in all the time she had been in the city, nothing could find its way onto her canvas but black-brimmed flashes of what had been in this city, dark eyes, arches and arches and arches of Old Assembly Close. She knew it would haunt her until she returned, until she saw with her own eyes, once more, that

Rae Women's Apothecary no longer sat there, waiting, and neither did the Rae women.

Nellie stopped before the alley. The stones that built the arch looked lighter, cleaner than its neighbors, but not by much. The life Nellie had lived there was the far past, already built over and with so many new lives stacked atop it. Someone who did not know what had happened to this place, who did not see the red flames of hell swallow it whole, burn through it like the stone was nothing more than paper, would not even notice the difference. But Nellie did not have the luxury of ignorance.

Even in the dark she could just barely make out the words on the sign at the close's curve, bearing its name in bright iron letters, fresh and untouched, as if nothing had happened here at all.

Edinburgh was brighter now, the night dotted with lights of white, green, red, that stretched and glimmered in the haze of darkness. The lights of modernity had replaced the heavy blanket of smog that once nestled upon the bricks. But the streets that webbed off the city's heart bore shadows. The closes were still where Edinburgh stored its secrets. Nellie stepped into the darkness of Old Assembly, counting herself once more among the city's many untold stories.

Everything was different, and yet nothing was at all. The stones had been rebuilt, a line of new flats stretching into the sky, space for a little shop tucked into its base. The hum of the city was muffled by the buildings that rose like a barrier. The only sound was Nellie's footsteps and the echoes of Jean calling her *Nell*, of Ari's laughter and Mary's soft words and Anne's patience, of Jean calling her a witch for the very first time. Nellie pressed her palm flat against the little deer around her neck, holding the copper to her skin.

If wanting something was enough to have it, if wishing

could change the past, Nellie would have had the power to rewrite it all.

And perhaps she did, or maybe time was never a line but a circle repeating, because there was a little shop there. No longer a sign for the Rae women, but a new black one, swirled gold writing marking *Beira's Market,* printed over an illustration of a snow-topped mountain peak. Nellie recognized the name Beira instantly, a name for the Cailleach used in Scotland in the more recent centuries.

Things are never quite the same as they were, but they are never so different as one may think.

Nellie had spent two centuries avoiding anyone who might be one of the Cailleach's hags, but there she was, undeniably standing before a place for those just like her. And despite the tightness in her chest and the tremble of her hands, Nellie reached for the shop's door.

As somewhere else in the city her girl unknowingly headed toward the very worst night of her life, the one that would never allow her to be the same woman again, Nellie crossed into the past and the future.

Stepping across the threshold felt like breaking some sort of spell. The shop was as dim as it had always been, though this time because the walls were painted true black and the sky beyond the large windows let in only the darkness of nightfall. It was different, of course, entirely, but this place looked like a natural descendant of the one Nellie had known.

Everything in the shop was made from the earth of Scotland; candles made of bee's wax and herbs, books on nature-based remedies and plant foraging and mythology, tarot cards that displayed Loch Ness and the Salisbury Crags in their background. A table in the center of the room displayed the detailed, colorful art of several decks, five high priestesses staring up at Nellie. Shelves housed rows of candles that lent themselves to the soft, earthy scent on the air.

"Hi there, you all right?" A young woman stood behind the

counter, nearly as tall as Nellie, her white skin holding on to the last remains of a summer tan. Golden blond curls were twisted in a bun atop her head as she pulled a dripping candle from the steaming pot before her. She was maybe a few years older than Chani, if Nellie had to guess, her smile open and polite beneath a pair of wide-set dark eyes.

Another customer pushed out through the front door, a little bag of goods in her hand and a smile on her face, leaving Nellie alone with the girl behind the counter.

"I'm good, yeah, thanks." Without thinking, Nellie spoke softly, gripped by the memory of how easily words echoed against these walls, how many of the words spoken in there were dangerous and secretive and bonding. She lifted a candle to her nose and breathed in the heady scent of chamomile and grass and gorse, stomach clenching at the familiarity of it. The smell of home, lost.

"Can I help you find anything?"

Before Nellie could answer the sound of a three-noted, swaying set of steps rang through the room, a door on the far wall softly clicking shut. Nellie finally noticed the chill that tightened her skin. Not the autumn weather, but the presence of other of the Cailleach's witches.

"Sorry, we're actually shutting up shop for the night," the newcomer said. "If there's anything you want to grab, Fiona can ring you up."

The shop, the world, tilted on its axis. The candle, heavy and solid, nearly slipped from Nellie's hands. In the two centuries since she had last set foot in this shop Nellie had met many people, heard many voices. But that was one she would never forget.

Afraid to hope, Nellie looked up into the very alive, very real face of Jean Rae, leaning against the counter. Her wide, dark eyes were steely and locked on Nellie.

☾

Nellie was a decent witch—not great, she knew, but good enough to stay alive this long and give the Cailleach at least a bit of power. So she knew she had not brought the woman before her back from the dead by magic or wishes or any other means. She knew such a thing could not be done.

But there seemed to be no other explanation for why Jean— who Nellie had seen burn to smolders in the wreckage of this very building, whose second and last life had burned among the flames—stood across the room from her now. The long curtain of her black hair had been cut short and severe, landing just below her pointed chin. She was still slender with those sharp elbows and sharper features that the little age lines around her eyes and mouth could not ease. Nellie wanted to run her fingers across every line of Jean's face, to feel that they were real, that she had lived and aged and *was alive*.

"We're closed. Please leave."

Even after all this time Nellie knew Jean well enough to hear the anger simmering beneath her words, flooding across her tight-jawed face, older, softened, but still the same. But Nellie could make no sense of it, any of it.

"Jean . . ." She breathed, sure that if the other woman heard her voice maybe she would recognize her too, even if Nellie's face had morphed beyond the young woman Jean had once known. She could not feel the ache of being unrecognized or worse, forgotten, through her own shock.

"You have some nerve coming here," Jean scoffed. "*Leave*, Nellie."

There was no softness in Jean's voice or her face, and Nellie could not understand what had happened, what was happening now. All she knew was that her Jean was finally in front of her after centuries of wishing, fruitlessly, for a moment like this. And yet, Jean looked at Nellie with nothing but the kind of unbridled hatred reserved only for those we held closest and were burned by.

"Jean, it's me," Nellie insisted, stepping forward, as if somehow the other woman didn't understand either, as if there was some miscommunication that could be fixed, despite already hearing her name leave Jean's lips. "How are you alive? I thought—"

"I don't care what you thought, frankly. Go."

This was not how this moment, this unbelievable moment, was supposed to go.

"The fire and . . . I saw it. I thought you died—"

"Well, I didn't. Turns out the fever didn't kill me when I was a girl after all. But you wouldn't know that, would you, because you abandoned us."

Through the haze of surprise and misunderstanding Nellie saw the blond girl leave through the door, casting a confused glance between Jean and Nellie, standing on opposite sides of the room. To Nellie it was a gulf she did not know if she could cross but longed to, to touch the other woman, to feel her and know she was real. But it seemed that to Jean the distance was not far enough, not enough space to hold the burning anger that radiated from her.

"I didn't know—*Jean.* I thought—I couldn't have stayed. I thought I'd only make things worse, put more people in danger. I thought you all were dead, and what could I have done, I—"

"Well, I was still here, Ari was still here!" Jean coughed roughly—a remnant of the dark smoke that had killed her centuries ago, Nellie realized—but it did nothing to tamper the power of her anger. "Every woman was still in this city, suffering, and where the fuck were you?" Jean tipped toward Nellie in her anger, her weight leaning heavily atop the black cane she held in her hand, trembling with rage beneath her touch. Jean was as terrifying and beautiful as she had always been.

It was two centuries of resentment bursting forth from the dam, and it was not supposed to be like this, but some reunions are forged by the same fire that created their distance.

"If I had known you were alive, I would have stayed!" Nellie did not become so small in the face of anger anymore, age like an armor around her. But Jean had been angry since the day she was born; she was better at it. And Nellie could not understand anything before her, her thoughts a screaming whir of wind trying to make sense of a senseless situation. She was busy trying to accept that everything she had believed and grieved for two centuries was not real. That it all could have been different, that it *was* different.

Jean guffawed, a searing, humorless sound.

"God, you still don't get it! That's fucked-up, Nellie. You abandoned your brother, you abandoned the Cailleach! You knew full well she needed her witches here. That's what her hags are supposed to do, charge into battle with her to bring about winter if we must! But you only cared for yourself! You abandoned her, you did exactly what he wanted. And what about *Ari*? Did you never think of her or all the others you were leaving behind? You're still such a coward. I've seen you making your way through the world for decades, hiding behind your art, not helping anyone but yourself."

The wind of Nellie's thoughts became a tornado. It felt like the world was slipping away from her. Every time her daydreams had scripted this impossible scenario it had never gone like this. It was never supposed to be reality, let alone be like this. She had thought Ari was safe, that Jean was gone. But she could not find words to explain herself, could not find her footing.

"You knew I was alive too? All this time?" She knew that Jean heard the third question she was not brave enough to ask. *And you didn't come find me?*

"N Rae isn't so subtle an alias." Jean rolled her eyes, crossing her arms across her chest, another layer of her unending armor.

Distantly Nellie's chest panged to see it, on the outside again.

"I saw some collection of yours down in London two decades ago. I would know your hand anywhere."

Even as Jean threw vitriol at her, Nellie's heart surged with longing, like it was tied to the other woman's with some pulsing, unbreakable chain, drawn toward her, even if she knew she may be burned. Nellie had decided long ago that it was worth it.

"But you never said anything? You could have told me you were alive; I would have come back for you if I had—"

"Come back for what? It had been a century and half, Nellie, I'm not the same woman you knew then. I'd changed. And it was clear you hadn't. You've always been like this, Nellie, even then," Jean huffed. "Especially then. Every morning you'd come into the shop more pink-cheeked and infatuated with me than when you'd left the night before. Even then I feared it was the idea of me you were creating that had you hooked more than the real thing. And look at how easily you fled—clearly none of it was ever real. You never cared about any of us."

The words stung across Nellie's skin, and for all her years she wasn't sure she had grown any wiser at all. For Jean was probably right and Nellie had never even realized, and she felt like a fool, like a child.

"Just *go*." The other woman's eyes were as hard as her stance.

Jean was right—she hadn't changed. For Nellie could feel herself shrinking and hiding as if she was that twenty-three-year-old girl terrified that every inch of space she took up was too much. Jean wasn't being entirely fair, but she was right—Nellie had chosen herself over all others, over the Cailleach. She loved the deity, yes, but she especially loved the protection that gave her. It was herself Nellie protected above all others.

She felt like a chastised child, but at least she had enough dignity now to not want Jean to see it.

Nellie turned toward the door, her mind twisted into knots and her heart crumpled between her feet. But she was fool enough, or perhaps brave enough, to look over her shoulder as she stood on the precipice of stepping outside. Jean did not look back at her. She did not even linger in the room any longer, for once leaving before Nellie could do it first.

CHAPTER 28

Edinburgh, Scotland
5 October, 2022

The air was heavy with a complex merging of scents from the mug on the little table to Nellie's right. Steam coiled above it, slow and twisty, defying gravity in that way that was customary to craft-made teas. It scented the air with the zesty oil of witch hazel for soothing wounds, inside and out. There was the prominent, earthy smell of chamomile, to aid with anxiety. The sweet lick of honeysuckle for brightening and soothing the spirit. Tart hawthorn berries for strengthening, lending the brew it's deep, purple-red hue. Rich rosemary for love had and love lost.

Heartache tea—Nellie's own specialty, perfected over the centuries once her hands became steady in the ways of the craft.

The Cailleach's craft was just a series of little actions, little lifestyles, little moments. But Nellie was too old to believe that this kind of ache would be a little moment too.

Nellie could hardly feel the charcoal on her fingertips, her body numbed down to nothingness. There are so few ways to cope with a world cracking open, and Nellie's favorite way, only way, had always been avoidance. Not that it mattered much, for her hands had been able to create nothing at all for days. The white canvas before her haunted her as much as Jean's words.

It was amazing that someone could live so long, walk in so many places, and yet see nothing at all. Understand nothing at all. Jean was cruel, senselessly so, and Nellie was realizing perhaps she always had been. Nellie had built two centuries of a life falling in love with a memory, with a hope for the future that had never come to be. Somewhere, deep down, she knew she couldn't blame Jean for not doing the same. To Nellie it was a future cut short, an immortalized *What if?* To Jean it was merely another of the world's betrayals.

But Jean could be callous and cutting. Unfortunately, Nellie knew that did not make her words any less true. That did not make Nellie any less of a coward. Any less selfish. But now Nellie could see the lies she had told herself, to qualify her fleeing. And Nellie had never once thought of all the other women she may not know but who she had left to suffer at the hands of that immortal being. She had not thought of how defenseless she'd left the Cailleach in Edinburgh, not a daughter left to give her power, to help welcome her season. Nellie had only thought of herself, her own ache, her own losses.

Nellie's studio, tucked away at the rear of their flat, was cast in warm lamplight. Day had long since faded into night, and the curtains were pulled tight to block out the view of the crags beyond. She had chosen this room, this flat, because she thought the view would comfort and inspire her. Her memories and her love were her art, even if it hurt.

But the sight no longer triggered the ache of memories. Now it just reminded Nellie of her confusion, of the flush of embarrassment that had lived deep in her bones for days. The shame.

Not just because of the choices she had made, once, but because of how horribly she had misjudged it all, how foolishly placed her affection was. Despite the fire and the anger and the cruelty, a deep part of her was still soft and tender for Jean. And now she suspected the other woman had never held the same for her.

Nellie recognized the familiar tread of Chani's steps coming up the stairs of the building before her key jingled in the lock. The door nicked closed softly, the girl's footsteps through the house as light and aimless as a ghost. She did not call out a bright-toned greeting to Nellie.

Nellie had been underwater for days, but not so much that she did not notice the shift in Chani too.

Nellie walked away from the blank canvas, feeling its presence, and that of the crags beyond it, as she moved through the house. Chani sat on the couch, knees tucked up to her chin, arms wrapped around her shins, trying to hold herself in, to protect herself. Nellie's chest tightened. She did not know what was wrong, but she knew something was. This was not her sprawling, happy girl.

"You're home from the lab a bit late." Nellie glanced at her watch. "The past few evenings actually. Everything all right?"

She sat down beside Chani, placing a hand on her knee. The girl didn't seem to feel it, though her face paled at Nellie's words.

"Yeah. All fine. I just . . . I've been taking the long way home is all."

"The long way?"

"Yeah. Around the . . . the Meadows, instead of through it."

Nellie's auburn brows pinched together, Chani looking past her toward the other houses visible through the bay windows.

There it is, Nellie's intuition seemed to whisper. Whatever it was that sat on Chani's chest, that she was keeping hidden in her middle.

"Why, love?"

Chani didn't answer for a moment, pulling her legs to herself, tightening, coiling inward. Nellie ran a hand over her head, down her hair, soft, the way she had done when Chani was just a girl. The way she had watched Rachel do to her daughter time and time again. Something splintered, Chani's lower lip trembling slightly.

The room felt too silent, frozen. Nellie's breath disappeared, the way it does when you know something is wrong, when you want to fix it, when you're terrified to look at the problem at all. She may think, too often, that it was better not to know. But that did not apply, never, where her girl was concerned.

"On Friday night I was, um, I went out to grab drinks with some friends from my lab, right?"

Nellie nodded, afraid to speak, afraid to breathe. She wished she could pause time, for she knew, bone-deep, that their lives were about to shift. That maybe they already had.

"I was heading home after and . . . Harry, he offered to walk me. You know, 'cause it was late and everything. You met Harry."

Nellie recalled the smiling blond man she had met briefly. "And we went through the park, and I know it was night and I wouldn't go through on my own, that's, like, the first thing girls learn when they move here, but he was with me, so I figured it was okay."

Nellie held her breath. Some stories do not need an ending. Some stories every woman knows by heart.

"And, I don't know." Chani squeezed her eyes shut, water brimming at their edges, her voice shaking. "He stopped and he tried to kiss me. And I just . . . I don't know, we're friends; I don't like him like that. But we were on one of the side paths, and they're not so well lit and . . . he just kept pushing it. I said no and I tried to joke my way out of it but . . . he thought I wasn't serious, or he didn't care, I don't know. He sort of pushed me over to one of the trees off the path, and we were in the dark and he just kept . . ." Her voice broke.

Nellie's heart fell to the floor like a shattering glass. She was just one woman, and she was no match for a world that had been shaped and distorted to hate them. She had held the horrors of the world off, but she could not stop them. They had found her girl.

"A few other people from our program happened to walk by and they recognized us and stopped. They were cracking jokes about us, no one even realized . . . I just went on with them, and Harry left," Chani breathed. "I don't know what would have happened if they hadn't walked by then."

But Nellie suspected she did know. Despite all she had done to shelter Chani, Chani was still a woman and women know, as though it's part of their blood and bones, what happens when a man decides he will take what he wants.

Chani held her arms so tight around her middle that Nellie was sure her ribs would crack. She wanted to open her arms, rewind the clock, make her girl soft and unafraid again, but she could not.

Nellie used to think that every crack losing her mother left behind had let all the horrors of the world in. But Nellie had kept Chani whole, she had raised her as a daughter of the Cailleach and a daughter of her own, and yet the hate of the world found her.

She pulled Chani to herself, and for a moment she feared that her touch would not provide the comfort it once had, that to Chani even her own body was now a thing to fear. Nellie knew the feeling well, that deep-seated strangeness of one's own skin after another has taken it for their own. But the girl leaned heavily against her, into the circle of Nellie's arms that were no longer their protective bubble.

We never should have come here. Only bad things happen here.

As if Chani could hear her thoughts, she spoke again, voice soft and unsteady.

"I can't leave. I can't . . . let him drive me out from what I want. I worked hard to get here. I'm staying."

It was not the answer Nellie wanted. Not the one she would have chosen herself. It was not the easy route; it was terrifying and challenging. But Chani was not Nellie. She was brave. Despite all the darkness, the heaviness on her chest, Nellie felt a wave of pride.

"I went to my professor, and I tried to tell him what happened. To, I don't know, report Harry. I couldn't—I can't see his face in my lab every day. I can't. But my professor just blew me off and passed me along to the head of the department, who told me that I could drop the class myself, but they could not unenroll Harry from it without any proof of misconduct."

Nellie did not naturally have anger running through her veins, fueling every beat of her heart and every thought. But as she heard those words it was like the very composition of her body changed, like a spark was lit within her and the fire of anger surged and swallowed her.

"So it's just my word against his. They won't even move either of us to another lab slot. And I can't drop the class. I won't. If I drop it, I have to drop out of the program because it's a required course, or be behind a year, but how am I supposed to . . ." Chani's words were swallowed by her tears.

Her brown hair fanned out across Nellie's chest, her tears wetting the shoulder of Nellie's shirt. She looked so young and small and defenseless, her round cheeks turning red. Chani had tried but the world had told her no. The world had told her, as it always did, that a man's place, no matter where, was promised. That a woman's was just a gift that could be taken back.

But Chani was not helpless. She was not defenseless—she had Nellie.

If there was one thing the Cailleach taught her children, it was this: do not let the world keep you small.

"I will take care of this. I will fix this," Nellie said.

And Chani, for all that she argued for her independence, for being treated as the adult she was, nodded gratefully. There were few things Nellie would fight for, but Chani was one of them. For Chani she would fight every time.

Nellie hadn't given Chani heartache tea since she was a little girl, awoken in the night by memories of shattered glass and aching for her mother. There had been no reason to—Nellie had ensured her girl never had to know heartache.

That night Nellie got up and poured Chani a cup of the tea.

CHAPTER 29

Edinburgh, Scotland
6 October, 2022

As Nellie passed beneath the heavy stone arch, her neck ached with the tension. She crossed by the bright green grass square in the faculty campus's center, dark stone buildings like a wall blocking out the world of non-academia on every side. The city thrummed distantly beyond the arch, but it couldn't quite penetrate the hush of the square. The sun was hidden behind Edinburgh's cloudy ceiling, but the air was just this side of warm for October.

Nellie headed straight toward the far building, its gleaming windows dulled by the cloudy afternoon. Despite the pattering in her chest, Nellie's steps were quick with determination, her boots ringing across the cobblestones like gunshots. Nellie would become whoever she needed to be for her girl. She let the world make her a coward in many ways, but not where Chani was concerned. Not when Chani needed her.

The tree at the base of the steps of the largest building bore a head of emerald leaves, its base crowded with unseasonably thriving flowers. The leaves rustling in the breeze was lost as Nellie passed through the heavy glass door and entered the building.

Her destination was easy to find, poorly marked as it was. This building wasn't intended for students or visitors, these rows of faculty offices made of glinting marble and floor to ceiling windows. Thankfully, Nellie's post as artist in residence gave her a bit more access than the average visitor. Or the average guardian of a student, the role she was there for that day.

Nellie pushed through the door of Principal and Vice-Chancellor Arthur Donoghue's office like it were her own. She knew that the vice-chancellor was recently appointed, this being his first term in the position. Nellie hoped it meant he would be eager to prove himself, to make friends within the faculty and students.

The room she entered seemed larger than its square footage due to the light that poured in through the wall-sized windows, heating the space immediately. As Nellie approached the man behind the receptionist desk, she felt the wool collar of her jacket scratch at her skin.

The man looked up, startled, clicking quickly through the computer blocking out half his face. There was a scattered, frantic sort of look in his eye as Nellie loomed above him.

"Hello, ma'am, how can I help you?" he asked but did not pause for her to answer. "The vice-chancellor doesn't seem to have any meetings scheduled for the day. Are you—"

"I don't have an appointment," Nellie's voice was cool and crisp. "But I need to see him promptly."

Classical music seeped out from beneath the closed door beside them, a dramatic crescendo muffled by the wood that marked the adjoining room as occupied.

When the man looked up at Nellie properly, there was a hard flint in his eyes, unmasked and pure in a way Nellie hadn't seen directed at her in centuries. It startled her back a step, memories flashing in her mind, the enraged, hateful faces of men who did not know her yet but had wanted more than anything to see her swing. Sweat pooled thick beneath her arms. She would have fled, were all those faces not worn out by the memory of Chani, face crumpled with a pain she should not have to bear, seeking help and being denied it again and again.

Nellie stepped back up to the desk.

"That's not possible." The receptionist's voice had a cold edge now. "Vice-Chancellor Donoghue sees visitors by appointment only. And, ma'am, he generally does not meet with civilians—"

"I am—" Before Nellie could finish, the door on the far wall cracked open. Though no face peered through, the simple gesture silenced Nellie and the receptionist both. A powerful man's presence can be felt even before he enters a room. To Nellie, the presence felt like inexplicable fear prickling along her neck.

"It's no bother. You can send her on in," the voice from within called, nonplussed.

Nellie did not even bother shooting the receptionist a glance as she walked into the adjoining office.

This office was larger, with deep hued bookshelves lining every wall that was not made of glass. The room was high enough up that it floated above the nearby buildings, a view of the city and the university main campus on the other side.

A middle-aged white man sat behind the desk, suit as clean and crisp as his posture, hands folded across the wood before him. Speckled gray-black hair was sleekly coiffed above cool blue eyes, distantly handsome in the way that intimidated rather than invited.

"Hello there, I'm Arthur Donoghue, principal and vice-chancellor. Please, sit." He tipped his chin to the chair across the desk.

Nellie sat perched on its edge, suddenly feeling the weight of what she was there to do too much, her skin flushing with anxiety. She could not resist the urge to shrug out of her coat, keeping her arms tight to her sides to disguise the moisture that bloomed there. She flicked her hair off her neck, but it did little to relieve the heat of nerves or the nausea pulsing in her stomach.

"What can I do for you?" There was a slight smile pulling at the corners of the man's mouth, though it seemed a bare flash beneath the stoicism on his face.

"Hi there. My niece, an undergraduate in the sciences department, recently reported that a classmate of hers attempted to," Nellie took a deep breath, "sexually assault her. *Did* assault her. Her professor, as well as the department head, seemed to take no issue and did not press the matter further, going so far as to suggest that my Chani drop out of her required courses so that she doesn't have to encounter her assaulter." The words came out in a rush, and all Nellie could do was hope they did not sound as nervous as she, for some reason, felt. Nellie realized she had not even introduced herself in her haste to get out the reason for her visit before the nerves robbed her of speech. But there was no going back now. "Meanwhile this young man is facing absolutely no repercussions. Surely this is not what the university stands for—being accomplice to assault and allowing the actions of its male students to prohibit the education of young women?"

The vice-chancellor sighed heavily, leaning casually in his seat, those clasped hands rising and falling by his side. Nellie's head pounded dully. Though the sun barely cut through the massive windows, the room was far too hot, and Nellie wished he would pull the curtains.

Chani, focus on Chani. Focus for Chani.

"My goodness," the vice-chancellor breathed, his voice as light and detached as it had been when Nellie walked in. "You have laid out quite the situation, haven't you?"

"I . . ." Nellie couldn't quite find words, not sure what to say as he seemed to subtly repaint the situation.

"I'm not quite certain what you'd like me to do. Surely, you're not asking me to take legal action on your behalf. To expel a student simply over a misunderstanding between two young people?"

The pit of Nellie's stomach dropped out. The conversation was sliding away from her, but she couldn't quite manage to get a hold of it again. She couldn't think around the roils of nausea that came in waves with the growing heat of the room.

"You say the professor's been informed as well as the head of the department. Squabbles like this are far below my jurisdiction, but since you've felt the need to bring it to me, I must assure you that I have the utmost trust in the judgment of my fellow academics," the vice-chancellor continued, shrugging. A slight, polite smile was clear on his face.

The air was too heavy, Nellie's clothes and skin were too tight.

"I advise you to let this be. Pick your battles, Ms. Duncan."

The nausea jumped up into her throat as Nellie's stomach dropped out beneath her. She had said many things to the vice-chancellor, she was sure, but her name was not among them.

And once she heard it, that knowledge he should not know, that slight mocking on his tongue as he said her name, it all clicked into place. Nothing made a hag servant of the Cailleach burn from the inside quite like the presence of the king of summer.

Nellie had been careless to bring Chani to this city. She had been a fool to come back herself. Because she was not the only one who had returned.

Perhaps this why the Cailleach had pulled her back to the city, why Nellie had kept her second life even after abandoning the Cailleach in Edinburgh centuries ago, only honoring her from afar. It seemed the deity would need all the servants she could get in Edinburgh, for her son was back.

Nellie's movements were quick with panic as she pressed to her feet, grabbing her jacket in fumbling fingers. The room swayed to its side as she did. It was only Nellie's anger that kept her upright, that kept her from falling to the floor, from giving into fear and fire.

She told herself to remain level, to remain calm. But she could not. Not as every one of her worst memories was searing itself to the forefront of her brain, as the thing she had spent her lifetime fleeing from had found her once more, here behind closed doors, once again in the spaces meant for men in power.

The man sitting behind the desk, watching her make her hurried way to the door did not sport the mocking, tilting smile she had last seen from Angus. He looked at her blankly, features pinched ever so slightly with confusion, looking like any other human man. But Nellie knew better.

The past—like hate, like Angus—is never really gone. It is merely lying in wait, ready to strike open old wounds anew.

Nellie could not make her heavy, dry, burning tongue say another word as she pressed out the office door. But behind her, the words burning through her skin like a brand, she heard Vice-Chancellor Arthur Donoghue, or rather the deity who wore his face, call to her one last time.

"It's wonderful to have you home, Nellie."

CHAPTER 30

Edinburgh, Scotland
7 October, 2022

Nellie's every urge told her to jump on a ship, a train, a plane, to flee. To leave, to protect herself and Chani, and let someone else try to handle Angus. Nellie had faced him before—she knew there was no winning. One man, maybe even one vengeful deity, could be weakened. But the hate he created that rippled and spread, jumping from the mind and heart of one person to the next, could not so easily be quelled. Even by witches. *Especially* by witches.

Nellie returned home from the vice-chancellor's office with sweat cooling on her skin as she thrust everything they owned into suitcases. She would put them on any plane she could, the first one out of here, no matter where it was going. But then Nellie caught sight of Chani moving about the flat like a ghost, hollow and haunted, watching her aunt without speaking. And Nellie knew that it was too late. No matter where they ran, no matter how far, Chani had encountered the horrors of man. She would spend her life as Nellie had, fleeing and hiding and rotting from the inside out. Leaving would not heal her girl, just as it had never truly healed her.

She thought of Tommy, left alone in a world with no mother and no sister. She did not see herself what had become of her brother, and it haunted her every day of her life. Even with all that had occurred, twice over, between her and Jean, leaving Tommy in favor of her cowardice was her greatest regret, the thing she would never forgive herself for. And Nellie knew that if she grabbed Chani and fled now, pulled the girl from her future and gave her back to a life of running from something that would never be escaped because now it was within—that would join the ranks of Nellie's regrets. She had not done better by Tommy, by the Cailleach, by herself, before. But she could do better for Chani now. For that was what it meant to love someone more than you loved yourself, to give your heart and bones to another like a mother, in whatever way you were one.

Nellie knew that a lot of people these days, especially down in the lowland cities, didn't depend on crops and farming for livelihood as much. So even if women may have more opportunity than they once did—and in turn the Cailleach may be seen more positively—people likely had less reason to honor her and her season, without the need to ask for her protection of their families and farms throughout the winter. In some regards, modernity was taking the Cailleach's power but in others, it was lending to it. But Angus, clearly, wasn't satisfied to let modernity evolve and shift, for natural balance to occur. He wanted everything.

The Cailleach still needed her witches.

An option occurred to Nellie that had not before. It made her chest grow heavy with the weight of fear and nerves, but it was there.

Angus had told Nellie to pick her battles. And so, she was. She would pick a whole war to give Chani a future she deserved. For her girl, for the Cailleach, and for herself, too.

So Nellie sat her girl down and told her the truth of her two-hundred-year life—all of it. She expected Chani to be confused or terrified. But she wasn't.

"It makes sense now," Chani said softly.

And yes, Nellie was sure it did. Why they had no choice but to live a life in motion, why they could have only each other and the craft. But that was not what Chani said.

"Why you're so afraid."

Nellie's chest pinched. Not protective, not cautious, but afraid. Her girl was not a girl anymore, had been grown for longer than Nellie had been willing to admit, and she saw the truth of Nellie now.

Afraid. She was, but this time she would try to be more. Nellie wasn't angry then. But she was angry now.

Nellie and her girl walked through the door of Beira's Market, seeking out the only other witches Nellie had ever known. She knew that Jean deserved to know that Angus was once more in Edinburgh, if she did not already.

The shop was empty of customers, the same young woman as last time behind the counter smiling at the two of them as they walked in. She must be a witch, for Nellie felt the telltale cool breeze that she had overlooked last time.

"Hiya, welcome back," the woman greeted, though there were questions behind her smile this time as she recognized Nellie.

"Hi." Nellie could feel how tight and unnatural her own smile was as nerves jangled through her. "I'm hoping to speak to Jean Rae. I assume she works here or . . ."

The girl nodded, face becoming stoic, niceties dropping away as protective skepticism fell in its place. A look as intimidating as Jean's own. Whatever drama Nellie had inadvertently brought to the shop last time, it was clear in the girl's face that she feared encountering it again.

"Um, sure. My mum should be up in the flat."

Nellie's thoughts flickered out for a moment, the reason she was there clouding over.

Nellie could see the similarities now that she looked. This girl had the same wide-set dark eyes as Jean, as her mother, a wicked glint off the rims of black, a challenge lying behind the pupils like a coiled snake. Nellie couldn't imagine Jean holding this girl, soft and newborn and so delicate, to her bosom with gentle hands. Couldn't imagine Jean cooing over scratched knees or wiping tears from cheeks after a nightmare.

Maybe she hadn't. Or maybe Jean had changed since Nellie knew her.

Maybe Nellie hadn't really known Jean at all.

"You both can come on up." The girl flipped the CLOSED sign over the door. Her eyes cut wearily across Nellie and Chani as she led them through the door on the far wall and up twisting stairs.

Nellie did her best to ignore the way her body seemed to be floating away from her as they climbed, the way these stairs haunted her with memories—new and rebuilt but rising behind the shop all the same. Nellie knew the welcome she received from Jean would be nothing like it used to be. It would likely not be a welcome at all.

The girl opened a door at the top, leading them into the warm entry of a sprawling flat, thankfully different from the one Nellie had once known atop the apothecary.

"Sorry, I didn't catch your names," the girl called over her shoulder as she led them down a carpeted hallway, light glinting off her blond curls.

Chani, usually the first to speak to strangers with exuberance and a smile, was silent at Nellie's side.

"Nellie Duncan," she answered. "And this is my niece, Chani."

Jean must have heard the exchange as she was already on her feet as they walked into the sitting room, eyes locked on

Nellie immediately. A steaming pot somewhere in the flat emitted a bitter, earthy scent, but Nellie noticed nothing but Jean.

"What are you doing here," Jean said, not a question but a demand.

It was still such a shock to see her, alive and there and not just in Nellie's imagination.

Nellie's chest panged, but the feeling was shallow. It was difficult to care about Jean's coldness when Chani was in danger. When they all were.

Jean stepped forward, wincing almost imperceptibly as she placed her weight on her right side.

"Is Ari in the city?" Jean seemed as surprised as Nellie was by her own question. "If there's any of us . . . of the Rae women left in Edinburgh, we need them now."

Jean's face fell into its glinting hardness, a layer of thorny protection.

"*We* are the Rae women. You gave that up two centuries ago." She gestured to herself and her daughter, as well as a friendly-faced girl about Chani's age sitting on the couch. The hair falling across her shoulders was dyed a soft dusk pink that offset the bright green of her sweater and her white skin. Now that Nellie knew to look, she saw Jean in the younger girl's face too; those same wide dark eyes, even if her face had a softness to it, a mouth that looked like it wanted to smile, though Jean's never did, not even in their most peaceful, blissful moments.

Nellie said nothing. She wouldn't rise to the bait of Jean's anger. She would not defend her past anymore—she wasn't here to discuss her past decisions but to affirm her current ones. Besides, after seeing Jean alive and enraged, after seeing Angus in the city and threatening her girl, Nellie found she couldn't defend her actions on that hot November night in 1824 the same way. She had abandoned her family, her friend, her deity, her city. She had run, and it had changed absolutely nothing.

"No," Jean finally answered. "Ari lives in France now with her spouse and her community of the Cailleach's children. She's safe. She's happy."

Good for her, was Nellie's first thought. Nellie's second thought was: *Her community*. Nellie's chest ached with a deep, unfamiliar want for that too. An ache that flared rarely but more and more with the passing years. She did not let herself look at it.

Jean stepped forward, ready to herd Nellie out the door. "If that's all you've come to ask, you should—"

"He's back."

Jean stopped, mouth hinged open. Nellie saw the way her chest started to rise and fall a bit quicker.

"Who is?" she asked.

"Jean. You know who."

Jean stood frozen, but her eyes darted around nervously. "And who . . . what . . . ?"

"The vice-chancellor of Chani's university."

"Well, fuck," Jean breathed, sagging into her seat. "Angus always did like a bit of power."

"Exactly. Can we talk? Please?"

"Yeah, all right." The anger seemed to fizzle out of Jean, shock filling its place. But Nellie knew Jean enough, or she thought she did, to know it was temporary. All she could hope was that when the anger returned it would be pointed at Angus and not at Nellie herself.

"Alone?" Nellie prompted, cutting her eyes to the three young women.

"I tell my girls everything." Even through the shock, Jean was a viper.

Before Nellie could say anything in return, the younger

woman in the corner stood, crossing the room toward where Chani lingered in the doorway.

"Come on. We were just brewing a restorative tea. We make it for a lot of folks who have dealt with PTSD and sexual assault." The woman's eyes roamed over Chani. "Do you want to help?"

"Yeah, all right." Chani nodded, following both of Jean's girls down the hall.

"I'm Nora, by the way. That's my sister, Fiona," Nellie heard the younger girl say.

She and Jean were left in stiff silence, the door to the room barely cracked on its hinges. Nellie was immediately impressed by the perceptiveness of Jean's girls, knowing what Chani needed without words. *Of course, they are Rae women after all. This is what they were raised to do.*

Without invitation Nellie perched on the chair opposite Jean's. She could not forget Jean's hostility, that terrifying, sharp piece of her that had always been there. Nevertheless, Nellie's breath shallowed just to be so close to the other woman. Her skin felt flushed as she shifted in her seat, unable to find steadiness under Jean's unwavering gaze.

How many times had that gaze taken her apart and put her back together again?

But there was no space for those memories now.

"God, now we've become my mum and Aunt Mary." Jean chuckled, breaking some of the tension in the room.

I hope we can be as good as them, Nellie thought. *They took in a scared girl and gave her the world. They did their very best until the end.*

Memories sat between them like smog, both women sitting in silence for a moment.

"Do you remember when we..." Jean started, voice fading.

"I remember it all," Nellie answered, finally daring to look Jean in the eye. There was so much looking back at her in that dark gaze.

They might not be what they once were to each other, but Nellie knew for certain the past never left. She could feel it in the weight of wanting on her chest. She could see it in Jean's gaze.

"So Angus has returned?" Jean's voice had a scratch to it that was not there before, and it was she who took her eyes from Nellie's first.

"Yeah." But Nellie did not start her story in the vice-chancellor's office, her skin burning her right through with fear.

No, Nellie started her story at the beginning, which she had once believed was the end. As the sun grew high and reaching in the sky and then settled into late afternoon and beyond, Nellie told Jean everything, from stepping foot on that boat in 1824 to hiding her face in every city in the world. She told her about meeting Rachel and Chani and feeling something, anything, again. About the accident that took two lives and changed Nellie's world forever. About raising Chani with the craft, watching her grow and fearing that the girl didn't have her second life, but fearing even more taking Chani to Scotland in order to get it. About when Nellie was sick, and the girl brewed her healing teas with her child hands. About the plants Chani grew in every fleeting home they had, about holding the girl so tightly that sometimes Nellie thought her ribs would crack. About returning to the place she said she never would because Chani was worth it, Chani would always be worth it. About every misconception Nellie had ever held and how raising her girl had shifted something deep in her. About the way Chani's body was taken like it was public property, about how Nellie had been ready to fight for her girl like a wild animal, about that deity in that office and the burning heat.

Nellie told Jean it all, not because she wanted Jean to understand her choice—it didn't matter so much now—but to know that Nellie was not the same as she once was. To know that she would not flee, not this time, because she would rather burn a hundred times than let the flames even lick at Chani. That she did not want her girl to see her as someone who was afraid anymore. She wanted Chani to know that there was more to the world than running. She was still trying to learn that herself.

Jean sat listening, silent for once, her beautiful, changed face attentive. And when Nellie was finally done, Jean did not ask about Angus's return as Nellie had expected. She gave her own story, offered Nellie a little piece of her past and herself. Perhaps an olive branch to mend an injury that Nellie had not even known she had inflicted until two centuries too late.

"After it all happened, when I awoke . . . it was the worst thing I've ever experienced. I didn't have my mother or my aunt or—" Jean swallowed *or you*, but Nellie heard it, and her chest tightened with guilt.

"Ari's family was supposed to leave the night of the fire, but they ended up delaying a day, some minor problem with their passage or something. But when she heard what happened, and saw that I was still alive, Ari stayed here with me. The two of us did our best to stay alive together. It took a long time for me to heal, from my damaged lungs and whatnot. Ari and her family took me in, took care of me. Angus left not too long after anyway," Jean continued. "I stayed in Edinburgh for another hundred and forty years or so. I didn't try to rebuild the shop. I didn't have the means. But Ari and I continued our services as best we could. Then Ari met her partner, Quinn. Quinn was studying at the uni and they, along with some friends, had learned about the Cailleach and taken up in her aid since moving to Scotland. Ari really found a sense of love and community with Quinn and that group, and when they all graduated and had to move back abroad for work, Ari went with them. They invited me along but . . . I couldn't leave Edinburgh yet. But I didn't know what to do with just myself." Jean shrugged, posture tense, as though admitting there were ever moments that she was not fearless and unabashed—that she had been lonely and afraid as Nellie was—was embarrassing.

"A decade or so later I heard whispers that Angus was nearby, in Glasgow. . . . I was alone, afraid. So I moved down to London, to reset a bit." Jean sighed, eyes falling to the ground. "I left too. I hid way back then until he left, and when I thought he would return, I ran. It wasn't so fair of me to say what I did to you the other day. You were afraid; you were trying to survive."

It wasn't quite an apology, but it was far more than Nellie expected. Yes, Jean too had run. But underneath the remorse, Nellie thought she still detected hurt on Jean's face; she wasn't sure if it was disappointment in herself or the lingering ache over Nellie's abandonment, much as she may understand the causes. "Thank you."

Jean cleared her throat and continued. "In London I met an older woman from Inverness, a child of the Cailleach. She took me in, taught me all the different kinds of the craft she knew. She was raised doing the craft through foraging and tending to wild winter growth, but living down in London she focused more on cooking. She saved me, I think." Jean paused for a moment, lost in thought, measuring her next words. They came out softer than before, softer than Nellie had ever heard her. Wistful.

"I met her son, John." A faint smile came across Jean's face, and Nellie's stomach swooped unhappily. "He was the best man I've ever known. Within the year he was my best friend, my partner, my family. We were everything to each other."

Nellie couldn't help the flare of jealousy that jumped in her, her blood whooshing in her ears. While Nellie had spent centuries burning a candle for Jean, the other woman's flame for her had extinguished in moments, lasting only as long as Nellie's bravery had.

"You were married to him?" So at odds with the norm, it

was Nellie's voice that held all the contradicting hard edges. But Jean quickly rose to prickled defensiveness.

"We never married, but we were partners his whole life. I'm bisexual, Nellie; I've always known it, even if I didn't have the word for it."

"No, it's not that. I am too! It's just . . ."

"What? That I allowed a man in my life?" There was a challenge in Jean's tone, that harsh, condescending way she used to speak down to Nellie for not knowing all she did, for not being unafraid and unfailingly open to everyone. "Being with a man or being a wife doesn't mean one can't be a child of the Cailleach. It's the patriarchy, the *systems*, you should resent. Have you spent your life fearing and avoiding all men, hiding yourself away from the world?"

Nellie didn't answer because she saw then that her answer was a foolish one. For yes, she had.

"That is not what the Cailleach teaches, and you know that," Jean pressed on, hearing the answer Nellie did not speak. "Besides, John was one of the Cailleach's children too. As is Quinn, who's nonbinary. Just as it is not only men Angus recruits, it's not only women who aid the Cailleach."

Nellie blinked, surprised. "It's not?"

"We were so narrow-minded and small-sighted then, tucked away in our little corner of the country. Just because the Cailleach's hags started as a group of women, or passed mother to daughter in our area, didn't mean it only could be women—or that it was the same elsewhere. John's community growing up had men who aided the Cailleach. Anyone can." Jean's dark eyes bore into Nellie's.

"It's not just women who embrace the Cailleach, or see the faults with how she was treated, how Angus has made sure her story is told, so biased; how he benefits because the world still says that her characteristics are not fitting for women, are an oddity. It's not just women who are negatively impacted by the patriarchal hatred Angus feeds off and worsens. So, of course, it's not just women who want to change it. The patriarchy harms and traps everyone, even those it also benefits. It's everywhere, beyond individuals."

Jean spoke with such assuredness and knowledge, these words and complex topics comfortable on her tongue. Nellie had hardly ever thought beyond herself and Chani's safety, hadn't given thought to systems and structures and the large-scale, deep-seated perpetuations. And here Jean was, again, thinking wider. Knowing more than Nellie.

Nellie was surprised, of course, and somewhere she knew that what Jean said made sense. But the other woman spit it at Nellie, made her feel small and foolish for doing what she thought she had to to stay safe. The difference between them was that, in the past two centuries, Jean had lived in the world; she had learned and met people and moved beyond the mindsets of the nineteenth century. And, Nellie now realized, she herself hadn't truly learned or opened her view. Because she wasn't living, she was running. Unlike Jean, she was never brave enough to push past the world she knew long ago. And, in turn, she realized that she had allowed Angus and the fear of him to control her life for centuries.

Nellie ached to think of how much sooner she could have known this, could have embraced other witches, if only she hadn't hidden herself away. "It makes sense. Of course it does."

The two women looked at each other a moment before Jean breathed out some of her indignant defiance.

"So, John"—the name burned Nellie's tongue with jealousy she knew was not hers to feel—"he was raised a witch?"

"He was, though he and his community didn't use that title. He was born in 1788. It wasn't an easy time to be supporting the Cailleach or the old stories, I'll tell you. But John devoted a lot of his life to learning, to aiding the Cailleach, and honoring and caring for the land. We were raised much the same, with the Cailleach, though we wouldn't meet for centuries. He was wonderful."

Nellie could not help but notice Jean's use of the past tense.

"We moved to Inverness. Our girls were born, first Fiona, then Nora. The first girl in my image, the second in John's. We raised our girls as children of the Cailleach, of course." *Our girls.* It made Nellie ache, not just that she was jealous of the role this man had played in Jean's life while Nellie had abandoned her. But because sometimes she too wished there was a third point to her and Chani's life. That she had someone to share smiles with as they watched their girl grow and blossom. But she always had Rachel's memory, held close to her chest alongside her guilt.

"John had died, the first time, as a child, drowned while playing in a bit of rough sea. And then . . ." Jean cleared the emotion from her throat. "In the late 1990s he got sick, and we came back down to London, to his mum. He did chemo; we did the craft. I think it kept him comfortable for a little longer. I hope. But he passed eventually. My girls may look young still, being witches with slowed aging and whatnot, but the first decade or so of someone's life, it seems they still age at the normal speed or close to it. They were both, physically, still so young when John passed. It was . . . hard, to say the least."

Nellie had questions, but she held them.

Jean continued, "We stayed in London for a while after John was gone, but it was too hard. And I couldn't silence the call to come home. There are plenty of reasons children of the Cailleach leave Scotland—some witches call it home for a lifetime, some only shortly. Sometimes life just brings them elsewhere, but they still practice her craft and aid her from afar. But she stays with you. *This place* stays with you."

Nellie knew, deeply, how true that was.

"I needed to come back here. And then John's mum passed

too, soon after. So I brought my girls to Edinburgh. A few years ago, I bought this building—" Jean gestured at the room around them. "And I opened the shop back up. I raised my girls as I had been, to take up the mantle of aiding the Cailleach."

Jean's face softened in a way Nellie had never seen on the other woman but had seen so many times in the mirror. A proud caregiver getting to talk about their children.

"My girls are just wonderful, you know. Fiona's in her final year studying to be a nurse, and she works at the shop most evenings. She loves our type of craft in a way I haven't seen since my own mum, always thinking of new salves and teas. Nora is doing her undergraduate in early childhood education; she wants to teach primary school and Gaelic to the young ones one day. They've already done such brilliant things, my girls."

Jean's story had reached its end, but both women knew a new, horrible story was unfolding in their city.

"I've met a lot of people who practice the Cailleach's craft in the past few centuries. The stories others have told of encountering Angus, of just living . . ." Jean's eyes were distant before returning to herself. "We have a safety net, privileges, and we owe it to others to use that, to—" Jean interrupted herself to take a deep, unsteady breath. "I will not allow Angus to take Edinburgh again. I will protect my daughters and the people of this city the way we couldn't last time."

Jean, fearless, brave, Jean.

They had lived such vastly different lives, but finally, they were back on the same team. Though Nellie couldn't deny she didn't quite share Jean's confidence in their abilities to weaken the deity's hold on Edinburgh.

"What do we do?" Nellie asked. It was only when she uncrossed her stiff legs that she realized how long the two had been sitting, how the sky beyond the window was streaked with golds and pinks of sunset now.

"What do you mean, what do we do? We rip the weed out at its root, we rise up against him before more people are harmed! There are so many who come into my shop, who have such an interest in witchcraft, or what they think they know of it. I mean, it's nearly an aesthetic these days; it's a trend because so many people are feeling the call of the power it can give them, young women especially, I think. They're interested in the craft; they *want* to embody the traits of the Cailleach. They're right on the edge of awakening—let's bring them over."

"I understand, I do." Nellie saw the moment Jean heard her disagreement, her dark brows pulling together in annoyance. "But unless you've reclaimed the power the first hags had and learned how to raise storms and winds—not to mention given the Cailleach human form again—then that's a death sentence. We can't just challenge him to some grand battle anymore."

Nellie breathed deeply, steeling herself. "He knows about Chani. I told him before I realized . . . who he really was. I can't risk acting too directly in opposition and having him come for my girl as punishment."

Jean's face softened, and Nellie suspected the other woman would empathize, but Nellie continued on her argument. "And we don't know what form Angus's control will take this time. He's older and much more experienced in this than we are. If we rush into the defensive, all we're doing is playing our hand before we even know what the game is. For now, we have to wait."

"It's going to get worse," Jean snapped.

"Yes, it is. But we don't know how. This isn't the nineteenth century; they're not going to start hanging witches in front of the pubs in Grassmarket this time. Neither of us have encountered Angus since, right?"

Jean shook her head, her face disgruntled to be agreeing to anything Nellie said. "But sometimes I see things, horrible things, happening around the country, and I suspect it must be him."

"Do you have a community here in Edinburgh? Of people . . . like us?"

"No, just me and my girls. It's likely there are others, but it's such a large city, so crowded. The Cailleach's children still maintain a low profile, to stay beneath Angus's radar. All the witches I've met in the city are no longer here."

Selfishly, she knew, Nellie was a bit pleased that Jean did not have her own community in Edinburgh. That, even if she did not love Nellie, maybe she needed her.

"I agree, the more witches who are on the same soil as Angus, the stronger the Cailleach's winter will get, and the weaker he and his summer will be. But I don't think trying to create more hags right now is the safest option. It's too overt, too public. Angus moves subtly, beneath the surface. We need to do the same to counter him," Nellie mused. "And you're sure we can't ask others to come aid us? From elsewhere?"

Jean paused. "Well, Ari and Quinn are in Montreal with their little one, visiting Quinn's sister, who's ill. I don't think they'll be able to come here at a moment's notice. Besides, even after centuries, the world is so dangerous for trans women. Scotland, especially, has been none too friendly as of late. It would be a big risk for Ari, but I'll tell her and let her make her own decision."

Jean thought for a moment. "There are plenty of the Cailleach's helpers around Scotland, but I doubt any would be keen to come down and help us. Generally, each community keeps to themselves, protecting their own bit of the Cailleach's land. Everyone's afraid to leave their own home unprotected. Even centuries on, no one knows enough about Angus, about what he does, to predict his moves."

"So, we don't know what his tactics are anymore," Nellie continued. "How he makes his horror spread."

"Exactly. If we can't call for the help of the Cailleach's witches elsewhere, then we need to make more here. Because what about when—"

"It'll get worse, yes, but we'll meet it when it does," Nellie interjected, firm. She could see the surprise on Jean's face. Could see the way it slipped into something like approval. Nellie ignored the fluttering in her chest. *This is not my Jean anymore. I'm not sure she ever was.* The mosaic of love in Nellie's life had been little more than a blip in Jean's. She would do her best to remember that. "With a plan that doesn't involve putting a target on us or anyone else. We're no good to anyone if we die a second time; that would just allow Angus to get his hooks deeper into folks' minds here so it's impossible for anyone to become a hag. We need to stay safe, for now."

The two women stared at each other, some of the hard edges that time and misunderstanding had borne between them softened, but many still pointed, ready to harm. They both saw this moment for what it was—the very crux of their differences. One wanting to act now, to strike with fire. One urged to wait, to hide, to protect the home before the village. But while Nellie's tactic may be the same as centuries ago, she knew her intent was different this time. Regardless, they would never find agreement here, only compromise.

"Fine." Nellie had expected it to be her who gave in to the battle of wills, but it was Jean who spoke, who nodded begrudgingly. "For now, we wait and watch. But waiting didn't serve us well last time. Let's just do our best to learn from the past instead of repeating it."

CHAPTER 31

Edinburgh, Scotland
16 October, 2022

Despite her words to Jean, Nellie had woken every morning expecting to find the city ablaze. To see the gallows reborn in Grassmarket. Men screaming vitriol in the streets. Or maybe the more modern brands of hate she saw all too often— women taken in streets or parks, daylight or night, vicious cat-calls, trusting a friend who would turn out to be anything but and being blamed themselves for being so foolish as to exist in the path of men. But there was no explosion of violent hatred overnight. The city did not rip apart at its seams to be re-stitched into a new beast. Edinburgh remained as it had since Nellie arrived. If she had not seen it herself she would not suspect Angus had returned at all.

That made her feel worse. She would have preferred ex-ploding hate to the simmering and slithering that she was sure Angus was spreading throughout the city beneath their noses. Anxiety lived in the pit of her stomach, growing larger and coiling tighter with each passing day. Nellie recognized the calm before the storm, and she lived in fear of it.

The girls in her class had grown something akin to comfortable, if not with her at least with one another. This room no longer sat in tense silence. Nellie could hardly hear her charcoal gliding across paper as the girls chattered over their own work behind her. She didn't mind though, for her fingers crafted once more, the dam of her creativity reopened. She had not understood how much the fear of Jean's hatred froze her, how she could move again now that at least some of it had been soothed since they lived on the same team once more. Nellie had not grasped how much the incomprehensible conversations of young girls made the tension release from her shoulders as she worked, the same familiar sound as Chani at her shoulder, talking and twirling her way through the house.

Maybe it was that that freed Nellie's creativity more than anything. Her girl was doing better again. Slowly, so slowly that Nellie was afraid to even think it and jinx it. But she was. They'd taken to brewing Nora's tea each night, and with every sip Chani seemed to soothe. She improved with every day she spent in the company of Jean's girls, the three growing into friends even though their weaving made Nellie's nervous in a way she could not explain. The ease of their union made Nellie jealous she could not achieve the same with their mother. Jean did not want Nellie anymore, and maybe she never really had. And Nellie would do her best to stop wanting Jean in return. So she'd keep her distance from the shop and the Rae women, even if Chani did not.

She could see that being around other children of the Cailleach was healing her girl. Even if she had to face that boy every week, present in her lab and unpunished. And yet, Nellie felt helpless because she knew she *was* helpless—Angus sat in power at the top of the institution. For now, there was nothing Nellie could do but be glad she had raised a girl who could find her strength, that was finding her community.

Nellie's hand was a blur before her as it moved across the canvas, charcoal in hand, like its own entity. That's how it felt at the best of times, like these visions were spilling out of her brain and her hand simply had to do its best to catch them all and pin them to paper. Dark eyes found their way to the canvas, Jean's usually, but they always did—portraits had become an accidental trademark of Nellie's, born naturally of her need to feel less alone in the centuries she was just that. Unconsciously she had committed the faces of strangers to the page, filling every makeshift, temporary home she had with people stitched together from canvas and charcoal. And once she realized all the faces were the same, once she sketched each face directly upon one another, again and again, until the features morphed and blurred into anyone, everyone—that was when the world had started looking. But there were some portraits, some people, that Nellie always let stand on their own.

Nellie was grateful to see that the face blooming out before her was not Jean's but Chani's, round cheeks and strong nose and that dark wash of hair down her shoulders. She was grateful she did not return to herself to find the glinting eyes of Angus beneath the skin of the vice-chancellor, the vacant, too-polite gaze of the boy who could shake Nellie's hand one night and grab for her niece the next.

Nellie ran a finger, featherlight, across the canvas, smudging the hard lines into dark mist, smudging Chani's hair into a cloud, until the girl's face appeared to be breaking free of the dark shroud around her. If Nellie could not free her girl in real life, she could free her like this.

"It's so warm in here." Nearby on Nellie's left Tia paused working to fan her face and neck.

"I know." Saba tied her long hair up in a bun. "If it gets any warmer out all the dry plants up on Arthur's Seat will catch fire. I heard it's happened before."

As Nellie floated up to the surface, the voices of the girls around her began to break through.

"No, I missed the entire party. My flatmate, Steph—you've met her, right?" Leila said on her other side. "Yeah, so, she was out at some club in New Town, I guess, and she was *drugged*. Thankfully some girl noticed in the bathroom and took her phone and called me. We spent the whole night in the hospital, and she was shaking and couldn't even stand. We were so scared. She's okay now, and no one touched her, but it was fucked."

Nellie stilled, charcoal-smudged hand poised partway to a stained rag. Angus wasn't here in this room, Nellie knew that, but a scorching heat flushed down her neck. The soft collar of her shirt felt too heavy, the cotton like a noose.

"Ugh, yeah, that's awful," Ella answered Leila, her voice calm and casual, her hand moving across the canvas tented before her. "Same thing happened to a friend of mine last month. At least it wasn't an injection, right?"

"Oh my god, I know. That happened to a girl in my course a couple weeks ago!" Worry crossed Leila's face as she answered, the two girls nodding in understanding. "She had this huge welt on the back of her arm where they jabbed her. She slept for like three days straight after. It's so scary."

Tia, overhearing, asked, "Is that a normal thing that happens here? Like a lot?" The first-year wore her confusion plainly on her face.

Mei leaned in, joining the conversation. "I remember hearing about drink spiking every once in a while, my first two years here. But in the past month it feels like everyone I know knows someone whose been spiked this year already."

Ella nodded her agreement while Leila said, "Seriously. What is going on lately?"

The girls continued their conversation as they worked, their tones as straightforward as if they were discussing some difficult coursework. Every horrible anecdote was met with a similar one, as if the young women of Edinburgh were so used to being the scientific experiments for the male desire around them that they hardly realized they were allowed to be angry. That they should be.

Nellie's stomach dipped like she was waking up to the world from a long sleep. And the world certainly had changed. This was no longer Angus's patriarchy that strung women up on rope and saddled them with fatal accusations. The rot was already in the soil, all across the world. All he had to do was stoke it. He had to ensure it kept spreading, out of control, snowballing, a decade's worth of misogynistic violence happening all at once. And these girls didn't even realize. They had become so used to all these little evils that they thought this was simply the way the world worked; they saw that things were worse than they used to be, but to them it just seemed a continuation of the norm, rather than the obvious sign of a being like Angus's presence. But Nellie saw it for what—or rather, who—it was.

Nellie understood Jean a bit more in that moment, as she could hardly swallow the anger that rose in her throat like bile. This was the world they were giving these young people, that they were letting them live in. If this was Angus, his game had improved. But much as Nellie wished she could change it, could stop it, what could they do? Just as before it felt so much bigger than them.

They said they would wait until they knew Angus's tactics, until they felt the ripple of the big bang, the explosion of his hate. So they would wait. But even Nellie, cautious, fearful Nellie, worried they would wait forever and look up to see the city already smoldering

CHAPTER 32

Edinburgh, Scotland
21 October, 2022

Nellie's steps clicked frantically, echoing down to her as she climbed the stairs to their flat. Her chest tightened from more than just her quickened exertion. She was home later than usual, her walk deterred by the flash and crowd of police that pushed her to the edges of the Meadows and around. And despite the extra ten, no, fifteen minutes, Chani had not answered her texts.

There was a moment where Nellie froze, key halfway twisted in the lock, at the sound of another voice beside Chani's from within their flat. Maybe in her moments of absence someone had come to the home—*Today was the day Chani had her lab, wasn't it? What if that boy had followed her, or the vice-chancellor, and*—but then through the warped wood Nellie heard the high pitch of the other voice, its soft Scottish lilt, and recognized it as Nora.

Nellie did not think that fearsome, gnawing need to protect

her girl would ever fade, no matter how many decades or centuries either of them lived. She wasn't sure she wanted it to. She wasn't sure who she was if she wasn't Chani's protector.

The girls didn't react as Nellie entered the flat. A small, embarrassing flair of jealousy swept through Nellie that Chani did not call out to her like she usually did. That she was too caught in conversation with someone else to maintain their little habits of love. She could not help it—Nellie wanted Chani to love her just as much as she loved the girl, wanted the safe bubble of them to stay closed, wanted Chani to always love and idolize Nellie as she had when she was young. But Chani was not a little girl anymore, and no amount of slowed bodily aging, no aiding the Cailleach, could turn back time.

Nellie found the two girls seated around the table in the kitchen, the herby scent of Nora's restorative tea heavy on the air. Worry puttered into Nellie's chest as she took in Chani's small hands wrapped around a mug, the frown on her face.

"What happened? Are you all right, love?" Nellie ran a quick hand over Chani's head. Her eyes flitted across Chani's face as her girl turned to look up at her, as if the damage the world did to women could be etched into their skin. Sometimes it was, Nellie knew.

"Yeah, I'm all right." Chani shrugged, her sunken body language not mirroring her words. "I'm not hurt."

Nora sat silently across from her, the friendly brightness that usually lived in her large eyes faded with concern. Two girls like rays of sunshine, but now clouds passed across their faces. Even Nora's effervescent hair seemed dimmed to a faded rose gold by the gloom of the kitchen.

Nellie folded herself into the third chair at the table, the wood creaking beneath her, stiff with disuse. It was only ever the two of them.

"The guys in Chan's lab are being assholes," Nora supplied, her soft voice pinched tight.

"Not just the guys," Chani said.

Nellie could feel the worry lodged in her throat.

"I guess . . . Harry told people we hooked up and then I, I don't know, changed my mind about it and tried to report him for it. But that's not what happened, I swear—"

"I know, love, I know." Nellie squeezed Chani's hand so tight her knuckle popped. Maybe she could hold her girl tightly enough that all the little cracks the world put in her would seep back together and become whole again. But no amount of hugs or love or witchcraft could undo what that man had done.

When Chani didn't go on, tea finding its way around the cotton in her throat, Nora picked up the story.

"And now they're all icing her out in the lab. Trying not to work with her, making all these snappy little comments about *ruining that guy's schooling* as if he's not a monster."

Nora had a kind face, a soft one, a radiance as delicate as the soft pink of her hair. But there was fire behind her words now, and Nellie recognized the girl's mother in each of them.

Otherwise, Nora looked so little like her mother—her hair lighter, even at the roots, her skin a touch warmer, her eyes a lighter brown—that Nellie could almost pretend that she was not Jean's, just as Nellie was not Jean's. It was selfish, Nellie knew, her throat tightening. There could be awful things in the world, close to home and afar, but it did not stop those selfish little aches of the things that happened only to her. Horror does not negate heartache.

"Is that what Angus does?" Nora turned to Nellie. "Is this all him?"

"I guess," Nellie admitted. "It's . . . he feeds off everything the patriarchy is, he stirs it. To keep us from embracing the traits of the Cailleach that women are told are *unladylike* and not for us; trying to maintain these rigid, harmful, outdated boundaries and binaries of what *men* should do and what *women* should do. Harming everyone in the process. All to keep his mother viewed as the villain of his story. The more we embrace the Cailleach, the stronger she gets and the harder it is for him to steal her power, to take all of Scotland and every season. So he steals our potential power too, aiming to keep small anyone who could choose to follow and aid her."

Nellie sunk into her seat, suddenly exhausted as she saw the worried looks on the girls' faces. "No one can practice the craft if they're too afraid to gather with others who'll teach or assist them. They can't be independent and angry and self-assured as they must to become a hag servant, if those traits mean a death sentence or ostracism. He tries to turn us against each other and ourselves."

Lady MacDonald's face flashed in Nellie's mind, and she shoved the image down, as she always did.

"So we're trying to stop an ancient deity who literally feeds off the patriarchy and makes it *worse*?" Nora sighed. "Great, as if it wasn't bad enough already. Besides, what does he even think will happen? He wants all of Scotland in some eternal summer he controls? We need *balance*. *The Cailleach* knows that."

Nora laughed without humor. "If Angus had his way, he'd be king of a burning, dying planet. God, no wonder he loves the patriarchy so much: so much effort to benefit himself and give himself power, without even realizing it'll eventually bite him in the ass too."

"But don't take the blame away from people like Harry either," Chani cut in. "They may have Angus in their ears, but, I don't know, they're still making their choices. The patriarchy exists everywhere, not just where he is. He makes it worse but—it's up to people how they act on it."

Nellie looked at her girl, at the way righteous anger made

her soft eyes hard, set her mouth in a line, tightened her jaw. Nellie had spent Chani's life hiding her, keeping her unaware and unexposed, and convincing herself that that was safety. Nellie had never known what to do with her own anger, so she had assumed that Chani did not either. But here the girl was, her anger replacing her sorrow and clearly, somehow, feeling better—feeling stronger—for it.

"True." Nora lifted her eyebrows, nodding appreciatively, though her next words were laced with sarcasm. "So we stop Angus somehow and then we try to convince people to dismantle their misogyny so we can upset the entire system of the patriarchy. Should be easy enough."

That intimidation, that seeming impossibility, Nellie thought, *was exactly what Angus was hoping for. Intimidate them all into inaction and passivity. If the hill seems too steep, why bother trying to climb? It would be easier and safer to just be quiet, obedient, everything the Cailleach and her witches were not, cannot be.*

Blue light glinted off the window, a searching strip that swept across their kitchen as a police car drove by, headed toward the direction from which Nellie had come. There was no rising and falling wail of emergency to accompany it. Whatever had happened in the Meadows that day was no longer urgent. Nellie's stomach dropped out just a little.

It wasn't Nellie's body whose boundaries were betrayed that night a few weeks ago, but regardless the sight of the Meadows, with all its open grass and twisting paths in tree-shaped shadows made her chest tighten. Made her breath shallow with the visceral reaction of a body reliving its trauma. She hated to think Edinburgh would become to Chani what it was to her—every sight of this place a reminder of fear.

"Have you girls heard anything about what happened in the Meadows?" Nellie asked, gesturing westward, where the presence of the park, and what had happened to Chani there, lived like a troublesome guest just beyond their door.

"What, today?" Chani asked. She and Nora immediately locked eyes in that way young girls do, conversations happening without a word. "I haven't heard of anything."

Nora reached for her phone, nails clattering against the glass for less time than it took for Nellie to shrug out of her sweater.

"Whoa," Nora breathed, and Chani leaned over eagerly to look down at the phone screen. "They found a body, in the far corner, behind that little tea stand thing. They aren't saying much yet, but the victim was a woman in her mid-twenties, found . . . strangled."

"What?" Chani's dark brows pinched together, her face becoming like that of a small child. Her eyes found Nellie's, as if her aunt could explain the horrors of the world, as if she could stop them.

But she couldn't. It is the worst moment when a child learns that a parent is just as afraid, just as confused, as they are. That adults do not have all the answers, that they will not always be able to keep their child safe. That the world always gets in.

For there it was, the other shoe Nellie had been waiting for, crashing to the floor. She hated herself for a moment as she felt a wash of relief that it was not her girl Angus's violence struck out at this time, that it was another woman, surely a stranger. Jean's voice popped into Nellie's head, as it often did for the past two hundred years, telling her that all women were theirs to protect as much as their own daughters. Nellie usually ignored that voice, that way of thinking, with ease. But this time, the shame and sorrow swept in after the relief. She'd heard those young women in her class talk—if it could be one of them, it could be any of them. In fact, it was already all of them, in small, creeping ways that permeated their lives, a system so normalized that Nellie knew even the shock of violence would wear off to just a warning soon enough. Angus hardly had to do anything; the world was made to keep him strong, and too many people no longer saw it as horror. It was merely the way things were.

Some dam that had held steady for two hundred years finally broke. Nellie had tried hiding, and it had done nothing at all—Angus and his horrors did not go away just because she outran him. And if she kept hiding, he would keep coming back to this city that was once more her home.

"Can we not do anything? Can we not even walk in a goddamned park without fearing for our lives?" Nellie's voice echoed off the walls of the kitchen, her anger reverberating.

She looked to Chani, who had never seen Nellie angry, ready to apologize for expressing it, for scaring her girl. But Chani was not a child anymore, and Nellie could see there was no apology needed—the girl's brows were lifted in surprise, her mouth a little circle, but her eyes were something akin to impressed. As if she had been waiting for Nellie to get angry. To do something.

And Nellie found she was ready for herself to as well.

"I should get home. My mum will be worried," Nora said, standing. "I think I'll get an Uber since . . ."

Since it wasn't safe for a woman to walk alone. But it wasn't safe for them to ride in cabs either, or with friends, or to do anything at all it seemed.

"We'll walk you home," Nellie said.

It wasn't because Nora was Jean's daughter that Nellie felt a surge to protect her. It was because Nellie could not bear to hear one more story about a girl hurt or violated or killed. She would have done it for any of them.

As the three women stepped out into the fading night Nellie did not fear encountering the vice-chancellor face-to-face. In fact, she almost wished for it. The flame of anger pulsed through her blood with each step, and she felt—she knew—that an angry witch on Scottish soil with everything to lose and nothing to fear was exactly what Angus most wanted to prevent, what he dreaded most of all. There is little opponent for an angry woman.

CHAPTER 33

Edinburgh, Scotland
23 October, 2022

Even though she knew it was silly—*they were beyond this now, weren't they?*—it surprised Nellie a touch when Jean greeted her with only mild hesitation instead of outright vitriol. Not only did Nellie find Jean exiting her shop as she arrived, but the other woman greeted her as though Nellie had been expected. Jean's dark brows rose for only a moment as she stumbled bodily into Nellie beneath the doorway of the shop. If she felt the way Nellie's heart slammed against her chest as Jean's body accidentally brushed hers, she did not show it. Just that slight expression of shock before Jean's angled face smoothed out in resigned weariness. Not because of Nellie's arrival, she quickly realized but because Jean had heard what happened, knew the path Angus had once more set their city upon.

"I was just about to come find you," Jean said. "I got your address from Nora."

Nellie's heart, which had not stopped its rattling at Jean's closeness, kicked up almost painfully against her bones, setting her body trembling. *You fool. What a shame to still be set aflutter by Jean when you know that she does not, has never, felt the same.*

Nellie swallowed her rising lovesickness. It went down smooth beside her pride.

"I take it you've heard, then," she said, somber.

The city was abuzz with the harrowing news of what had happened in the Meadows. The victim's name had not been released, boiled down instead to statistics: a white woman, aged twenty-five, a student at the university. Her death had already caused a media frenzy across the nation, constant coverage from outlets that only seemed to care about this sort of story when it involved a certain kind of victim: young and white and well-off. A statement had been released, gathered from eyewitnesses, that they were searching for a suspect, a white man aged thirty to forty-five. The descriptor did little to narrow down the occupants of the city. It put Nellie even more on edge, as she imagined so many others in Edinburgh felt now. A sense of fear had fallen over the city, freezing people; exactly, she suspected, what Angus was aiming for.

"Yeah." A breeze swept down the street, brushing Jean's black hair across her face. The woman, a cup in each hand, couldn't reach up and smooth it away herself but oh, how Nellie wanted to do it for her.

Fool.

Jean held one of the travel mugs out to Nellie, who did her very best not to let their fingers brush as she took it. Nellie ignored the spark that jumped in her when they inevitably did.

"Since you're already here—what do you think, should we walk and chat?" Jean asked.

Nellie contemplated asking if she thought it was safe to do so. But she knew the answer: no, it wasn't. But she didn't want

Jean to know that, still, all Nellie wanted to do was hide away. So instead, she asked, "Where to?"

"We'll wander. The city hasn't changed so much as you'd think. You'll know it well."

It will still feel like home, Jean did not need to say. So Nellie did not have to correct her.

"Are your joints . . . can you walk all right today?" Nellie asked, unsure if it was the right thing to say. If it was her place to worry about Jean anymore. But some things can't just be turned off.

Jean's face flickered for a moment, as if she did not expect Nellie to remember her struggles and pain, as if for a time they had not nearly been Nellie's own, so much had the woman cared for the other.

"Fibromyalgia, as it turns out. Not much to be done for it." Jean's face smoothed into neutrality. "But I'm not flaring up today. I'm good."

The two women fell into step, passing through the arch of Old Assembly Close, out into the bright bustle of the Royal Mile. On a few occasions Jean had to smother a cough in her elbow, and each time it panged at Nellie, a reminder of the long-ago death the other woman suffered. Nellie, too, often got deep headaches from her own death—the blow to the head that had killed her—but to be reminded of Jean's demise came with a shock of guilt still.

They turned right down the Royal Mile, headed toward Holyrood at its tail. The direction Nellie had not yet been brave enough to walk, the little street where she had once lived, had abandoned Tommy, hanging by its end, too fresh a reminder even after centuries.

They did not speak, silently sipping and casting their gazes to each passerby, Nellie's with concern, Jean's with something akin to camaraderie. Nellie shrugged out of her jacket, the air too warm on her skin, too heavy, even as a dense layer of cloud blocked out the sun, making the air gray as though this was still Auld Reekie with its crown of smog. It really was like slipping back in time, despite all the trappings of modernity. Some cities do not change, even if the people do.

Their pace was leisurely, not a word said between them, despite that being the very purpose of both women seeking out the other. Nellie could not find her voice, too afraid to speak and shatter this moment, this silent intimacy with Jean, this activity without animosity, so much more than she had expected to ever have again with the woman. It was Jean who finally broke the silence, her words nearly startling the cup from Nellie's hand.

"Maybe you should just gather everyone in this city and tell them to ignore him once and for all," Jean said, her lips pulling up at the edges.

"Oh? Is that all it takes to stop the whispers of Angus now? And why me?"

"Why not? That's your superpower, remember? That beauty that makes people listen to every word you say."

Nellie's chest tightened. The street beneath them sloped downward. She looked at the mug in her hand, so she did not have to look in Jean's eyes.

"Well, I'm not so young and beautiful anymore. The world doesn't listen to me the way it used to." She tried to put a chuckle behind her words, but she heard them fall flat.

How foolish Jean must think her, to miss her beauty, to miss the privilege it gave her, to see how much she loved being a beautiful face even as she resented it in turn.

But Jean's voice was not cutting as she answered. It was heavy with uncharacteristic sincerity. "Then people are more foolish than I thought. You're more beautiful now than you ever were, Nell."

And this time Nellie did not try to hide her smile or her pink cheeks, for she knew she couldn't.

This fire, it would not stop burning, at least not in her. She had held a candle for Jean Rae for two centuries, and she knew then that she likely always would. Whether or not it had been real to Jean, it had been real to her.

That cocky, arresting smile of Jean's returned, for the first time, as she took in Nellie's expression. Nellie did her best to hold her chin high, kept her gaze forward, roving over the weathered stone buildings on either side of them, as if pubs and tourist shops and museums were more interesting than Jean.

"I spoke to Ari yesterday." Jean shifted. "Quinn's sister isn't doing well. They can't leave yet. But you know Ari—" Painfully, guiltily, Nellie realized she was not sure she did anymore, and that was her fault. "She'll be here as soon as she's able. And she said she'll help in any way she can from afar."

She hoped that, if they all survived Angus this time, she could find a way to make it up to Ari. She didn't know if such a thing was possible. Her friend might be happy and thriving, but Nellie had cut her deep. Nellie might have thought Ari already safe and en route out of the country when she had fled, but really, she had not given much thought to the other woman in that moment, or what would happen when Ari returned to Edinburgh and found herself without another witch in sight. It was not just Jean and the Cailleach that Nellie had abandoned two centuries ago.

Nellie veered left, leading them down a narrow street that bloomed into a high stone wall perpendicular to it. Nellie had not been back there since she'd returned to Edinburgh. But it had changed so little, just like the rest of the city. She would recognize New Calton Burial Ground anywhere. Where it had all begun.

Jean's shadow at midnight, standing above her mother, returned to life. The sound of her husky voice, Grace Duncan's name on the wind, the first time the Rae women entered Nellie's world.

But then burning from the inside out on this side of the wall, hearing Angus within speak with the commissioner's tongue, Isobel buried deep in soil where they could not reach her.

This was where it all ended too.

Without thinking it was as if their feet had guided them there because there was nowhere else to go, not really. Because it was time for Nellie to stop running and look at her past.

"Hmm," Jean mumbled as they passed through the gates and into the cemetery. That was all Nellie needed to know that the other woman remembered it all too. That those memories, those horrors, were no longer Nellie's to bear alone. She found that she felt lighter even as they climbed the steep uphill of the cemetery, sticking to the path that wove between the dotted headstones.

The watchtower loomed in the corner, though its stones had cracked and tumbled, a rusted gate across its doorway barring entry. That was fine, Nellie had no wish to climb it again, to envelope herself in memory.

She cast an eye to the ornate headstones they passed, so many dated far later than Nellie's own years in this city, people who had lived and died in an Edinburgh that Nellie had never known. For each woman's name she saw in stone, Nellie hoped it had been a better city for them. They crested the top of the hill, passing a tree blooming in green, and it was only then that Nellie allowed herself to breathe, equal parts disappointed and grateful that Isobel's name had not jumped out at them.

They followed the path as it looped around, suddenly face-to-face with the beautiful backdrop of the crags beyond the walls of the cemetery, past Holyrood Palace. Those lush green rolls of land, reaching up toward the gray sky, so high above the city. As it always did when Nellie took in that sight, memory rushed back to her. She dared to cast an eye to Jean, so close Nellie could practically feel the hum of her body on her skin. Those dark eyes were fixed on the cliffs too and when they cut to Nellie, she could see that two hundred years had done nothing to fade that memory of a kiss on the crags.

It was Jean who pressed on walking, stepping away from Nellie to peek into a tilting tomb. For once, Nellie was not the coward.

Still, it was Nellie who spoke first, breaking the tension as they continued, boots pressing into soft, warm earth.

"Obviously Angus isn't being dormant anymore. It's . . . what happened to that woman is horrifying. But it's not even surprising, not these days. You think it's him, right?"

Jean scoffed, humorless. "Yeah, I'd say. Back then he just had to keep women down where they were. Now, it seems, he's trying to rip women out of any advantages they may have gained, including an education. Even if it means their death."

Nellie breathed deeply. "Last time he had the whole city. He could do anything he wanted. He has power at the university now, he's impacted the students, but . . . how far does it extend?"

Jean continued walking, her words flowing back to Nellie as she followed. "I don't know."

It was a few minutes before Jean spoke again, voice impassioned. "We *need* to make more witches. The more witches there are here, the stronger the Cailleach gets, and the weaker Angus is. It's the only option, the only move we have against him."

"Sure, but we're putting those new witches at risk," Nellie said, voice strained. "As far as we know, right now, Angus is acting beneath the soil, with little acts of violence against individuals and letting the fear that it could happen to them too keep people small. He's making the misogyny that already happens anyway worse. But if we introduce more witches, more power, he'll be angry. He'll rise to meet that. He'll act on extreme measures to wipe out all the Cailleach's followers. And if he starts something on the surface again, an overt act of oppression and war, like another witch trial that completely swallows the city . . . a bunch of new, barely trained witches will not be enough to help give the Cailleach strength. We'll be putting her at higher risk along with everyone in this city. And we would be responsible for that horror."

"You act like what he's doing isn't bad enough already! You said yourself you didn't think he'd go for a witch hunt in this day and age. And you're right, he won't. Clearly. But he's still causing death and harm, now. He's capable of anything. You shouldn't forget that," Jean fumed.

"For all we know, we could stand on our soapbox and tell the whole city about the Cailleach and that she needs their help and that they can live another life . . . and none of them will believe us. This world is far more skeptical of the supernatural than it once was—even then I wouldn't have believed all this if I hadn't seen it with my own eyes." Nellie brushed her hand along the stones of a crumbling, gated-off tomb. She collected her thoughts before continuing. "Besides, just like before, he's made it terrifyingly dangerous to be independent and have agency and push back. Those traits of the Cailleach aren't as villainized anymore here, so it's not as easy for him to warp perceptions of her. It seems instead he's aiming to make those traits impossible for humans to achieve themselves, make it so the Cailleach can't have new hags, and the ones already here are kept powerless. It would be hard to create witches, even *if* they believed us. Rather than trying to give the Cailleach more children, we first need to prioritize weakening the control Angus has on people, this hate he spreads that leads to violence. Make people less afraid, less separated—that alone will reduce what Angus can do."

Finally, Nellie spoke the words she knew would convince Jean, the concern that truly weighed the heaviest on Nellie's mind. Jean cared for everyone, wanted to help everyone. Nellie wished she was like that. She truly did. But there was one person she worried for above all others, and if that made her selfish or a coward so be it. "Even if we could make more witches . . . we'd be putting our girls at risk, being so vocal. Chani, Nora, Fiona. I can't risk doing something that inspires that targeted vengeance in him. We lost everyone last time, Jean. Mary. Anne, Isobel . . ." *Each other.*

Nellie saw her words land, concern burrowing deep and overt on Jean's face at the thought of her daughters coming to harm by Angus's hand. She didn't tell Nellie she was right, but she did sigh. "Yeah. Okay. We'll do what we must to protect our girls."

"There's got to be some other way, something we can do without being too loud." Nellie sighed. "I just don't know what. I don't know how to show these young people this isn't how things should be, that they have some power."

Jean nodded. "This is about more than just Angus. People are affected, whether or not they know the truth of him or the Cailleach. Everyone is at risk; people deserve agency. They need the traits of the Cailleach now more than ever, even if it's not safe to tell them everything."

"Sure, but how?" Nellie replied.

"Last time Angus turned women against each other, made us sell each other out and hide away and stay quiet. He made women silent and complicit in our own destruction. He gains power by making people scared, dividing them, turning them against each other." Jean's face was set, assured.

She paused, gaze far away, eyes looking out over the city, visible beyond the wall of the burial ground. "We need to break that cycle. And I think there's a way to do that without waking other witches. Show Angus that we're not letting history repeat, that people will come together and stand up for themselves. That it's still possible to embrace the traits the Cailleach teaches, despite what Angus has created, even if people don't know everything about her."

Jean's eyes, when they found Nellie's face, were lit with mirth. "I have an idea. Just trust me."

Perhaps she shouldn't, she knew that. But Nellie did.

CHAPTER 34

Edinburgh, Scotland
29 October, 2022

It took a while to get everything in place. And every day they planned, Nellie had to convince herself not to lose her nerve. The plan was a true compromise—all of Jean's daring combining with Nellie's caution. But Nellie found that her hesitation was waning. There was no room for it anymore alongside the anger, the indignation, the fierce protectiveness that was growing in her. It couldn't compete with her need to show not just Chani but all the young girls in this city that they did not have to accept the way they were treated.

The girls in her art class had gotten used to her, no longer sitting in nervous silence when Nellie entered a room. But the space was hushed that day, the young artists casting glances around at the newcomers in their space, the four extra easels propped up, making a circle. Nora and Chani, Nellie knew, lent the space no intimidation—the girls sat side by side in their bright hues, smiling pleasantly at the confused faces looking at them. Fiona and Jean, however, were the very picture of accidental intimidation, mother and daughter sitting so identically with their crossed arms and stern, tight-lipped expressions. Nellie knew neither meant to be daunting. Where Nellie used fleeing and cowardice as safety, it seemed Jean and her oldest layered themselves in thorns to keep the world out.

Neither worked though. The world had found them. And now they were there to maybe, hopefully, soften the damage. Maybe even change the tides, though Nellie had hardly let herself hope once over the past six days.

The girls had blinked like owls as she spread out stones gathered from across Scotland along the windowsills, naturally-made holes in their bodies marking them as hag stones. She'd set locally made charcoal sticks on each easel. All gifted by Beira's Market, of course.

Despite the chill caused by five witches in one place, Nellie opened the windows wide, allowing the sights and senses of the Cailleach to spill in, the view of the crags in the distance, the trees on the far side of the street.

Nellie did her best to ignore the weight of the extra gazes upon her as she sat at her spot and took a deep breath.

One easel sat open and empty on the far side of the room.

Catherine Baker.

The police had finally released her name, the woman who was just walking home from dinner with friends, whose life and body was taken by a man who did not even know her and left her abandoned in the park before nightfall. Nellie had recognized the name immediately, before she saw the accompanying picture the news had released: the small, quiet girl who had sat in Nellie's class for weeks.

Nellie and Jean had planned to do this before Nellie knew it was one of their own who was taken, before she saw the tension and sorrow that weighed heavily on the classroom and everyone in it. Nellie had suspected the girls in her class would need a way to express their fear and anger before—but now that they all knew that the girl whose life had been violently stolen was a familiar face, was one of their own small group, Nellie *knew* they would need this. There was so little she could offer these girls, her hollowness mirroring theirs. But she could offer them this, with Jean's help—not an awakening as witches, but a guidance into a way to do *something*.

Catherine was like a silent fifteenth woman in the room, in every room and street in Edinburgh where women dwelled. Her name seemed to be on the wind that moved through the city, wind that was too hot, choking the very same women who said her name.

Nellie made sure Catherine's name would be in this room too, in the space the girl herself should have been.

"I'm sure you've all heard about the recent passing of your classmate Catherine Baker," Nellie began, guiding all eyes to that empty easel.

"Murder," Jean corrected, voice hard as stone so no one would hear the quiver of sorrow. But Nellie heard.

"Yes, she was murdered. It was a terrifying, senseless act of violence within our community." Nellie felt nervous of every word she said, so much more comfortable to let her art do the speaking for her. She was even more uneasy as she felt the eyes of Jean and Chani behind her, the flaring need to impress them both. To be brave for both. And for Jean's girls too, and for the nine young women whose faces looked up at her with their own unease and sorrow and, beneath it all, flickers of anger. For all the people in this city who may not know about Angus and what he spread but knew too well the fear and shrinking and terror patriarchy cast, like a cloud over Edinburgh. Inescapable and choking.

Most of all, Nellie wanted to be brave for Catherine.

"Though none of us have experienced what Catherine did—and I pray never will—I imagine we're all feeling a sense of helplessness. Of anger. Sometimes it feels like that is what it means to be a woman. Today I'd like you all to let yourself feel those emotions deeply, here in this room of your peers, and with those emotions create self-portraits. It can be your whole face, body, just your eyes. Whatever you please. I also ask you to draw the people who make you feel empowered and safe. The people who ease those feelings, as much as they can be eased."

The nine faces staring at Nellie bobbed slightly, eyes already catching on the canvases before them, artists spinning and stewing.

She told the girls exactly what she intended to do with their art, an unorthodox sort of exhibit, a kind of rebellion, a site of gathering. Nellie knew she was asking these girls to trust her, asking them to use their art not only to express but to make a statement. She knew that many of the girls in this class did not have the safety of privileges Nellie did—her white skin, having English as her first language in this country, the consistent income of her art that acted as a safety net, a second life, and so much more—that gave her protection from much of Angus's spreading cruelty in this city. But she knew how helpless these girls must be feeling in the wake of such violence so close to home, knew that they could feel the heavy absence in that empty desk.

So Nellie offered the girls the chance to use their art as a voice, knowing she would use her privilege and knowledge of the craft alike to protect them and raise their voices as much as she could. Nellie suspected she did not need to lay out the risks of being vocal to these girls, but she did anyway. It was too risky to tell them about the Cailleach and a feud as old as this land that they were all unwillingly trapped in. But they did not need to know the truth of the deity to know the risks of the world. When Nellie had asked if they were willing to partake in what she and Jean had thought up, they'd all said yes. The weight of their grief and trust was not lost on Nellie.

Nellie gestured behind her to where Jean and her daughters sat beside Chani. "I've brought some friends in to work with us. Feel free to talk through anything you would like to or need to. Let yourself feel your art. I'll be walking around if anyone needs a hand."

When Nellie breathed out it was a fragile, trembling sound.

She feared the girls would do nothing, stare at her with closed-off expressions and silence. Instead, one by one, they picked up their charcoal. It wasn't long before their voices were moving across the room.

Nellie did not reach for her own charcoal right away. Instead, she paced through the room, lips growing white where she gnawed on them. Even as she did her best to empower these girls, in some way, she feared she was just putting them in danger. But she reminded herself she wasn't awakening them to the Cailleach, wasn't teaching them the craft, wasn't painting a target on their backs.

It wasn't the craft, it was merely art, as if art could be *merely* anything. As if it was not just as powerful.

Nellie's footsteps were well practiced and soundless as she wove between the easels, peering over the girls' shoulders. There were portraits of eyes so close that, even with charcoal, the ring of moisture could be seen on their edges. There were full bodies, arms braced protectively across their middles, faces blocked out from view by an invisible breeze lifting dark hair across them. As if these portraits could be anyone and everyone. Each stroke of charcoal was vulnerable, as raw as the medium that expressed it.

And the words of the girls floating on the air that day were such a contrast to what Nellie had overheard just weeks prior. No longer were their conversations passive and accepting. One sentiment seemed to echo across the room again and again.

"She was just trying to walk home."

Nellie circled to the top of the room, Nora and Chani leaning toward each other as they worked. Both girls shook with quiet laughter as they looked at one another's canvases, neither artists but doing their best. It made Nellie's chest a little lighter, that some hardships could still be faced with smiles, that Angus had not yet stolen all joy from the people of this city, despite all he had done and did. To her girl. To all of them. Nellie remembered all too well what it was like for the women of Edinburgh to think of happiness as nothing but a distant memory, eradicated by the fear of their present moment.

Fiona did not share the ease of her sister, the charcoal nub gripped so tightly in her long fingers that Nellie was certain it would snap in two. The anger seemed to radiate through her skin as she slashed the black stick across the canvas like a sword, as if she was ready to ride into battle. She was Jean's girl after all, so perhaps she was.

She looked up as she heard Nellie come to pause over her shoulder, a streak of black powder dusting her blond curls as she brushed them from her brow.

"It's just . . . I'm just so *angry.*" Fiona sighed, and Nellie could see that, like her mother, she wore an angry face so the world would not see the sorrow beneath. But it was there on the canvas, in the way that the lines seemed to have adopted the tremble of her hands.

"As you should be," Nellie responded, and meant it. For once, she did not fear anger, did not see it as a terrifying thing to be smothered down. Anger didn't just have to put a woman in danger—it could make her dangerous too. "If you're angry, be angry. Put that in the art. Don't hold back."

Fiona breathed for a moment, her jaw held in a tight line. Then a loud crack resonated through the room as she snapped the stick of charcoal in half, attacking the canvas in violent streaks of night across the image of her face, of her mother's and sister's beside it.

Jean looked over at her daughter with a blank face, but Nellie could see the little upturn of her lips, felt it arrest and seize her for a moment. Then Jean looked up. She caught Nellie's eye as she stepped closer to where the other woman sat, a half-finished self-portrait on the canvas before her.

"Hmm, turns out I'm shite at this." Jean chuckled. "I used to think your drawings at the shop were so easy, but I'm not so sure anymore I could've done them myself."

"Trust me, you could have. That work was . . . I always wondered why you lot brought me on. Any one of you could have done what I did there." The vulnerability in the room must have gotten to Nellie; she pulled forth words she had thought about for too long, afraid to hear any answer, to have a confirmation that she was not needed at Rae's, not really.

Jean paused her scratching on the canvas to look up at Nellie properly.

"Maybe, sure. But we wanted to help you. We didn't take the chance awakening many women back then. It was too risky. But we could tell you needed this. That you had little to lose and so much to gain. That you felt like you didn't deserve *more*. We wanted you to find women you could trust. *That's* why we brought you on." Jean shrugged, as if it was the easiest thing in the world. And just like that, it was.

Nellie felt a swelling in her chest as she leaned over, her hair brushing Jean's shoulder. Nellie's face hovered just an inch from Jean's as she ran her finger above the canvas, where the force of Jean's hand had driven a notched line into the white.

"You don't need to press so hard. Charcoal requires a gentle hand. Trust that it will find its own way to where it needs to be. Imperfection is part of the process."

Jean turned her face to Nellie, their breath on the air and not another soul in the room. Her dark eyes darted down to Nellie's neck, where the little copper deer had slipped free of her neckline, swinging in the air between them like a pendulum. Jean's gaze followed it, hypnotized, as it swung softly. Her eyes grew wider as Nellie watched her understand what the jewelry was and what it meant that Nellie still wore it, had always worn it, had scorched her hand reaching into a fire to get it just so she would have a piece of Jean with her always.

The room was sweltering, just as all the city was these days, but the flush of red that swept down Nellie's face and neck had nothing to do with the unnatural warmth. Embarrassment nestled deep in her ribs as she stood up, stepped away, returning to her own easel without another look at the other woman.

Nellie knew she was pushing, was reaching, for something that Jean did not ever intend to give back. She was only ever hurting herself by still burning for the other woman.

As Nellie looked over her own blank canvas, she felt Jean's eyes on her. As she rolled up her sleeves, settled atop her stool, tied her red hair into a knot at the base of her neck, she felt Jean's eyes on her.

But then the charcoal was in her hand, sliding across the little grooves of canvas. And there was nothing in the world beyond her hand and the black ash and the deep ache and anger and indignation in her chest.

When Nellie rose to the surface an hour later, the girls around her talking to one another, passion laced in their voices, there were four sets of eyes staring back at Nellie from the canvas.

There was Nellie's own, large and doe-like but haunted, tired with all she had seen and feared she would see again. Mary's, small and assessing, that downward tilt at the corners.

Anne's, each dark stroke of lash and pupil blooming with kindness and beneath it, a stern, protective fearlessness.

Grace Duncan's, eyes drawn from memories so far gone Nellie was amazed she held them at all—round and loving and brave, so like Nellie's own, like Tommy's. For once, seeing herself in her mother did not make Nellie ache.

CHAPTER 35

Edinburgh, Scotland
8 November, 2022

Nellie had spent so long shrinking and hiding herself, it was hardly a challenge to make her steps across the cement soundless. Jean, walking along beside her, fell in and out of the shadows between the lampposts that lined the main walkway of the Meadows. The twisted fingers of branches, like aged hands, made Nellie feel the Cailleach's presence as surely as she felt Jean's at her side.

The bright orb of the full moon sat heavy in the black sky above them, and Nellie whispered a silent call for help to the Cailleach. A thank-you for being with them, for protecting them. They had waited until this night, midnight on the first full moon of the Cailleach's season, to do their deed. Samhuinn came and went without the warm weather breaking. Bonfires were burned and performances were given, to mark the shift from the warm season to the cold, like the one they attended up on Calton Hill. Unfortunately, Jean assured Nellie somberly, it was much less attended and elaborate than years past, Angus's smothering affective.

But, even with time to prepare, mentally and logistically, Nellie could not quite assuage her nerves. She was just glad Chani was elsewhere, safe, that the girls had finally agreed to allow just Jean and Nellie to take on the dangerous part of their task.

It was through the two of them that this all began. It was by their hand that it should end. Well, hopefully, if all went according to plan, which Nellie could not help but speculate it would not, as it never really did, did it?

"I can practically hear your nervous thoughts from here, Nell," Jean said from within the darkness.

The nickname did what it always did, sending Nellie's stomach swooping.

Jean is over it, she chastised herself. *In fact, there was nothing for her to get over. It only ever meant anything to me.*

"Yes, well, we're doing something . . . dangerous. It's normal to be nervous," Nellie whispered, eyes casting over the dark shapes of trees against the night sky, searching for the right one. Searching for a deity amid the nightfall. But Nellie knew better by now—Angus was not the type of being that had to lurk in the shadows. He was the summer, the sun, and his evil could be done by daylight, so normalized it had become.

"Why are you whispering?" Jean cracked, her voice the only sound beyond the distant whizz of a passing car beyond the park.

"Because we're doing something dangerous," Nellie repeated.

"Oh, come on. It's not like this is illegal." Jean paused. "I think."

"That feels like a technicality. There's a reason we're doing this in the middle of the night."

"Sure. For the shock factor. You've done plenty of exhibits before, you should know all about this by now."

Before Nellie could come up with a retort she came to a stop beneath the shape of a large tree just to the right of the path, halfway down the park's central trail. It was the busiest, most obvious spot in the park. The tree was slightly at odds with the others around it, a bit stouter, branches more knobbled. It was an old blackthorn tree, a plant with a storied association with witches and crones. It was perfect.

"If anything, we're doing something good actually." The sight of Jean accompanied her voice as she stepped up beside Nellie, near enough that she could make out the dark-haired woman even against the dim night.

The grate of Jean's voice, the way the night knit itself into her hair and eyes, her stone-cold face and devious smile—Nellie was twenty-two in New Calton all over again and her life was about to begin.

Nellie tried to hold on to her bravery as she carefully placed the bag on her shoulder onto the grass by the tree's roots. It landed with a soft thud, Nellie looking over her shoulder reflexively. There was no one there to hear them, no one to stop them.

Still, Nellie whispered, "Let's be quick, yeah?"

"Aye, aye, captain," Jean quipped.

Nellie pulled out the contents of the bag, careful to keep her grip on the edges of each piece, so as not to smudge the charcoal she knew was on them, though the black lines were made invisible by the darkness of midnight. She was grateful Jean had been cooperative enough to let Nellie come up with a plan for this part, the pieces passing from her hand to the other woman's with a well-thought-out efficiency.

Nightfall would last for several more hours, but their luck might not.

Ribbon passed smooth as water through Nellie's fingers as

she unspooled it from the bag like a magician, twisting and knotting and tying, an incantation in each pull. Jean had wanted to use rope, had insisted ribbon was too beautiful and "there is nothing beautiful about what is happening." But Nellie couldn't bear the thought of seeing sunlight glint off hung rope. Not in Edinburgh, not again. She had not had to say the words to Jean before the other woman paused and seemed to understand. Despite all the ways they were different and had morphed even further apart in two centuries, some things keep people bound for good.

As the moon sat heavy and bright in the sky like an approving mother, Nellie and Jean reached and crouched and tied, canvas and charcoal and ribbon, rough tree bark skating across their fingers. By the time the final knot was pulled taut, the moon had shifted overhead, and Nellie's watch told her it had taken exactly one hour, just on time.

She backed up onto the path to admire their work. It was little more than shadows dangling off the hulking darkness of the tree's form but still Nellie's chest tightened. With fear a little, but also with pride. Even in darkness, Nellie could tell it wasn't perfect. But it was an offering to the women who came before them and to the Cailleach. A dedication and, hopefully, so much more.

Even the night before Fiona had faced Nellie and her mother and asked, tentatively, "In the nicest way, do you really think this will . . . fix everything?"

"No. Of course not," Nellie had answered. "But we would have given anything to have a show of community and support in 1824. It's important we give that to people now." She meant it.

Whatever would come next—and Nellie hoped desperately it was not fire and horror and death—they had done something. This time, they had tried. It felt exhilarating and thrilling and terrifying. It felt *good* to fight back, even if it did not mean awakening everyone in the city. They had done what they could to help them, to empower them, while keeping them safe.

For now, it was enough.

Jean's shoulder brushed Nellie's as she stood beside her, four eyes locked on their work but two minds all too aware of the faintest brush of skin and fabric. Aware of the closeness of the past that had somehow, miraculously, become the present.

"We should go," Nellie said, bending to scoop up her now empty bag. "We don't want to linger."

"Should we head to yours?" Jean asked.

Nellie stopped, the two women facing each other, knowing their homes lay in opposite directions but neither moving either way down the path.

"What?" Nellie breathed.

"I thought we were going to do the little protective luck ritual." Jean rustled the bag of supplies strung across her own body. "And since Chani is spending the night at mine with the girls, I figured we should go to yours. For a bit of privacy."

Nellie was glad it was dark enough that Jean couldn't see her cheeks rush with blood.

"Right, yeah." Her voice was too breathy. *Damn it all.* "Of course."

"Of course," Jean repeated, and Nellie could hear that serpentine smile in her voice. It seemed no matter how much time passed Jean Rae would never stop being able to read her like an old favorite book.

"Lead the way." Jean gestured toward Nellie's house. Shoulder to shoulder they set off down the narrow path, the past a third companion left to trod on the grass behind them.

CHAPTER 36

Edinburgh, Scotland
8 November, 2022

Nellie felt twenty-three again, sneaking through the city with a secret. Her building was silent as she and Jean climbed the steps to the flat. She was grateful for the many stairs they'd had to tread, grateful that it covered the true reason for her breathlessness.

Nellie felt almost giddy with excitement—Angus maybe none the wiser of their little rebellion, the full moon drifting in and out of clouds beyond the window. Jean in her house, shrugging off her jacket, settling herself into Nellie's kitchen like it was familiar. Like she belonged. Nellie wasn't sure if it was a delirious sort of giggle or pure nerves that she swallowed down as she moved about the kitchen, plucking the tea blend she'd made just that morning from the cabinet.

Rosemary for prosperity and loyalty, heather to attract luck, cinnamon to inspire action and provide protection, some honey and lemon to sweeten. Nellie's good luck tea wasn't the most delicious of her brews—the wrong side of earthy and spicy—but she knew they'd need it. Usually, Nellie added some marigolds to break up the heavy taste, but she had none left in her stock and could not manage the bravery to return to the crags, where she knew the yellow and orange blooms crowded the base in the unnaturally warm season.

"Wow, you've really updated your craft. Not just teas and tonics anymore," Nellie laughed as Jean unpacked a stack of velvet-wrapped tarot cards and a heavy candle onto the kitchen table.

Jean smiled, almost self-deprecatingly, and Nellie couldn't stop the little twist in her stomach.

Jean shrugged. "This stuff has all been around for a while in lots of cultures, but there's a reason it's so popular globally now. It's accessible and easily studied. And beautiful. People like beauty."

As Jean's long fingers unwound the swath of fabric protecting the cards she cast a quick glance to Nellie, whose cheeks flushed and whose hands, suddenly quaking, dropped one of the tea bags on the counter with a wet splat.

That's fine, she told herself, *spilled tea is good luck*.

"Besides, I find they help me communicate with the Cailleach more directly. In my own way," Jean continued. "My cards are custom-made, hand-painted by a witch up in Pitlochry, with paint made from local plants. That's her form of the craft, her art—like you."

Nellie startled. She had never thought of it that way, but she realized it was true. Even while far from the Cailleach's land for centuries, she still felt close to the deity, remained a daughter with two lives. There was a reason her portraits began with the Cailleach's face, why those features permeated every piece she made, why, still to this day, Nellie always ordered her supplies naturally-made from Scotland, telling herself it was simply habit. But, no, Jean was right; that was her craft, her connection.

"Fancy," Nellie tried to joke, to cover the way she ached,

seeing that, still, in some ways Jean saw Nellie more than she could see herself.

The air crackled softly as Jean struck a match, lighting a glass-cupped candle in the center of the table.

Tiny bubbles floated up on the edges of both teacups, like a protective circle. Nellie knew what that meant—romance, a kiss for each little droplet. She gave both cups a gentle jostle as she set them down on the kitchen table and settled herself across from Jean.

Jean lifted her steaming mug before her, and Nellie mirrored the movement, the two cups clinking edges.

"Cheers—to many lives and many loves." Jean's smile was the kind Nellie had spent centuries dreaming about. They drank, eyes locked over the rims of the cups, the tea getting stuck in Nellie's throat.

Jean picked up her tarot deck, shuffling them quickly between her hands, the illustrated eyes on the back of each winking at Nellie as they passed in and out briskly.

Nellie lost herself in the quick flick of Jean's hands across the cards, fingers rapidly slipping between them. Age had softened Jean Rae, not just in the way her elbows and clavicle no longer jutted out like rocks beneath her clothing. But in her eyes, in the way her fire blazed but not as though it would recklessly burn everything in its path. In the way she'd forgiven Nellie enough to be sitting there together. Working together.

That is all it is, Nellie reminded herself. She knew it was fruitless. For two hundred years Nellie thought Jean was gone—her affection for the other woman burned perhaps too long, lit from a naive place, she knew that now. But it had been with her long enough that Nellie had already learned to tuck the affection away into a hidden part of her chest. It did not matter if everything was different and yet the same. She would keep her love there for safekeeping.

Two cards jumped out of the moving stack, sliding face

down across the table. A beat passed and then a third fell out, landing on the table face up. Nellie's heart sank through her stomach, landing among the worn floorboards at her feet. The cards were bright-hued and vivid, beautifully made. But what they depicted was anything but.

A figure made of swirling lines hung from a tree by a thick strip of rope. They were trussed up by the ankle not the neck, head hanging down toward the grass. But there was no denying it, the meaning of this card labeled as the Hanged One.

Jean's eyes caught on the card for a moment, but she moved on quickly, flipping the other two without flourish.

A tall, narrow turret of a building, bright red flames spilling out of its little windows, the stones crumbling from it, the building destined to fall by any and all means—the Tower. On the other was a looming being, bare-chested and with a split face. One half was topped with curly sun-colored hair, bright blue eyes, and an alluring, smiling mouth. But the left side of the face was horned, the beautiful face twisted with unmasked fury, with taloned feet gripping the throne upon which it sat. There was an angry set to its eyes, hands dripping in chains linked from the being to two naked figures that stood before it. The Devil. Of course.

Nellie may never have touched a tarot deck in her life, but she knew these could mean nothing good. The mockery of their past was there on the table threefold, telling them it would be their future too. The little bubble of hope she'd preserved in her chest like a sacred thing was deflating. Nellie took a hefty sip of her tea, wishing it was something a bit stronger.

Jean took a deep breath, eyes roving across the colorful spread of doom between them.

"It's not the most obviously positive draw," she admitted. Nellie raised her eyebrows as if to say *Oh, really, who could have guessed.* Despite the heavy weight the air had taken Jean cracked a smile for just a moment before it fell away again.

"The Hanged One is about being suspended in time, that many may not understand or agree with what you're doing. Self-sacrifice. But it can be affirmative too, a reminder to trust yourself and your wisdom. The Devil is a symbol of living in fear, domination . . . bondage. The physical and material world being valued over the spiritual. It's all a bit on the nose."

"And the Tower?" Nellie reached out toward the third card, those flames staring up at her. Her hand hovered above it, too afraid to touch, as if the painted fire could still burn her.

"The Tower is about danger and destruction. The norm, the way of life, completely crumbling. Usually as a result of selfishness and hubris."

"Oh no—"

"No, no, it's a scary card. Obviously. But it can be quite positive. It's about change. Isn't change what we're aiming for?"

Nellie nodded reluctantly. *Hopefully this time change can come about without fire and brimstone.*

"I'll just—" Jean swept the three cards to the side, moving the remaining stack in a quick shuffle again. Immediately Strength fell forth, and Jean smiled.

"That's the Cailleach's card for me. It's about a conclusion to a problem. Whatever happens, she's with us," she said, her hands still shuffling.

The Strength card depicted the Cailleach how Nellie had always thought of her: an old woman, age living in the wrinkles of her face and her snow-white hair, looking directly out of the card. Her single ice-blue eye was as steady and powerful as the swirling snow and mountaintops painted in the background.

It took much longer for more cards to spill out. Nellie watched, eyes jumping between Jean's hands and her stoic, focused face. The air smelled earthy and almost sweet, the candle between them jumping and swaying its orange-blue flame.

Finally, three more cards tumbled out from the stack all landing face up on the table between them.

A fair-haired goddess, silver wings filling the card behind

her, a wineglass in each hand, held upside down, yet somehow a silver liquid flowing between each.

Two women, chest-deep in a pond, the sky behind them a swirl of colors to match the water, their dark hair flowing down across their bare breasts, a cup in the hands of each, clinking between them.

The profiles of another two women like mirror images of each other, bound at the mouth in a soft kiss, though black hair trailed from one and auburn from the other, mingling beneath them into a swirling, abstract circle.

Temperance.

Two of Chalices.

The Lovers.

Before Nellie could register the little skip in her chest, Jean laughed.

"Not so subtle." Her dark eyes moved from the cards to the image of the moon and crags hanging heavy beyond the window.

If Nellie spoke to the Cailleach like a mother, a protector, Jean spoke to her like an old friend.

Jean tapped on the face of the fair-haired goddess gently.

"Temperance is very much about healing old wounds and balance being restored. It could be about a number of things happening for us at the moment."

It could, they had plenty going on. But Nellie's mind stuck on the word *us*.

Jean laid a finger on the Lovers and the Two of Chalices, sliding them both toward her.

"In conjunction these two usually mean . . . a reconciliation between lovers, finally seeing and understanding each other entirely."

Jean did not look at Nellie, her eyes locked firmly on the tabletop. But Nellie looked at her. She felt a little shock fall through her body, and she loved to see the way Jean's cheeks turned pink.

She was so focused on the woman across from her she was

amazed she could even notice the smell on the air, wafting from the candle, somehow suddenly grown so strong Nellie could not ignore it. The fresh scent of cold air, a harsh breeze tinged with salt spray. The earthy hues of the grass across rolling hills. The unmissable sweetness of coconut and vanilla, the unique, impossible smell of wild gorse.

Nellie's breathing stopped as she reached toward the candle. Hope—it inflated again in her chest, sang through her blood.

She spun the candle toward her, eyeing the white label stuck to its front. The proud mountain of Beira's Market marked it as one of Jean's creations, hand-made. And there beneath it, the candle's name that marked it as a piece of Nellie's own heart.

Kiss on the Crags.

"It was the first candle we sold in the shop, nearly a decade ago. It's been a bestseller since," Jean said quietly.

Nellie could do nothing but nod, her skin tingling so much she felt she would fall out of her body if she did not move, if she did not touch Jean. Because she knew now that she could. The candle, Jean's words, Nellie recognized them for what they were. Beneath Jean's anger and loss and feelings of betrayal, there was still that little flame that burned for Nellie. All along, while Nellie had kept a piece of Jean Rae tucked in her chest, Jean had held a piece of her in turn.

Nellie found she liked the way bravery fit in her bones, so she continued to be brave. She rose slowly from her chair, walking around the table to kneel between Jean's legs, which opened to allow her to press close to the other woman. They were face-to-face, near enough that Nellie could feel Jean's quick breaths across her lips. Blue eyes locked on brown, and for once Nellie was glad that she remembered everything, that there was not a single memory that she did not carry with her.

It was Jean who pressed forward first, always the bravest of the two of them, her Jean. *Her* Jean.

When Nellie's mouth met Jean's, it was as she had spent centuries imagining it would be. It was as it always had been.

Lips and tongues moving in tandem, soft and gentle and then pushing, because that was what they had always done, wasn't it, push each other? Nellie had forgotten what desire felt like, but it rose in her chest like a surge.

She pressed her tongue along Jean's, pressed her chest to the other woman, reveled in the feeling of soft flesh meeting its mirror. Reveled in the way Jean surged forth too, gripped her hands in Nellie's hair, linked her calves across Nellie's lower back, pressed her in closer. Nellie could scarcely breathe, but that didn't seem so important anymore.

She ran her hands up Jean's body, different but so much the same, just as she knew her own body was. Nellie guided the other woman up onto the table, every bit of fabric, of skin, under her fingertips like a shock to her system. As Jean spread herself across the table, those omens of death and destruction and love beneath her, Nellie forgot about anything else in the world but the woman before her.

Change was inevitable, but it seemed less so here, in this cyclical city. Edinburgh looked at it always did. And Jean tasted as she always had, earth and water and fire. Nellie was happy to burn for her.

CHAPTER 37

Edinburgh, Scotland
9 November, 2022

She knew it was a cliché, but Nellie was certain Edinburgh seemed brighter that day. The sun had hardly cracked through the clouds as she'd awoken, tangled in sheets and damp air and Jean's limbs. As if the city had finally woken up. Or maybe Nellie had.

But even the brightness of her morning could not quell her nerves as her feet carried her to the edge of the Meadows. Chani bumped her shoulder against Nellie's, smiled up at her with not a hint of fear, only excitement. Only hope.

Her brave girl stepped onto the park's main pathway, clustered with people. Nellie followed her.

They were only a few steps into the park but there was no missing it.

At first it seemed like time had slowed in the Meadows, all the dotted figures along the path moving in a crawling slow motion. But as they got closer Nellie realized most of the park-goers were not moving at all. Traffic slowed and stopped before the tree just to the right of the path, as though the old blackthorn was an assessing traffic cop, calling the people of Edinburgh to attention.

At a sight like that, it'd be hard not to pay attention. Nellie's pulse drummed in equal parts fear and joy—she'd been so worried no one would see it, that no one would care. She was worried now about what would happen if they did. For people certainly were seeing.

Jean had told Nellie about a memorial tree that had gone up in the Meadows the previous year to honor a woman who had been murdered down in England; even without Angus, these horrors were everywhere. Jean shared how local students had started the memorial tree by tying ribbons on it, and other passersby had added their own colorful bows to the branches too—perhaps a nod to the old healing ritual of clootie wells—along with flowers to its base. This city, these students, had already shown that they longed for a place to come together within this park that they had long been told was dangerous for them.

And now sorrow and horror and hopelessness were on this very soil, under Angus's eye—so Nellie and Jean had devised their own form of protest. One that heralded back to, honored, and expanded on not only the students' recent show of community in the modern history of the Meadows the year before, but also to the witches' two-centuries-old history with this city. A display that would speak directly to Angus and to all those passing by in the park. They did not expect others to get involved, to add anything. They simply wanted people to *see*.

Strung up on ribbon from the oldest tree in the Meadows hung a dozen portraits like inflated ornaments on a Christmas tree. Portraits crafted in charcoal, protection and fear and anger in their gazes. There weren't many, but the deep-hued ribbon, the pure white canvases, the scratching black lines—they stood so at odds with the uniform line of green and brown trees that guided each path in the park.

Every person who walked down the center of the Meadows would feel those eyes on them. Watching, assessing, protecting—like all art, the way the portraits made people feel depended entirely on who they were. But no matter what, it sent a message, to each other, to Catherine's memory, to the Cailleach: *If you are here, in this park, you are not alone.*

Deep-red ribbons like dripping blood flapped in the warm breeze, dozens of eyes dancing and turning, casting their protective glances on every corner of the park. People Nellie knew and those she didn't watched her from the sturdy white paper hanging from the branches, others that she and Jean had cut and pasted right onto the bark, as though even the tree itself looked out for the people here.

By daylight Nellie recognized Ari's familiar smiling face, reproduced in Jean's amateur hand, alongside another drawn figure that Nellie assumed must be Quinn. There was Grace Duncan, holding hands with the son she never got to meet. Mary and Anne and Isobel, Rachel and Chani and Fiona and Nora, Jean's and Nellie's own faces drawn by their girls. So, so many other faces made by the young artists in her class, their mothers and sisters, fathers and brothers and partners and friends.

Hung from the highest branch, the unmissable crux of the display, was a portrait of Catherine Baker, sketched by the girl's own hand during one of their earliest classes. The canvas was the largest of them all, an undeniable message that Catherine Baker deserved to be safe, that she should still be here, that she was not and won't be forgotten.

And to be absolutely certain, there, right in the center, flaked with charcoal still, a sign in Jean's thick, angry hand:

YOU ARE NOT ALONE

That final touch had been Nellie's idea only the night before they set out, an undeniable marker that those hanging portraits were meant to be protectors and reminders both, for Catherine's memory and for all those within the community that felt at risk. Beyond anything else, that sign made Nellie nervous. It could have been some unique modern art exhibit, the Meadows made a medium. But that piece, that declaration of rage and desperation and grief, surrounded by so many warm faces, Catherine looking out at the whole of the park from her perch—that made it clear that this was a protest. To the patriarchy and its normalized violence. To Angus. Nellie thought of the large windows of the vice-chancellor's office, the way he was able to look down upon the city.

Chani took Nellie's hand, pulling them both into the crowd of people that stood in a wide circle around the tree. All around them eyes squinted to get a better look at the charcoal ones that looked back at them. Shoes pressed into grass as onlookers trod around the tree, seeing the drawn faces swinging there. Voices whispered, quiet and private, but fervent.

Fiona, tall as she was, could be spotted easily among the crowd, her scrubs visible beneath a light sweater. As they drifted over to her side, Nellie caught the eyes of Tia, Saba, and Gabby, who stood together, open-mouthed in awe at their own art hanging from the tree, at the larger piece it had come together to make. At the intrigue of the people around them. They smiled at Nellie, their earlier nerves around her replaced by the familiarity born of mutual achievement.

Nellie and Jean had thought they weren't teaching these girls the craft but, thinking back to the previous night's conversation with Jean, Nellie realized that wasn't true. This was, perhaps, some form of the craft, this art—at least for those who knew the truth of the Cailleach, who knew they were acting in her favor, to connect with her. Using the tree, using their voices, the Cailleach's tools and presence in the room with them as they created. And judging by the way the display grabbed and moved people—Nellie thought maybe this form of the craft did have the Cailleach's extra bit of effectiveness in it after all.

Or maybe, craft or no, people just needed this.

Fiona wordlessly held her phone out toward them, some social media site Nellie didn't recognize on the screen. But Chani's eyes grew with understanding as she took it in.

"People are already talking about it," Fiona explained. "They're calling it the 'You Are Not Alone' tree. It doesn't exactly roll of the tongue, but it's sticking already."

Fiona looked at Nellie stoically, eyes so like her mother's that Nellie felt compelled to confess all her sins and more. "They want to know who made it."

"People want to add to it too," came a voice from Nellie's shoulder. It was Tia, the other girls beside her, Mei and Liv now joining them too.

"My flatmate recognized my mom," Gabby said, pointing at the charcoaled face of a middle-aged woman, looking upon them. "Other people want to add something to the tree. Is that, like, allowed?"

Nellie's instincts screamed no. They had already pushed; they shouldn't push more. But fate decided for her.

"Did you lot do this?" An unknown woman who looked to be in her early thirties leaned over to join their conversation. Other heads quickly turned their way. Nellie felt it all slipping away from her grasp. But there were no accusatory tones, no vitriol directed at them.

People were intrigued. People were moved by the art piece, moved enough to want to express themselves too.

"It's all just so fucked-up, right?" A young redhead in a university sweatshirt jumped in, gesturing to Catherine's sketched face. "I'm a shite artist but I'd like to chip in. I think a lot of my friends would as well."

Nellie couldn't quite find her voice, found herself freezing under the collective eyes around her that swiveled from the tree to her.

The purpose of this had been to not be silenced, to show support and community. And they hadn't awoken any of the girls involved to the Cailleach, hadn't made them specific targets to Angus. Surely others deserved to have their voices heard too.

"Yeah, all right. Maybe we could . . ." Nellie's mind raced. "We could host a big art collective in the park in a few days' time. Anyone who would like can come create and add something. We'll bring the supplies."

The small group around them nodded appreciatively. Nellie caught an excited smile pass between Liv and Mei, a smiling whisper from Saba's mouth to Tia's ear.

"Is it just for girls or can guys add to Catherine's memorial too?" A group of university-aged boys leaned in, brows pinched together as they looked over the tree.

A memorial to Catherine. Exactly what it was, exactly what it was meant to be. Their art, but her tree, her memory taking roots. One and the same.

From the horrors created in Angus's wake, they were managing to grow something good. Something united, collected from the ashes of that very same flame, the Cailleach's creations, her trees propping them and their voices up.

"Of course," Nellie said, "All are welcome. I'm not sure when would work yet, maybe in a few days' time? Give us a bit to set it all up and you all can invite your friends. Maybe we can post a date and time on a flyer or—"

"On it." Fiona waved her phone at them, a newly created social media profile on the screen. "Follow @YouAreNot-Alone_Edinburgh. We'll post updates there."

Fiona turned to Nellie, shrugging. "Too late for a rebrand. Might as well lean into it."

It took Nellie a moment to put a name on what she was feeling. Accomplished. Settled. She hadn't been certain she was someone with a right to feelings like that anymore. Perhaps ever.

For once she did not wait for the other shoe to drop.

She should have.

CHAPTER 38

Edinburgh, Scotland
12 November, 2022

Nellie had tried not to get her hopes up too much. Old habits die hard.

She thought maybe there'd be one or two groups awaiting them, had assured Chani and Nora that they did not need to clear out the local art-supply shop as they had. Surely, she thought, there would not be many people here anyway. Despite living through its predecessors and beyond, Nellie had never had much interest in social media. She didn't realize how intensely powerful a tool it could be.

So Nellie found her footsteps frozen with shock when she'd entered the main path of the Meadows at the set eleven o'clock time to find a large crowd eagerly waiting beneath the—now regularly called—"You Are Not Alone" tree. It was as if the people of Edinburgh could not wait another day to send a message to Catherine. To send a message to each other. And, without knowing, to Angus, who may not have slain a woman by his hand, but who undoubtedly encouraged and fed upon the patriarchy that allowed such horrors to happen.

Nellie thought perhaps he had underestimated the people of Edinburgh. Perhaps she had too.

Her words had not fallen on unwilling ears, were not just in her own mind and heart. The sheer number of people who crowded the Meadows because they too had something that this tragedy had triggered, that they could not keep in, showed as much.

Many of them were university students, of course, but nearly all ages made an appearance. Nellie walked among the people as they worked, providing not just charcoal but pen and water-color, oil paint, and even a typewriter. Prompting some of the shyer among them to create whatever they felt called to, to get out their anger, their shame and fear, however they must. The working crowds merged and joined, chatter heavy on the air.

More drawings joined those hanging from the tree, self-portraits and mothers and fathers and friends, eyes, or faces, or full bodies, one person alone or many drawn together— from talented hands and exploring novices alike. A large num-ber of the white strips hanging from the tree bore snatches of sentences and phrases, with and without portraits. Some of the papers held positive tales, the beautiful and connecting parts of girlhood, times the writer had felt safe or empowered, odes and thank-yous to those who made them feel that way. Some people simply scrawled statistics, the percentage of peo-ple who would fall victim to violence for their gender, the amount of young women who had experienced sexual assault, the number of reported drink spikings in Edinburgh in the past year alone. Notes intended for Catherine, from those who knew her and those that simply felt connected to her. Some of the writings simply broke Nellie's heart. Lines of grief and abuse, times when women had had their bodies stolen by men who felt they deserved them.

Women of color portrayed the times they were fetishized,

diminished, stereotyped as too angry or too meek. The ways they felt that feminism too often did not make space for them and spoke over them, how daily life involved being met on all sides by aggressions both overt and underhanded. Images and stories detailed how, Angus or not, misogyny did not and had never looked the same for many of them as it did for their white counterparts, and the extra danger that came with that intersection.

Men and boys who held the guilt of not standing up to a friend's joke that was anything but, of having their own bodies made victims, of being told their worth was solely in protecting and earning, of feeling smothered and shamed every time they were told to "be a man" and banish the very existence of emotions, as if feelings were a gendered, embarrassing thing.

Nonbinary and gender nonconforming people used words and images to detail their own experiences of the patriarchy: the suffocation of society's gender binary and the laws that tried to exclude and invalidate them, the violence of their identity being misunderstood, ignored, by people who did not want to understand them and did not try to, people who did not believe they had the right to exist as themselves.

People shared how their experiences with the patriarchy were inextricably woven with racism, sexuality, ableism, religious discrimination, capitalism. How it all bled into and fed on everyone's lives, some more than others, and always in different ways. How, because of this, some names did not get remembered or publicly mourned.

Nellie saw Chani's story there too, right here where it had happened, the university just beyond where her assault continued in the classroom, despite her effort and Nellie's. She had seen the way saying those words—what had happened to her—had brought the light back to her girl's face. Nellie hoped it would do the same for all of them. There were so many stories hanging from the tree that were nearly identical to Chani's, so many instances where the university had chosen to preserve reputation over the safety of their students, ignoring the desperate cries of young women. It ached to read those words on the breeze, dangling from every branch. But it did not put sorrow on the air. It put freedom. Pain can rot away if it sits inside.

From every branch there was an illustrated reason of why it was so difficult to embrace the traits of the Cailleach, why Angus did what he did. The tree was a place for grieving, for anger, for joy, for hope, in words and in drawings. Whether it was a statistic or a story of horror or joy, you were not the only one. You were not alone. And in memorializing Catherine, in creating unity in the very place that her life was taken, the people of Edinburgh were not allowing her, her memory, to stand alone either.

The tree did not create world peace, nor did it solve everything. Nellie knew that it did not aim to. But it gave people a place to speak and see their words and experiences there, unhidden. Undeniable. That they were not alone in them. That in this city, on this soil, they had a space for their voices. In doing so, in just acknowledging it all and coming together, they were depleting Angus's hold on the city.

By late afternoon Jean had to run to the shop for more ribbon. The old blackthorn held its position proudly, reaching branches unwavering under the heavy weight of confessions and unity, more paper leaves added to it by the minute. It was almost as though, with each new addition, each reclamation of unapologetic agency and anger, the Cailleach's power grew, her tree standing taller and stronger.

It was like a beacon, a monument of white canvas catching the eye from every corner of the flat park. Nellie thought it might even be visible from the crags beyond, this spot of white paper in the sea of green and stone that was Edinburgh, looking as if, on this one tree, winter had arrived at last.

As she stood observing two groups of young girls helping each other to reach a branch, their earlier sorrow now cracked with laughter, Nellie felt a hand slide around her waist.

"It's helping. It's powerful," Jean said softly, her short hair tickling Nellie's cheek as she leaned in.

Nellie felt so pleasantly warm, the flutters in her stomach for once those of excitement.

"It is," Nellie breathed.

Nellie's eyes were on the tree, but Jean's were on her.

"I hope you're not afraid. For you or them," she said.

"I worry, I suppose." Nellie shrugged.

"You? No, never."

Nellie answered Jean's serpentine smirk with a smile of her own.

"But I'm not afraid," Nellie finished.

"I'm proud of you, you know?"

"It was your idea." Nellie felt her cheeks pinken and not from the too-warm air.

"Maybe," Jean said dismissively. "But you did this, Nell."

"So, you don't hate me for abandoning you anymore, then?" Nellie wished she could swallow the words as soon as she said them.

"No." Jean's tone was uncharacteristically somber. "I know you wouldn't run again. I hope you know that too." With a parting kiss Jean drifted away, among the groups sitting on the grass at work, unaware she had let Nellie atone for sins that corroded her just as much as any horror she had once seen in this city.

It was true, Nellie realized. She would not run anymore. From this city or herself.

She folded herself down onto the grass, a small white paper before her, and a nub of charcoal in hand. The crags loomed over the many treetops of the Meadows as Nellie lost herself to her second kind of craft.

It was many hours later when a shadow grew out before Nellie, everywhere it darkened rocked by a blistering heat, as if the grass beneath them had been set on fire. Nellie did not need to turn to know who had arrived—it felt like the very depths of summer breathed down her neck, roiling her stomach, acid crawling its way up her throat. She swallowed heavily and turned to look up at the vice-chancellor, blocking out the sunlight. His face was lost to shadows as he looked down at her. But Nellie could feel the mocking expression that sat there.

On instinct she moved her eyes across the field, ensuring Chani was far from her, hidden among a group of newly made artists at work. Though she offhandedly wiped sweat from her brow, her girl did not look up.

Nellie pushed herself to her feet even as her skin felt like it was melting from her body, as the world tipped sideways around her as heat burned inside her head. She did not care if the extreme warmth burned straight through her, Nellie refused to look up at Angus.

Jean materialized beside her, a white-knuckled hand weaving through hers. Jean was not steady herself, but they would steady each other.

She lifted her chin and waited for the being to speak.

"How sweet, that you two are still such close friends," he said, eyes falling to their clasped hands.

Nellie never thought she'd roll her eyes at a deity, but there was a first time for everything.

"Quite the little show being put on out here," Angus continued when they didn't respond.

He smiled, but Nellie could see its strain. This was not her first time facing down someone who wished her harm.

"Why am I not surprised to see you two at its helm?"

"And proudly too." Brave, brave Jean crossed her arms across her chest.

"It is something," he said dismissively. "But unfortunately, that something is illegal, dear."

Nellie's blood boiled, and not from that creature's nearness. This must be how Jean always felt.

"This is community-owned land, is it not?" Nellie countered.

His dark brows flicked up in surprise as she spoke.

"That may be"—the vice-chancellor gestured to the looming buildings of the university nearby—"but you're awfully close to my campus. And many of the folks you've gathered here are students under my care. As the principal and vice-chancellor of the university"—he smirked, like they were all in on some joke together—"that makes your incessant rule breaking very concerning to me. In fact, it makes it my problem to eradicate."

"Have you not done enough of that?" Jean snapped, pointing at the sign on the center of the tree, the now hundreds of others blooming around it.

He did not so much as look at the living piece of art, of defiance. He did not mock or gloat. Perhaps he was not so proud, so sure, as he had been two centuries ago. Nellie suspected that, to an ageless being, the passing of time meant nothing. But still, how had he not tired of his own hateful quest? How could he still not see the benefits of balance, that the people and the land needed winter and summer both, a time and place for everything?

But his voice was steely.

"I advise you to take down this indiscretion at once. Or it shall be done for you."

With one last silent, weighted look, he continued past them, steps heavy and sure toward the university. Neither Nellie nor Jean looked away from his retreating figure until it was lost among the buildings.

Surprising them both, it was Nellie who spoke first.

"Let's get back to work, then."

CHAPTER 39

Edinburgh, Scotland
14 November, 2022

From: Principal and Vice-Chancellor Arthur Donoghue

To: University Faculty and Staff; Undergraduate Students; Postgraduate Students

Subject: University-wide Curfew and Restrictions

To all members of the university:

I am certain that, by now, most within our community have heard of the recent passing of one of our students, just off campus in the Meadows park. Though the investigation is ongoing and not yet fully released to the public, as vice-chancellor I have been privy to many of these details; it is believed that this student was walking through the park, alone, around nightfall. Due to this incident, as well as other allegations of sexual misconduct recently perpetrated in the

Meadows—true or false—I, on behalf of the university, am putting into place a **mandatory curfew for all female students, staff, and faculty**.

All female members of the university community are hereby strictly prohibited from being out of doors past nightfall. This mandate is intended to help these vulnerable members of our community keep themselves safe. **It is in effect immediately.** Any female students, faculty, or staff members found out after sunset—without specific approval from the vice-chancellor—will receive repercussions in the form of **docked grades and enrolment status and, where applicable, suspended work without pay**.

The health and safety of our university community is paramount to the administration. We also care deeply for ensuring that all our students get the most out of their educational experience. For this reason, the administration is also putting into place a **ban on the gathering of students in groups larger than five**. The sole exception is active course hours. Though they may not always be in the classroom, students should always be prioritizing their learning, and therefore large gatherings are strictly prohibited in all aspects of the students' lives. Recent large gatherings have increasingly distracted from students' ability to focus on their coursework and, most concerningly, stirred up a sense of causeless disgruntlement and fearmongering within the community.

The Meadows is also strictly prohibited to all members of the university, considering all the aforementioned points.

Though this unfortunate event has rocked our community, the best, and only way to move forward is for individuals to take responsibility for their personal safety and well-being.

Arthur Donoghue
Principal
Vice-Chancellor

The room was hauntingly silent. Nellie could not stop replaying the vice-chancellor's email in her mind, like a torturous song she could not escape, burning her thoughts again and again. She knew the girls around her, sitting silently, staring at blank canvases, were likely doing the same.

When the email had pinged into her inbox that morning, Nellie's stomach had fallen away upon seeing the vice-chancellor's email address. The message itself had only made her sink further.

It was so absurd, so impossible, that Nellie was amazed everyone around her did not immediately realize that the vice-chancellor was being worn by a deity intent on smothering the agency of women in order to debilitate and steal from his own mother. Because this could not be normal. This was, so obviously, absurd, ancient vengeance.

Every new restriction was a blatant quelling of the Cailleach-esque traits, to keep new people from aiding her—stripping independence, agency, smothering power, muting and downplaying anger, keeping people from gathering, especially in the outdoors, where they could embrace the Cailleach's land. It was such an overt, unmasked, widespread attempt to stop the Cailleach's aides from acting and, perhaps even more so, from creating more.

But there was one particular point of the email that gave Nellie a slight, twisted hope that Angus was not as informed as they were. It was only the female students banned. Nellie suspected that Angus still thought it was only women who could aid the Cailleach and be her witches. He likely did not yet realize that even those that seemingly benefited from the systems he fed off and spread, in many ways, suffered for it too and wanted to end it, and that there were so many people who existed outside this binary of man and woman. In the face of all the vice-chancellor's power and restrictions it didn't seem like much, but regardless, this little bit of an advantage of knowledge gave Nellie a buoy.

And she desperately needed it. She just wished she could share it with her students.

Leila, directly in front of Nellie, stared at her canvas like she wasn't seeing it at all. Her dark eyes were far off, wandering the confines of her mind. It was such a stark opposition to a few days ago in the Meadows, the girl's face lit up with mirth and pride as she stood beside her classmates and looked at their art, their protest. Or the compassion on her face as she sat with other students as they created their own piece to hang upon the tree, community rising around her like mountains, firm and protective. Now Leila held the charcoal loosely in her hand, forgotten. It was no longer an instrument of empowerment. For any of them.

Nellie dug around in her bag until she emerged with the syllabus she'd written up months ago. It had, largely, been foregone, allowing the girls to lead their own artistic education and, later, to focus upon the Meadows project. But that day, there was no crackle on the air of emotions rising in each of them, desperate to make its way onto the canvas. Nellie trailed her eyes over the plan, seeing that day's session was meant to focus upon shading work, practiced by re-creating still lifes.

Nellie had not brought any objects for the girls to draw. Her mind, too, was far away.

But there was no point. There was no sense forcing these girls to drag charcoal across canvas when it felt like a chore, when even existing in the world at the moment felt like such a monumental, draining task.

That was what Angus did; it was like decades of violence and hopelessness and control happened all within a week.

Any positivity, any unity they had created seemed stamped out in a moment.

Nellie's privilege was such that the bans only angered her,

rather than upending her safety. She could not help but think of the women who would be so much more affected than herself: those who needed to work at night to earn their living; those who had unsafe housing situations that they were now stuck in. The girls in front of her, or the slew of female students who were now being policed, their university experiences and freedom hindered, simply because of violence others enacted on them.

Nellie's inbox pinged with a few new emails from other confused, horrified members of the faculty. Nellie knew—could see—that so many other staff and faculty at the university were opposed to what the vice-chancellor was doing. That they were perplexed as to how he ascertained the power to put these restrictions in place. This was never what the institution had stood for. It was unprecedented, unbelievable. And, of course, it was, for this was far more abnormal and vengeful than any of them could truly understand.

But he had not consulted with others before sending the email. Likely the vice-chancellor did not have the sole authority to make such declarations, especially concerning movement off campus. But the message had been sent, literally and figuratively, and it could not be unsent.

Even if they did manage to withdraw the restrictions Angus wanted in place, Nellie almost felt it was too late. Seeing that message in their inbox, seeing how someone in power over their education wanted to blame and restrict them—she could see on the faces of the girls around her that Angus had already achieved the hopelessness he wanted to cause.

Nellie's eyes were pulled from the somber faces of her students as her phone lit up on the desk before her. Jean's name was bright on the screen along with a preview of her message, a string of all-caps expletives in response to the screenshotted email Nellie had sent along earlier. She flipped her phone face down. She did not quite feel able to meet Jean's anger right now. Nellie just felt numb. She did not want to admit feeling beaten by Angus, but it was hard to summon rage at the moment; it felt like every little bit of ground they gathered, he ripped out from under them, and much more besides. Like always. They were always fighting this uphill battle.

Tia fidgeted nervously behind her canvas, untouched, as they all were. Beside her Ella's eyes lingered on the window, mindlessly twirling her strawberry-blond hair around a finger. On Tia's other side Saba cut a glance from the window to Nellie and back again.

Beyond the glass the sky was slowly tilting into deep pink. Though it was barely four in the afternoon, and another thirty minutes of class remained, night would soon fall upon Edinburgh.

"Uh, Ms. Duncan," Saba said, one more glance at the sky beyond. "Should we leave . . . since, you know."

Nellie wanted to talk to the girls. To tell them that it was messed up, that the vice-chancellor was bigoted and wrong and had no right. To tell them not to be numb but angry instead, to gather, no matter what new rules stood in their way, and refuse. But she, too, felt powerless. She could hardly encourage these girls to put themselves at further risk, not only their bodies and minds and hearts, but risk their educational standing too. Nellie may be an adult, a visiting professor, a witch—but she felt just as helpless.

She knew she couldn't save anyone, and it was never her place to. That was not what the Cailleach was about, but rather giving people the tools to help save themselves, to create change and community. Yet, Nellie, in her fearful silence, knew she was keeping those tools from those that needed it most.

She remembered Chani that morning at their kitchen table, staring down at the email on her laptop. Chani was so much better and brighter than Nellie but in that moment her girl had reminded her so much of herself, two centuries ago in this city. Chani trembled with deep-seated fear, feeling small and afraid and ashamed of her own body. It had cracked Nellie. And she could imagine these girls felt so much of the same.

Nellie sighed. There was no point risking this new curfew when the girls were not even able to create anyway. Angus had stolen so much from them.

"Yeah, I guess we should all set off then." Even as she said it, Nellie felt the heavy presence of Catherine's still-standing, honorary easel—Nellie could not help but feel that by acquiescing, they were letting the young woman and her memory down.

She began to pack up her things, the nine girls doing the same. As much as they all disagreed with the new bans, they all, too easily, fell into line with it. They, Nellie included, packed quickly, casting anxious looks at the sky, racing time so that they could lock themselves up at home, punished for the actions of those with far more power than them.

Nellie wanted to give them some sort of encouragement. But she felt so raw herself. She did not have the words, though she tried. "It'll . . . it'll pass, girls." She did not tell them it would be all right. Or that they should ignore these restrictions. She did not know what to do.

Nellie did not expect her words to offer much comfort, and they didn't. Ten silent women emerged from the room, voiceless.

CHAPTER 40

Edinburgh, Scotland
15 November, 2022

Over two centuries Nellie had been plagued by dreams of raging fire countless times. So when she drifted up toward waking to see a too-bright orange hue behind her eyelids, she was certain it was just her night terrors clinging to her half slumbers. Until she heard Chani's voice, frantic and searching, breaking through to Nellie.

She was on her feet before she was fully awake, nightdress tangled around her middle. She turned toward the door, toward where Chani's shouts echoed from the hall. But as she spun, mind frantic and not yet gripped to reality, Nellie caught sight of the window. Or rather, what was beyond it.

Nellie's world seemed to freeze. It was like no time had passed at all, as though two centuries had been nothing. For Nellie would recognize the sight of Edinburgh burning anywhere.

And though all she could see was angry red flames licking

the sky, Nellie knew it was the Meadows that sat beyond the windowpane.

Nellie and Chani were both hastily pulling on coats and shoes when they crashed into one another in the hallway.

"We should—" Nellie's tongue was a bundle of nerves in her mouth.

Not again, not again.

"I already called Nora," Chani cut in, reaching for the door. "They'll meet us there."

It had to be well into the early hours of the morning, but they were not the only shadows taking harried steps toward the park. Moths to flame. Ghosts to doom.

Nellie could feel the heat on her face before they crossed the street. The park burned from the inside out, every tree swallowed by flames, like the Meadows had been stuck with a hundred pinpricks and hell had seeped up through the holes. Like the sun had reached down its flaming hand to brush the leaves.

One tree burned brighter than the rest, its flames fueled by paper and charcoal and vengeance.

Distantly she heard Chani greet Nora and Fiona, felt Jean appear at her shoulder. But Nellie could not look away from the fire. She clenched Jean's hand so tight her knuckles shone white in the darkness. It was all the same, but Jean was there. She was there by her side, alive.

Nellie did not have a single doubt in her mind that this was Angus's doing.

He had acted by fire again to mock them, without a doubt. It had worked—Nellie felt like her chest was cleaving in two and she could easily identify the telltale quiver in her bones that told her to do as she always did. To run, to flee, to protect herself and hers. She could not save them all.

But she was not that twenty-three-year-old girl anymore, shunned and scared of the world. She would not let herself return to it.

People around them whispered softly to their friends, words inaudible but the concern in their voices clear. Some held up phones, blocking their faces. But there were so many more who were visible; young people wandered out from the student halls down the street, their features painted red by the flames across from them. They did not know, but this fire was a message to them, each and every one.

Nellie's head swiveled, eyes squinting through the darkness between buildings. She half expected the deity with the vice-chancellor's face to stroll out of the flames, untouched. But the fire burned, eating everything in its path, and this time Angus made no appearance. He did not need to come and gloat, did not crave the look on Nellie's face when she saw all that was stolen from her, saw the woman she loved like a mother who had taken it. He knew he had succeeded, had burned not only the memorial tree but every single one alongside it. He had burned the Cailleach down to her roots. The stories may say the Cailleach's frost froze the ground and leeched the life from plants—but clearly Angus's heat could do the same.

His message was not lost on Nellie.

Distantly she positioned herself between Chani and the flames, felt her girl bump her forehead against Nellie's shoulder in assurance. It was not enough to shame his female students, to keep people from gathering to remember Catherine or share their stories. Angus had to have everything. He had to burn it all to the ground.

Nellie watched the burning trees, the grass beneath turning black. She watched the Cailleach's creation and theirs be charred and destroyed, once again. They had failed her, once again.

Nellie scrubbed a hand across her chest, but she could not smother the ache there. She gripped the copper deer until her hand hurt.

It is not the same. You are not the same.

"Maybe we should leave," Jean said, her voice so soft it was nearly lost to the crackling black air. The crowd stepped away as one as the flames climbed higher. There would be nothing left. "For a while, at least. Leave Edinburgh. Leave Scotland."

"What?" Nellie turned to her sharply, certain she had misheard.

"He's responding to us. We did this." Jean gestured to the jumping fire, though the tree was no longer visible. "He is not playing around. Last time my mother and Mary they—" Jean choked on a sob, a sound Nellie had never heard from the other woman.

She reached to tuck Jean against her chest, but the dark-haired woman's armor quickly returned, her spine straightening.

"We can't let what happened to them happen to our girls," Jean's voice cracked.

Nellie wanted to protect those she cared for, just as she had before. But this was not the same, and neither was Nellie. She had Chani now, a girl she would have walked through these flames to protect. A girl she would not do wrong by as she had done to Tommy.

Nellie was almost tempted to agree with Jean. To take Jean and the three girls and flee. To save themselves and be done with it. To let Angus win Edinburgh again. But fleeing had not saved Tommy, left alone in the world, Nellie never seeing what had become of him. Fleeing would not protect Chani this time either.

Nellie had lived this story before. She knew how it ended, and she had seen history repeat. They could leave, but Angus would not. This was his home as much as it was theirs. Even if he too fled the city, he would return one day, and more helpless people in this city would keep paying the price. The Cailleach would keep paying the price.

Nellie had fled before, and it had not saved herself or her loved ones. The crumbling look on Chani's face, skin lit red by the flame, told her fleeing had nearly broken them. She would not do it again.

"If we do nothing, he might feel he's won and leave Edinburgh. For now." Nellie could feel the ash coating her throat as she spoke. That was okay. The fire was already in her. "But he'll be back. We'd just be letting him continue this cycle. So, we have to break it. Or, I guess we have to start a new cycle."

Jean's face, beneath the fear, flickered with pride. But it lasted only a moment. "How?"

Nellie knew, just as Angus surely did, that a figure like the vice-chancellor was too big to fall; they could never simply accuse him of this crime and be believed. Again and again, he had robbed her of a voice.

Nellie knew he would not stop at this. He would keep going and going.

Knowledge was power, and people deserved to know exactly what they were up against. They deserved all the tools, all the power, that could be given to them. The Cailleach needed help in Edinburgh. There was only one thing left to do. They would share the truth of the Cailleach, allow it to bring them together, like the smoldering tree once had.

Nellie turned to Jean. "We need to tell the story of the Cailleach; introduce people to her tale, remind others of her importance. There might be other hags in this city with no ties to the uni, who don't even realize Angus is here—we need to be loud enough, finally, to find them and all come together. And we need to awaken more to her aid. Show others how to support her, how helping her is helping themselves too, and each other. It's time."

It was the only way.

Of course, Nellie could not help but worry. Who would ever believe them? Who would ever, when the night looked like burning soil and confessions, dare to push back?

CHAPTER 41

Edinburgh, Scotland
16 November, 2022

Turned out, Nellie was wrong. It seemed people were coming together all on their own already.

Nellie blinked. Then she blinked again.

Jean, lying beside her in bed, head propped on Nellie's shoulder to get a better view of the little screen breathed out, "Holy shit." Nellie couldn't have said it better herself.

The video playing on her phone came to an end. Nellie pressed play, starting it at the beginning of the forty-three second loop. But barely forty seconds was more than enough, it seemed, to prove that it was the vice-chancellor who had lit the community exhibit, Catherine's memorial tree, on fire, burning the Meadows with it.

Nellie's phone screen showed a dark nightscape of the Meadows, taken by the shaking hand of a student and passed around the university at large already, spreading like the fire it recorded. The video was dim except for the center, where a shadowy figure held a lighter up to one of the hanging bits of paper from a low branch, dumping gasoline over the art before taking the little flame to more pieces. The park, so dry from the unnatural warmth of the season, burned quickly. Within seconds, the tree bloomed with fire, and, with the light, the figure's face came properly into view.

"Whoa, what are you doing, man?" said the voice of the faceless videographer.

Another voice off-screen said, "Wait, I know that guy."

But Vice-Chancellor Arthur Donoghue, clearly there on-screen, was too far to hear them. Nellie was impressed by just how good cameras were these days, even zoomed in across a park.

The video continued, showing the vice-chancellor methodically moving on to the next tree, draping its branches and roots in gasoline before lighting it aflame. He seemed to be muttering to himself, but the students recording the video were too far to catch his words. But Nellie knew that it wasn't to himself that the vice-chancellor—Angus, really—was speaking. More likely, it was his mother. Nellie could only imagine he was mocking the Cailleach as he burned her creations, as he burned the pieces of art that were meant to stand for the same things she did, that were the resistance to the smothering he created.

Once more, the video came to a sudden stop as the students recording, with alarm, took off away from the park as the flames spread closer to them. It was a short video, but it was unbelievably damning.

Almost as unbelievable was the email that had accompanied the video in Nellie's inbox. Though it had come from Gabby, it had also been signed with the names of the other eight girls in the course. Gabby said that she wasn't certain who had originally taken the video, but it was being passed around the university, and students were enraged by what they saw there.

Not fearful or hopeless like they had been just two days before but angry. And, Gabby informed her, that anger was driving the students to action. Already, starting today, students were intending to protest the actions of the vice-chancellor by conducting a sit-in on the green outside his office. This group of students—the number of which Nellie could not be certain— would be foregoing attending any classes until the vice-chancellor was either fired or forced to resign by the university. For that reason, none of them would be in Nellie's class that day. And they hoped that she—their instructor who had so tried to give them and other students a place to connect— would now support this space they were creating for themselves, and join them in their protest of all university responsibilities until the actions of the vice-chancellor were publicly acknowledged and remedied, as much as they could be.

Nellie's eyes scanned over the email again until they rested once more at the bottom.

We hope to see you there, Ms. Duncan.
Gabby, Leila, Ella, Saba, Mei, Charlotte, Tia, Sam, and Liv

The warmth of Jean's body disappeared as the other woman pushed herself out of bed, grabbing her cane from where it rested against the bedside table. She turned to look at Nellie over her shoulder, dark hair frizzing around her head. "Well, let's go. I'd love to see Angus finally get in some hot water."

☾

Nellie put her ringing phone to her ear, already knowing it would be Chani without having to glance at the screen.

Before Nellie could even say hello, her girl was talking. "Come on, Auntie Nell. I keep getting texts from the group chat that people are going."

Nellie sighed. "This isn't a social event, Chani. Angus could be dangerous. He *is* dangerous."

"Seriously? I'm not a child. I don't want to go to the sit-in because I'm scared of missing out on fun with my friends. I'm angry. I'm hurt by what he did too—as vice-chancellor, like everyone else is, even if they don't know who he really is. I'm part of this."

Nellie and Jean paused at a crosswalk, a biker zooming past them, cars humming steadily down the busy road. Even with Jean's joints aching, the other woman had insisted on taking the longer road, going wide around the Meadows. Neither one of them was ready to look at the carnage directly yet.

Nellie's stomach was in knots, but she knew she was in the wrong. "I know, love. I do. Just, please, let me go first. Make sure it's safe. I just want to keep you safe."

They continued walking, the phone pressed to Nellie's ear. She could hear Chani breathing on the other end. Nellie and her girl knew each other well enough by now to know what the other was thinking; that Chani was already unsafe, and she deserved to try to change that herself.

But compromise had always been their strong suit. "Okay. Once you get there and check it out a bit, let me know. Nora and I will be over as soon as we get the okay. And I'm not going to class."

"Of course, you shouldn't. Thank you, Chan. Love you."

"Love you," her girl responded. Nellie hung up just as she and Jean approached the stone-arched entrance to the square. Without a word, they passed through.

Both women's steps came to an abrupt stop. Usually, the large rectangular green reaching through the center of this part of campus was pristine and untouched, probably to a super-stitious degree, as so many university greens were. Typically, within the square between the massive, aged buildings there was an academic hush, the bustle of a main road at its back a light din.

Not that day.

That day, the green in the center looked anything but. There were so many people sitting atop it that the color could only be seen in the small gaps of space, few and far between. And it was certainly not quiet. There was the sound of many overlapping voices in discussion, words that Nellie couldn't quite pick out. But it reminded her so much of that first day that the girls in her class had created their protest art, those eyes and portraits, anger and community and finally, finally, demanding more.

For that's exactly what these students were doing. Nellie and Jean walked on, quickly spotting the girls from her course seated together in the middle of the square, their numbers bolstered by a few faces Nellie dimly recognized from the day of creation in the Meadows. Mei spotted Nellie first, a smile splitting her face. She got the attention of the other girls before enthusiastically gesturing Nellie and Jean over to them.

They made their way over, weaving between seated groups of students. Nellie recognized the faces of a few other faculty members: the older classics professor, the lecturer on Scottish history, three other members of the art department, and so many more.

"Hey, Ms. Duncan! Jean! Come, sit." Leila said as they reached the girls, lowering themselves to sit among them.

The other girls greeted her warmly, Charlotte introducing the others to Nellie, bragging about the older woman's role as the latest face of the N Rae collective. For just a moment, entirely unexpected and unfamiliar, Nellie felt an incredible urge to tell them the truth. She looked at these young people who were demanding safety and change for themselves and others, and she wanted them to know everything. She wanted to step out of the shadows.

Before she had a chance to say a word, Jean caught sight of the poster boards lying in the center of the group. They were half-created, markers and charcoal and paint in the students' hands.

Gabby, following her gaze, spoke. "The vice-chancellor clearly wants to silence students. We're not going to let him."

Jean and Nellie were passed art supplies.

Nellie looked up at the window of the vice-chancellor's office, the head of the square, that all the protestors sat facing. He wasn't visible within, and Nellie imagined he wouldn't be. She had overheard that he had made his way into the office that morning before the protestors had arrived, but they certainly had him barricaded in there now. If he wanted to leave, he'd have to face the people who he had, as Gabby said, thought he had the right to violently silence.

The helplessness so many had felt in the wake of the vice-chancellor's restrictions had given way to anger. Perhaps Angus thought that by burning down the tree he was simply adding to his control, his silencing. Clearly, he had not realized that it was the step that pushed people too far; he had taken action and now they would all take action in return.

Still, even this close, Nellie had to shrug out of her coat. She sent off a quick text to Chani, just three words. *Come on over.* She paused before sending a follow up. *You're right. You should be here.*

The sun was high in the sky above them, seeming magnified as it beat down onto the square between buildings. But the people were undeterred. A chant began in the square, rippling quickly up through the numbers. As the many voices became one, Nellie knew that, even shut away behind stone and glass, Angus could hear them. He would not be able to ignore the sound of them all.

CHAPTER 42

Edinburgh, Scotland
20 November, 2022

By day five it wasn't a sit-in anymore. There wasn't enough room to sit.

Too many people were pressed into the square, tucked shoulder to shoulder, looking over one another's heads toward the largest building that housed the office of Vice-Chancellor Arthur Donoghue. Despite the growing numbers, their objective remained clear; to see the Vice-Chancellor dismissed from his position for his violence that allowed, and minimized, harm against already ill-protected students. For silencing students when they tried to come together. The objective was for the university to acknowledge how it, at large, allowed and protected these figures and this academic culture.

Nellie stood in the crowd, just one voice among many. Jean was by her side, as she always would be. A few feet ahead she spotted Chani—even now, she could not resist the urge to keep an eye on her girl—standing with friends, Nora by her side. Following the coldness and harmful words of her lab mates Chani had fallen in with a new group of students, many of them introduced to her through Nora. Nellie had already met them, a group as outgoing and warm as the two girls. Chani had excitedly told Nellie that a few of the group were Jewish too, and they had been helping Chani connect with her heritage, were giving her that community she had so longed for.

Despite everything going on around them, Nellie felt her body settle, in a way that she had not known it was able. Or maybe it wasn't despite what was around them, but also because of it. It was, in short, unbelievable. But it was real.

Every day the group of people in the square had grown, their voices louder and louder. It was not just women, and it was not just students. It had become of interest beyond the university, to the city at large. There were also news vans along the square and beyond. It was—they were—unignorable. A few times Nellie and Jean had even felt a distant chill sweep in, had known that, somewhere in the crowd, other of the Cailleach's children stood with them.

White signs dotted the crowd, jutting up above their heads, pointed toward the window of the Vice-Chancellor's office. There was one just a few feet ahead of Nellie that faced her as the holder turned to talk to a friend. The poster board was densely packed with numbers. Nellie squinted, trying to make it out through the glint of the sunlight and her own waning eyesight. She may age slower than many, but she certainly aged still. For the first time, that realization came with a sense of peace.

Eventually she was able to make out the numbers clearly and, a moment more, with a shock she realized what they meant. It was lines and lines of dates, percentages. It was every incident of sexual assault, harassment, misconduct, or intimidation that had been reported at the university and been ignored. A line at the bottom, written in a thick, bolded hand read:

This is just in the 2022 academic year. It's November.

Other similar signs were all over the crowd. It made Nellie think of Chani immediately, knew that her girl's horrifying experience was represented there. But Chani, too, held her own sign. It had three names on it. Not that of her assaulter but the three university officials she and Nellie had tried to report to, had turned to for help, and been ignored by. Their names needed to be said too. They, too, should not be allowed to hide behind their seats of power.

The signs around them did exactly as they were meant to. They were staggering. They were horrifying. They showed, without a doubt, the way that the university silenced and ignored its students. Even without the vice-chancellor, even without Angus, this was a problem. And the people gathered here would no longer let it be ignored.

Nellie realized how foolish she had been to think young people there didn't notice or had accepted the deep claws of patriarchy. This protest was crowded with many, but it had started by the hands and mouths of the students, and it was them at its helm. They did not know of Angus, but they could feel what he did. They didn't need to be awakened to the Cailleach or know the truth of Angus to see these horrors and want to stop them. And they did not need Nellie or Jean or even witchcraft to aid and empower them—they were already doing that themselves, together. They may not know of the Cailleach, but they were, in every way, exemplifying her independence, her anger, her agency; but also her creation, her destruction, her protection. And, like her witches, they were fighting back and standing their ground, not letting those qualities be used to make them villains or shamed into silence.

Progress was not simple. But it was so clear that it was happening. Because it was being demanded. To see these people here, protecting themselves and others—it was such a foil to the Edinburgh Nellie used to know. This was nothing like the city of two centuries ago, where people gathered to watch a woman's violent demise, made entertainment of others' suffering. The world was not perfect now, by any means, but Nellie's chest filled to see people gathered to help one another. To *care*.

Jean gripped Nellie's arm, capturing her attention. "Look." Jean gestured up to the window that Nellie knew was the vice-chancellor's office. Briefly, a figure flickered past the pulled curtains. It was clear that, even though the door of the office had been picketed by protesters since dawn, he had somehow managed to surpass them and get into the office.

"How?" Nellie asked.

"There must be another door somewhere," Jean answered. "Come on." She grabbed Nellie's hand, guiding her through the crowd and out onto the stone pathway, less crowded, that ran along the front of the buildings. They tucked into a small gap of an alley between the vice-chancellor's building and the one beside. They followed the opening down to its end, finding themselves on a busy street. They also found themselves face-to-face with a barely marked door on the back of the main building, exclusively for deliveries and the like.

Without so much as a word, Jean leaned over the lock, plucking a clip from her hair, and making quick work of it. There was a panel of buttons to buzz, but Jean seemed entirely unconcerned with typical means of entry. Nellie, shocked, automatically stepped behind Jean, blocking her from the eyes of passersby.

"What are you doing?"

"Getting us in, obviously," Jean said without looking away from her work. The sound of the protesters echoed distantly through the other side of the building.

"*Why* would we want to do that?" Nellie had stood among that crowd for days. She had felt the energy of all these different people coming together for a purpose. She knew the power in that, nearly mythical itself. Nevertheless, she had no desire to get nearer to Angus.

With a small click that could hardly be heard over the crowd, the lock turned. Jean pushed the door open, stepping inside. Nellie followed. If Jean was going to face Angus, she would not let her do it alone.

"What floor?" Jean asked.

Nellie answered, the other woman quickly taking off up the steps, Nellie at her heels.

"Again, why?" she asked.

Jean paused as they reached the floor Nellie had indicated. "Because the people down there are calling for the dismissal of the vice-chancellor. As they should. But we also need to call for the dismissal of the being within him. It's time for Angus to realize he's lost Edinburgh this time. It's time for him to go."

They stepped out onto the floor, walking down the hall toward the vice-chancellor's office door.

Nellie couldn't deny that she agreed with Jean, but she also could not deny that fear gnawed at her. But she no longer admonished herself for her fear. One cannot be brave if one is not afraid first. And Nellie was ready, finally, to be brave.

They entered the office. The receptionist Nellie had encountered her first and last time there was gone, the desk sitting empty. Sweat immediately bloomed along Nellie's neckline, but it was no longer suffocating. He was growing weaker; his season was waning.

The two women pushed through the far door into the vice-chancellor's office without asking for permission because it was not his to grant. Arthur Donoghue, or the being wearing his face, rather, sat behind his desk. His graying hair was disheveled, his tie hanging loosely beneath the collar of a white shirt that was not so crisp as it once was. He looked up at them with those sharp blue eyes, but he did not seem at all surprised to see them.

"Come to gloat, ladies?" he said with a mocking eye roll. "Perhaps a bit early for that, isn't it?"

Neither woman answered for a long moment, letting the voices of the crowd below the window speak for them. Angus took a deep breath, clearing his throat with a sound like gravel.

"I don't think it's too early, no." It was Nellie who made the cutting comment with a honey-sweet smile. "You know, two hundred years ago, you managed to have this entire city in your grip. You were strong then, that was clear."

She took a step forward, unafraid of the air around him, lukewarm at best. "You're not now. Now, all you have is the university." She gestured to the window, the people beyond it. "And even that, you are losing. We will make sure of it. Or, I guess, the students will. Your way of thinking, your old tricks, may just not be the normal way of life soon enough. It might take a while. It might take centuries. But progress is coming. And I think you and I both will stick around to see it, don't you? I'm so glad I have a long life."

Nellie thought perhaps she *was* gloating. Maybe she was tempting not only fate but Angus, furthering his rage, driving him toward more dangerous, extreme acts to quell the Cailleach, her hags, her traits. But Nellie felt confident, beyond doubt, that even without a whole city of witches aiding the Cailleach, he was being pushed out.

And as the man simply sat there, deflated, looking between them and the window, not a returned word of mocking, Nellie knew she was right. She had nothing more to say to the vice-chancellor, to Angus. She was simply ready to see him leave. So she took hers first.

Lacing her fingers through Jean's, Nellie guided them out of the office and through the building. Within a minute the electrified, powerful energy of the crowd enfolded them once more. They were not surrounded by witches, but Nellie felt cooler still.

CHAPTER 43

Edinburgh, Scotland
23 November, 2022

"Come on, Auntie Nell!" Chani called over her shoulder.

Nellie watched the girl surge up the green slope, the purple heather parting to let her pass. Her puffy periwinkle coat was as bright as the girl herself, her face split by a beaming smile. Chani looked so like she used to, a little girl playing in her garden, always a smile for Nellie and for the plants. Nellie ached to see it but she was learning sometimes revisiting the past can be sweet, even if the bitter notes do trail beneath.

As she always would, Nellie followed Chani, happy to let her girl lead.

The gorse and heather of the crags drooped, its stalks fatigued and its petals dying. Autumn was finally coming to Edinburgh at last. Late but welcome all the same.

Nellie could hardly believe her eyes that morning, when Chani had broken the cardinal sin of interrupting Nellie at work to thrust her phone in her aunt's face. Nellie had read the university email once, twice.

But the text never changed. Vice-Chancellor Arthur Donoghue had been forced to resign from his post. A former law professor from Edinburgh, a woman, had taken up the role in his stead.

It had not been the Cailleach's hags who had driven back Angus. It had been the people of this city, looking out for themselves and one another, refusing to let the hate in the soil continue to grow. Nellie knew it would not last forever, Angus's absence. As always, he would be back to try again; such was the nature of the seasons, of the years, always a cycle. But as Chani's phone was still in her hand a cold breeze creeped in through the window, and Nellie knew his departure was assured, for now. That was enough.

Nellie had already contacted the new vice-chancellor—by this time next week she and Chani would be in her office, fighting for her girl's case. Chani would not leave or shrink or rewrite history in her mind so that a man could continue to prosper.

Nellie had not dared step foot on the crags since her return, the very sight of them arresting her. But horror had been rewritten and so had the past, and Nellie knew she could return to the most beautiful, free spot in the city with the person she loved most.

Her joints ached as she pressed up and around the bend running along the base of the slope Chani already disappeared behind. Gorse-spotted green earth swelled up beside Nellie, high-reaching walls of stone behind it. It was massive and wild and true, and Nellie was happy to feel small beneath it. The grass swayed in the chilly air, clinging to its post until the very end, for surely autumn's arrival would be soon and swift.

The wind beat against her face, stinging Nellie's cheeks pink and numb with the pure cold. She was so happy to feel it, she couldn't be certain if the moisture in her eyes was just the breeze. As Nellie turned the corner, the entire city unfolded for her.

The side of the crag leveled, rolling fields stretching out beneath it before the high stone buildings of the city took over, so very like the ones she had known, the home that had made her and broken her and made her again. Behind the buildings the ocean reached out as far as the eye could see, flat and blue in the early morning light. And in the far distance sat the mountains, finally topped in a thin layer of white. The stories said that when the Cailleach prepared to begin her season she washed her white cloak in the Corryvreckan whirlpool before laying it across the mountains to dry, appearing to the human eye as little more than snow. She was here. Nellie smiled at her, in the mountains, in the frigid air, in the stones, in the soil.

Chani perched on the cliff's edge, her feet dangling over. Nellie's chest jumped at the sight of danger, but she said nothing. Her girl was stronger than she knew.

If it had all brought her to Chani, then it had all been worth it. Nellie suspected that's what having a child was. Not keeping out every inch of the world, the good and bad alike in the name of protection. But making a better world for them to move through. Teaching them the strength to do so themselves, without ever losing their kindness.

They had nowhere near defeated Angus or solved the millennia of hatred in the minds of so many people. But it was, if nothing else, a beginning.

"Oof. I am not getting any younger," Nellie quipped as she folded herself to sit beside Chani, a knee cracking in support of her statement.

"I mean, you're not really getting any older either." Chani laughed.

She was, of course, but only at the rate a witch should.

Nellie breathed deep, the air stinging her lungs with the smell of gorse and sea and the earth dying so it could start anew. She looked out over the city and found that she loved every piece of it.

Nellie pulled out her phone, typing a quick message to Jean. It was a plan she never thought she would call into place, words she never thought she would be brave enough to say. But things were different now.

She would help return the story of the Cailleach to the roots of Edinburgh, where it would grow and bloom, a cycle like seasons, unending.

The sun emerged from beyond the sea, banishing the shadows that clung to the crags, painting the grass and the stone houses in the distance golden beneath a cerulean sky. Morning rose and fell upon the people of Edinburgh.

Nellie kept Chani's hand in hers as the blistering Scottish wind tangled brown and red hair into one.

Nellie Duncan returned home, eyes lifted to the sky.

EPILOGUE

Edinburgh, Scotland
24 November, 2022

Nellie hadn't stuck around last time to see the smoldering wreckage of the Rae Apothecary in daylight. She was almost grateful for that as she took in the sight before her. If it had been terrifying by night, it was simply sorrowful by day.

The entirety of the park and the university and crags beyond were easily visible now that every tree had been razed down to ashes. It was worse than a barren field threaded with blackened cement paths—it was a wasteland, a hellscape. The once green grass was scorched black, the air so heavy with the scent of ash that Nellie worried she'd be sick.

The occupants of the park seemed to mirror its face. Fiona had used social media as her gathering tool once more. Nora and Chani had brought their friends and friends of friends. Nellie had invited the girls from her class. The park was full of people, but it was devoid of life.

People strolled about the space like zombies, slow and sorrowful, confused. Nellie caught the eye of many of the people

she had sat beside for days outside the vice-chancellor's office
or had drawn with in this very park weeks ago. Now their
shoes were brushed with burnt earth and their art, their confessions, their hearts, were burnt into nothing, as though they
never were. As though remembering and honoring Catherine
did not matter and neither did they.

The vice-chancellor might have been held responsible—
though to such a small degree—for his actions, but it was clear
from the faces around the park that, seeing this damage, they
were not yet settled. If they were confused and questioning
and angry . . . Nellie knew they were ready. If she was was another question.

The girls from Nellie's class appeared, drifting toward her,
swaddled in winter coats for the first time that year. Nellie felt
Jean's hand slide into hers. She was glad Jean did not ask if she
was certain, did not offer to awaken them all by her own
words.

It was Nellie who had failed this city and the Cailleach before and carried the grief of it on her shoulders for centuries.
She deserved to be rid of it.

Nellie remembered what she was fighting for. That she was
fighting this time.

She would do for the people of this city what the Rae women
had done for her so long ago, telling her everything, encouraging her, taking her beneath their wings. Saving her even if it
meant putting themselves at risk, putting her at risk, because
Angus ensured that women always were in danger and always
had been. But these people did not simply have to accept their
past and present as their future. Nellie had seen them fight for
themselves and each other. They did not need witchcraft to
face the patriarchy, but Nellie was going to give it to them regardless.

Though Angus may not have realized it, there was more to
the Cailleach, and therefore her helpers, than just anger, independence, and agency—there was loyalty and protection, fair-

ness and caring, accepting growth and death and change. And so those traits, too, would be nurtured on this soil, would thrive in this community. Those traits, too, gave power.

Time is perhaps an illusion, but Nellie was done allowing it to be circular.

For the first time in a decades-long body of work, Nellie Duncan stepped forth before an exhibit of art and claimed it as her own. Not a collective known as N Rae, cycles of artists taking up the moniker. One woman who had died and come back again. One woman who could live for centuries.

Nellie stepped forth and gave the people of Edinburgh the chance to do the same. Nellie spoke, and she awakened.

She did not hop on a soapbox, preach and scream and demand. She did as women did, had always done. She told one woman—or rather, nine, those in her class—and knew that soon all the others would know. Gossip was a woman's currency, after all, and too long had means of women's power been used to shame them.

There are few things in the world as powerful and underestimated as young girls. And social media was like a weapon in their hands.

As the sun rose high above Edinburgh into the afternoon, Nellie and the others kneeled in the charred grass, digging up earth and planting new seeds. With each hour the sun ticked higher in the sky, the group of curious people—the Cailleach's hag servants now, or soon enough—grew.

The blackened grass was still hot beneath their skin, but it was no matter. They put in those seeds, giving the earth, the Cailleach, another life. It would take a while for them to grow—hundreds of years maybe. But that was okay, these people might now be around to see it. They planted not just blackthorn trees and winter plants, but the plants of Angus's and Bride's season too because the Earth needed to bloom and fade, balance, to thrive. Nellie dug and planted until her wrists and knees ached, but they were worth it.

As they worked, she told them everything she knew. The tale of the Cailleach and all its variations, all true, as long as they were believed. Nellie told them of every herb and remedy, every whisper to the Cailleach's moon, every tip and trick to live a life for themselves. To make their life their own. To protect each other.

With each word and each seed Chani was at her side. Nellie and her green-thumbed girl spoke in soft tones about the long lives they had lived—all Nellie had seen and lost and learned. Chani told them of how she connected to the Cailleach through gardening, how she could feel the deity in every patch of Scottish soil she dug and watered and cared for, her own way of aiding and connecting to the queen of winter. Some of the newcomers circled Jean on a patch of grass as she told them of the power of the Cailleach's earth, of anger and aggression and the beautiful things that it can form when balanced with kindness.

Nellie expected these young people to not believe her, these youths who could so easily be made skeptics by having the world in their phones. And some did, of course. But many, many more listened eagerly, ate up each word as if they were starving for it as fresh earth nestled beneath their fingers. Maybe they simply wanted it to be true. Or maybe they knew, deep in their bones, that this was their truth, their destiny. Many had heard the stories of the Cailleach already, could easily connect those tales to what Nellie told them, had known family or friends that were among her helpers already.

Like calls to like, even if Nellie had long ignored its call. The Cailleach deserved to be believed and helped and honored, and these people deserved the chance to do that, and all that came with it.

The witches of this city joined together, no longer in hiding.

Nellie squeezed Chani's hand, soft earth pressing between their palms. She wished Rachel could be there with them. Nellie wished her own mother could be too. But present or not, living or dead, it was Grace Duncan who had started it all, whose name on the wind had carried Nellie to the Cailleach.

When the moon began to rise in the sky, silver and bright, as people listened and shared and learned, the air, slowly, began to grow a chill.

The Cailleach gained many new children that day.

Let Angus return, let the number of these newly formed witches call him like moths to flame. They would face what they must.

They would stay right there to watch the trees grow.

HISTORICAL NOTE ON "WITCHES," MYTHOLOGY, AND MISOGYNY

Witch trials are a deep-seated and impactful part of Scotland's history, as well as the history of so many European countries. As someone who lived in Edinburgh for years, and particularly studied Scottish literary history and society, I have long thought on and researched its witch trials, and contemplated what it was that made people—an approximate 84 percent of whom were women[1]—be singled out as witches.

It is difficult to pin down dominant commonalities between those accused as witches, but there were many traits that were arguably underlying in why certain people—particularly women—were socially othered and therefore accused, in Scotland and beyond. Many of these characteristics are still, and have long been, ingrained in the way we think about "witches" and are indicative of the larger patriarchal structure: older women, "unattractive" women and/or people who did not present themselves in accord with demanded expectations of gender appearance, poor women, those who may have defied gender roles, women who lived and worked independently (often in the aid of their community, such as midwives or healers), unmarried women, women without children, people with disabilities, those who could serve as a warning to others or a scapegoat for powerful men in times of economic or religious wavering. Too often, accusations of witchcraft were domestic

---

[1] Julian Goodare, Lauren Martin, Joyce Miller, and Louise Yeoman, "The Survey of Scottish Witchcraft," witches.hca.ed.ac.uk, accessed 2 October 2023.

or neighborly squabbles turned deadly, rooted in classism, ageism, and misogyny.

Though of course not stated directly during the real trials—unlike the fictional witch trials in this book, in which it is more overt—one could validly argue that the dominance of the patriarchy was inextricably woven with witch trials.[2] I was fascinated by these traits that have been associated with "witchiness," and the enduring nature of this association.[3]

The more that I thought on and researched these traits deemed "witchy," the more it brought to mind the story of the Cailleach. I don't remember when I first heard her story, but I know that it really spoke to and stayed with me and was a topic I dove into learning more about. As is common in folklore, the story of the Cailleach varies depending on the source, region, and time.[4] My postgraduate studies centered on analyzing (primarily Scottish) history, culture, and politics—particularly during the Enlightenment, Romantic, and Victorian periods—through the lens of those periods' literature, both oral and written; in other words, looking at what literature could tell one about the social thoughts and politics of the period in which it was produced and how those social norms affect a story's creation and reception. So, of course, I was fas-

---

[2] Julian Goodare makes a wonderful and compelling argument for this in "Women and the Witch-Hunt in Scotland," *Social History* 23, no. 3 (1998): 288–308, in which he concludes that "witch-hunting helped to divide women—by encouraging some women to accuse others—and helped to unite men by demonstrating that the ultimate evil was female and not male" (p. 308).

[3] For more information on the modern-day movement for the Scottish government to forgive and pardon those accused of witchcraft throughout Scotland's history, I would encourage you to visit www.witchesofscotland .com.

[4] The Cailleach is a prevalent figure across Gaelic folklore, though her story varies regionally. I focused this book primarily on a version of this folklore specific to Scotland—one version in particular, in which the Cailleach is more of a singular figure as opposed to a shared title or descriptor, as is seen in other iterations.

cinated by how the evolution of the story of the Cailleach could be indicative of shared societal thought and shifts over time.

This book is really a reimagining of one particular version of the Cailleach's story—a version that is oft questioned due to its divergence from earlier folklore. The version that fascinated me was one by folklorist Donald Alexander Mackenzie, "The Coming of Angus and Bride," published in the early twentieth century[5]—and the way that more modern sensibilities, Christianity, growing class divides, and misogyny (among other things) potentially affected the way she was portrayed in this tale.[6] And, notably, this version of the tale with its battle between the Cailleach and Angus over seasonal control seems to be unique to Mackenzie's version—yet it is arguably one of the most persistent versions of the mythology in modern day.

Mackenzie's tale focused upon a binary battle between the Cailleach and Angus that paints the female deity as feared and vengeful, the clear antagonist of the story. The Cailleach was often a powerful and respected (and more neutral) creator figure in earlier stories, particularly pre-Christianity—if still slightly feared and mistrusting of humans. Of course, it makes sense that the Cailleach was a complicated figure, due to her association with winter and the danger that the colder season brought to people and their crops and livelihoods. Still, I found it fascinating that Mackenzie's more modern version seemed to lean into her villainy, and that is why I focused pri-

---

[5] Note: Mackenzie refers to the Cailleach as "Beira."
[6] Explorations of the way that the growing dominance of patriarchy transformed folklore, specifically that of the Cailleach, is discussed in sources such as J. G. McKay, "The Deer-Cult and the Deer-Goddess Cult of the Ancient Caledonians," *Folklore* 43, no. 2 (June 30, 1932): 144–74, and Gearóid Ó. Crualaoich, "Non-Sovereignty Queen Aspects of the Otherworld Female in Irish Hag Legends: The Case of Cailleach Bhéarra," *Béaloideas* (1994/1995): 147–62, which also discusses the Cailleach as the "personification of cosmic female agency."

marily on it.[7] The Cailleach and her hag servants are put into the role of villain when in connection to Angus[8], in ways that really called back to these "witchlike" traits—whether it be the constant reminders of her old age and being called a "hag," her lack of traditional beauty, her coldness toward humans literally and figuratively, her independence and sheer power, or her cruelty toward Bride due to jealousy of the other woman's beauty. Mackenzie's version also really fascinated me because of the way its battle over seasonal shifts could be explored through a modern-day lens amid the growing impact of climate change.

In this version of the tale, Angus's ambition in bringing warmth during this time of flux between seasons is portrayed as a heroic act done in the name of love for, and saving, Bride and mankind from the Cailleach and her hags' abuse in the form of an angry winter. In opposition, I thought that the Cailleach and her hags holding on to winter was not portrayed as the natural other side of Angus's actions—simply a battle over this fluid seasonal time—but rather done primarily out of anger, stubbornness, jealousy, and revenge. Within this version, the Cailleach is the one portrayed as wanting to continue a perpetual winter, enraged by the signs of spring and desperate to have seasonal control, by any violent means necessary—and this was an idea I wanted to play with and subvert within

[7] Mackenzie himself acknowledges that some later evolutions of the Cailleach's story highlighted her villainy and human men's ability to outwit her more than earlier versions, in *Scottish Folk-lore and Folklife*: "Stories of this type were evidently of comparatively late literary development . . . they emphasize the meanness of the food-denying winter deity and the cleverness of men who make use of poetic charms" (p. 179).

[8] Angus has counterparts in the Irish figure Aengus (also called Óengus and Aengus Óg). In these tales he is a deity of love, youth, and sun, with distinct folklore in each location, often tied to a story of true love, and in some versions, described as cunning and shapeshifting. Within these stories he is often more neutral than the mainly heroic way Mackenzie portrays him. Within Scottish folklore, Angus primarily appears in Mackenzie's version of the story, connected to Beira and Bride.

the lens of how patriarchy affects story evolutions, and how often male figures are given grace that female figures are not granted, especially ones who do not physically present with ingrained concepts of "goodness" aka expected beauty and youth.

"Witch" has historically been a title put onto individuals—with negative connotations and attached danger—that exhibited these aforementioned traits or lifestyles. The association between the Cailleach and witches is of comparatively later development, hinting at the way the deity's villainization via these "witchy" characteristics is one that has evolved and grown with shifting social views. Mackenzie even notes this connection, saying that "after beliefs in witchcraft were introduced into the Highlands, these were mixed with local beliefs. Memories of the Cailleach appear to account for the Highland beliefs regarding witches raising storms and drowning people, and appearing as various animals . . ."[9] That connection and what it represented, socially, was one I wanted to explore in my alternate versions of Edinburgh.

I could not ignore how many of these "witchy" traits, lifestyles, and ideals are still used today to villainize and control women and those of marginalized genders, and are integrated into our current society, surviving due to the persistence of the patriarchy. Though I focused largely on misogyny and these "witchy" traits in this book, in the case of Scotland and the story of the Cailleach, there were many connected factors that likely contributed to the evolution of this story, including industrialization and violent attempts to stamp out Scottish folklore and language throughout history, as well as the connected growth of Christianity and biblical stories.

There were many other books and articles I read in the process of my research including (an absolutely incomplete list):

[9] Donald A. Mackenzie, *Scottish Folk-lore and Folk Life* (London: Obscure Press, 2013), p. 159.

Enemies of God: The Witch-Hunt in Scotland, by Christina Larner; *Witchcraft and Belief in Early Modern Scotland,* edited by Julian Goodare, Lauren Martin, and Joyce Miller; *Witchcraft & Second Sight in the Highlands & Islands of Scotland: Tales and Traditions Collected Entirely from Oral Sources,* by John Gregorson Campbell; *A History of Women in Medicine: Cunning Women, Physicians, Witches,* by Sinéad Spearing; *Where Are the Women?: A Guide to An Imagined Scotland,* by Sara Sheridan; *In Defense of Witches: The Legacy of the Witch Hunts and Why Women Are Still on Trial,* by Mona Chollet; "Continuity and Adaptation in Legends of Cailleach Bhéarra," by Gearóid Ó. Crualaoich; and "Legends and Traditions of the Cailleach Bheara or Old Woman (Hag) of Beare," by Eleanor Hull.

I would highly recommend reading some of the works mentioned throughout this note and its footnotes to get a fuller picture of the many iterations and evolutions of the Cailleach's story and the history of witch trials in Scotland—and the way that misogyny interacts with both.

Author's Note

Edinburgh as a city often feels like a living being, and the nature that is interwoven into the city is no exception to that. To walk down the street in Edinburgh in the twenty-first century can look very similar to how it did in the nineteenth century. Though it is a modern city, somehow it is still a place that seems both frozen in time and timeless. This story's main character, Nellie Duncan, very intentionally shares a last name with a young girl killed for witchcraft in Edinburgh in the sixteenth century, Geillis Duncan, and one of the last people in Scotland to be prosecuted under the Witchcraft Act of 1735, Helen Duncan during the twentieth century—violence and resistance are continuing, and the ways and mindsets of the pasts are never too far from the present.

This is the same reason that I chose to fictionally set a witch trial in 1824, long after Scotland's real final witch hunts—even the nineteenth century, a time of comparative modernity and industrialization, could still resort to unfounded, communal violence in the name of history and posterity. With this book I wanted to integrate the rich history and folklore of the city, as well as its dualities, into a tale that examined the violence of the patriarchy and the different, insidious forms it takes in different times.

There are many parts of myself that I wanted to put into this story: my deep love for Edinburgh; my studies; being queer; being Jewish; having fibromyalgia; losing a parent at a young age; coping with the trauma of sexual harassment and assault; being an aunt, a daughter, a sister; being a woman—

and the many things that, in my personal experience, come with being a woman. The daily fear, the shame, the hopelessness at feeling like your body is owned by the world and not yourself, the disenfranchisement, being told time and time again that these things that you, and so many others, face are in your head, are not real, are not actually so bad. And this, my own experience as a cisgender woman living in Western Europe, comes with massive, intersectional privileges that many other women, trans, and genderqueer and gender nonconforming people are not granted, as well as people who exist in so many other intersections of marginalization.

I felt so sad that, from my own experience, and speaking with other femme-presenting people in my life, these negative things were a uniting element of how we lived in and moved through the world. But even in those negative shared experiences there was a sense of community, and I wanted to explore not only how patriarchy seems cyclical and persisting but also how communities have and can form around these shared fears and horrors. It was important to me to also make very clear that these communities *must* be actively intersectional and explicitly include trans and nonbinary people.

In addition to various global art exhibits that explore the impact of the patriarchy and gender-based violence—such as Yoko Ono's "Arising: Testaments of Harm," amongst others—the "You Are Not Alone" tree in the second half of the book was also partially inspired by the Sarah's Tree memorial created by students Martha Reilly and Imogen Luczyc-Wyhowska in 2021. The memorial—in which people tied ribbons to a tree in the Meadows allocated as "Sarah's Tree" and left flowers or cards at its base—was a response to a gender-based murder that occurred in the UK. The tree was intended not only as a space to honor this woman, but also for those in Edinburgh to rage about her life taken too young and the patriarchal norms that allowed this to happen, as well as the many instances of gender-based violence and fear that occur in the lives of far too many. While, within the story, I touch briefly on the way that tree impacted many people in the city, I felt that impact firsthand in my real life. It made so many of us feel seen and heard, creating a sense of community, and prompting conversations about the impacts of the patriarchy. With this book I wanted to honor and explore Edinburgh's history, and, to me, Sarah's Tree is an integral and moving part of modern Edinburgh history, especially modern feminist history. This memorial was deeply impactful to me, hence my wanting to honor and pay homage to it within this story.

Though this book's alternate 1824 and 2022 Edinburgh is more "history inspired" than a work of pure historical fiction, there are many parts of the story that are rooted in real events: Maggie Dickson waking up alive after being hung, graves being dug up and bodies stolen and sold, cemetery guards, the horrific North Berwick witch trials, a surge of drugging by injection across the UK in modern day, the Great Fire of Edinburgh on 15 November, 1824, and much more.

As much as all of the above, this book is a love letter to Edinburgh. It was an opportunity to explore and weave together years of my research, studies, curiosities, and experiences during my time living there, though the story was drafted primarily during the final year I lived in the city; it was, in many ways, a way to say goodbye to a place I had called home for a good chunk of my early adulthood and that drastically shaped and changed my life.

September 2023

THE LAST WITCH IN EDINBURGH

TIMELINE

1590 -1592	North Berwick witch trials
Anne Rae hung Nellie meets the Rae women	**1824** *18 September*
1824 *29 September*	Helen Gordon hung
Isobel hung	**1824** *16 October*
1824 *24 October*	Nellie and Jean encounter Angus at St Giles
Great Fire of Edinburgh	**1824** *15 November*
2022 *10 September*	Nellie and Chani return to Edinburgh
Nellie and Jean reunite	**2022** *30 September*
2022 *6 October*	Nellie encounters Angus as the Vice-Chancellor
Catherine Baker killed	**2022** *21 October*
2022 *9 November*	You Are Not Alone memorial begins
The Meadows burned down	**2022** *15 November*
2022 *16-20 November*	Protest against the Vice-Chancellor
Vice-Chancellor resigns Angus leaves Edinburgh	**2022** *23 November*
2022 *24 November*	The Meadows rebuilt

ACKNOWLEDGMENTS

Authors often talk about the distinct challenge of writing a sophomore book, and I can say that that was, absolutely, the case with *The Last Witch in Edinburgh*. Getting this book to where it is took a great deal of effort and empathy from so many people. Many, many thanks to:

My editor, Shannon Plackis—every suggestion you made for this book made me go "OMG, that's *exactly* what the story was missing." Thank you for your sharp editorial eye, your patience, for chatting with me about everything from our favorite fanfics to dark academia trends, and for always trusting me and my ideas.

My agent, Jill Marr—I could not have asked for a better partner and support system during the chaos of creating a sophomore book. Thank you for your excitement about this book (and all my ideas), your wisdom, and for always advocating for me and my stories and the space and time I needed to write them.

The wonderful team at Kensington, specifically Adam Zacharius, Steve Zacharius, Jackie Dinas, Lynn Cully, Kristine Noble in Art, Alex Nicolajsen and Lauren Jernigan on the Digital Team, Shannon Gray, Vida Engstrand, Kristen Vega, production editor Carly Sommerstein, and Michelle Addo in Publicity.

The staff and librarians at the National Library of Scotland, for providing a work space and documents, books, and maps, that were essential for much of my research. And for your curiosity as to what I was working on—and meeting the answer with such enthusiasm and encouragement.

The Jolly Judge pub, just off Lawnmarket, for providing ciders and the perfect ambience while I bore through much of the early draft of this book.

Black Moon Botanica on Candlemaker Row for making their "Witch Wood" homemade candle, the scent I kept lit throughout working on this book.

Readers and bookstagrammers who reached out to tell me you enjoyed my debut and the ways it resonated with you. Genuinely, it means the world. Thank you, thank you, thank you for reading.

Mikaela Moody, for authenticity reading this book and sharing your insight and lived experiences, helping me bring Ari—and all the other witches—to life.

Natalie Kiki and Mikayla Bridge, two wonderful writers and friends, for reading a draft of this book in its earliest and rawest form.

The welcoming community of Gothic fiction writers—particularly Paulette Kennedy and Hester Fox, who have been so supportive and encouraging.

My therapist, for taking a crash course in how publishing works and for keeping me (mostly) calm.

My pals in Edinburgh—whether it was weekends in the Highlands or in the Meadows, or weeknights at the pub, you made sure that every cobblestone in the city carries a happy memory for me. And thanks for listening to years of me talking about the history of witch trials, local cemeteries, and grave robbings (and people reawakening), long after others would have tuned it out.

My former course mates, turned friends, for your unending enthusiasm for the stories I write and for sharing yours with me.

My tremendously supportive in-laws, who have welcomed and loved me more than I could have dreamed of.

Jim and Nermin, for letting me stay in your home during a good chunk of this revision process, and for having a home full of so much poetry and art that it was easy to stay inspired.

My mother and aunts for providing a lifelong example of an independent, loud, and slightly terrifying community of welcoming women. My sister, for always accepting me without question and for being both sister and very best friend. And my brother, the kindest and most supportive person I know, for thinking every story I tell is wonderful, ever since I was little and talking about "wicked witches" who were actually the good guys. Juni, for being the best niece anyone could ever ask for, for changing my life for the better by making me an auntie, and for asking me if I wanted to start a coven with you (obviously, yes).

Finally, Beau—it was an emotionally grueling process getting this book to publication and, wow, I was lucky to have you by my side during it. Thank you for helping me turn half of this book from a sprawling mess full of plot holes into something that is hopefully a bit more coherent. Thank you a million times for your support, your calmness, and your love.

The Last Witch
in Edinburgh

ABOUT THIS GUIDE

The suggested questions are included to enhance
your group's reading of this book.

DISCUSSION QUESTIONS

1. Having lost her mother at a young age—and having an abusive father—Nellie has a very complicated relationship with family. However, throughout the book we see her find a new family, first in the other women at the apothecary, and later with Chani, who she raises like a niece. Discuss the roles that homesickness and chosen family play in the story.

2. Isolation is a recurring theme in Marielle Thompson's works. In what ways did you see the theme of isolation explored in *The Last Witch in Edinburgh*?

3. What preconceived notions about historically accused witches or witch trials in Scotland—and Europe at large—did you have before reading the book? After reading it and the historical note, how have those thoughts changed, or not?

4. Nellie and Jean's relationship in the nineteenth century is often unbalanced; Nellie idealizes Jean, and Jean holds Nellie to a standard that is sometimes unfair. How do you think that being apart for two centuries, and growing in that time, allowed them to come together again?

5. The modern-day part of the book focuses on how the patriarchy is often interwoven with academic institutions. What are some other facets of modern-day patriarchal impact that you think can be explored?

6. Though there are a few brief chapters set in other areas, almost the entire novel is set in Edinburgh. Elements of

the city's real history, folklore, notorious figures, and geography are woven into the story. Edinburgh itself becomes a character—a place that Nellie loves but cannot help but resent, being the site of so many painful memories. What part do you think the city of Edinburgh played in the story? How do you think it would have been different were it set elsewhere?

7. Why do you think the author chose to set a witch trial in an alternate version of nineteenth-century Edinburgh, rather than setting the story in an earlier period that actually experienced witch trials?

8. Nellie and her art students create a memorial tree in a park in response to the gender-based murder of a local student that occurred there. They, and many others, add pieces to the tree: drawings of those that make them feel protected, written statistics about assault and gender-based violence, stories of how the patriarchy has negatively affected them or times that their community helped them feel empowered. If you were to add an art piece or story to the "You Are Not Alone" memorial tree, what would it be?

9. Legacy is a recurring theme in the story—including through Nellie and Jean's relationship with their daughters, and the impact that they leave on Edinburgh. With that in mind, why do you think the book is titled *The Last Witch in Edinburgh*?